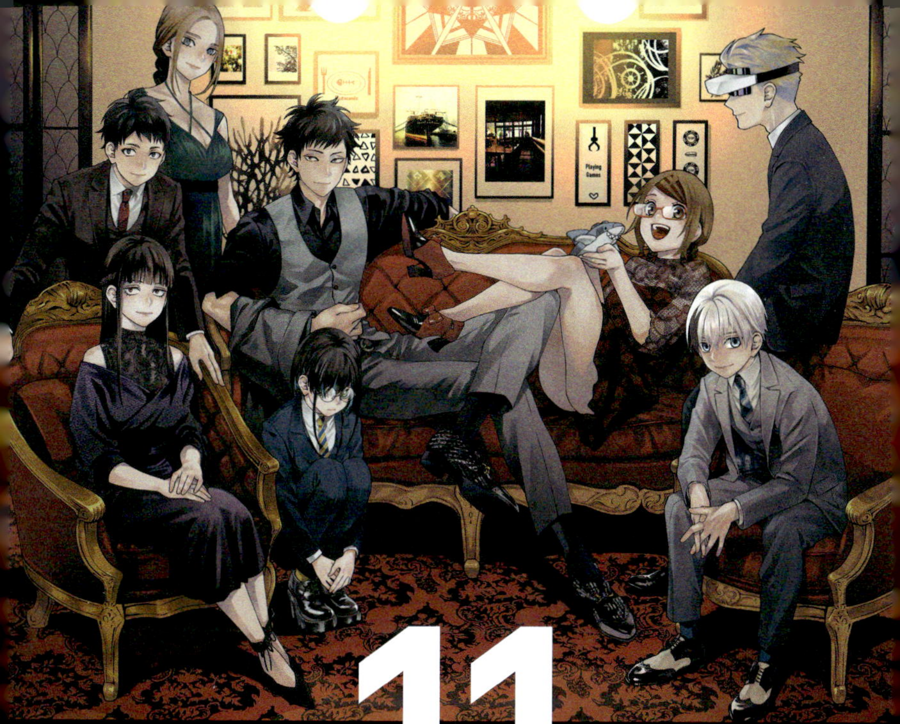

# 11

# DEAD MOUNT DEATH PLAY

#88 03

#89 27

#90 51

#91 73

#92 85

#93 107

#94 133

#95 155

CONTENTS

DEAD MOUNT
DEATH PLAY

# #88

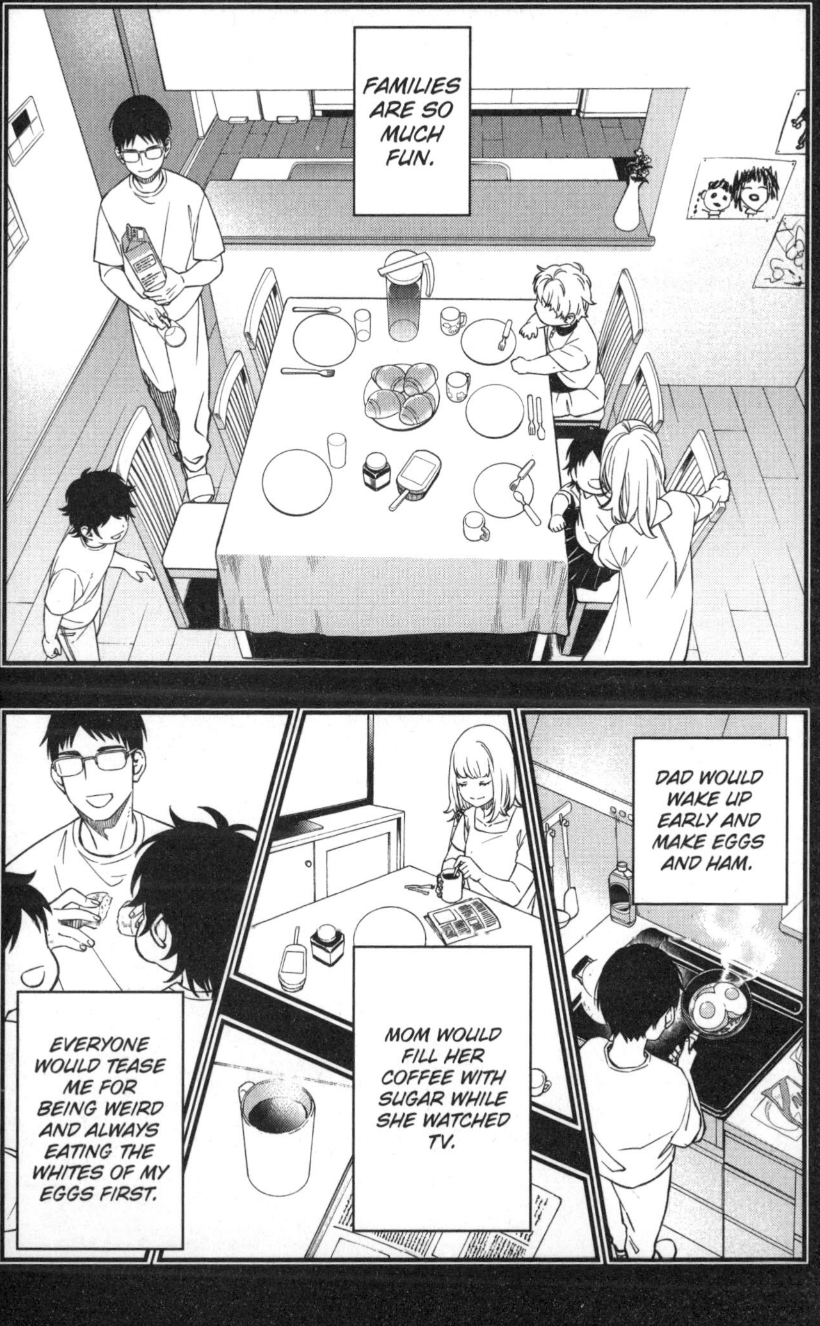
FAMILIES ARE SO MUCH FUN.
DAD WOULD WAKE UP EARLY AND MAKE EGGS AND HAM.
MOM WOULD FILL HER COFFEE WITH SUGAR WHILE SHE WATCHED TV.
EVERYONE WOULD TEASE ME FOR BEING WEIRD AND ALWAYS EATING THE WHITES OF MY EGGS FIRST.

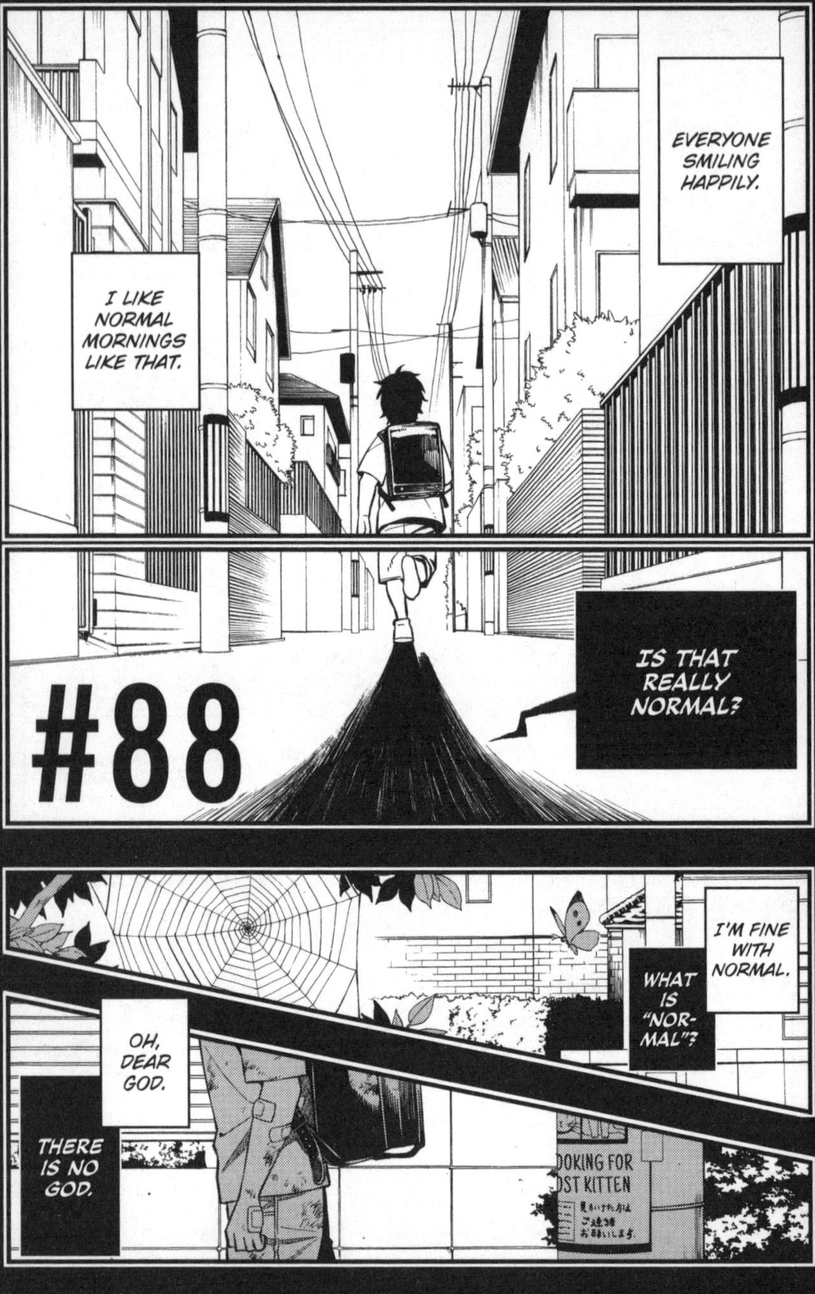
EVERYONE SMILING HAPPILY.
I LIKE NORMAL MORNINGS LIKE THAT.
IS THAT REALLY NORMAL?
#88
I'M FINE WITH NORMAL.
WHAT IS "NOR-MAL"?
OH, DEAR GOD.
THERE IS NO GOD.

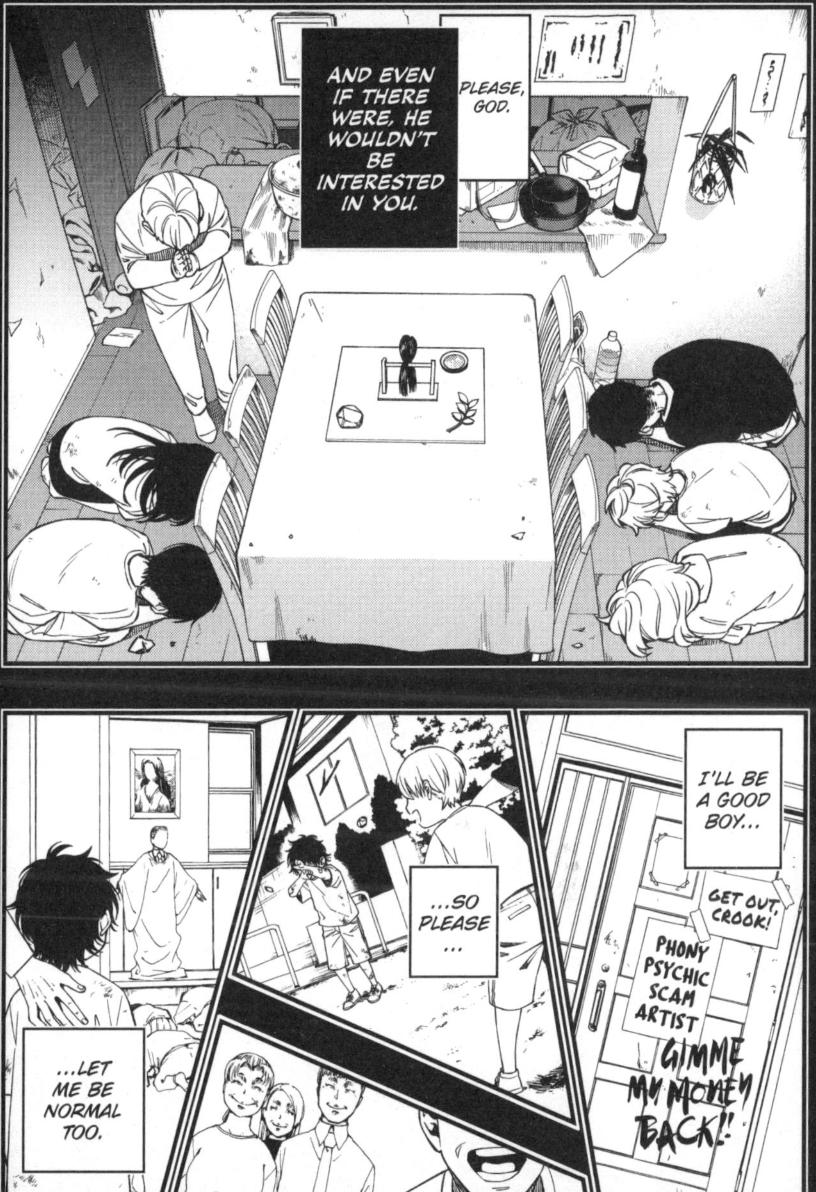
PLEASE, GOD.
AND EVEN IF THERE WERE, HE WOULDN'T BE INTERESTED IN YOU.
I'LL BE A GOOD BOY...
GET OUT, CROOK!
PHONY PSYCHIC SCAM ARTIST
GIMME MY MONEY BACK!!
...SO PLEASE...
...LET ME BE NORMAL TOO.

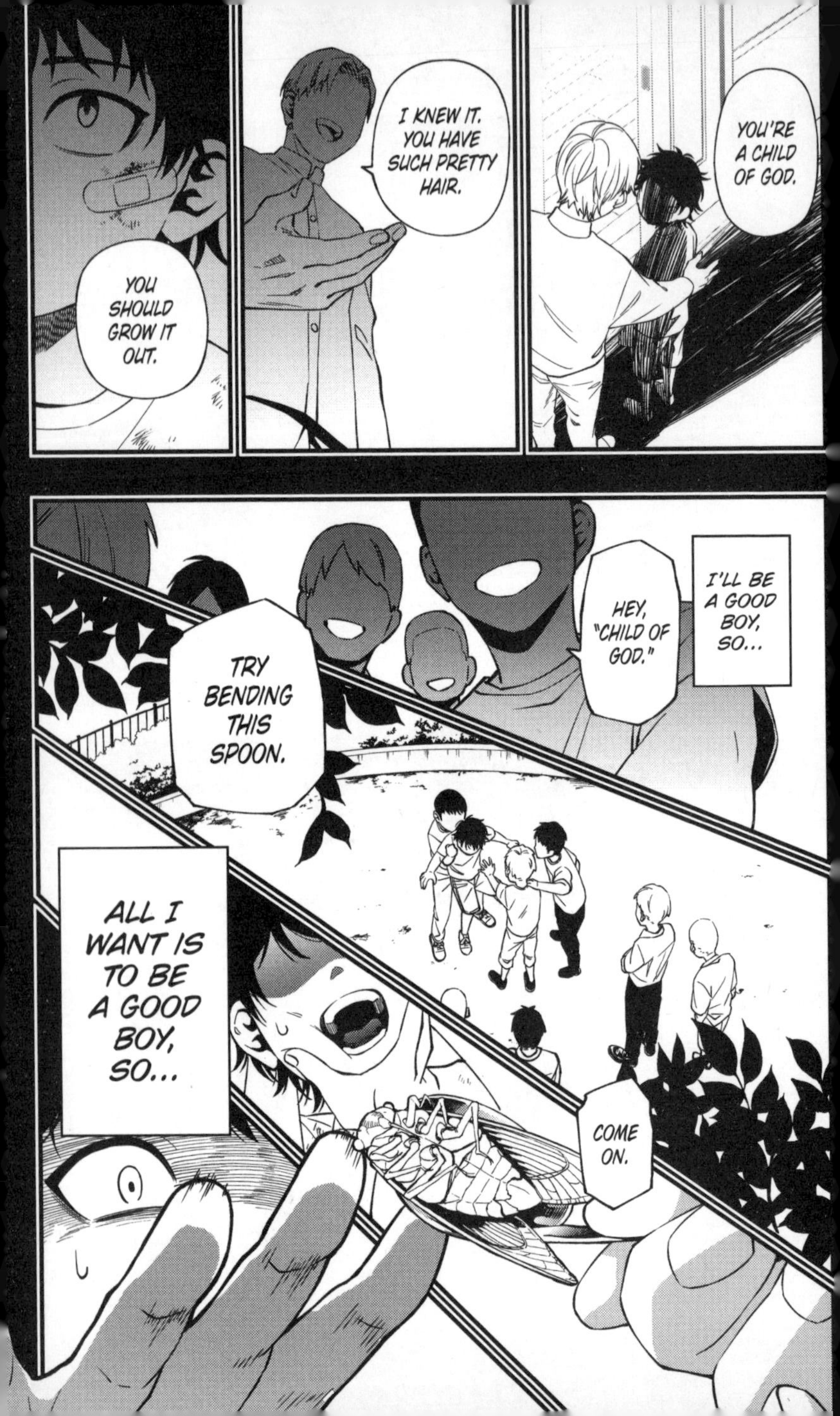
YOU'RE A CHILD OF GOD.
I KNEW IT. YOU HAVE SUCH PRETTY HAIR.
YOU SHOULD GROW IT OUT.
I'LL BE A GOOD BOY, SO...
HEY, "CHILD OF GOD."
TRY BENDING THIS SPOON.
ALL I WANT IS TO BE A GOOD BOY, SO...
COME ON.

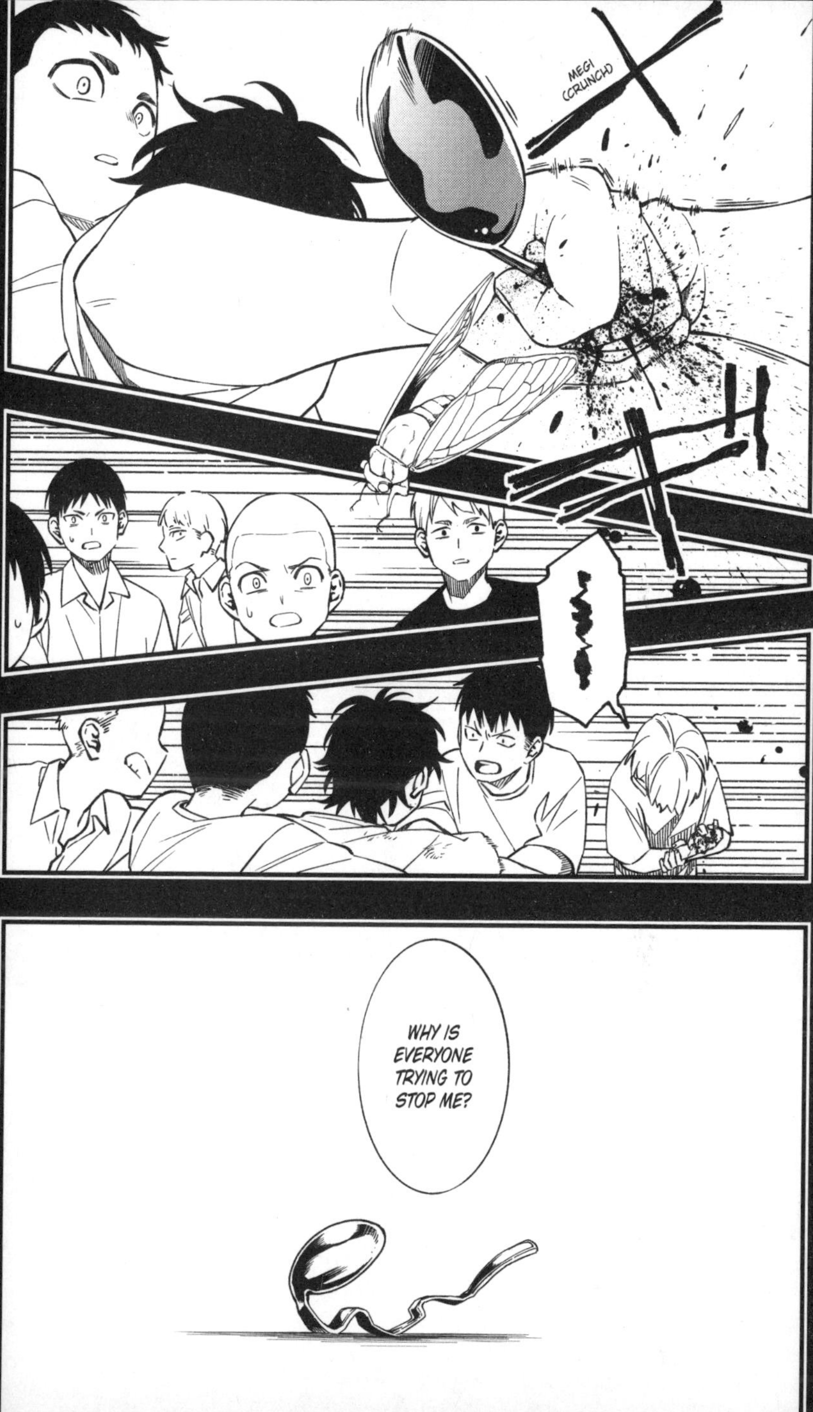
MEGI (CRUNCH)
WHY IS EVERYONE TRYING TO STOP ME?

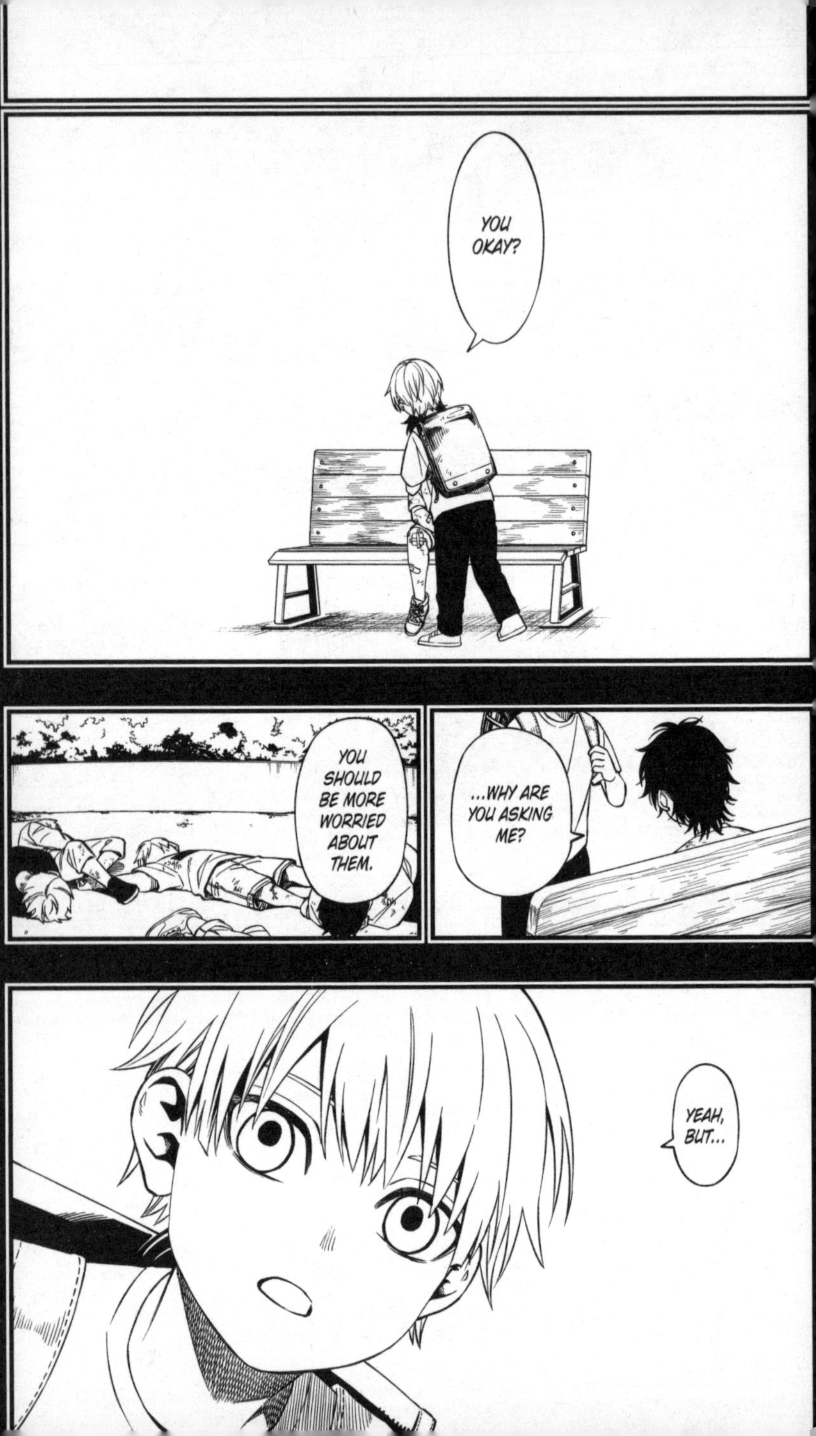
YOU OKAY?
...WHY ARE YOU ASKING ME?
YOU SHOULD BE MORE WORRIED ABOUT THEM.
YEAH, BUT...

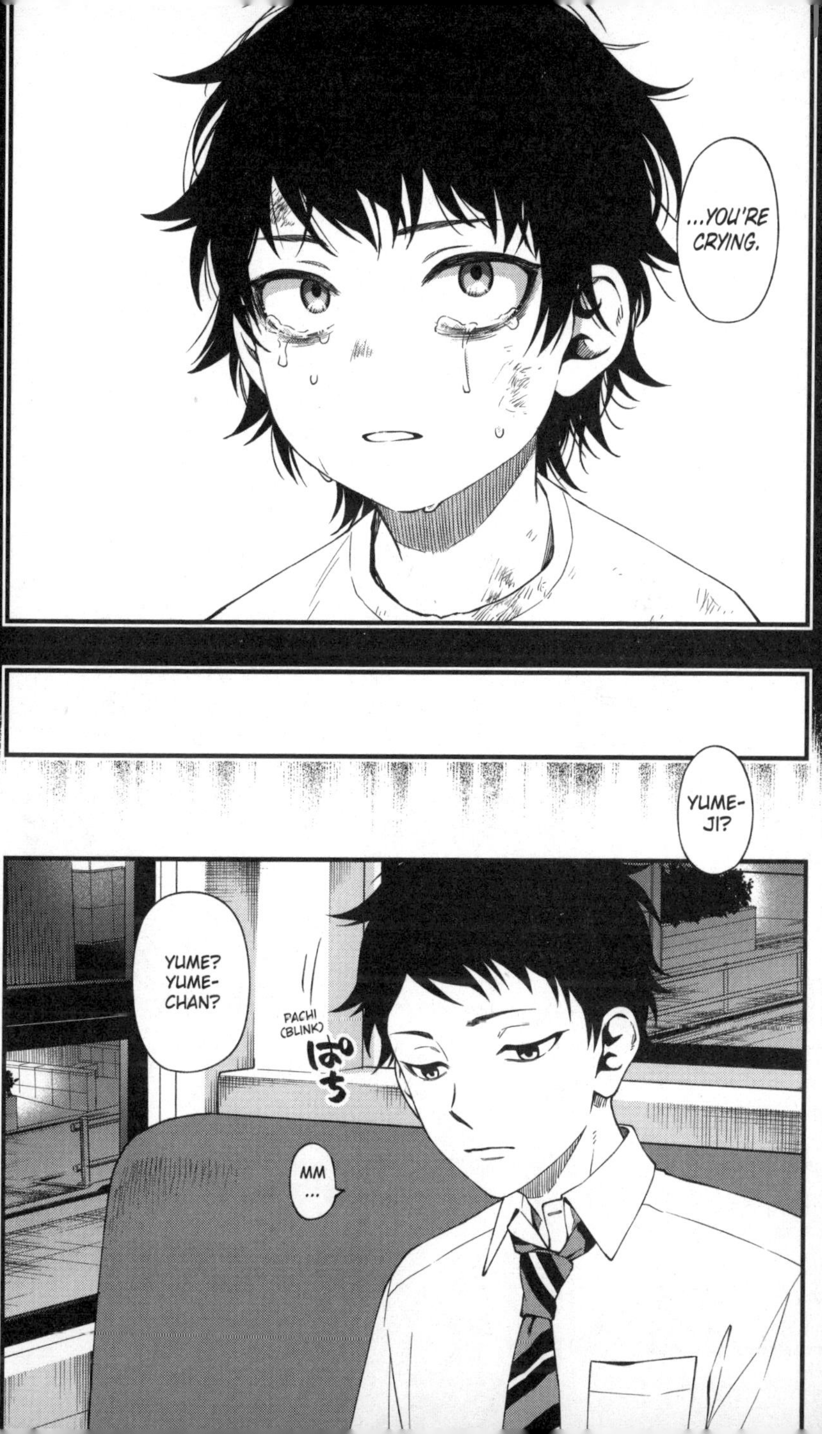
...YOU'RE CRYING.
YUME-JI?
YUME? YUME-CHAN?
PACHI (BLINK)
ぱち
MM ...

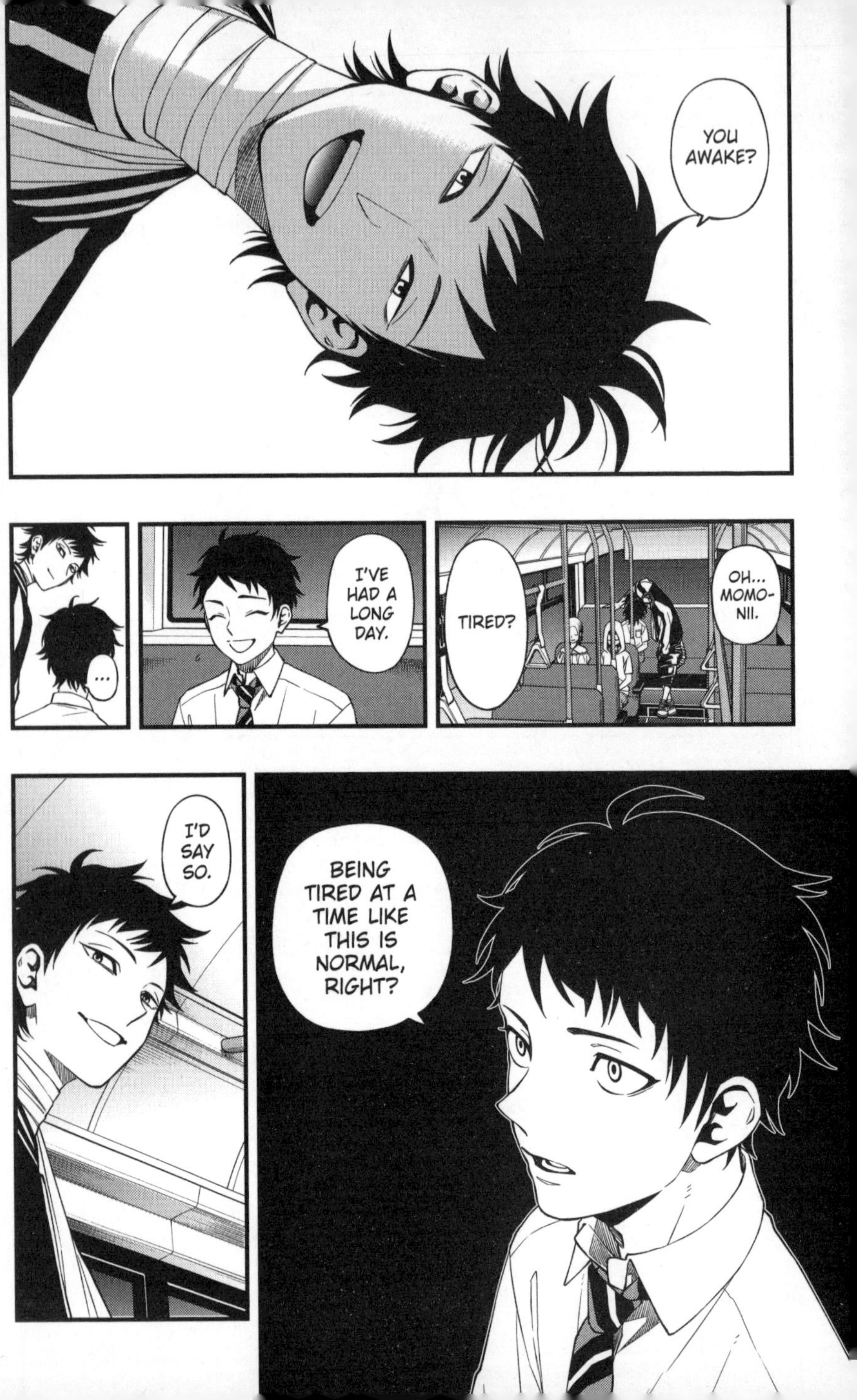
YOU AWAKE?
OH... MOMO-NII.
TIRED?
I'VE HAD A LONG DAY.
...
BEING TIRED AT A TIME LIKE THIS IS NORMAL, RIGHT?
I'D SAY SO.

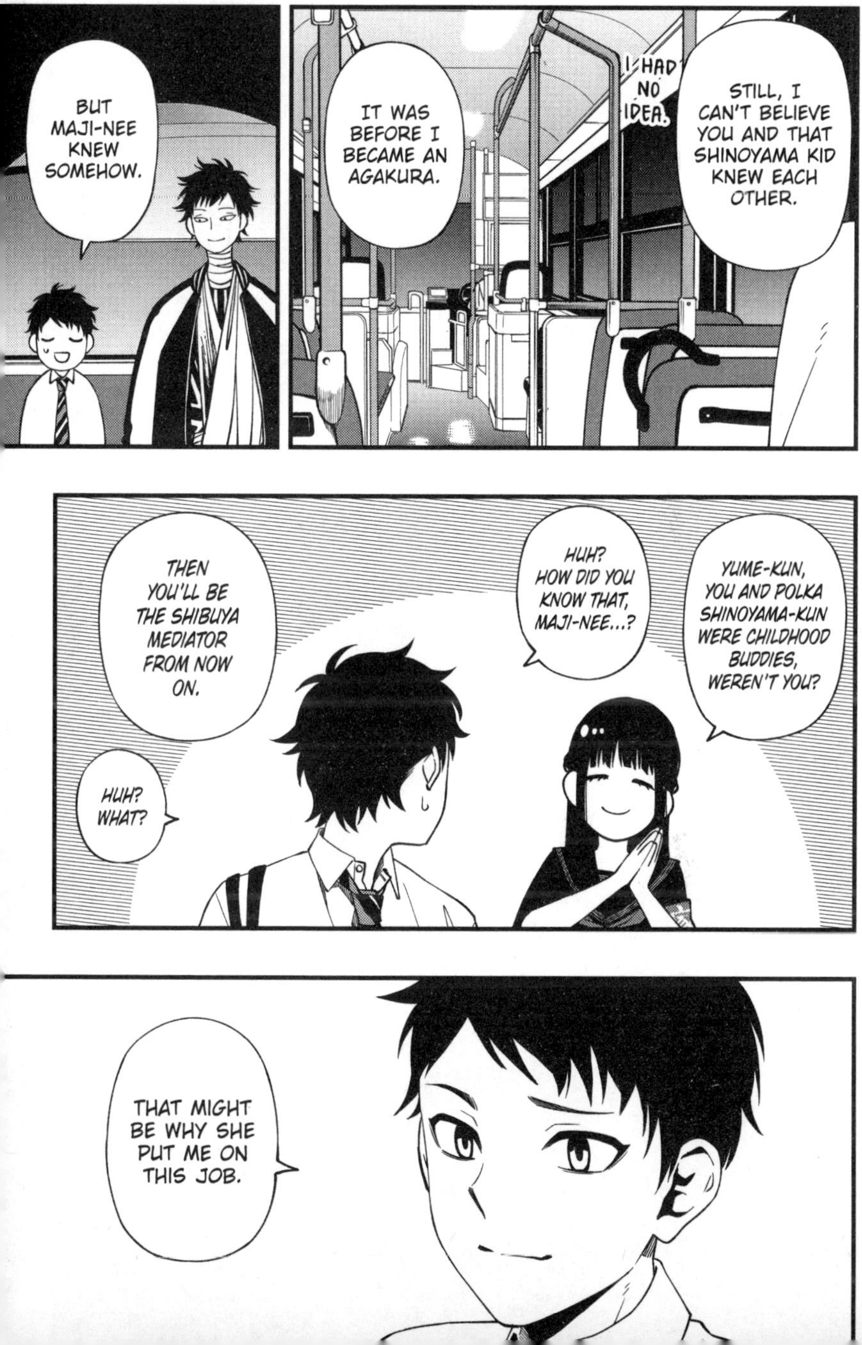
STILL, I CAN'T BELIEVE YOU AND THAT SHINOYAMA KID KNEW EACH OTHER.
I HAD NO IDEA.
IT WAS BEFORE I BECAME AN AGAKURA.
BUT MAJI-NEE KNEW SOMEHOW.
YUME-KUN, YOU AND POLKA SHINOYAMA-KUN WERE CHILDHOOD BUDDIES, WEREN'T YOU?
HUH? HOW DID YOU KNOW THAT, MAJI-NEE...?
THEN YOU'LL BE THE SHIBUYA MEDIATOR FROM NOW ON.
HUH? WHAT?
THAT MIGHT BE WHY SHE PUT ME ON THIS JOB.

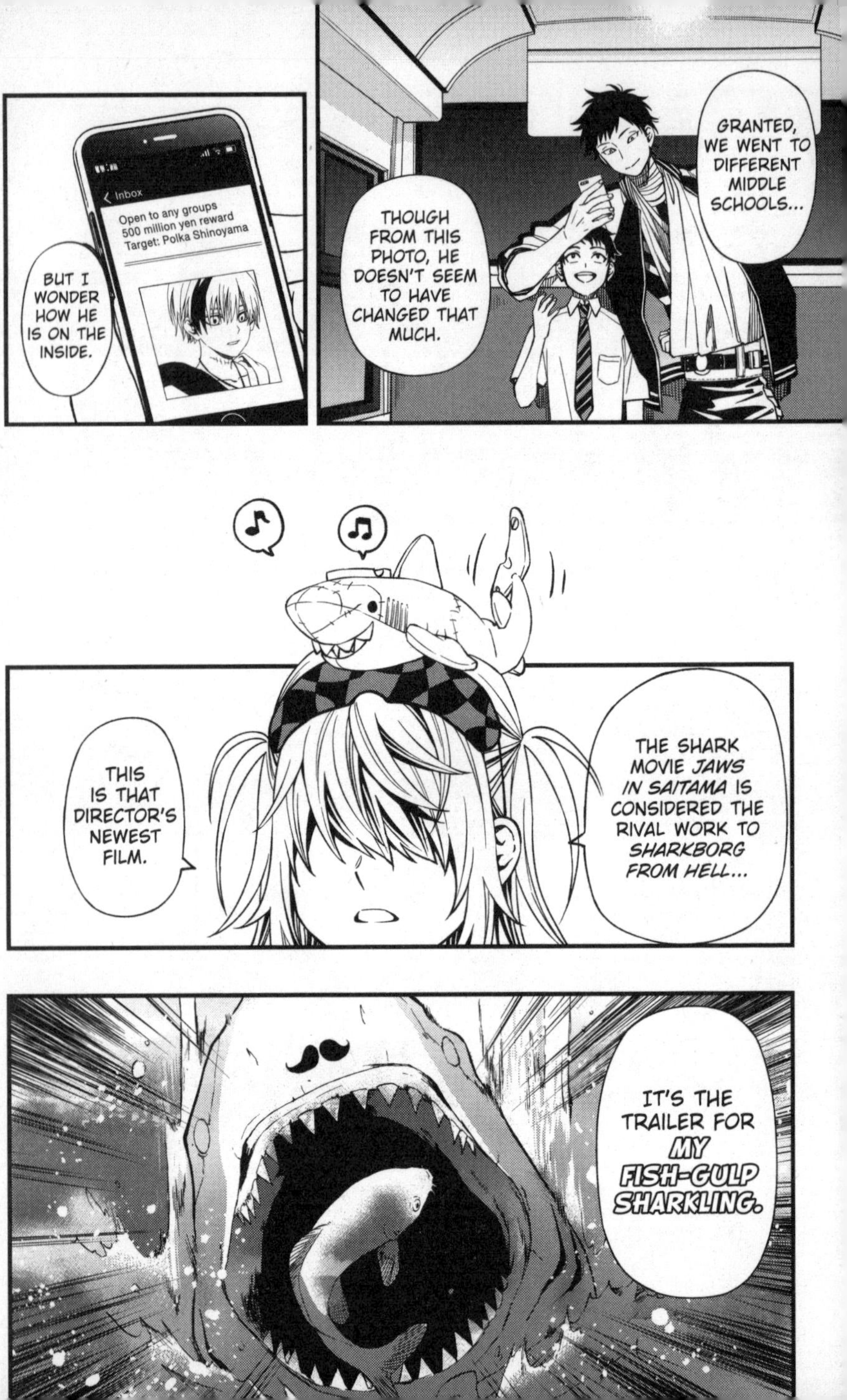
GRANTED, WE WENT TO DIFFERENT MIDDLE SCHOOLS...
THOUGH FROM THIS PHOTO, HE DOESN'T SEEM TO HAVE CHANGED THAT MUCH.
Inbox
Open to any groups
500 million yen reward
Target: Polka Shinoyama
BUT I WONDER HOW HE IS ON THE INSIDE.
THE SHARK MOVIE *JAWS IN SAITAMA* IS CONSIDERED THE RIVAL WORK TO *SHARKBORG FROM HELL*...
THIS IS THAT DIRECTOR'S NEWEST FILM.
IT'S THE TRAILER FOR *MY FISH-GULP SHARKLING.*

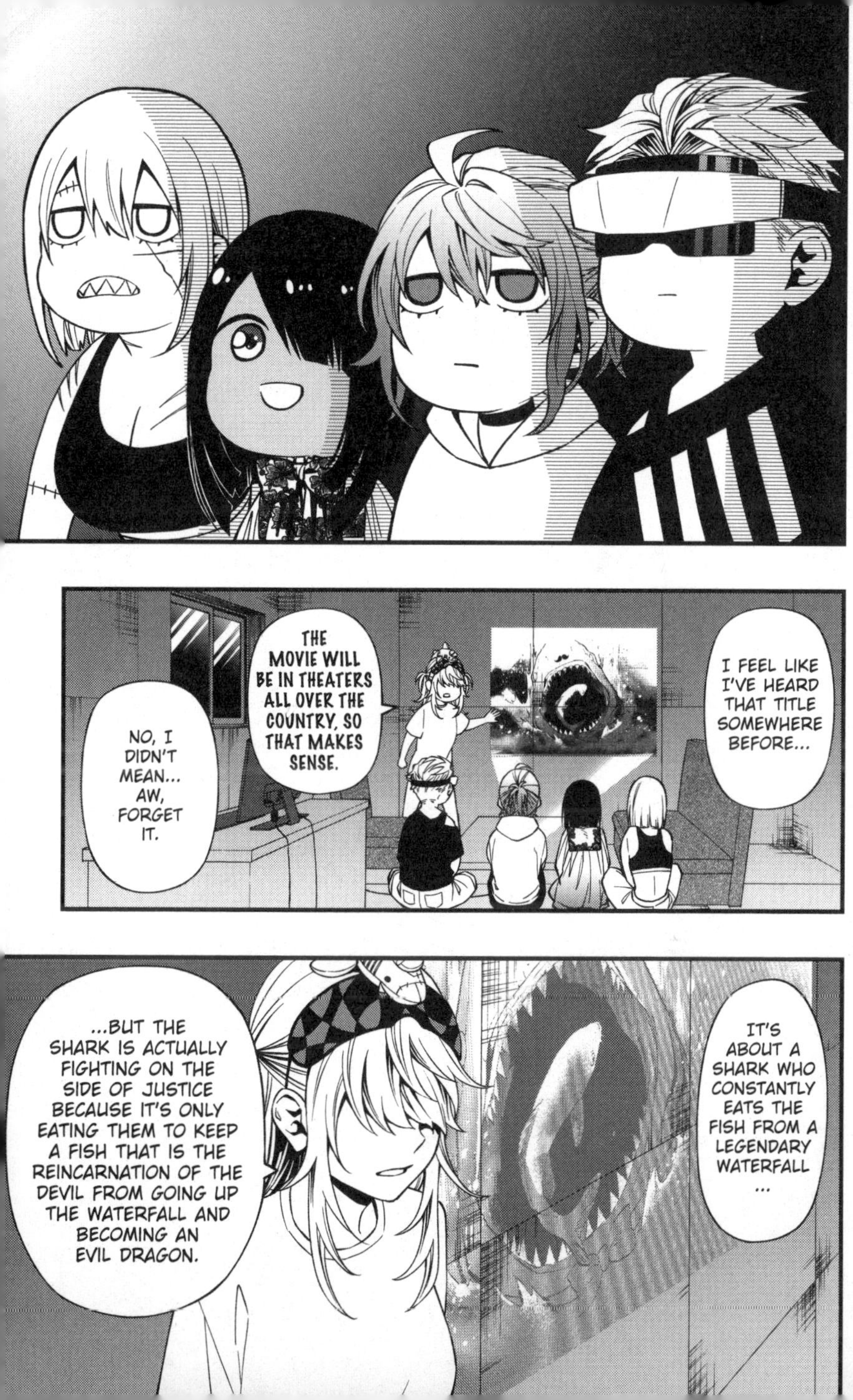
I FEEL LIKE I'VE HEARD THAT TITLE SOMEWHERE BEFORE...
THE MOVIE WILL BE IN THEATERS ALL OVER THE COUNTRY, SO THAT MAKES SENSE.
NO, I DIDN'T MEAN... AW, FORGET IT.
IT'S ABOUT A SHARK WHO CONSTANTLY EATS THE FISH FROM A LEGENDARY WATERFALL ...
...BUT THE SHARK IS ACTUALLY FIGHTING ON THE SIDE OF JUSTICE BECAUSE IT'S ONLY EATING THEM TO KEEP A FISH THAT IS THE REINCARNATION OF THE DEVIL FROM GOING UP THE WATERFALL AND BECOMING AN EVIL DRAGON.

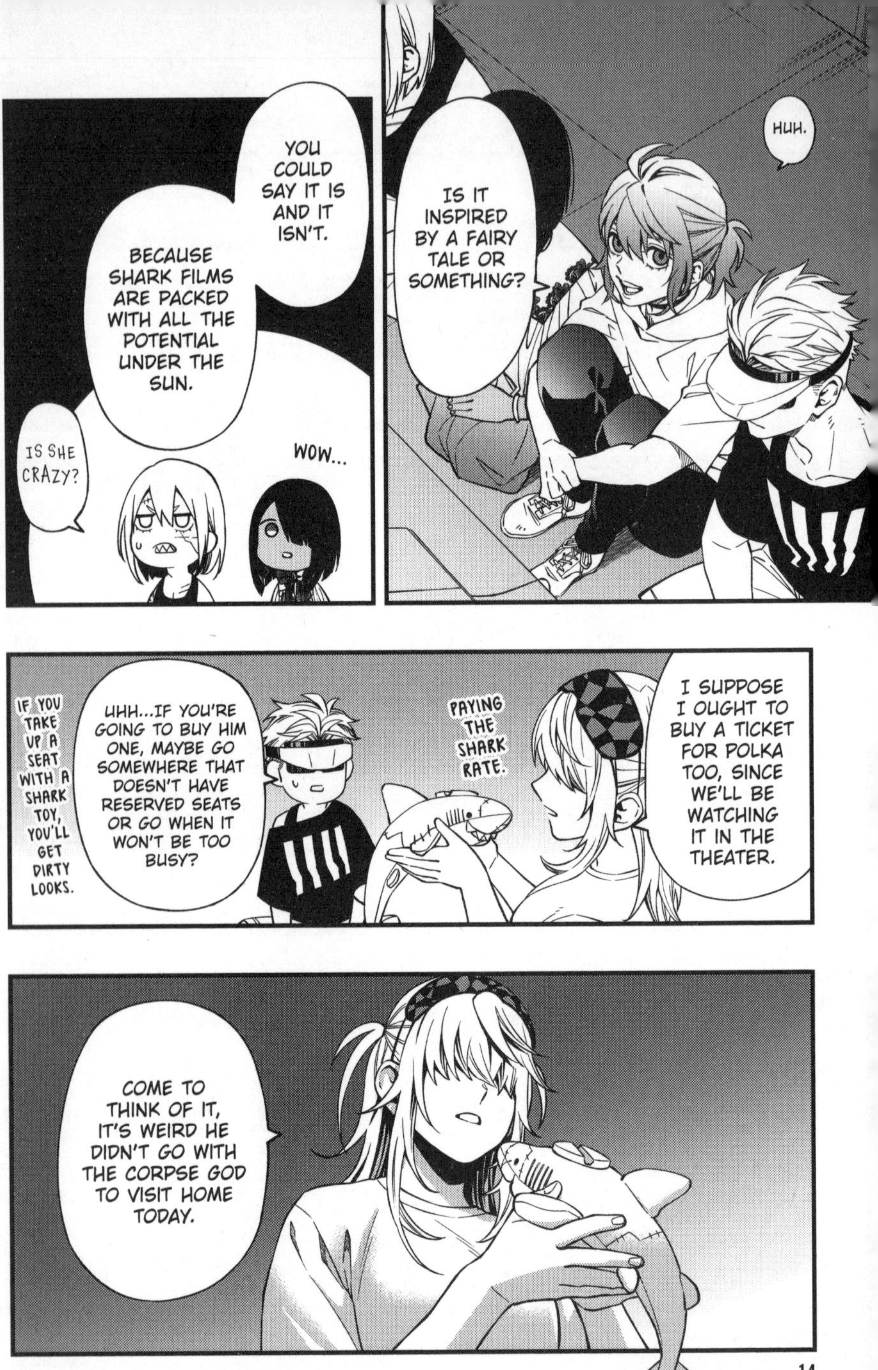
HUH.
IS IT INSPIRED BY A FAIRY TALE OR SOMETHING?
YOU COULD SAY IT IS AND IT ISN'T.
BECAUSE SHARK FILMS ARE PACKED WITH ALL THE POTENTIAL UNDER THE SUN.
WOW...
IS SHE CRAZY?
I SUPPOSE I OUGHT TO BUY A TICKET FOR POLKA TOO, SINCE WE'LL BE WATCHING IT IN THE THEATER.
PAYING THE SHARK RATE.
UHH...IF YOU'RE GOING TO BUY HIM ONE, MAYBE GO SOMEWHERE THAT DOESN'T HAVE RESERVED SEATS OR GO WHEN IT WON'T BE TOO BUSY?
IF YOU TAKE UP A SEAT WITH A SHARK TOY, YOU'LL GET DIRTY LOOKS.
COME TO THINK OF IT, IT'S WEIRD HE DIDN'T GO WITH THE CORPSE GOD TO VISIT HOME TODAY.

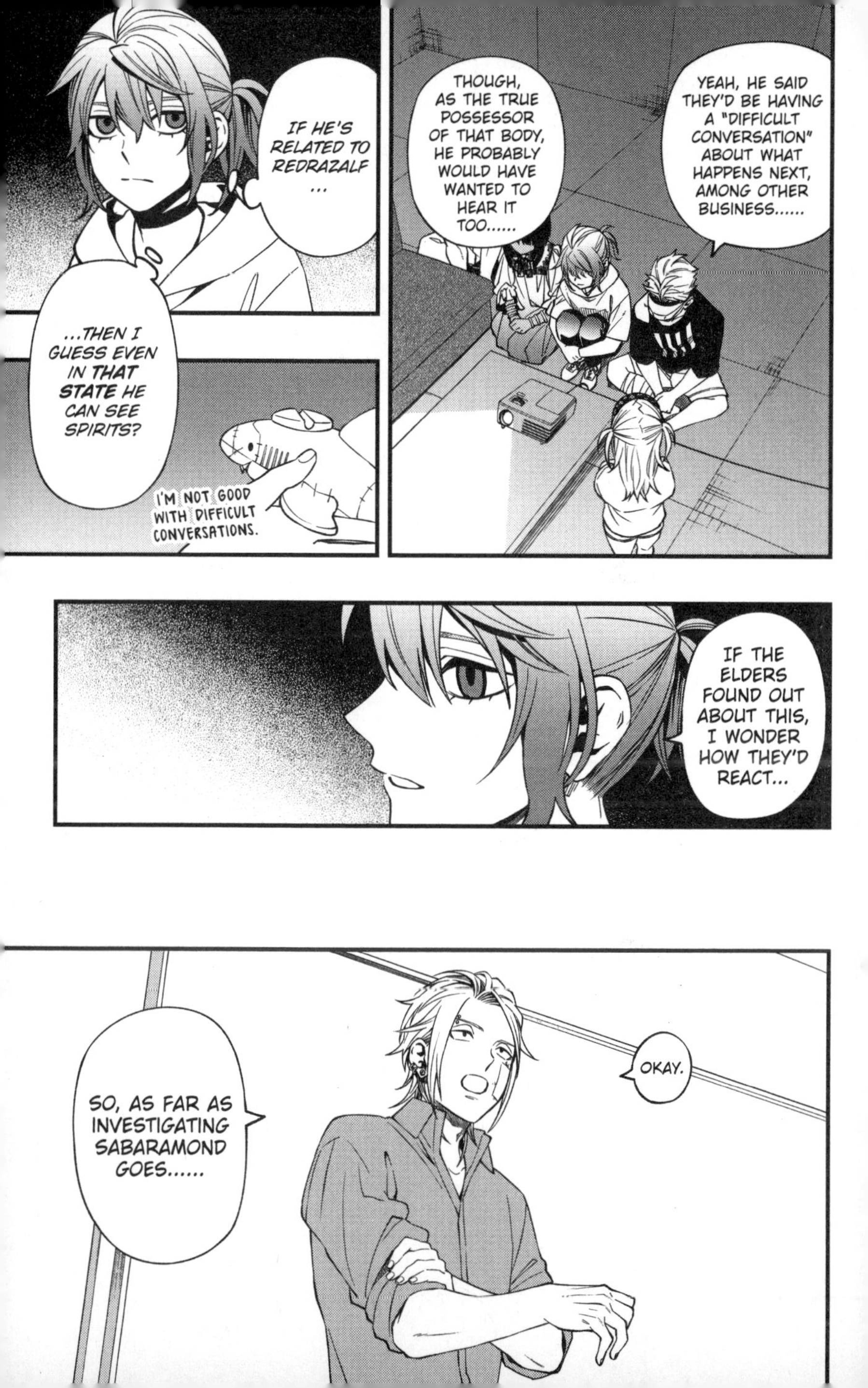
YEAH, HE SAID THEY'D BE HAVING A "DIFFICULT CONVERSATION" ABOUT WHAT HAPPENS NEXT, AMONG OTHER BUSINESS......
THOUGH, AS THE TRUE POSSESSOR OF THAT BODY, HE PROBABLY WOULD HAVE WANTED TO HEAR IT TOO......
IF HE'S RELATED TO REDRAZALF...
...THEN I GUESS EVEN IN THAT STATE HE CAN SEE SPIRITS?
I'M NOT GOOD WITH DIFFICULT CONVERSATIONS.
IF THE ELDERS FOUND OUT ABOUT THIS, I WONDER HOW THEY'D REACT...
OKAY.
SO, AS FAR AS INVESTIGATING SABARAMOND GOES......

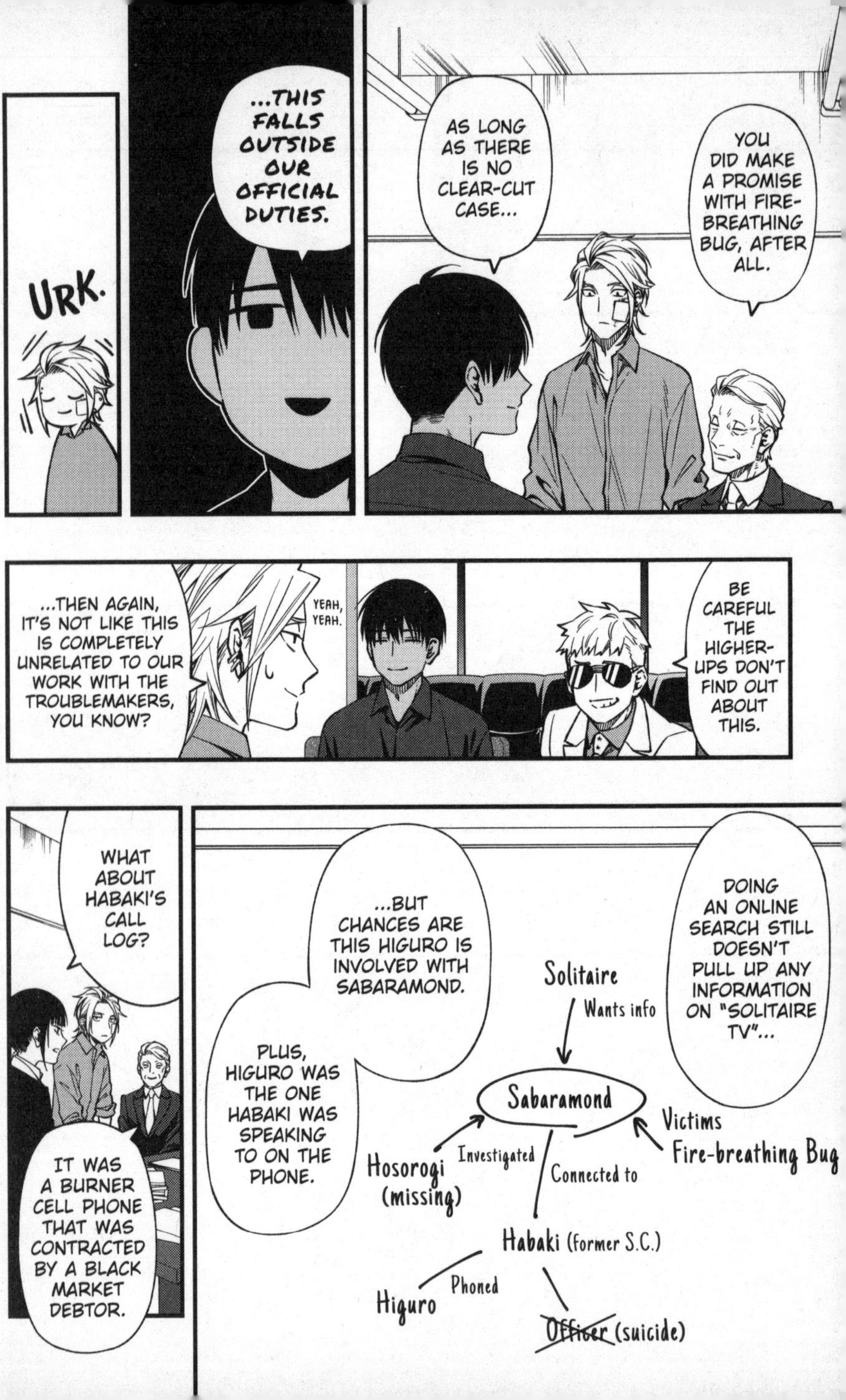

YOU DID MAKE A PROMISE WITH FIRE-BREATHING BUG, AFTER ALL.
AS LONG AS THERE IS NO CLEAR-CUT CASE...
...THIS FALLS OUTSIDE OUR OFFICIAL DUTIES.
URK.
BE CAREFUL THE HIGHER-UPS DON'T FIND OUT ABOUT THIS.
YEAH, YEAH.
...THEN AGAIN, IT'S NOT LIKE THIS IS COMPLETELY UNRELATED TO OUR WORK WITH THE TROUBLEMAKERS, YOU KNOW?
DOING AN ONLINE SEARCH STILL DOESN'T PULL UP ANY INFORMATION ON "SOLITAIRE TV"...
...BUT CHANCES ARE THIS HIGURO IS INVOLVED WITH SABARAMOND.
PLUS, HIGURO WAS THE ONE HABAKI WAS SPEAKING TO ON THE PHONE.
Solitaire
Wants info
Sabaramond
Victims
Fire-breathing Bug
Investigated
Hosorogi (missing)
Connected to
Habaki (former S.C.)
Phoned
Higuro
Officer (suicide)
WHAT ABOUT HABAKI'S CALL LOG?
IT WAS A BURNER CELL PHONE THAT WAS CONTRACTED BY A BLACK MARKET DEBTOR.

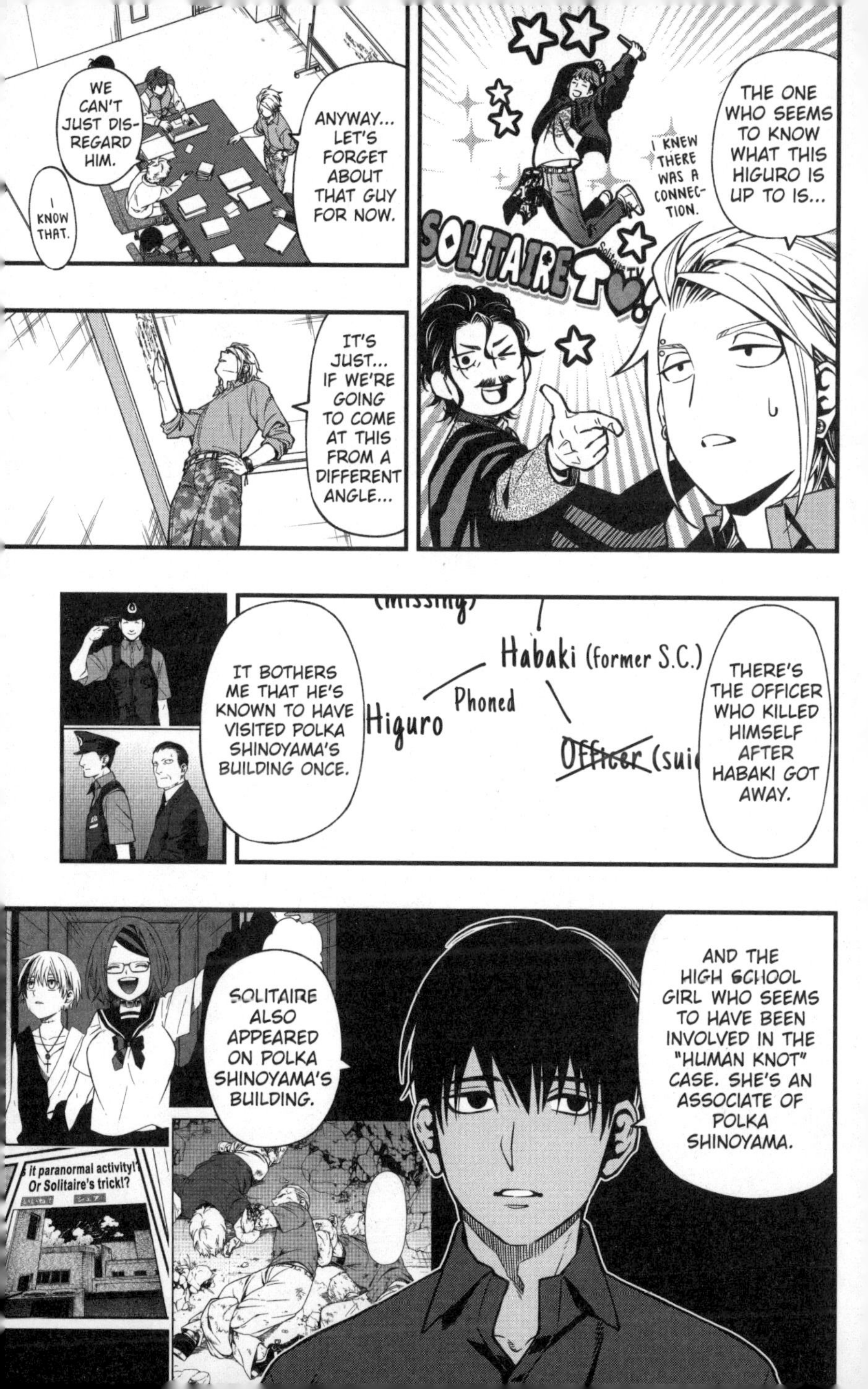
THE ONE WHO SEEMS TO KNOW WHAT THIS HIGURO IS UP TO IS...
I KNEW THERE WAS A CONNECTION.
SOLITAIRE TV
ANYWAY... LET'S FORGET ABOUT THAT GUY FOR NOW.
WE CAN'T JUST DISREGARD HIM.
I KNOW THAT.
IT'S JUST... IF WE'RE GOING TO COME AT THIS FROM A DIFFERENT ANGLE...
THERE'S THE OFFICER WHO KILLED HIMSELF AFTER HABAKI GOT AWAY.
Habaki (former S.C.)
Phoned
Higuro
Officer (sui
IT BOTHERS ME THAT HE'S KNOWN TO HAVE VISITED POLKA SHINOYAMA'S BUILDING ONCE.
AND THE HIGH SCHOOL GIRL WHO SEEMS TO HAVE BEEN INVOLVED IN THE "HUMAN KNOT" CASE. SHE'S AN ASSOCIATE OF POLKA SHINOYAMA.
SOLITAIRE ALSO APPEARED ON POLKA SHINOYAMA'S BUILDING.
s it paranormal activity!? Or Solitaire's trick!?

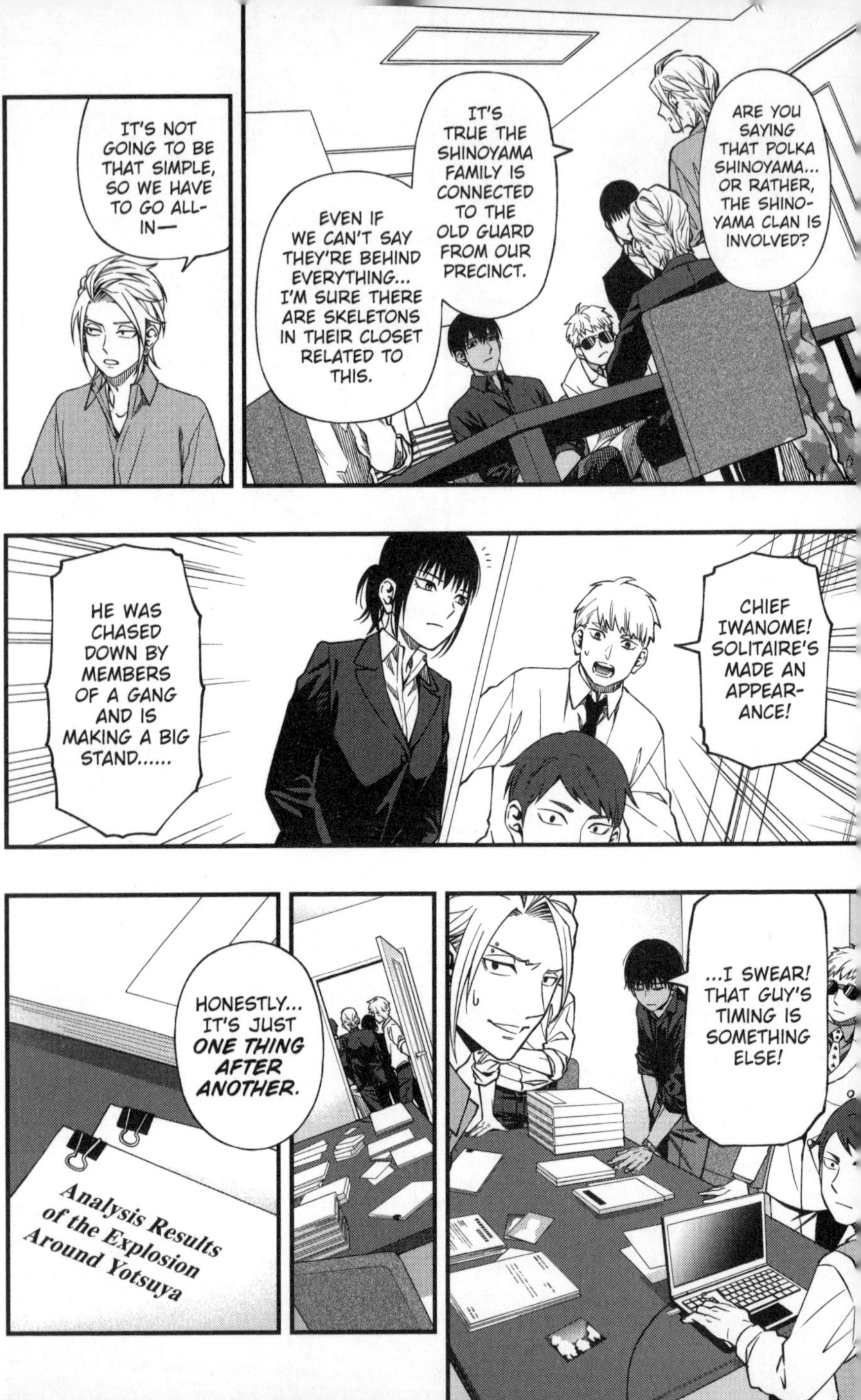
IT'S NOT GOING TO BE THAT SIMPLE, SO WE HAVE TO GO ALL-IN—
EVEN IF WE CAN'T SAY THEY'RE BEHIND EVERYTHING... I'M SURE THERE ARE SKELETONS IN THEIR CLOSET RELATED TO THIS.
IT'S TRUE THE SHINOYAMA FAMILY IS CONNECTED TO THE OLD GUARD FROM OUR PRECINCT.
ARE YOU SAYING THAT POLKA SHINOYAMA... OR RATHER, THE SHINOYAMA CLAN IS INVOLVED?
HE WAS CHASED DOWN BY MEMBERS OF A GANG AND IS MAKING A BIG STAND......
CHIEF IWANOME! SOLITAIRE'S MADE AN APPEARANCE!
Analysis Results of the Explosion Around Yotsuya
HONESTLY... IT'S JUST ONE THING AFTER ANOTHER.
...I SWEAR! THAT GUY'S TIMING IS SOMETHING ELSE!

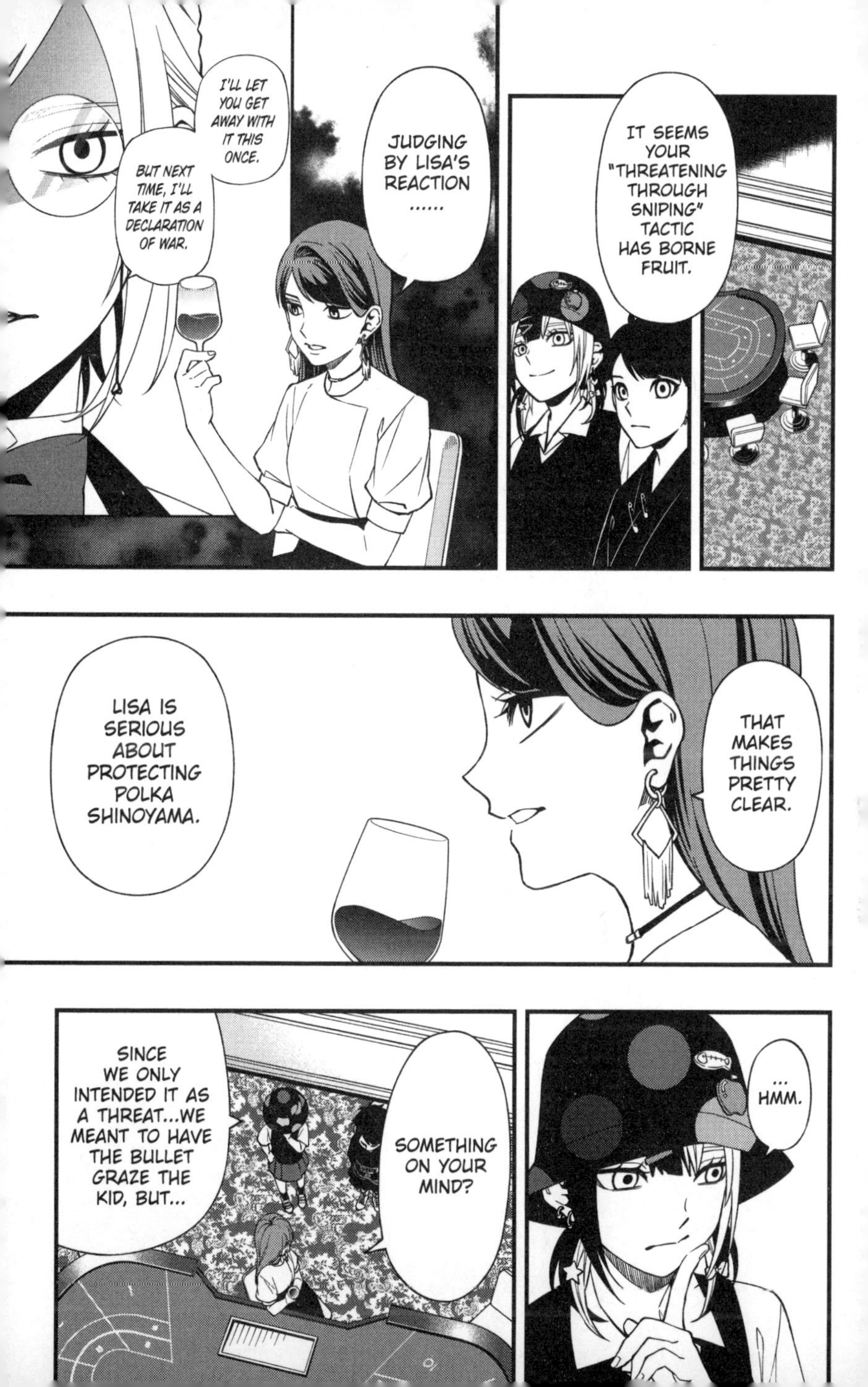
IT SEEMS YOUR "THREATENING THROUGH SNIPING" TACTIC HAS BORNE FRUIT.
JUDGING BY LISA'S REACTION ......
I'LL LET YOU GET AWAY WITH IT THIS ONCE.
BUT NEXT TIME, I'LL TAKE IT AS A DECLARATION OF WAR.
THAT MAKES THINGS PRETTY CLEAR.
LISA IS SERIOUS ABOUT PROTECTING POLKA SHINOYAMA.
... HMM.
SOMETHING ON YOUR MIND?
SINCE WE ONLY INTENDED IT AS A THREAT...WE MEANT TO HAVE THE BULLET GRAZE THE KID, BUT...

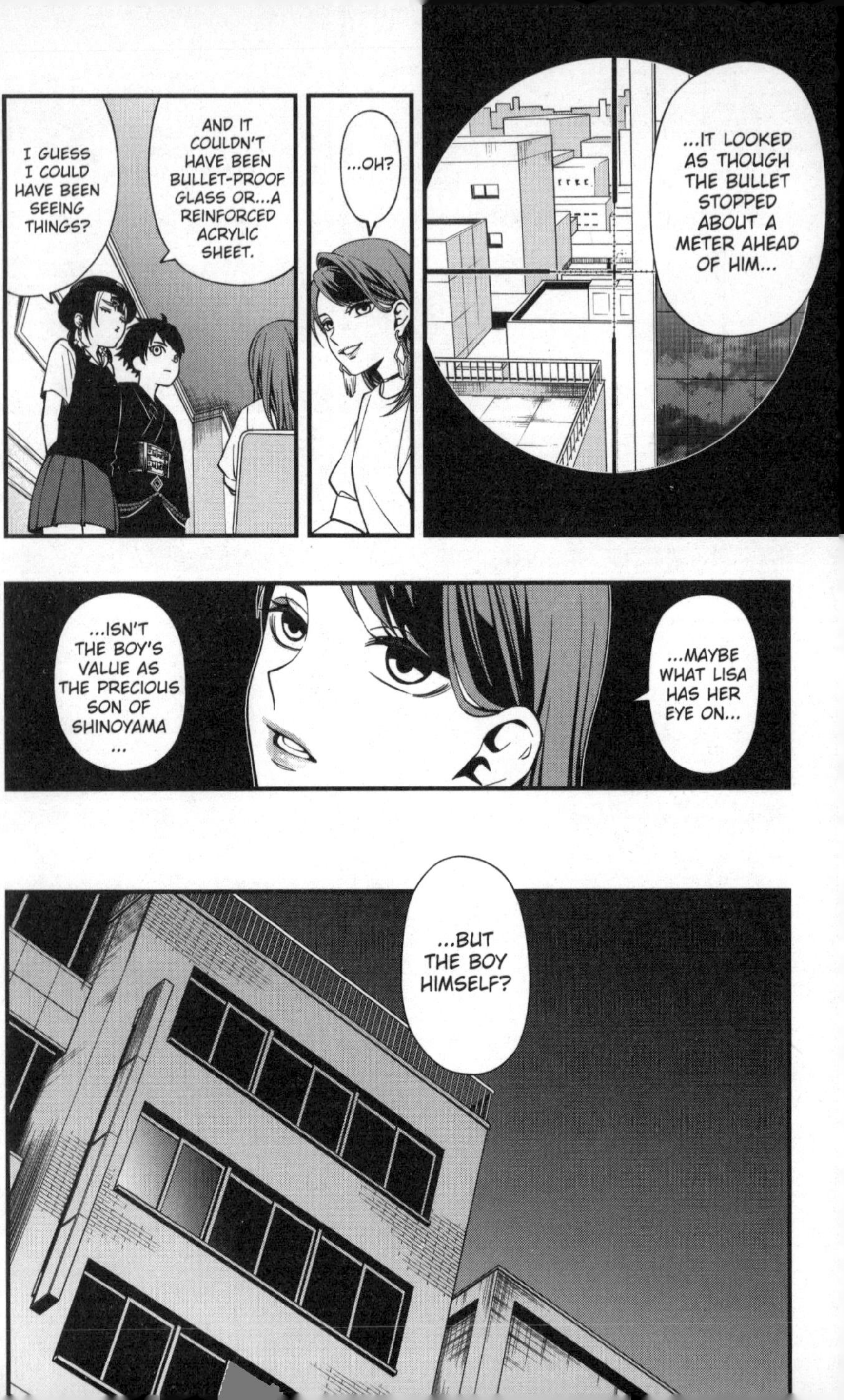
...IT LOOKED AS THOUGH THE BULLET STOPPED ABOUT A METER AHEAD OF HIM...
...OH?
AND IT COULDN'T HAVE BEEN BULLET-PROOF GLASS OR...A REINFORCED ACRYLIC SHEET.
I GUESS I COULD HAVE BEEN SEEING THINGS?
...MAYBE WHAT LISA HAS HER EYE ON...
...ISN'T THE BOY'S VALUE AS THE PRECIOUS SON OF SHINOYAMA...
...BUT THE BOY HIMSELF?

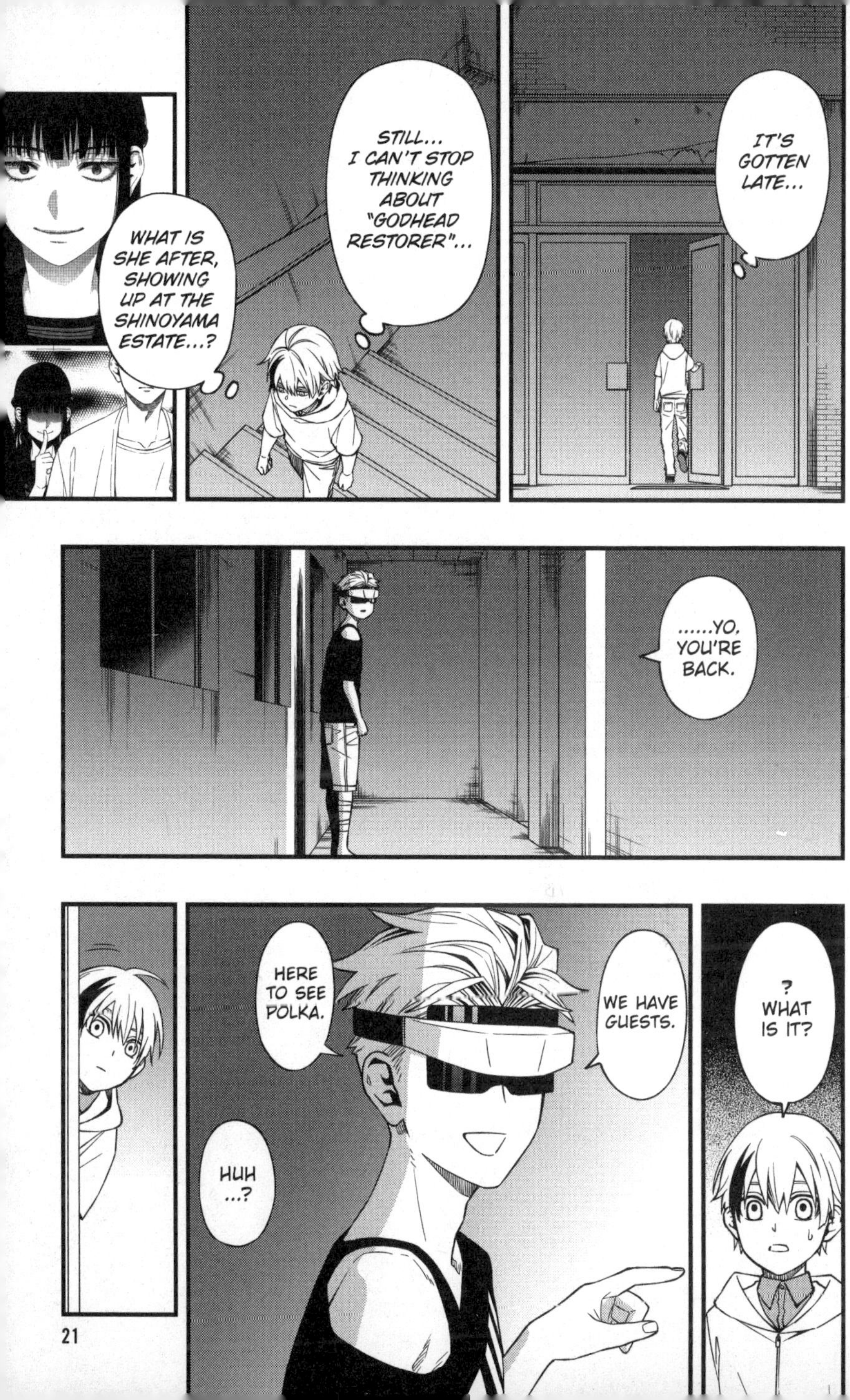
IT'S GOTTEN LATE...
STILL... I CAN'T STOP THINKING ABOUT "GODHEAD RESTORER"...
WHAT IS SHE AFTER, SHOWING UP AT THE SHINOYAMA ESTATE...?
......YO, YOU'RE BACK.
? WHAT IS IT?
WE HAVE GUESTS.
HERE TO SEE POLKA.
HUH ...?

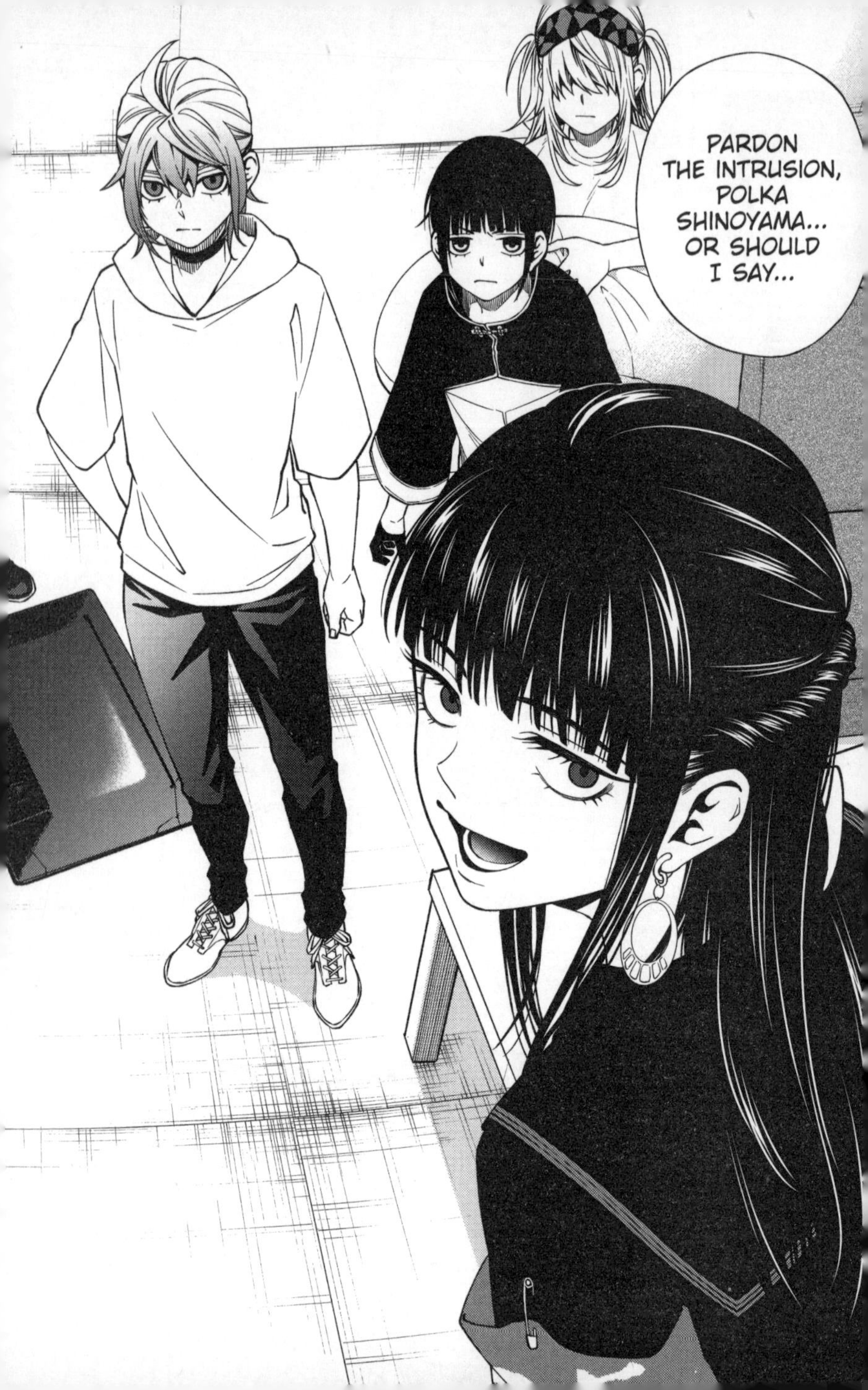
PARDON THE INTRUSION, POLKA SHINOYAMA... OR SHOULD I SAY...

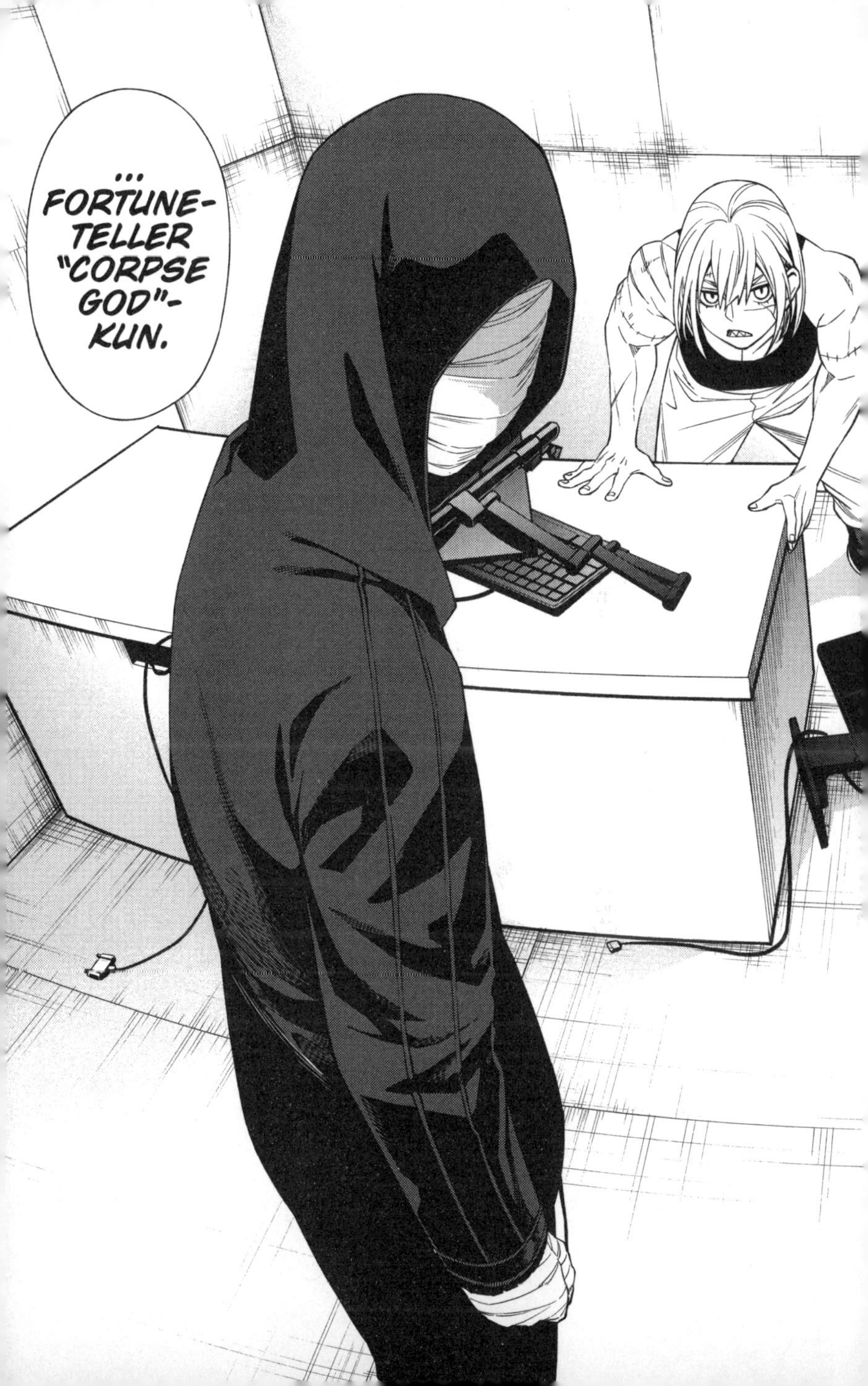
... FORTUNE-TELLER "CORPSE GOD"-KUN.

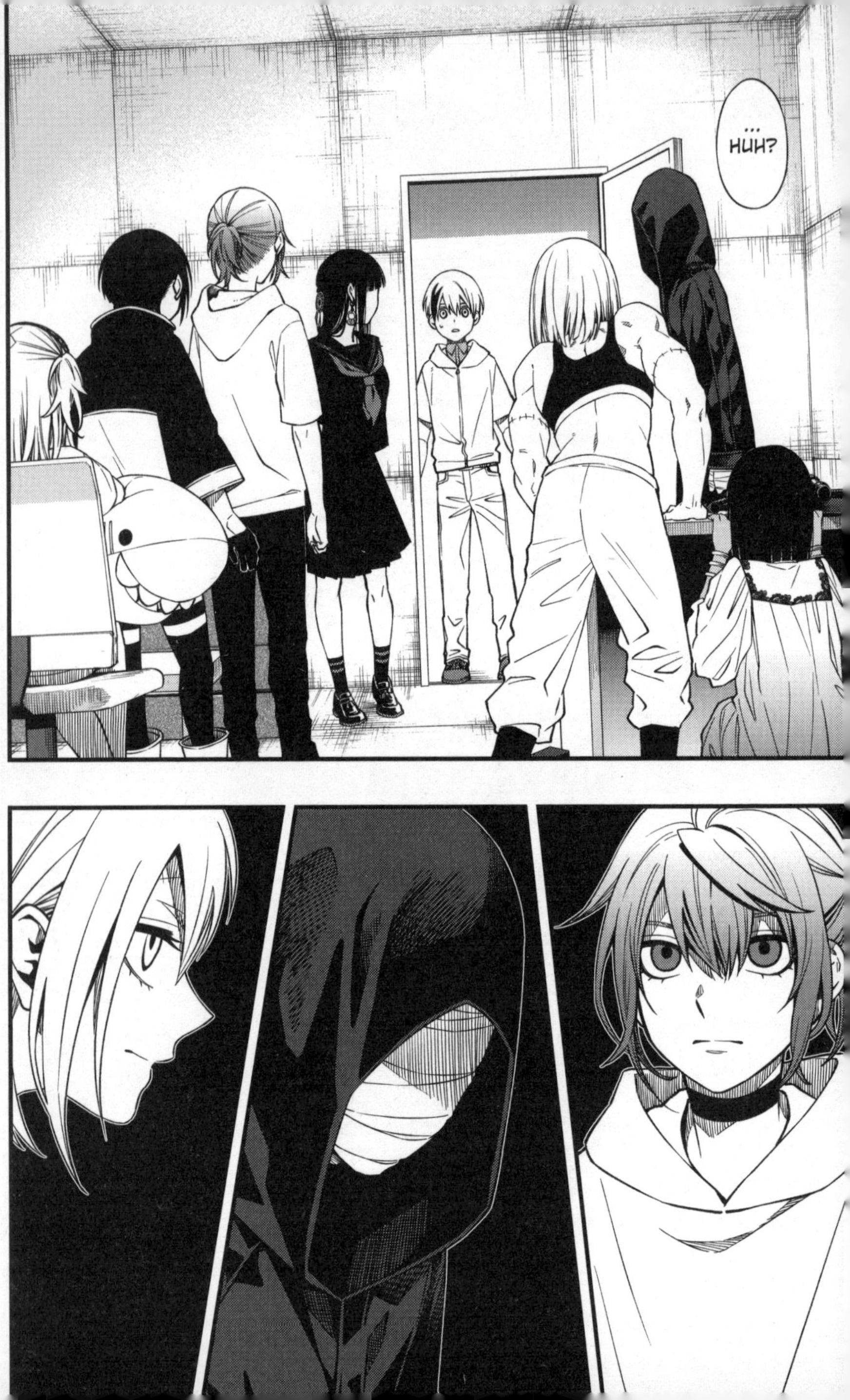
...HUH?

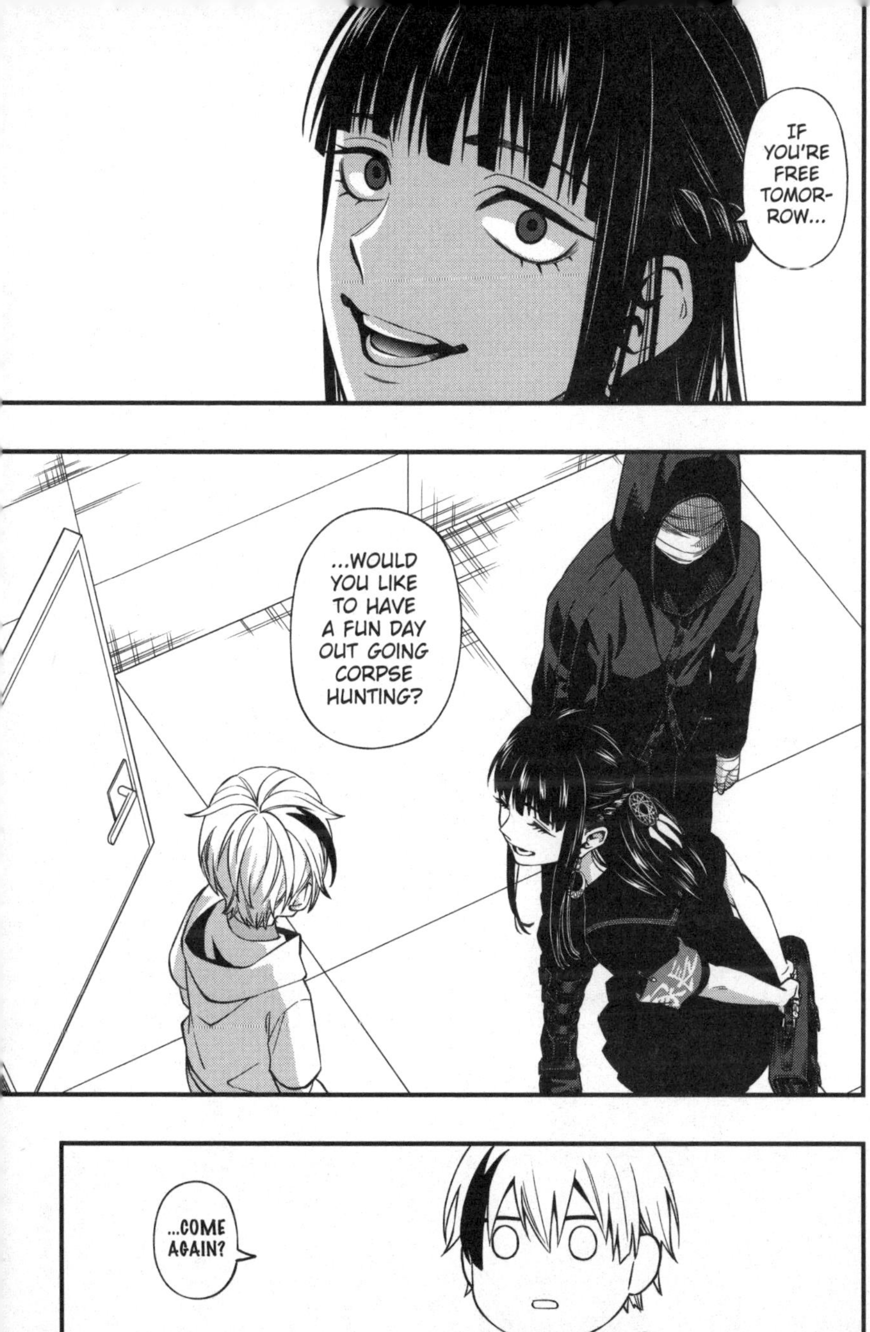
IF YOU'RE FREE TOMORROW...
...WOULD YOU LIKE TO HAVE A FUN DAY OUT GOING CORPSE HUNTING?
...COME AGAIN?

# DEAD MOUNT DEATH PLAY

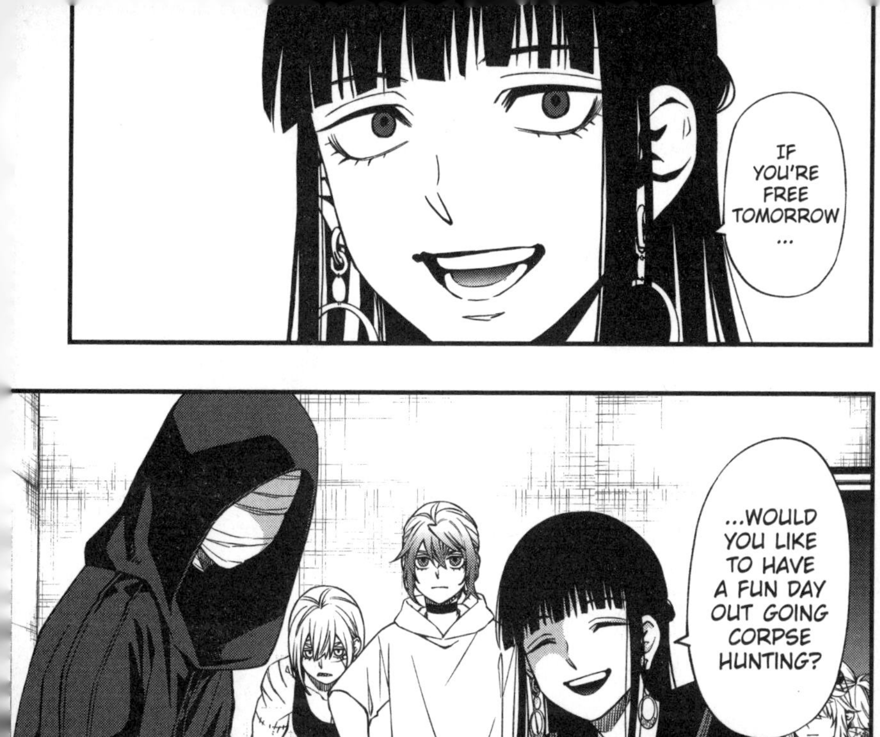
IF YOU'RE FREE TOMORROW ...
...WOULD YOU LIKE TO HAVE A FUN DAY OUT GOING CORPSE HUNTING?
...COME AGAIN?

# #89

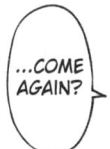

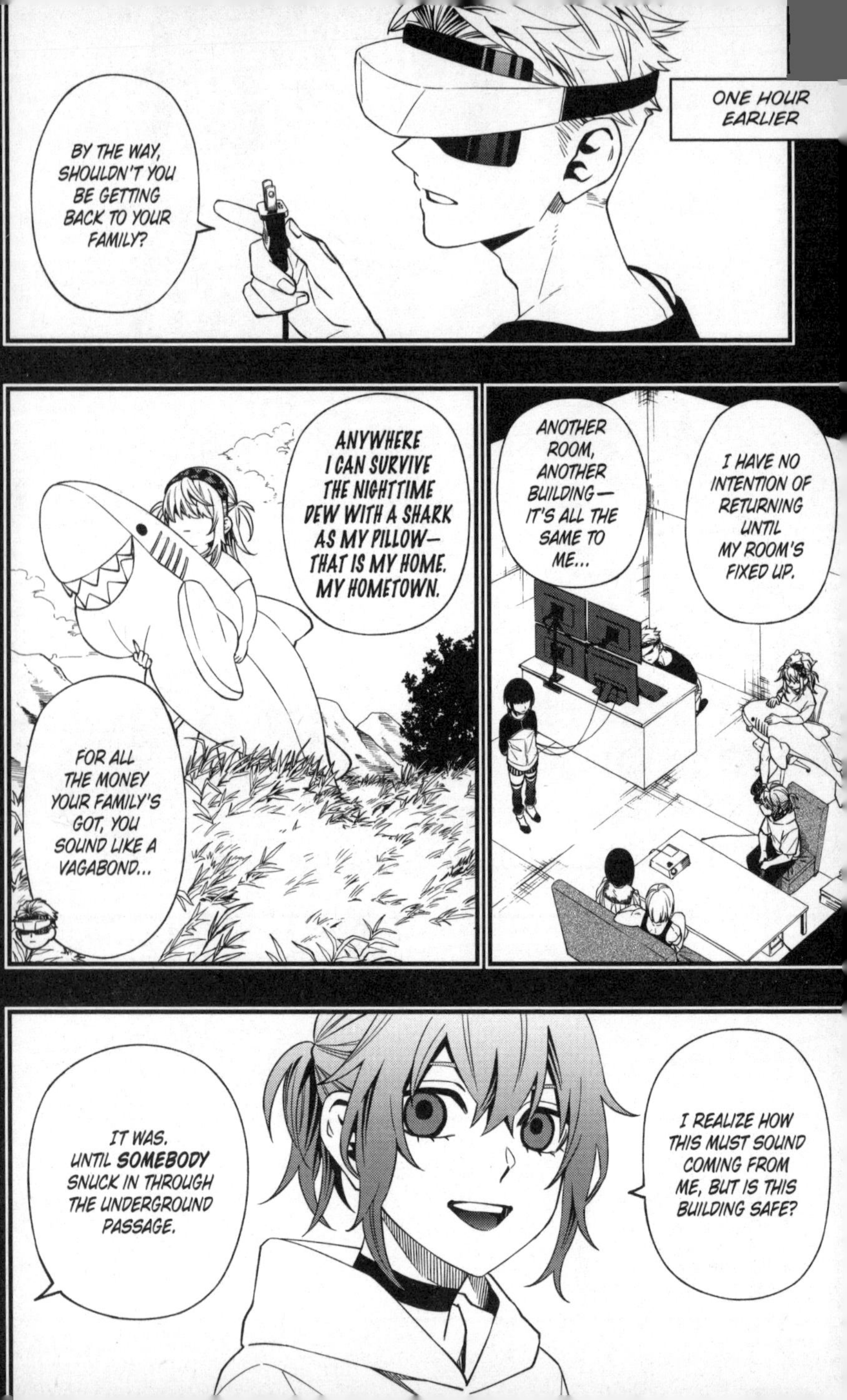
ONE HOUR EARLIER
BY THE WAY, SHOULDN'T YOU BE GETTING BACK TO YOUR FAMILY?
I HAVE NO INTENTION OF RETURNING UNTIL MY ROOM'S FIXED UP.
ANOTHER ROOM, ANOTHER BUILDING— IT'S ALL THE SAME TO ME...
ANYWHERE I CAN SURVIVE THE NIGHTTIME DEW WITH A SHARK AS MY PILLOW— THAT IS MY HOME. MY HOMETOWN.
FOR ALL THE MONEY YOUR FAMILY'S GOT, YOU SOUND LIKE A VAGABOND...
I REALIZE HOW THIS MUST SOUND COMING FROM ME, BUT IS THIS BUILDING SAFE?
IT WAS. UNTIL SOMEBODY SNUCK IN THROUGH THE UNDERGROUND PASSAGE.

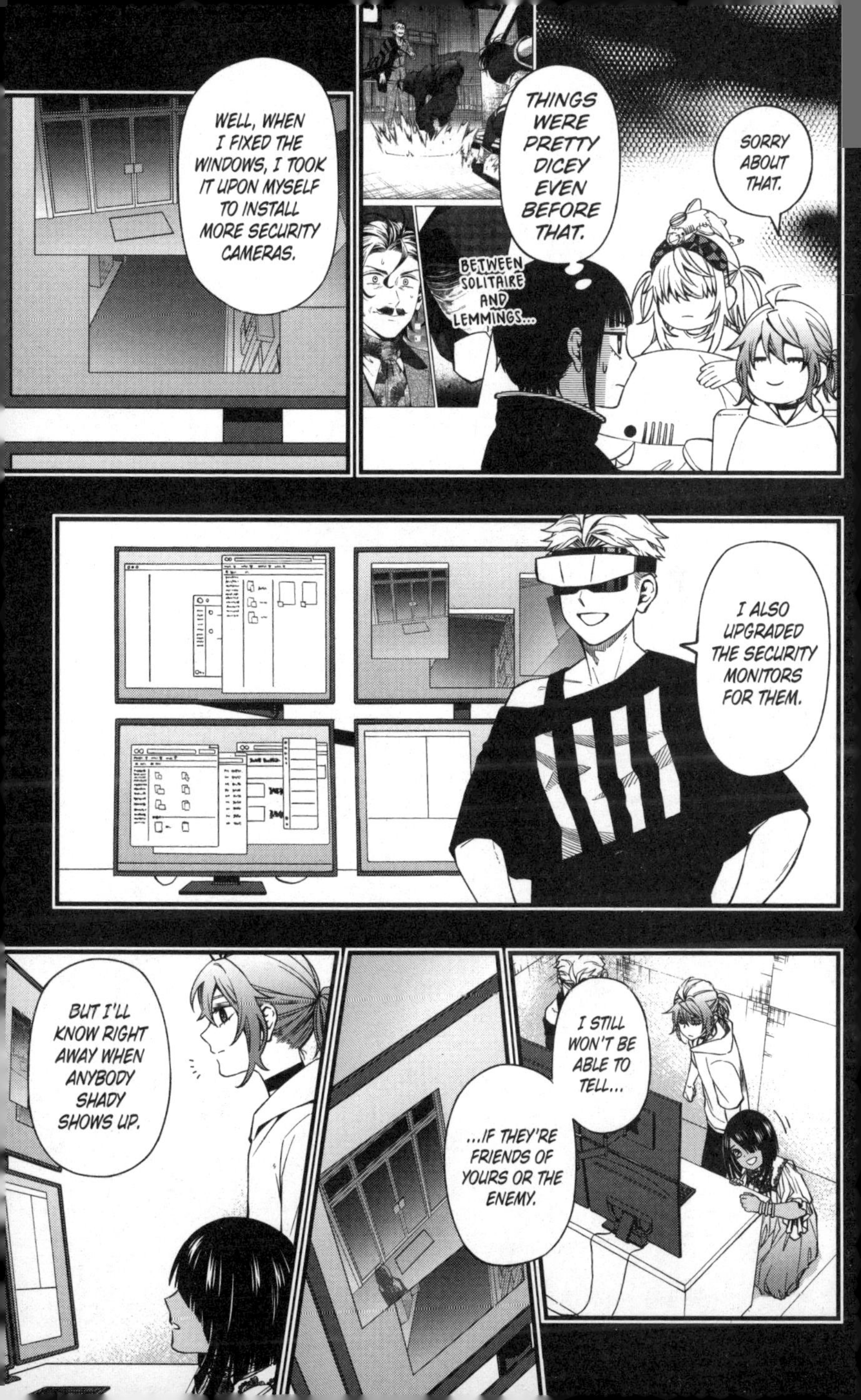
SORRY ABOUT THAT.
THINGS WERE PRETTY DICEY EVEN BEFORE THAT.
BETWEEN SOLITAIRE AND LEMMINGS...
WELL, WHEN I FIXED THE WINDOWS, I TOOK IT UPON MYSELF TO INSTALL MORE SECURITY CAMERAS.
I ALSO UPGRADED THE SECURITY MONITORS FOR THEM.
I STILL WON'T BE ABLE TO TELL...
...IF THEY'RE FRIENDS OF YOURS OR THE ENEMY.
BUT I'LL KNOW RIGHT AWAY WHEN ANYBODY SHADY SHOWS UP.

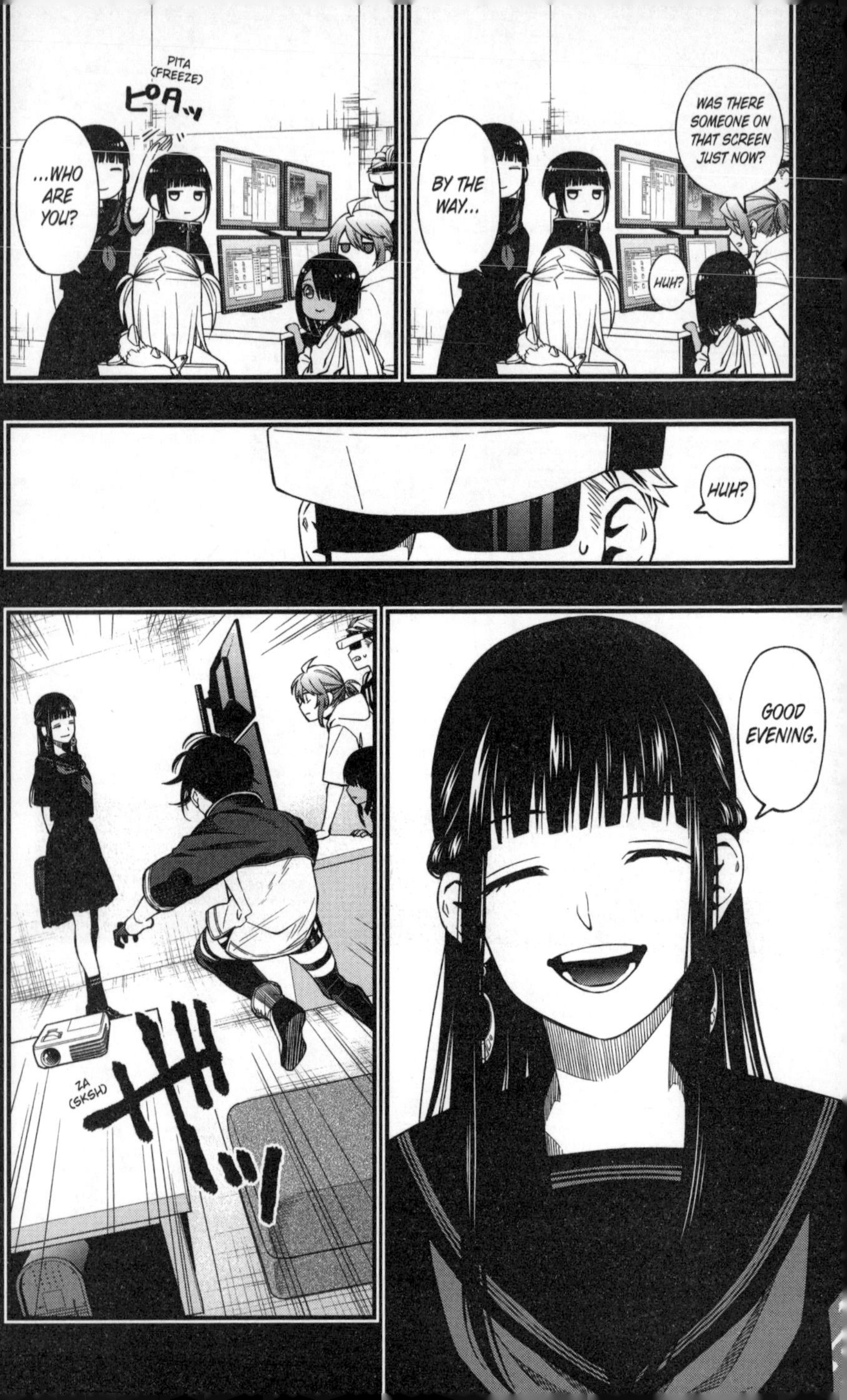
WAS THERE SOMEONE ON THAT SCREEN JUST NOW?
HUH?
BY THE WAY...
PITA (FREEZE)
ピタッ
...WHO ARE YOU?
HUH?
GOOD EVENING.
ZA (SKSH)
ザッ

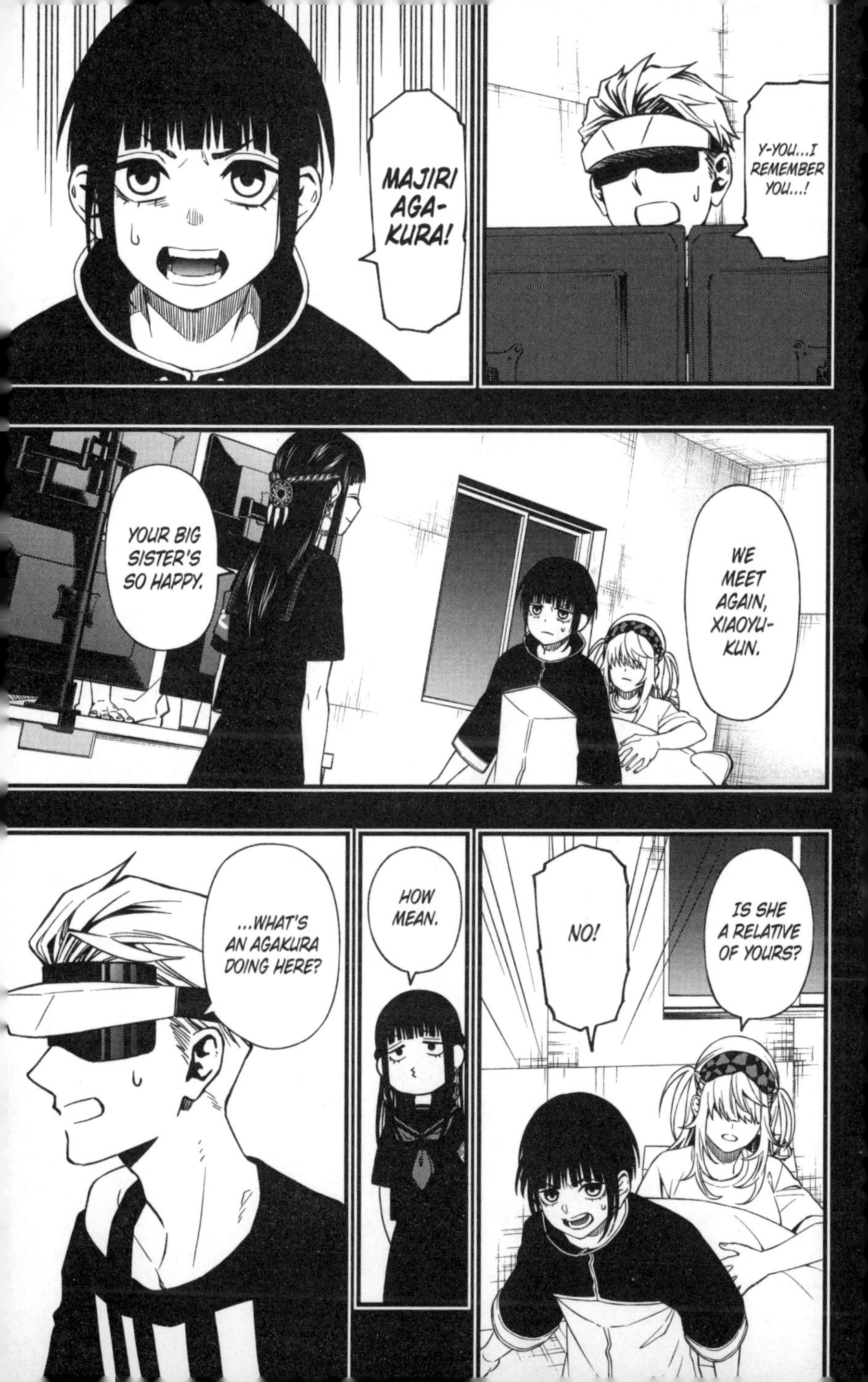
Y-YOU...I REMEMBER YOU...!
MAJIRI AGAKURA!
WE MEET AGAIN, XIAOYU-KUN.
YOUR BIG SISTER'S SO HAPPY.
IS SHE A RELATIVE OF YOURS?
NO!
HOW MEAN.
...WHAT'S AN AGAKURA DOING HERE?

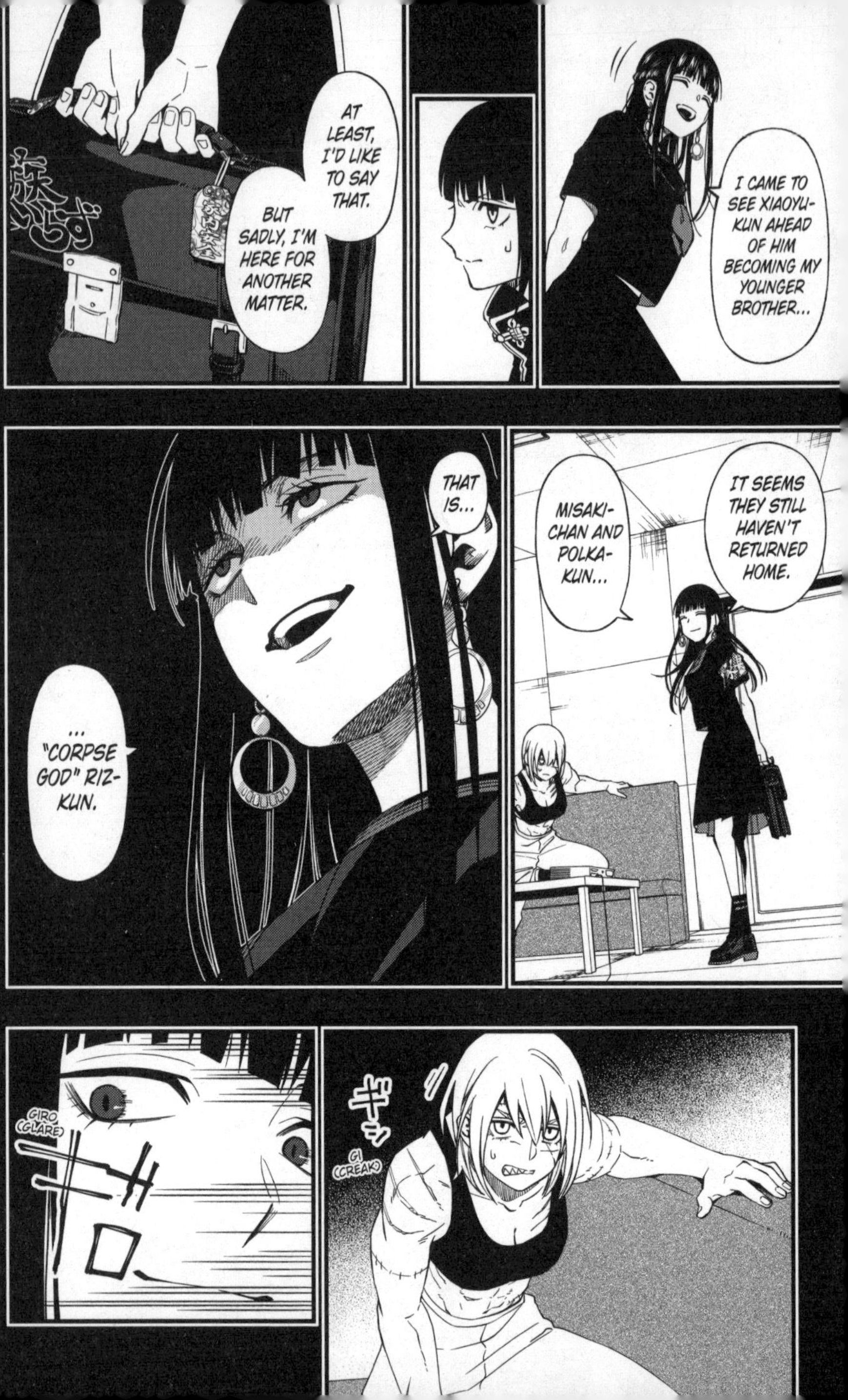
I CAME TO SEE XIAOYU-KUN AHEAD OF HIM BECOMING MY YOUNGER BROTHER...
AT LEAST, I'D LIKE TO SAY THAT.
BUT SADLY, I'M HERE FOR ANOTHER MATTER.
IT SEEMS THEY STILL HAVEN'T RETURNED HOME.
MISAKI-CHAN AND POLKA-KUN...
THAT IS...
..."CORPSE GOD" RIZ-KUN.
ギッ
GI (CREAK)
ギロ
GIRO (GLARE)

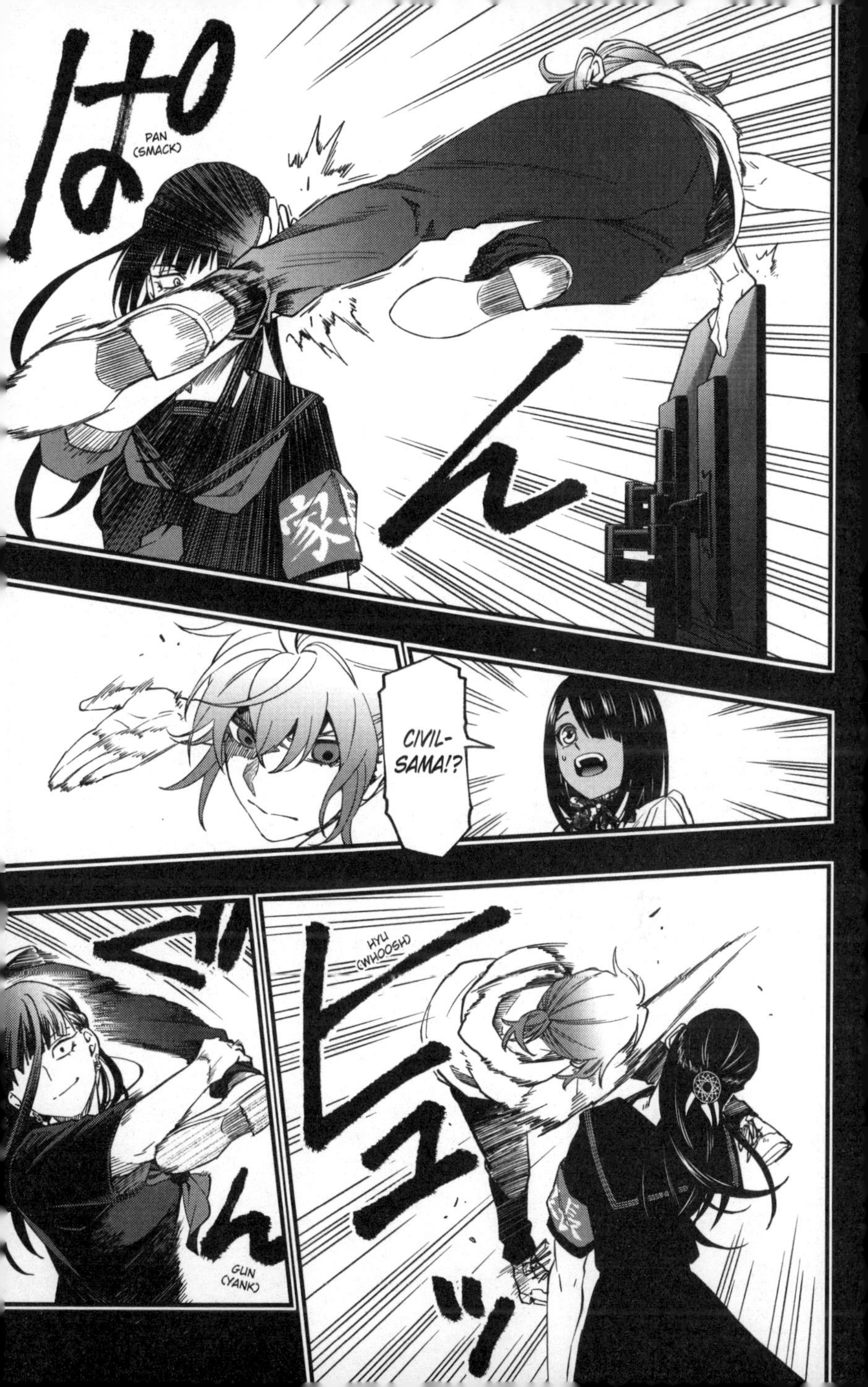
PAN (SMACK)
CIVIL-SAMA!?
HYU (WHOOSH)
GUN (YANK)

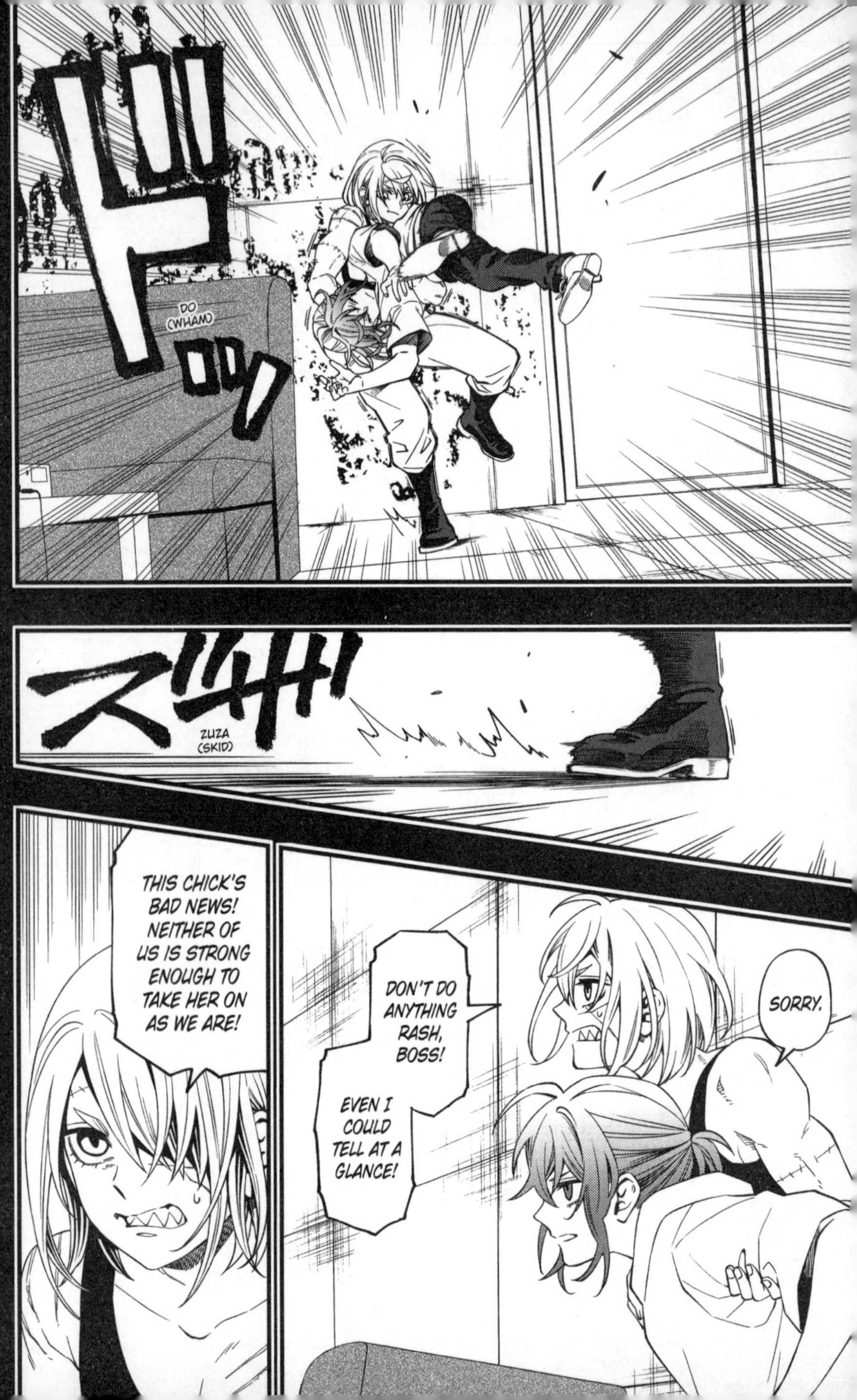
DO
(WHAM)
ZUZA
(SKID)
THIS CHICK'S BAD NEWS! NEITHER OF US IS STRONG ENOUGH TO TAKE HER ON AS WE ARE!
SORRY.
DON'T DO ANYTHING RASH, BOSS!
EVEN I COULD TELL AT A GLANCE!

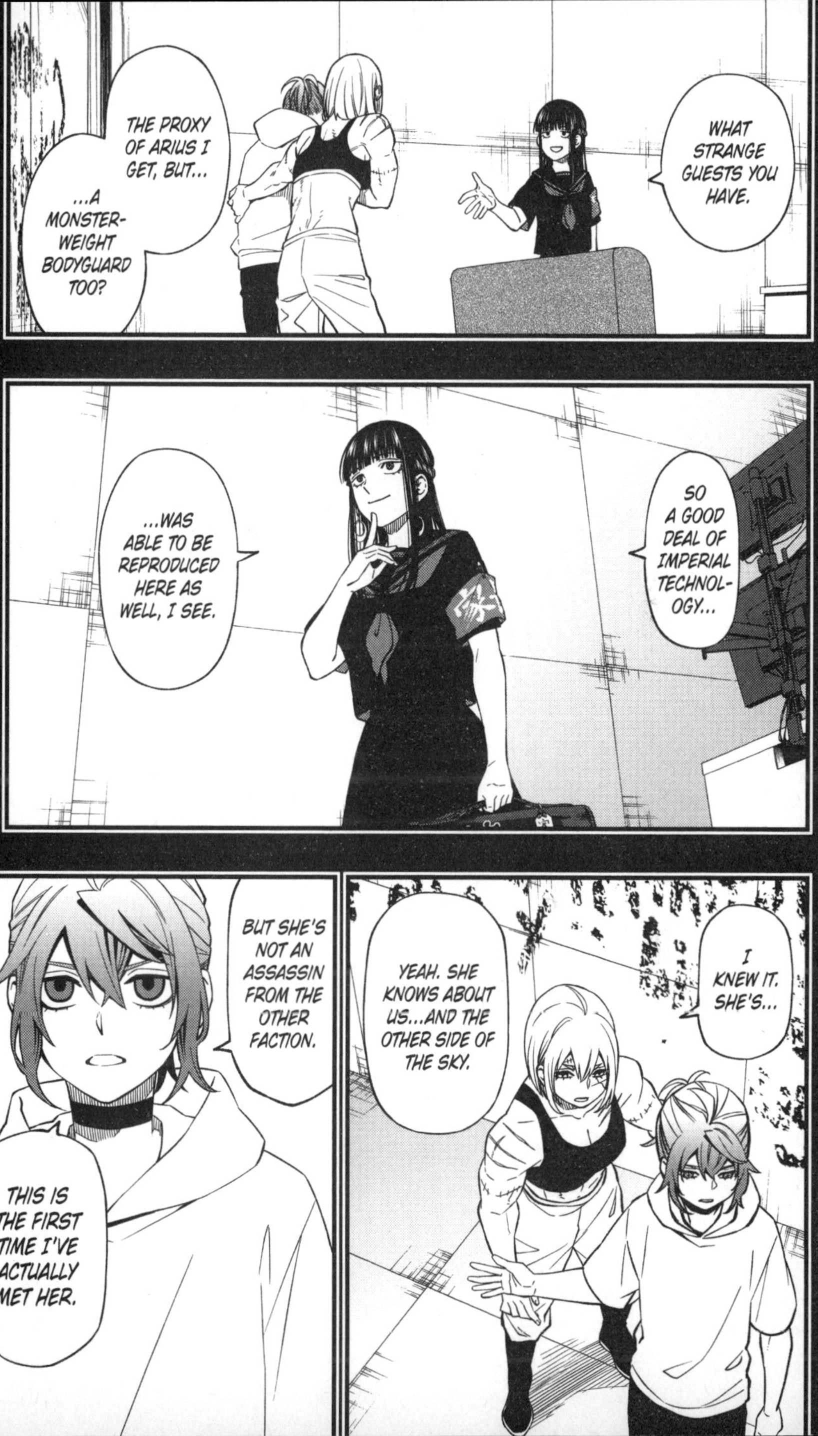
WHAT STRANGE GUESTS YOU HAVE.
THE PROXY OF ARIUS I GET, BUT...
...A MONSTER-WEIGHT BODYGUARD TOO?
SO A GOOD DEAL OF IMPERIAL TECHNOL-OGY...
...WAS ABLE TO BE REPRODUCED HERE AS WELL, I SEE.
I KNEW IT. SHE'S...
YEAH. SHE KNOWS ABOUT US...AND THE OTHER SIDE OF THE SKY.
BUT SHE'S NOT AN ASSASSIN FROM THE OTHER FACTION.
THIS IS THE FIRST TIME I'VE ACTUALLY MET HER.

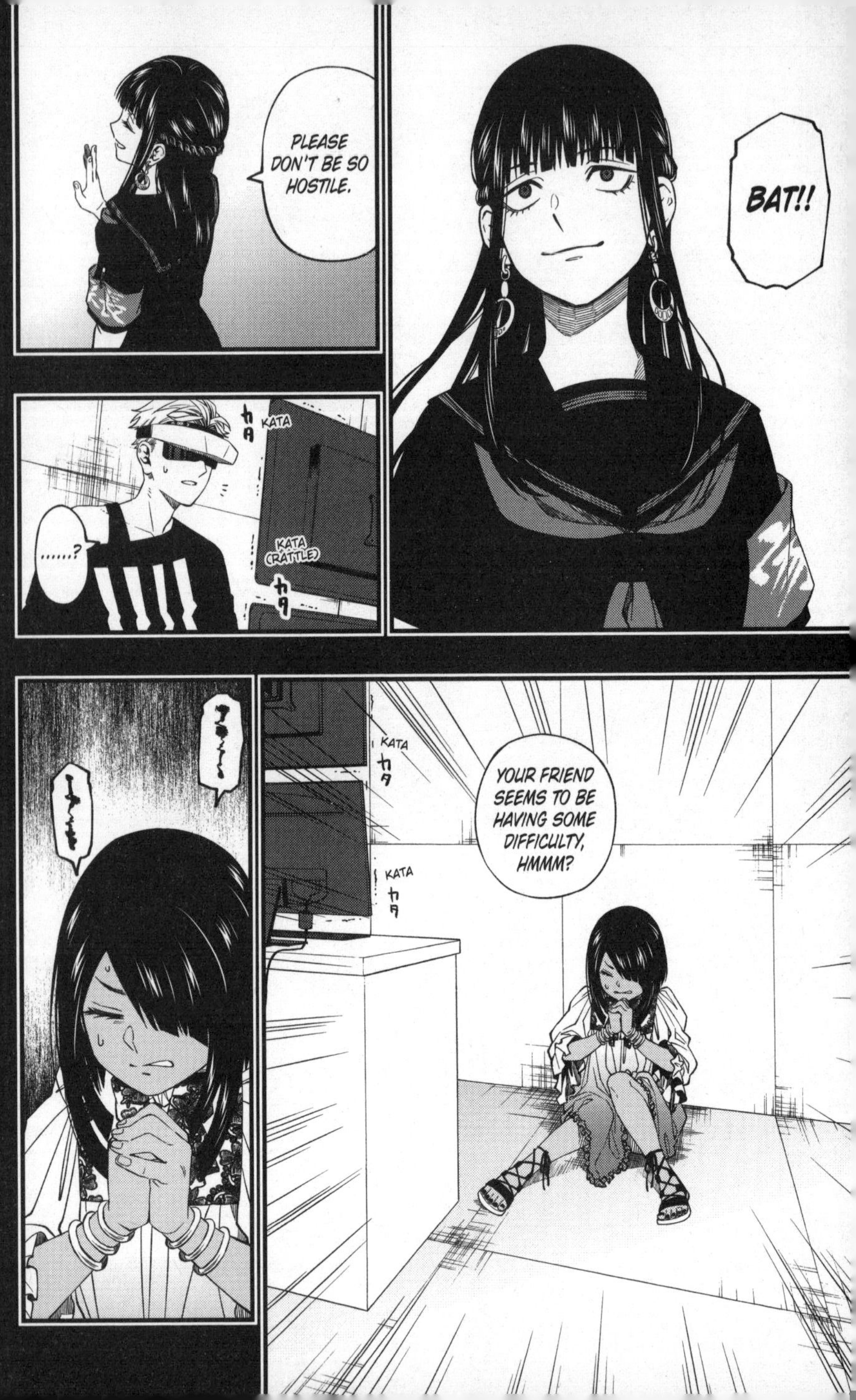
BAT!!
PLEASE DON'T BE SO HOSTILE.
KATA
カタ
......?
KATA (RATTLE)
カタ
KATA
カタ
YOUR FRIEND SEEMS TO BE HAVING SOME DIFFICULTY, HMMM?
KATA
カタ

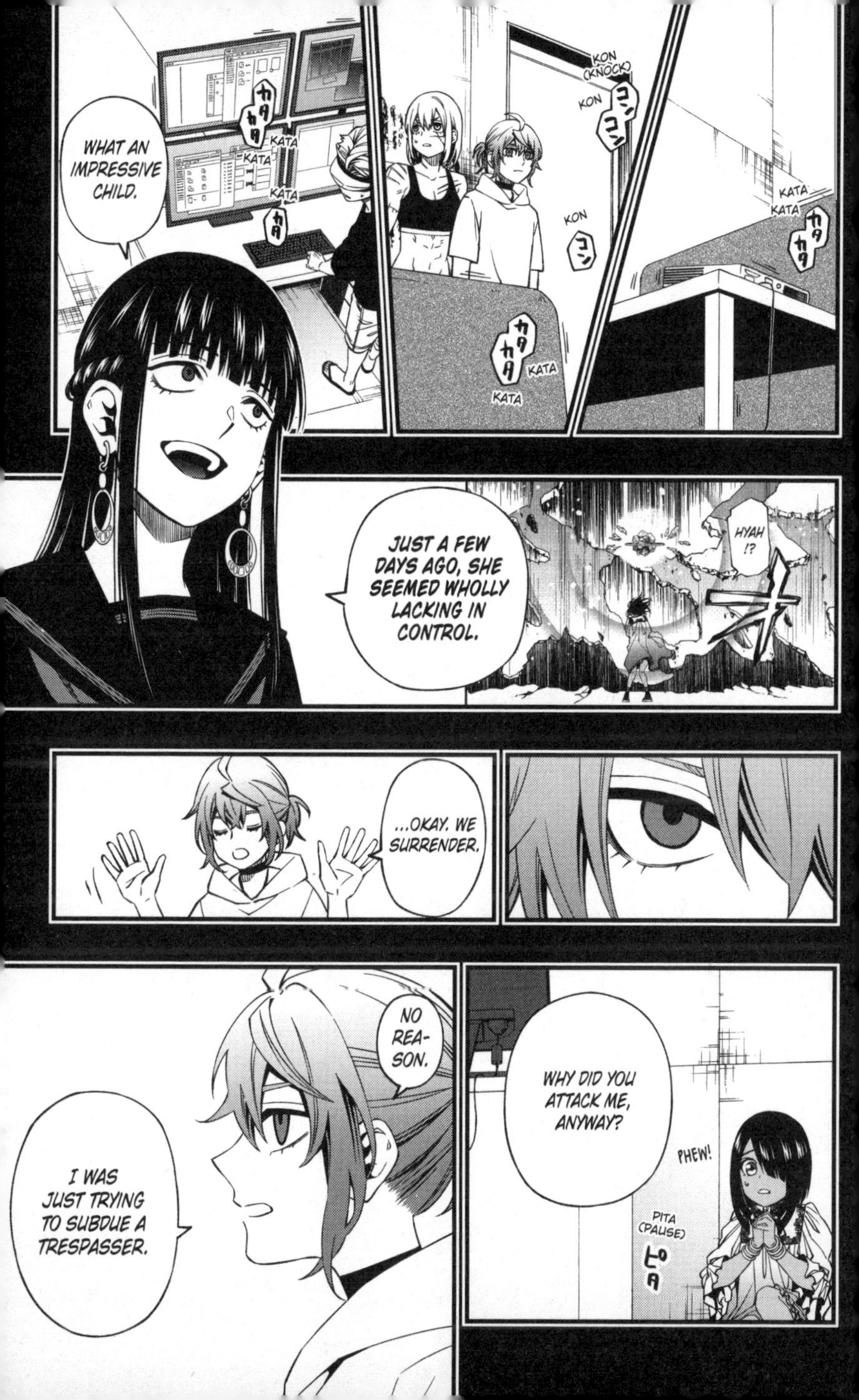
KATA KATA
カタカタ
KON (KNOCK)
KON
コンコン
KON
コン
カタカタ
KATA
KATA
WHAT AN IMPRESSIVE CHILD.
カタカタ
KATA
KATA
KATA
カタ
HYAH!?
JUST A FEW DAYS AGO, SHE SEEMED WHOLLY LACKING IN CONTROL.
...OKAY. WE SURRENDER.
WHY DID YOU ATTACK ME, ANYWAY?
PHEW!
PITA (PAUSE)
ピタ
NO REA-SON.
I WAS JUST TRYING TO SUBDUE A TRESPASSER.

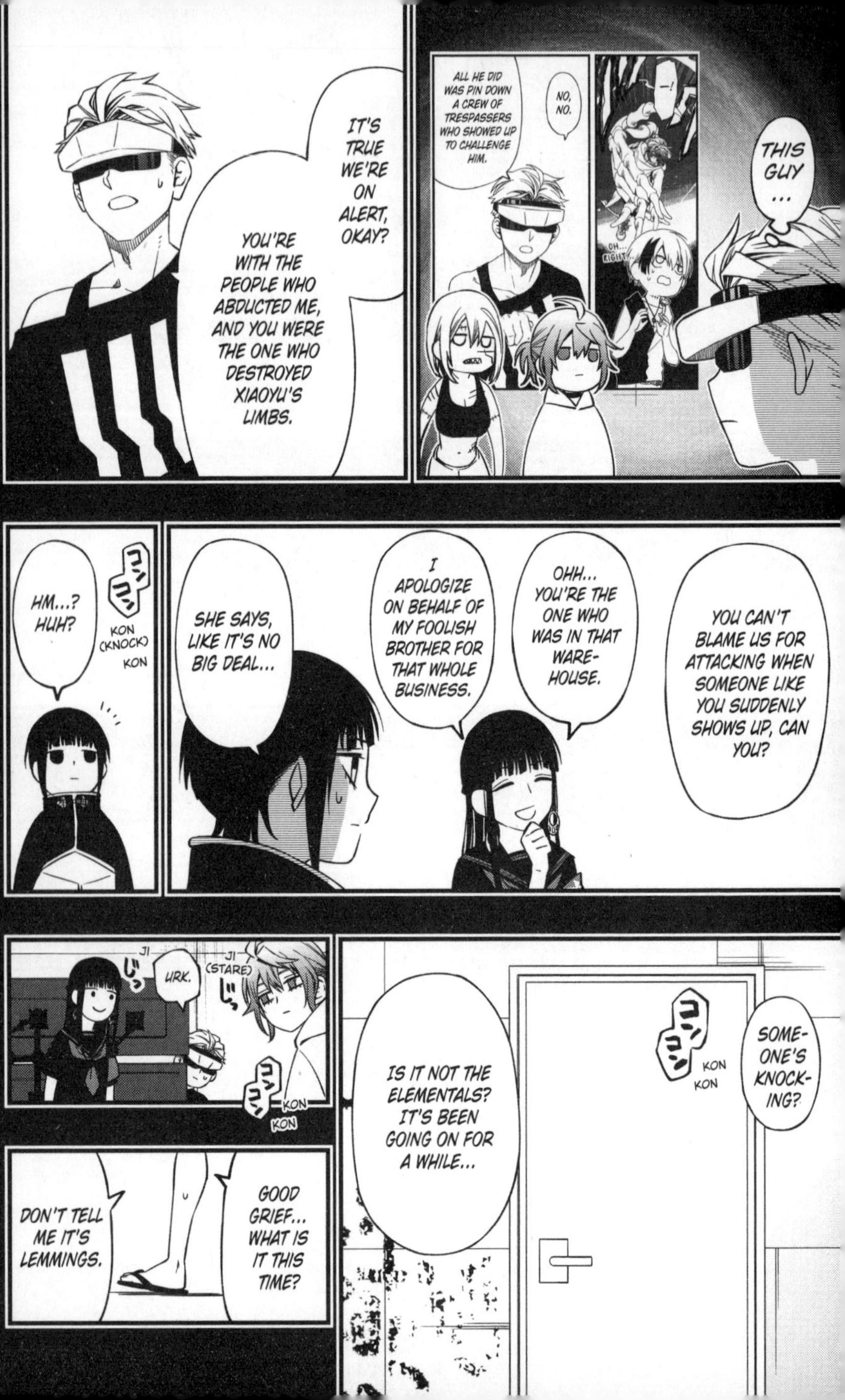
THIS GUY ...
NO, NO.
ALL HE DID WAS PIN DOWN A CREW OF TRESPASSERS WHO SHOWED UP TO CHALLENGE HIM.
—!
OH... RIGHT...
IT'S TRUE WE'RE ON ALERT, OKAY?
YOU'RE WITH THE PEOPLE WHO ABDUCTED ME, AND YOU WERE THE ONE WHO DESTROYED XIAOYU'S LIMBS.
YOU CAN'T BLAME US FOR ATTACKING WHEN SOMEONE LIKE YOU SUDDENLY SHOWS UP, CAN YOU?
OHH... YOU'RE THE ONE WHO WAS IN THAT WARE-HOUSE.
I APOLOGIZE ON BEHALF OF MY FOOLISH BROTHER FOR THAT WHOLE BUSINESS.
SHE SAYS, LIKE IT'S NO BIG DEAL...
KON (KNOCK) KON
HM...? HUH?
SOME-ONE'S KNOCK-ING?
KON KON
IS IT NOT THE ELEMENTALS? IT'S BEEN GOING ON FOR A WHILE...
JI (STARE)
URK.
JI
KON KON
GOOD GRIEF... WHAT IS IT THIS TIME?
DON'T TELL ME IT'S LEMMINGS.

ガチャ
GACHA (KCHAK)
ぱたん
PATAN (SHUT)
コンコンコンコン
KON KON KON KON KON KON
ゴンゴンゴンゴン
GON (BAM) GON GON GON
UWAAH !?
ガチャ
GACHA

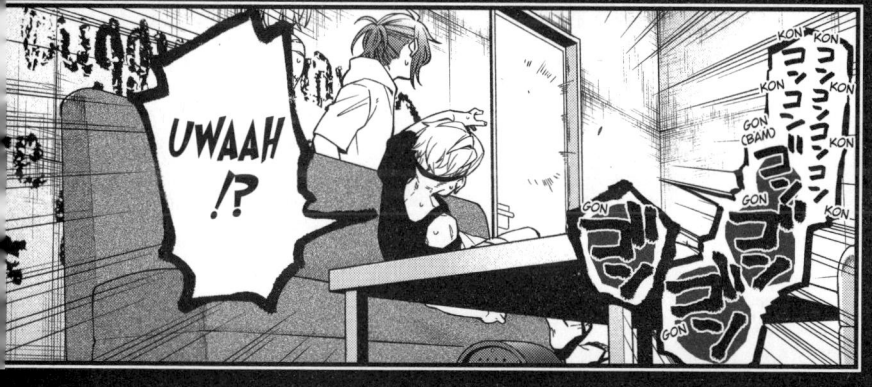

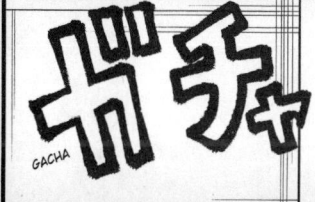

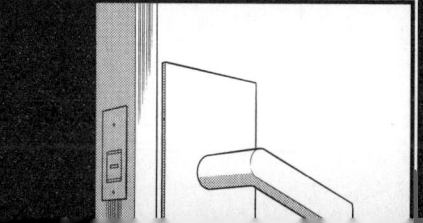

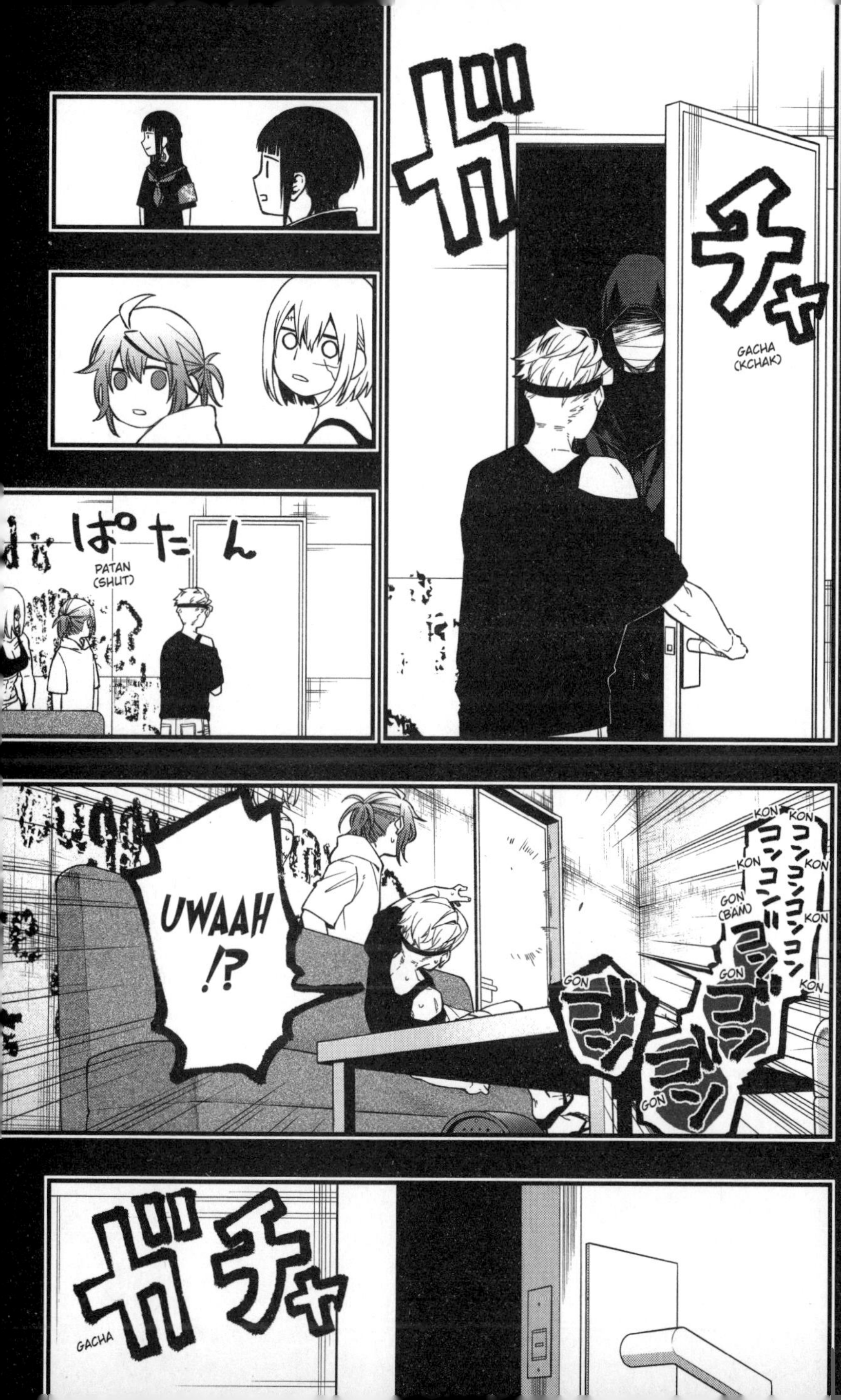

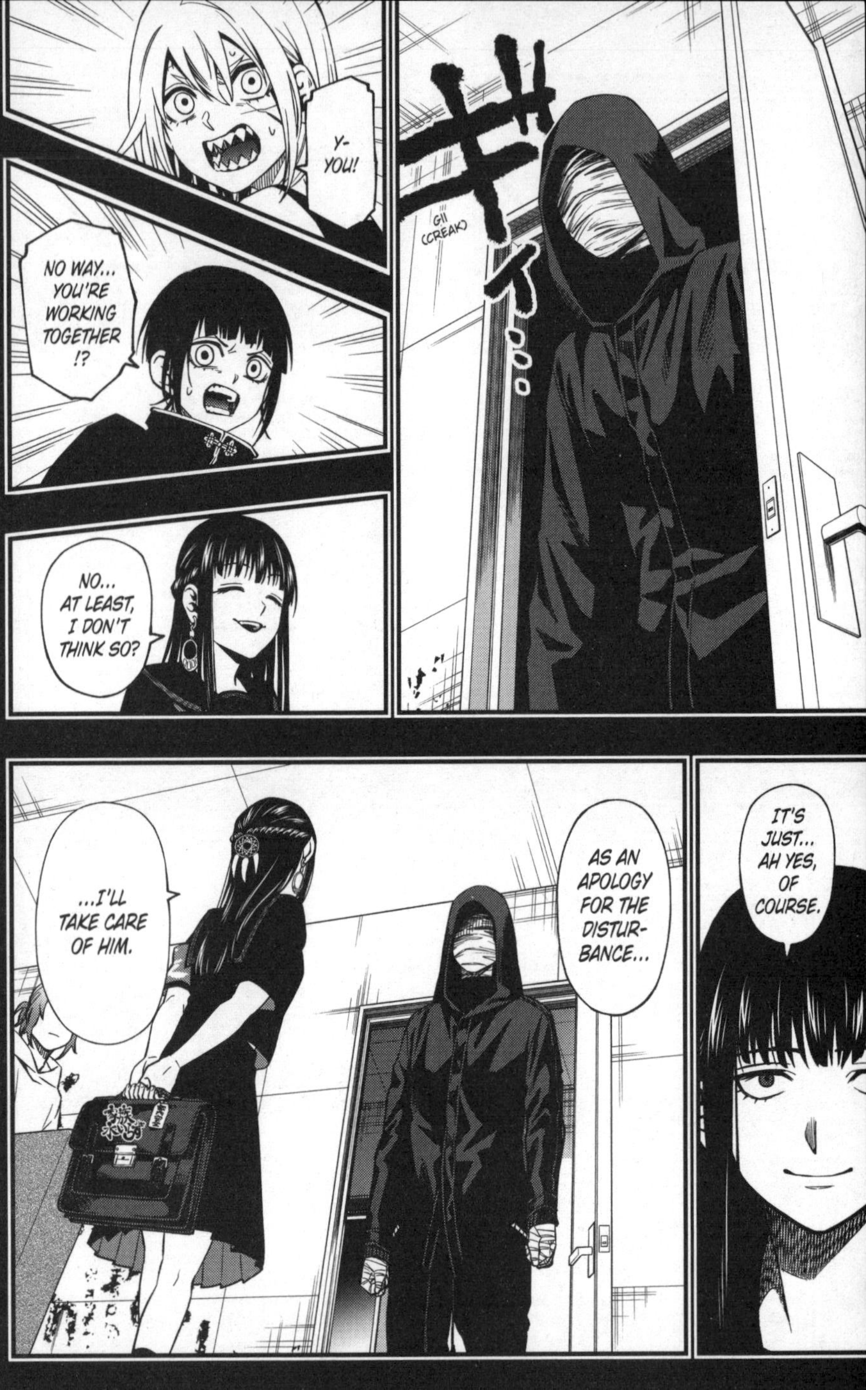
GII (CREAK)
Y-YOU!
NO WAY... YOU'RE WORKING TOGETHER!?
NO... AT LEAST, I DON'T THINK SO?
IT'S JUST... AH YES, OF COURSE.
AS AN APOLOGY FOR THE DISTUR-BANCE...
...I'LL TAKE CARE OF HIM.

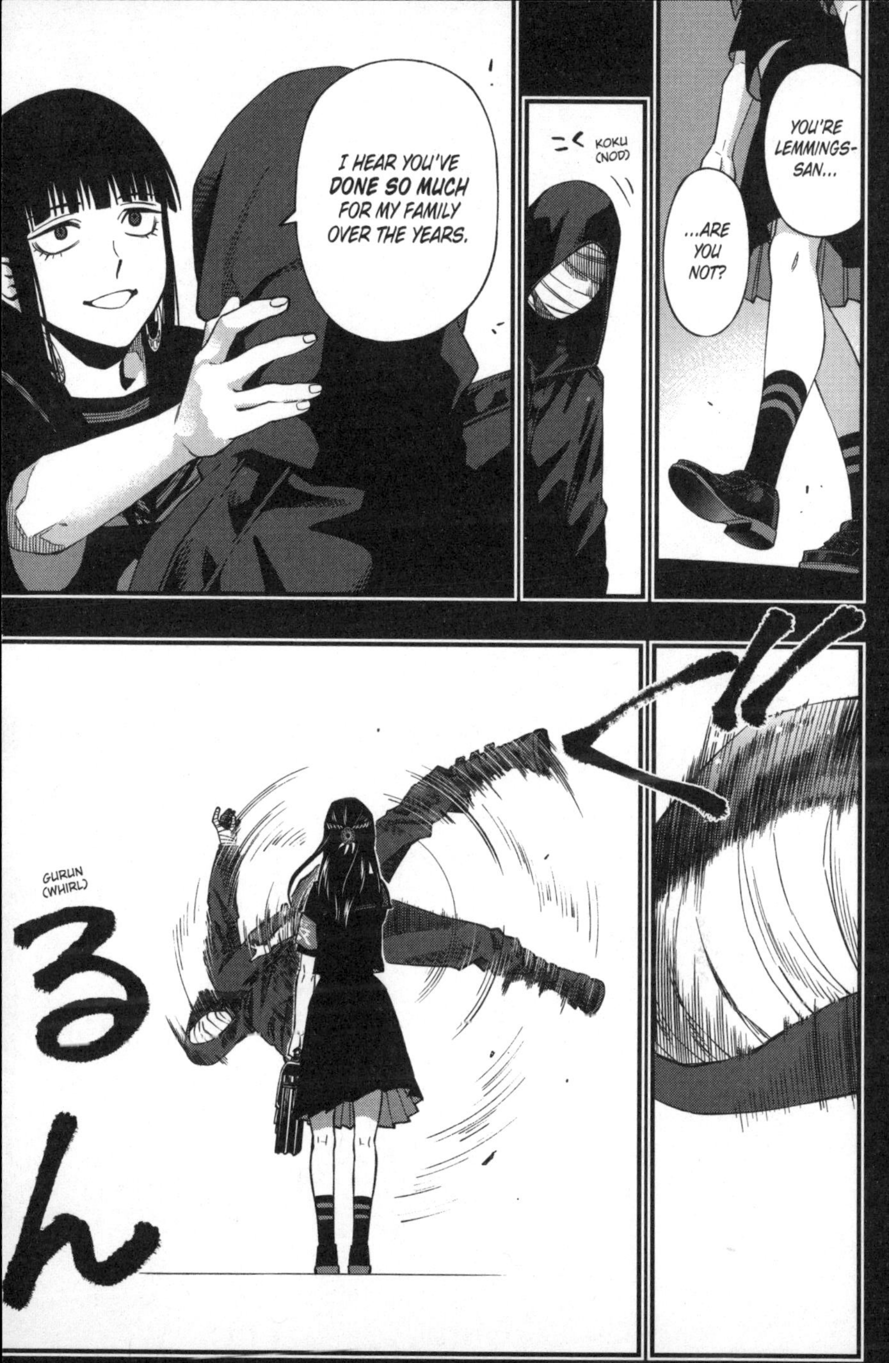

YOU'RE LEMMINGS-SAN...
...ARE YOU NOT?
KOKU (NOD)
I HEAR YOU'VE DONE SO MUCH FOR MY FAMILY OVER THE YEARS.
GURUN (WHIRL)
るん

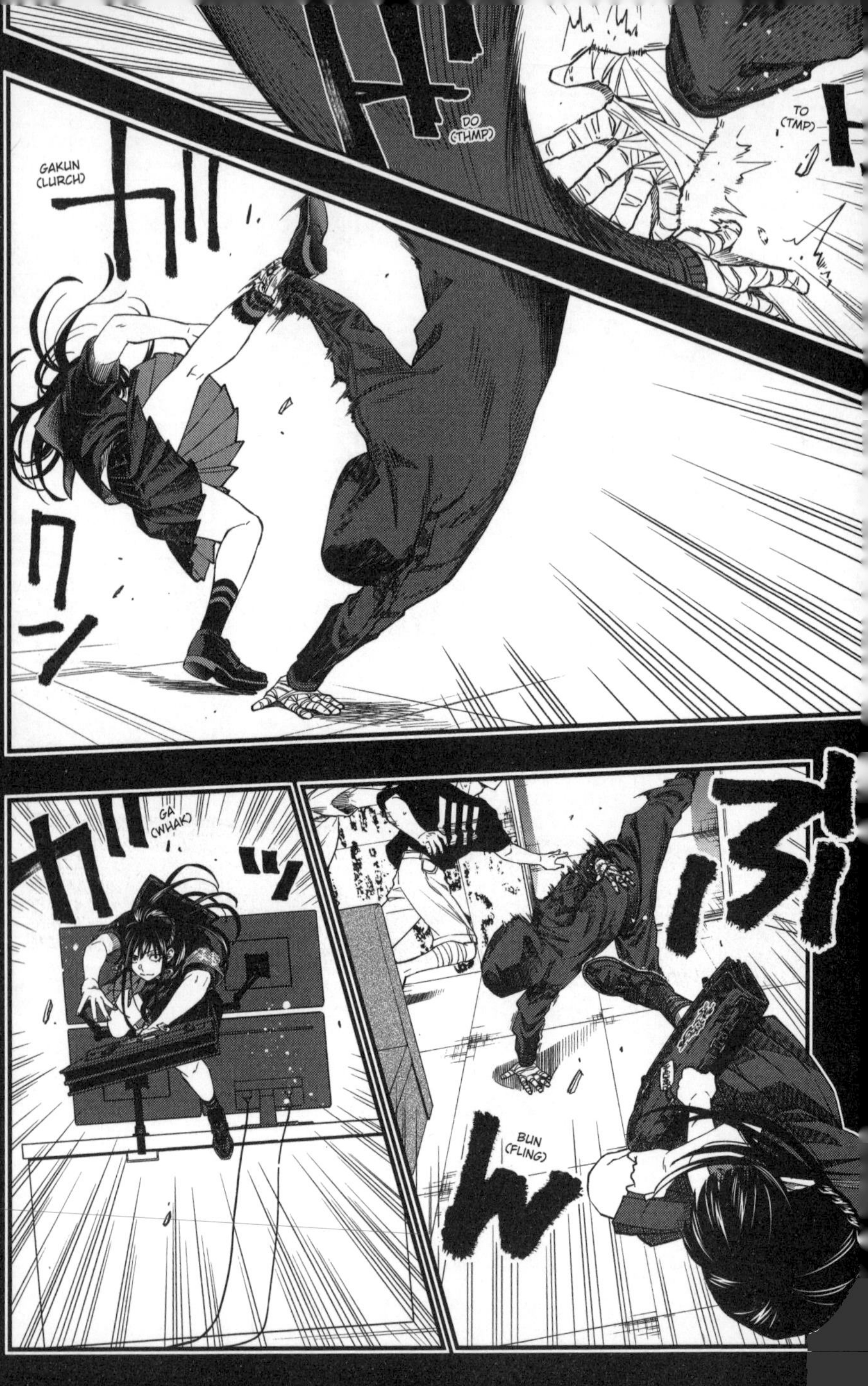
TO
(TMP)
DO
(THMP)
GAKUN
(LURCH)
BUN
(FLING)
GA
(WHAK)

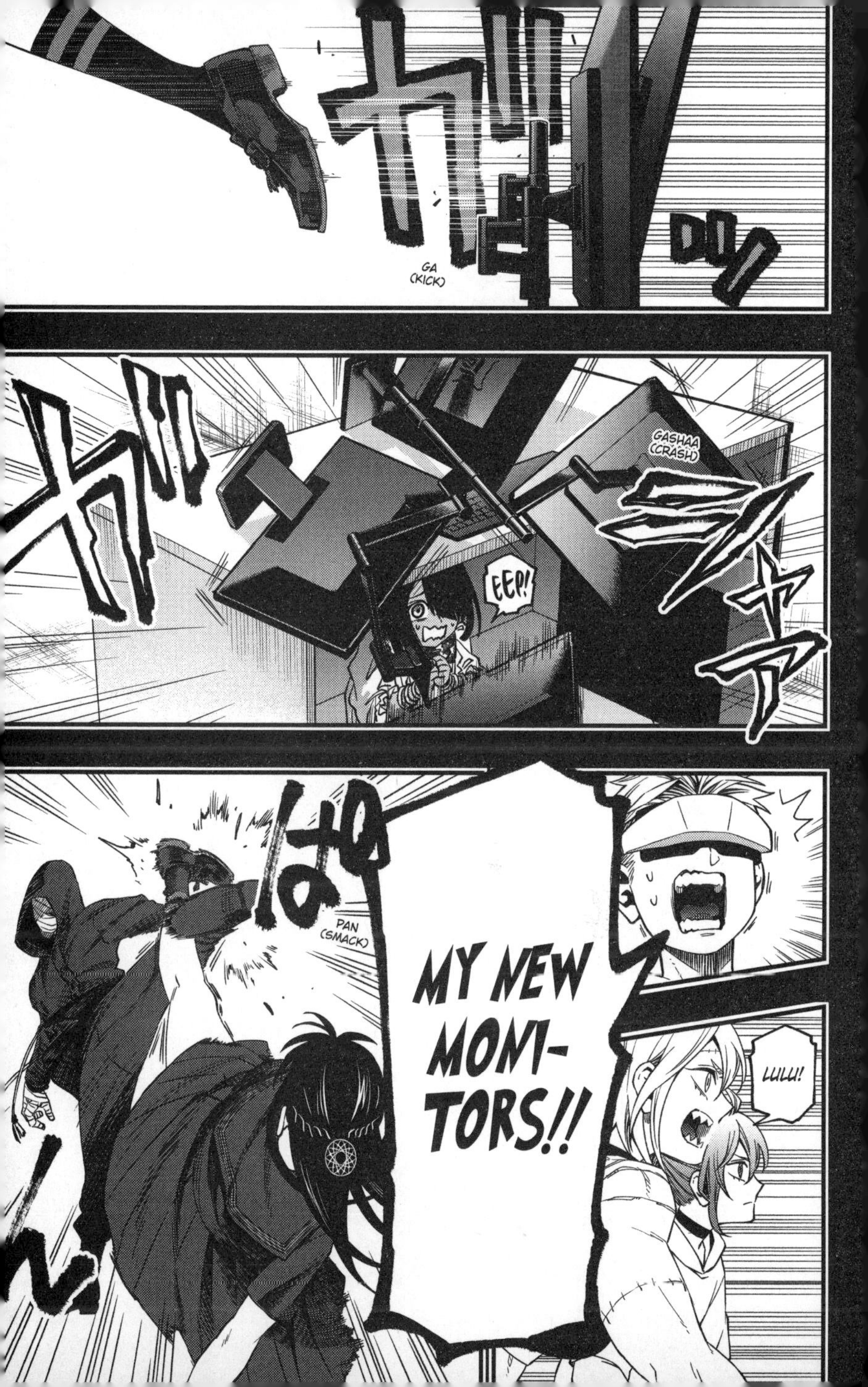
GA
(KICK)
GASHAA
(CRASH)
EEP!
MY NEW MONI-TORS!!
LULU!
PAN
(SMACK)

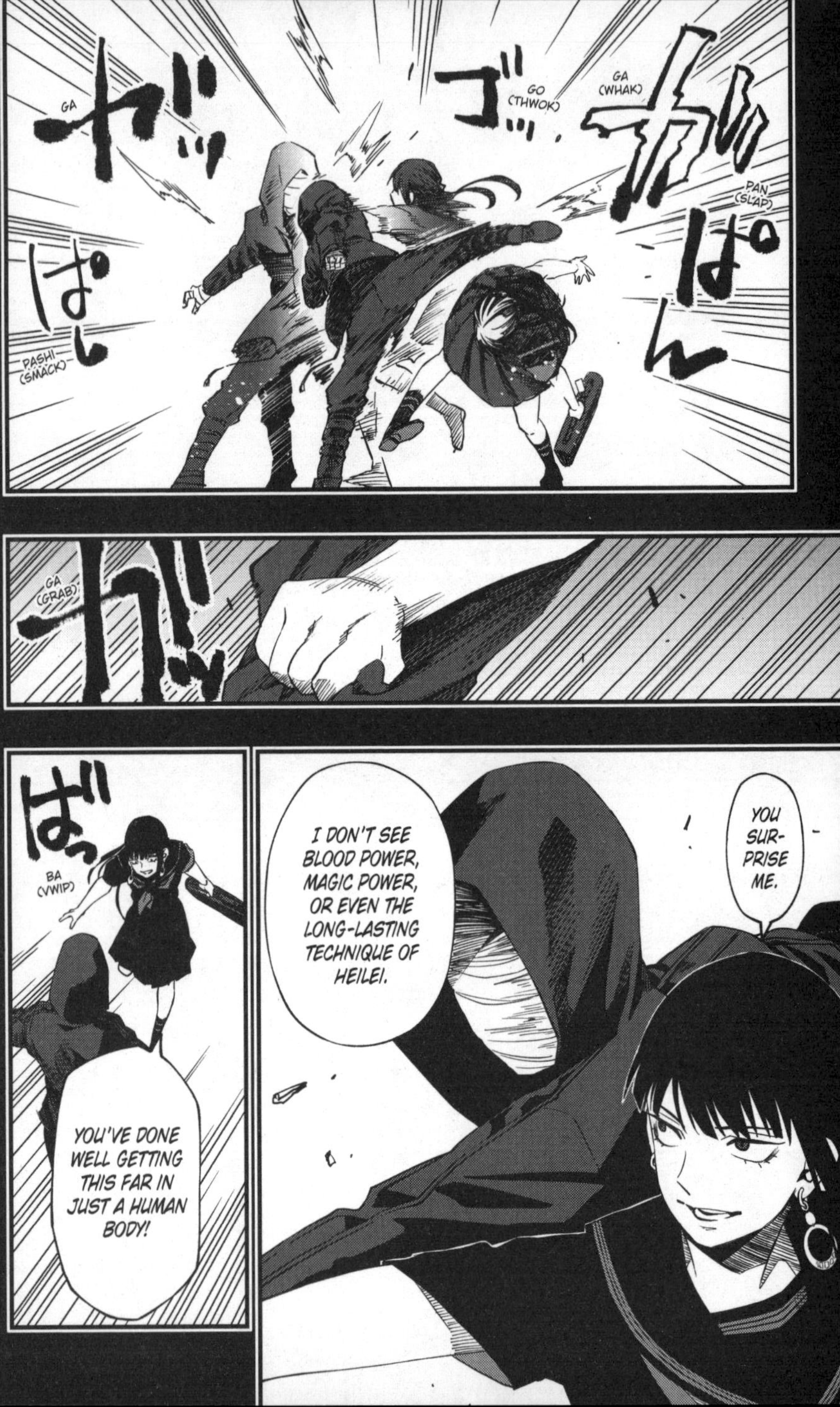
GA (WHAK)
PAN (SLAP)
GO (THWOK)
GA
PASHI (SMACK)
GA (GRAB)
YOU SURPRISE ME.
I DON'T SEE BLOOD POWER, MAGIC POWER, OR EVEN THE LONG-LASTING TECHNIQUE OF HEILEI.
BA (VWIP)
YOU'VE DONE WELL GETTING THIS FAR IN JUST A HUMAN BODY!

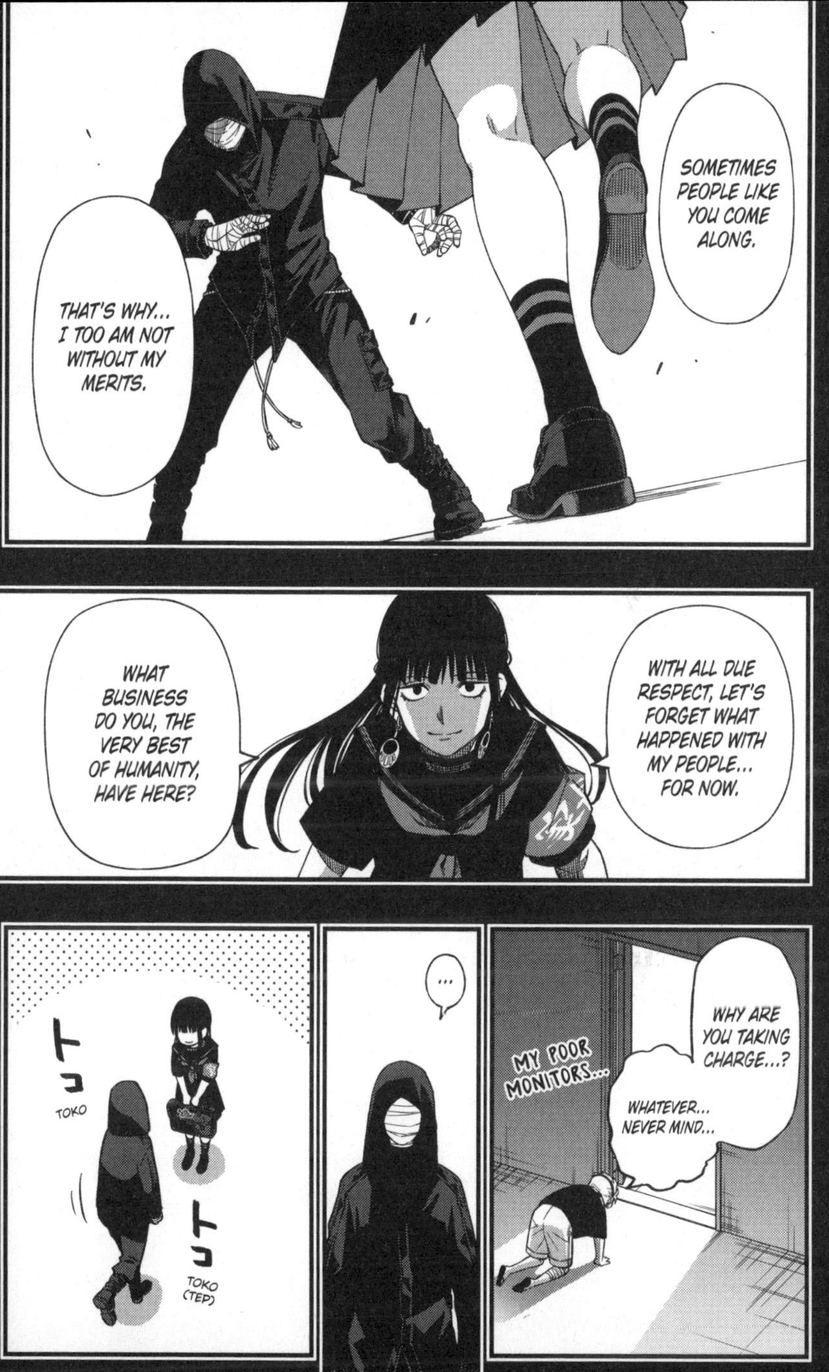
SOMETIMES PEOPLE LIKE YOU COME ALONG.
THAT'S WHY... I TOO AM NOT WITHOUT MY MERITS.
WITH ALL DUE RESPECT, LET'S FORGET WHAT HAPPENED WITH MY PEOPLE... FOR NOW.
WHAT BUSINESS DO YOU, THE VERY BEST OF HUMANITY, HAVE HERE?
WHY ARE YOU TAKING CHARGE...?
MY POOR MONITORS...
WHATEVER... NEVER MIND...
...
トコ
TOKO
トコ
TOKO (TEP)

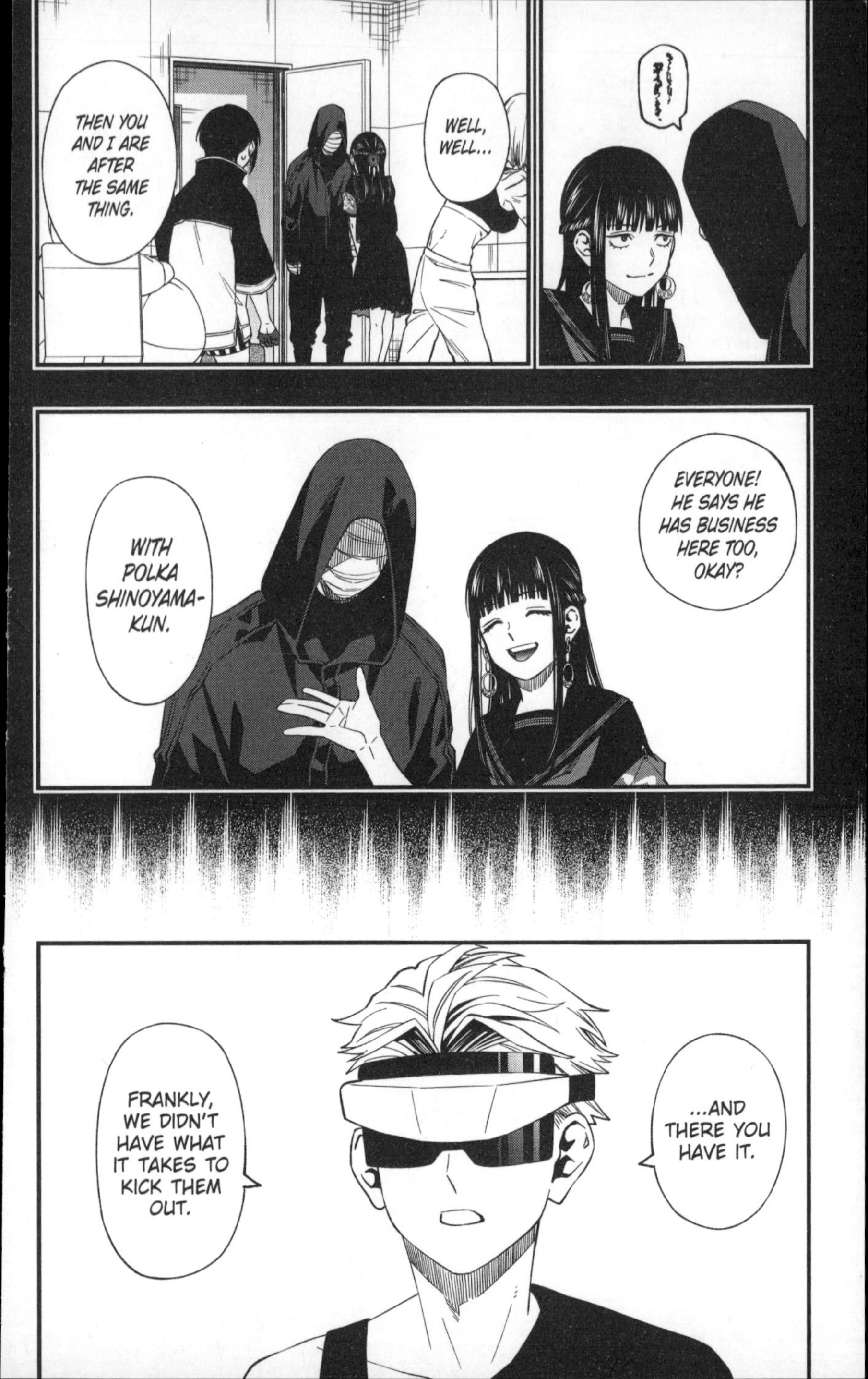
WELL, WELL...
THEN YOU AND I ARE AFTER THE SAME THING.
EVERYONE! HE SAYS HE HAS BUSINESS HERE TOO, OKAY?
WITH POLKA SHINOYAMA-KUN.
...AND THERE YOU HAVE IT.
FRANKLY, WE DIDN'T HAVE WHAT IT TAKES TO KICK THEM OUT.

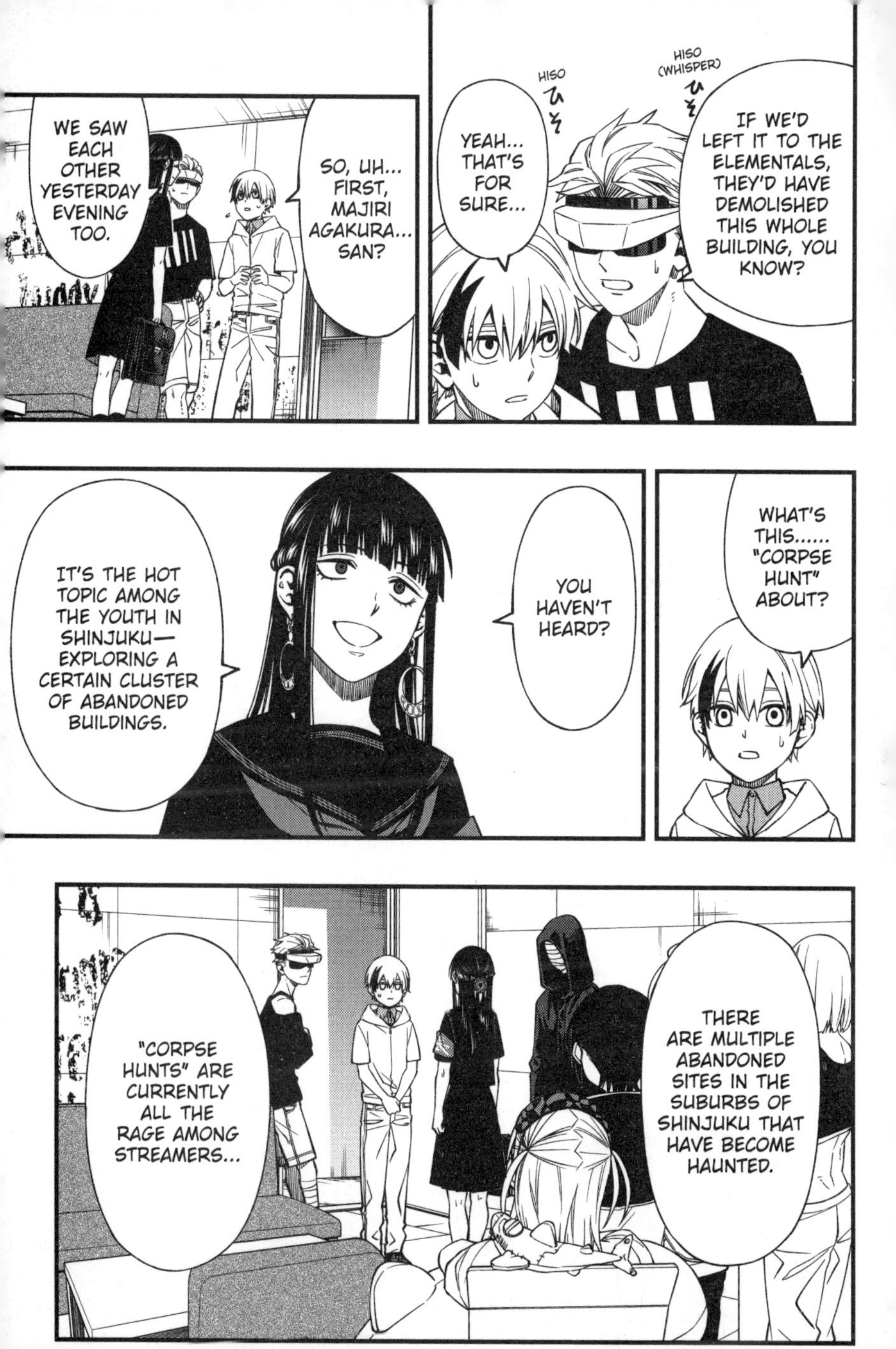
HISO (WHISPER)
ひそ
IF WE'D LEFT IT TO THE ELEMENTALS, THEY'D HAVE DEMOLISHED THIS WHOLE BUILDING, YOU KNOW?
HISO
ひそ
YEAH... THAT'S FOR SURE...
SO, UH... FIRST, MAJIRI AGAKURA... SAN?
WE SAW EACH OTHER YESTERDAY EVENING TOO.
WHAT'S THIS...... "CORPSE HUNT" ABOUT?
YOU HAVEN'T HEARD?
IT'S THE HOT TOPIC AMONG THE YOUTH IN SHINJUKU—EXPLORING A CERTAIN CLUSTER OF ABANDONED BUILDINGS.
THERE ARE MULTIPLE ABANDONED SITES IN THE SUBURBS OF SHINJUKU THAT HAVE BECOME HAUNTED.
"CORPSE HUNTS" ARE CURRENTLY ALL THE RAGE AMONG STREAMERS...

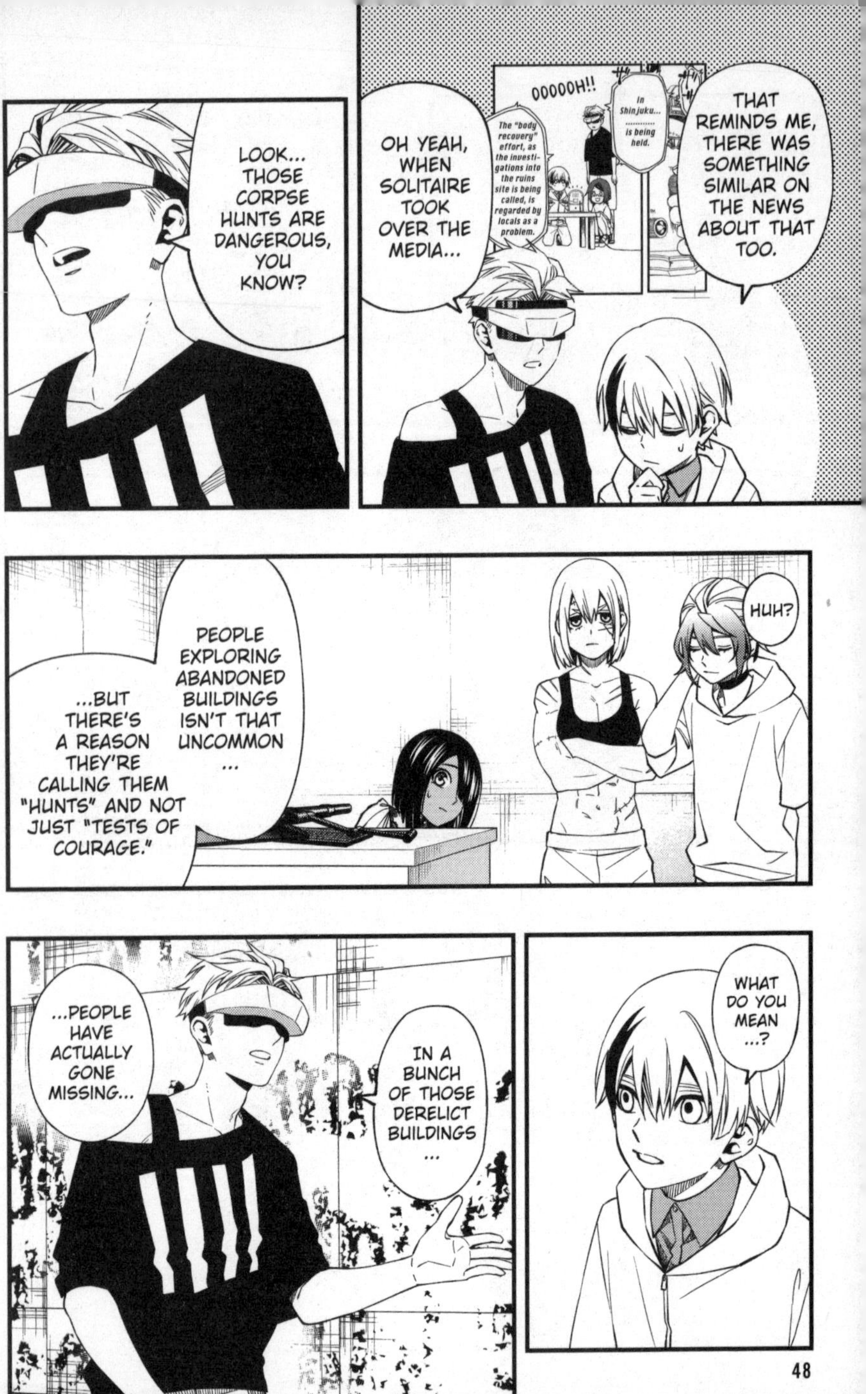
THAT REMINDS ME, THERE WAS SOMETHING SIMILAR ON THE NEWS ABOUT THAT TOO.
In Shinjuku... is being held.
OOOOOH!!
The "body recovery" effort, as the investigations into the ruins site is being called, is regarded by locals as a problem.
OH YEAH, WHEN SOLITAIRE TOOK OVER THE MEDIA...
LOOK... THOSE CORPSE HUNTS ARE DANGEROUS, YOU KNOW?
HUH?
PEOPLE EXPLORING ABANDONED BUILDINGS ISN'T THAT UNCOMMON...
...BUT THERE'S A REASON THEY'RE CALLING THEM "HUNTS" AND NOT JUST "TESTS OF COURAGE."
WHAT DO YOU MEAN...?
IN A BUNCH OF THOSE DERELICT BUILDINGS...
...PEOPLE HAVE ACTUALLY GONE MISSING...

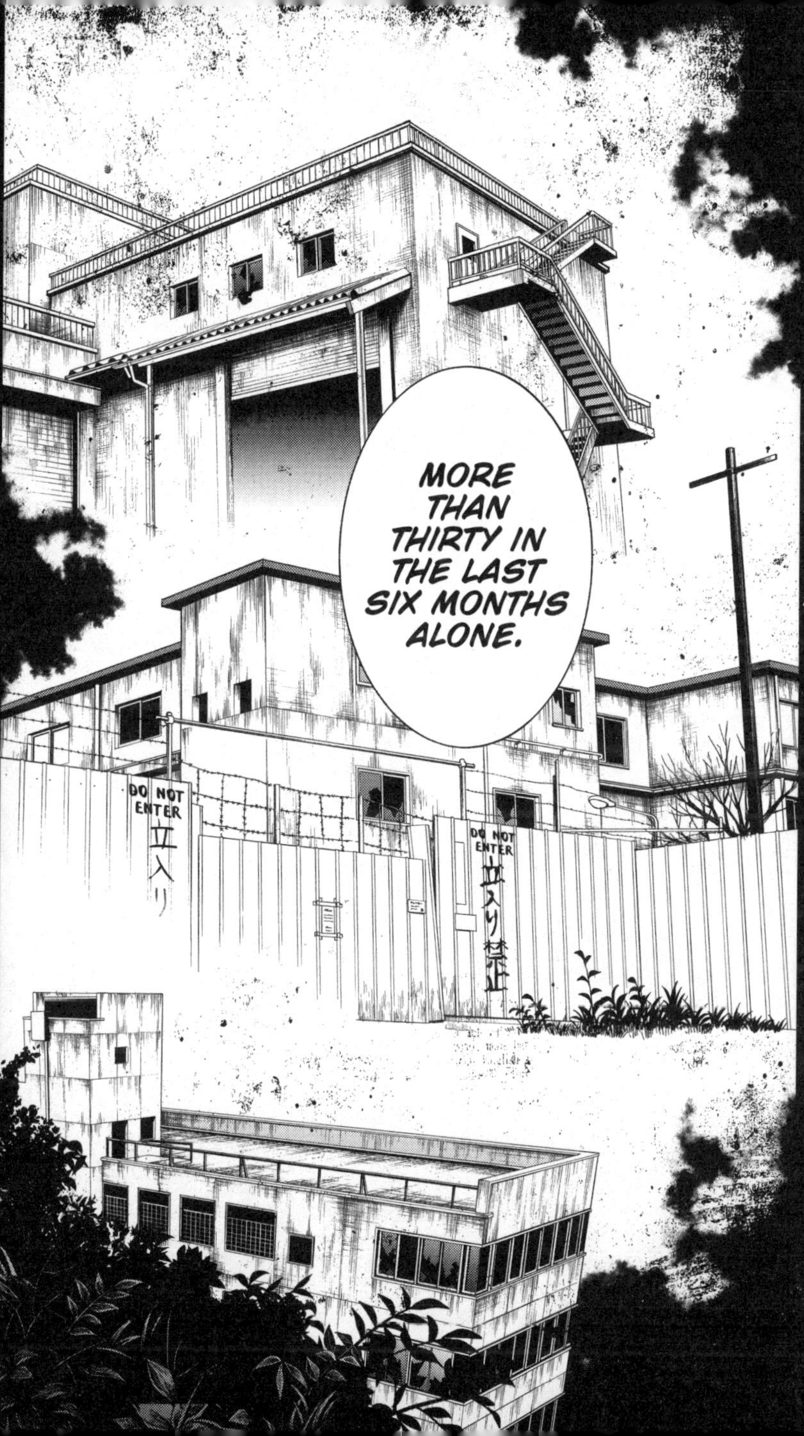
MORE THAN THIRTY IN THE LAST SIX MONTHS ALONE.
DO NOT ENTER
立入り
DO NOT ENTER
立入り禁止

# DEAD MOUNT DEATH PLAY

# #90

THE TALK OF THE TOWN!

# CORPSE HUNT

**Difficulty Level** ★★★★★

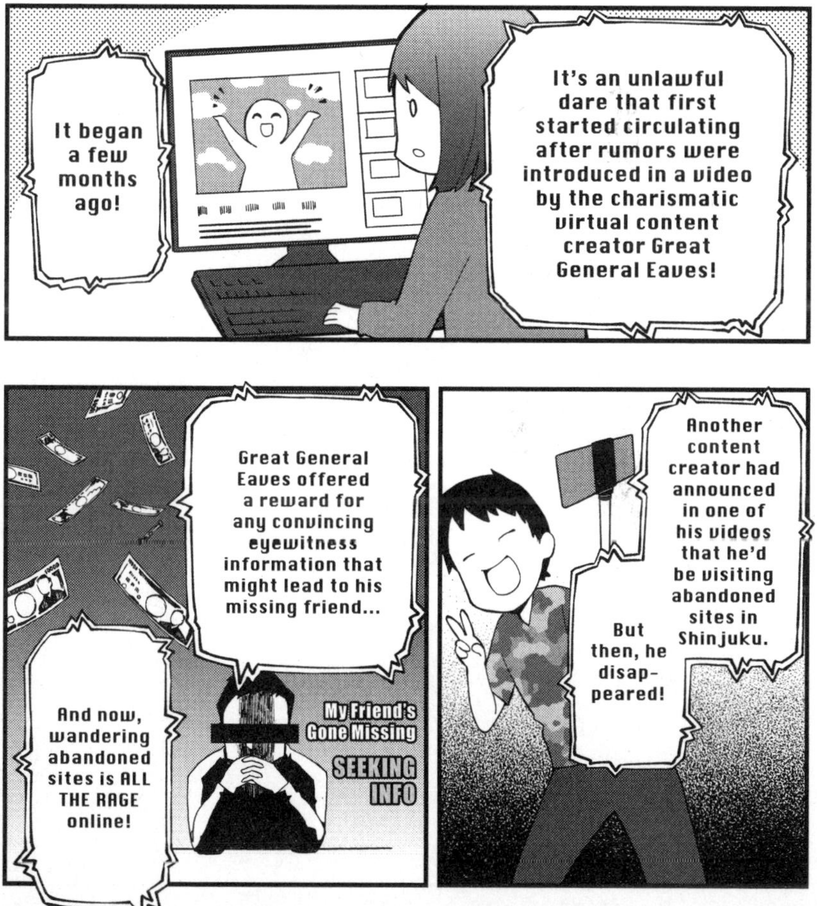

It's an unlawful dare that first started circulating after rumors were introduced in a video by the charismatic virtual content creator Great General Eaves!
It began a few months ago!
Another content creator had announced in one of his videos that he'd be visiting abandoned sites in Shinjuku.
But then, he disappeared!
Great General Eaves offered a reward for any convincing eyewitness information that might lead to his missing friend...
My Friend's Gone Missing
SEEKING INFO
And now, wandering abandoned sites is ALL THE RAGE online!

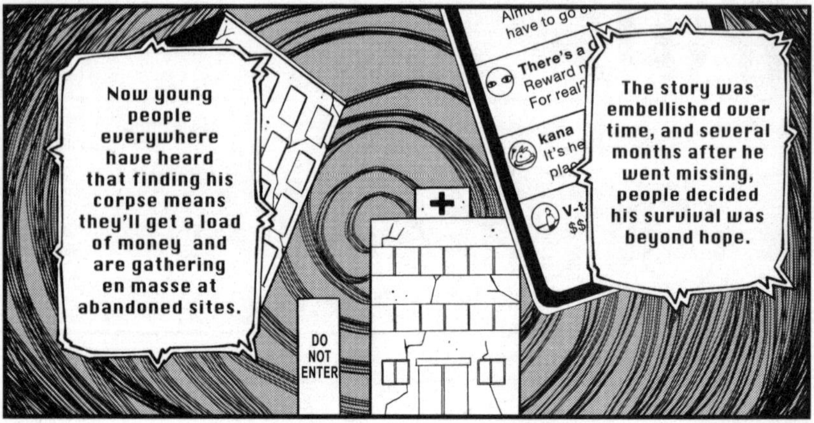
The story was embellished over time, and several months after he went missing, people decided his survival was beyond hope.
Now young people everywhere have heard that finding his corpse means they'll get a load of money and are gathering en masse at abandoned sites.
have to go
For real?
kana
DO NOT ENTER

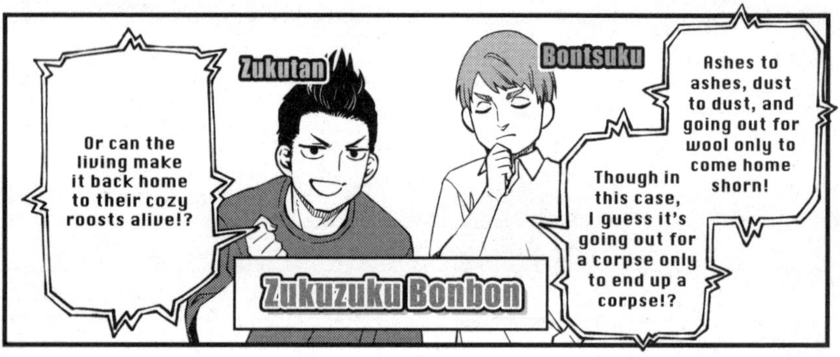
Bontsuku
Zukutan
Ashes to ashes, dust to dust, and going out for wool only to come home shorn!
Though in this case, I guess it's going out for a corpse only to end up a corpse!?
Or can the living make it back home to their cozy roosts alive!?
Zukuzuku Bonbon

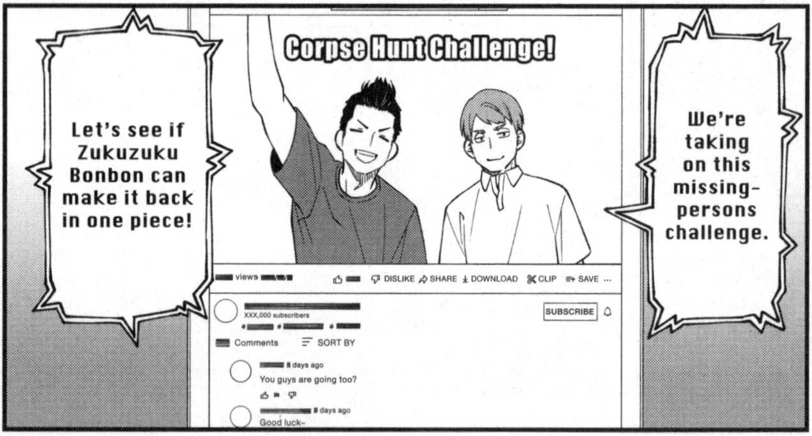
We're taking on this missing-persons challenge.
Corpse Hunt Challenge!
Let's see if Zukuzuku Bonbon can make it back in one piece!
views
DISLIKE
SHARE
DOWNLOAD
CLIP
SAVE
XXX,000 subscribers
SUBSCRIBE
Comments
SORT BY
days ago
You guys are going too?
days ago
Good luck~

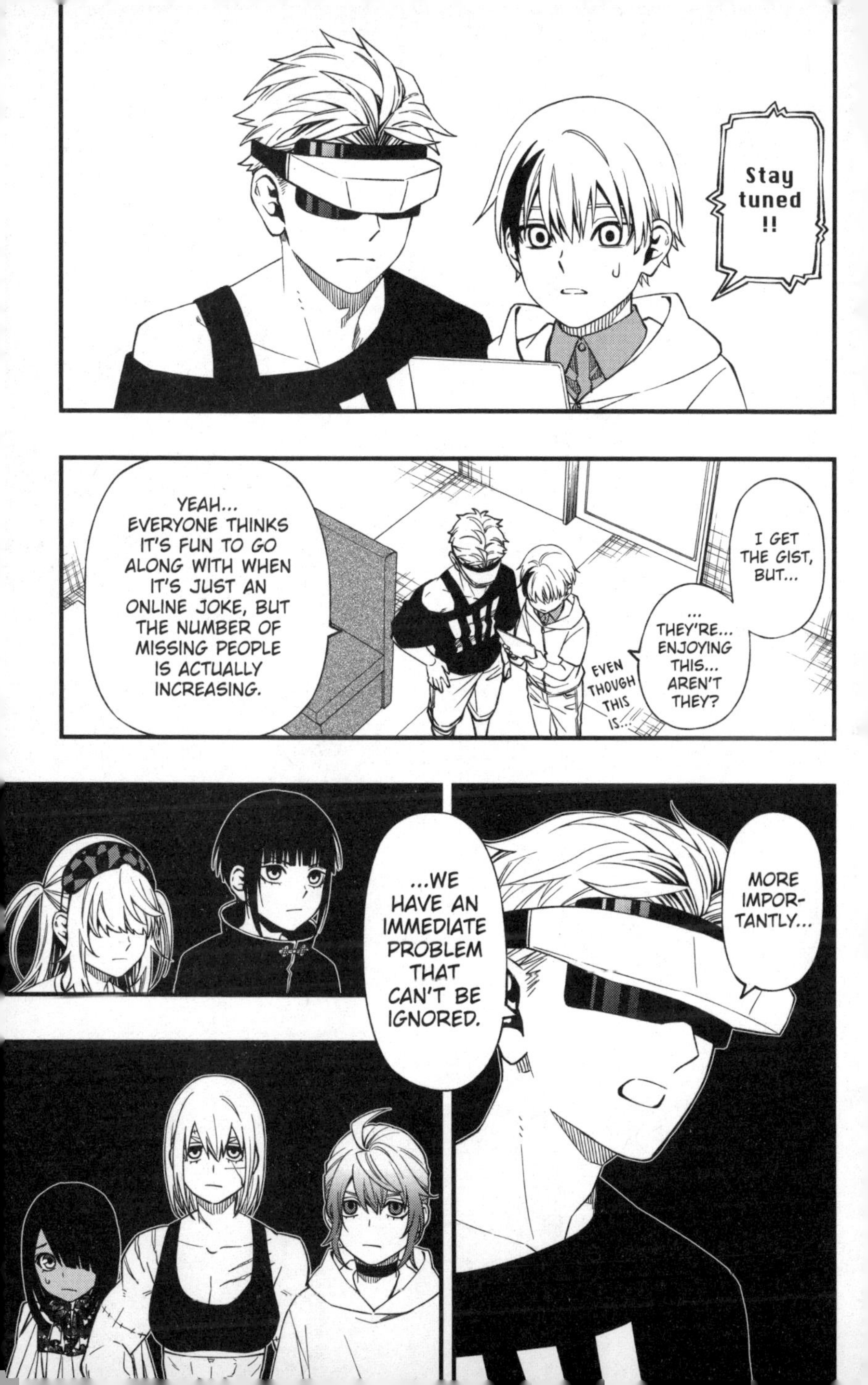
Stay tuned !!
I GET THE GIST, BUT...
...THEY'RE... ENJOYING THIS... AREN'T THEY?
EVEN THOUGH THIS IS...
YEAH... EVERYONE THINKS IT'S FUN TO GO ALONG WITH WHEN IT'S JUST AN ONLINE JOKE, BUT THE NUMBER OF MISSING PEOPLE IS ACTUALLY INCREASING.
MORE IMPORTANTLY...
...WE HAVE AN IMMEDIATE PROBLEM THAT CAN'T BE IGNORED.

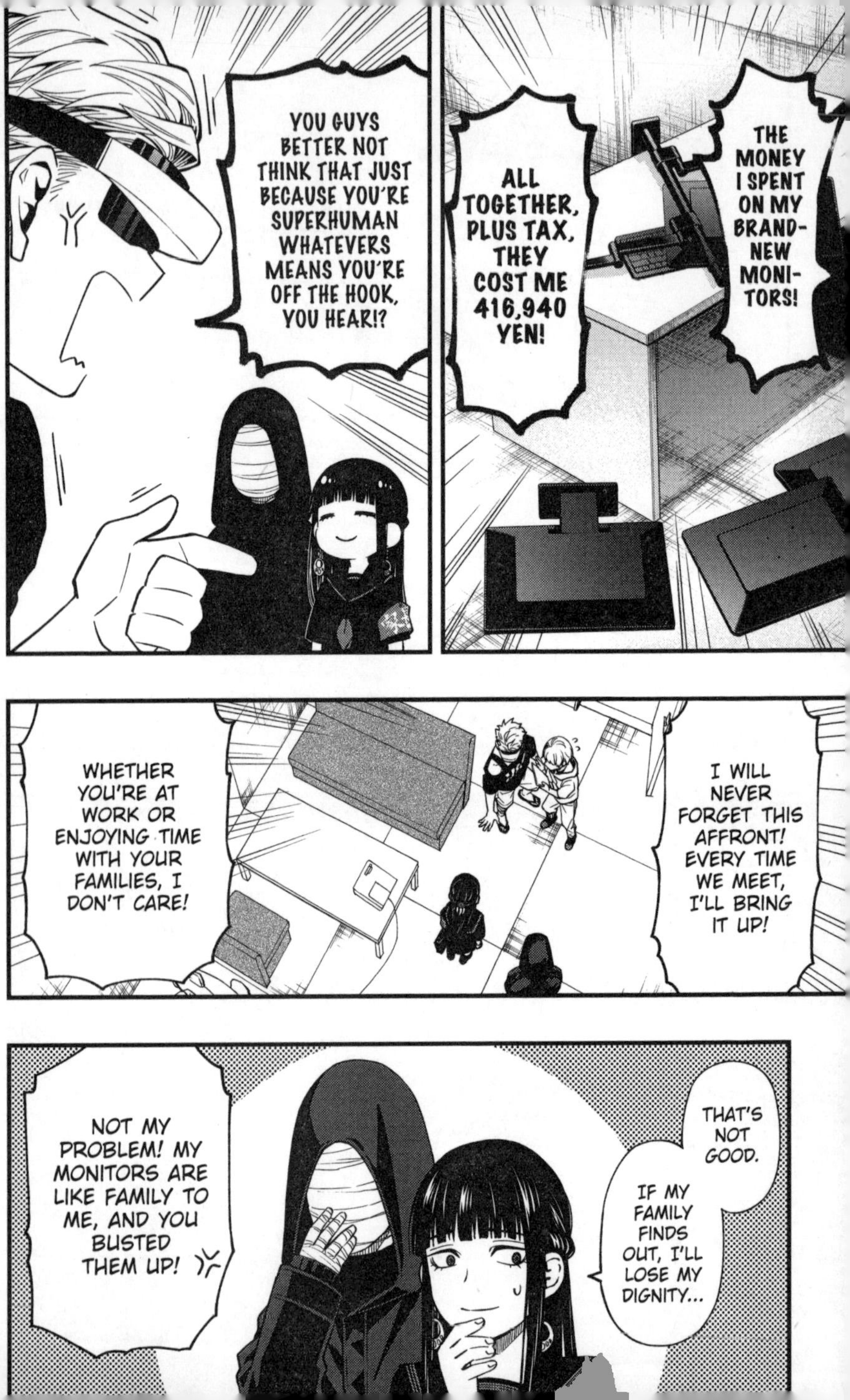
THE MONEY I SPENT ON MY BRAND-NEW MONI-TORS!
ALL TOGETHER, PLUS TAX, THEY COST ME 416,940 YEN!
YOU GUYS BETTER NOT THINK THAT JUST BECAUSE YOU'RE SUPERHUMAN WHATEVERS MEANS YOU'RE OFF THE HOOK, YOU HEAR!?
I WILL NEVER FORGET THIS AFFRONT! EVERY TIME WE MEET, I'LL BRING IT UP!
WHETHER YOU'RE AT WORK OR ENJOYING TIME WITH YOUR FAMILIES, I DON'T CARE!
THAT'S NOT GOOD.
IF MY FAMILY FINDS OUT, I'LL LOSE MY DIGNITY...
NOT MY PROBLEM! MY MONITORS ARE LIKE FAMILY TO ME, AND YOU BUSTED THEM UP!

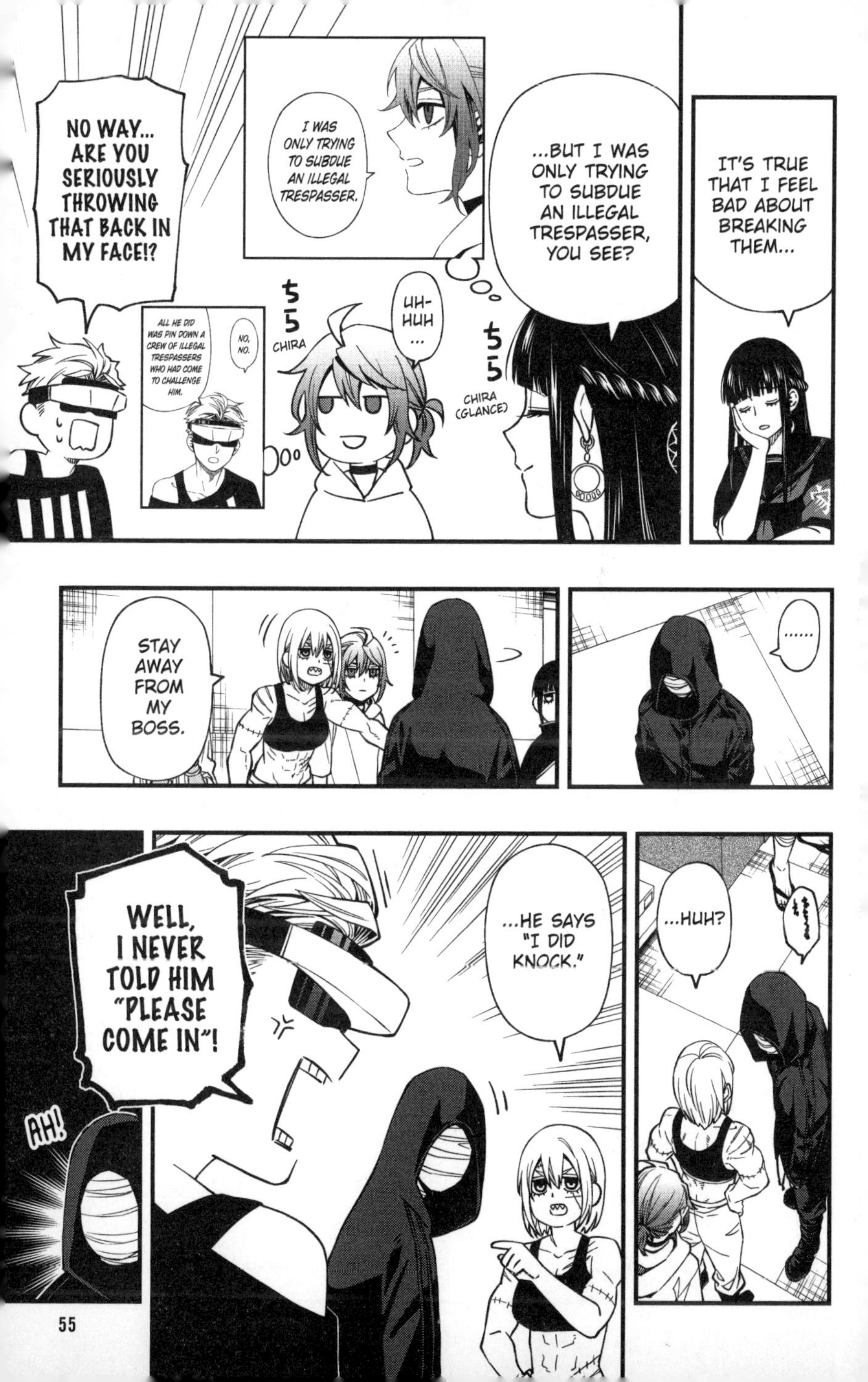
IT'S TRUE THAT I FEEL BAD ABOUT BREAKING THEM...
...BUT I WAS ONLY TRYING TO SUBDUE AN ILLEGAL TRESPASSER, YOU SEE?
I WAS ONLY TRYING TO SUBDUE AN ILLEGAL TRESPASSER.
CHIRA (GLANCE)
UH-HUH...
CHIRA
NO, NO.
ALL HE DID WAS PIN DOWN A CREW OF ILLEGAL TRESPASSERS WHO HAD COME TO CHALLENGE HIM.
NO WAY... ARE YOU SERIOUSLY THROWING THAT BACK IN MY FACE!?
......
STAY AWAY FROM MY BOSS.
...HUH?
...HE SAYS "I DID KNOCK."
WELL, I NEVER TOLD HIM "PLEASE COME IN"!
AH!

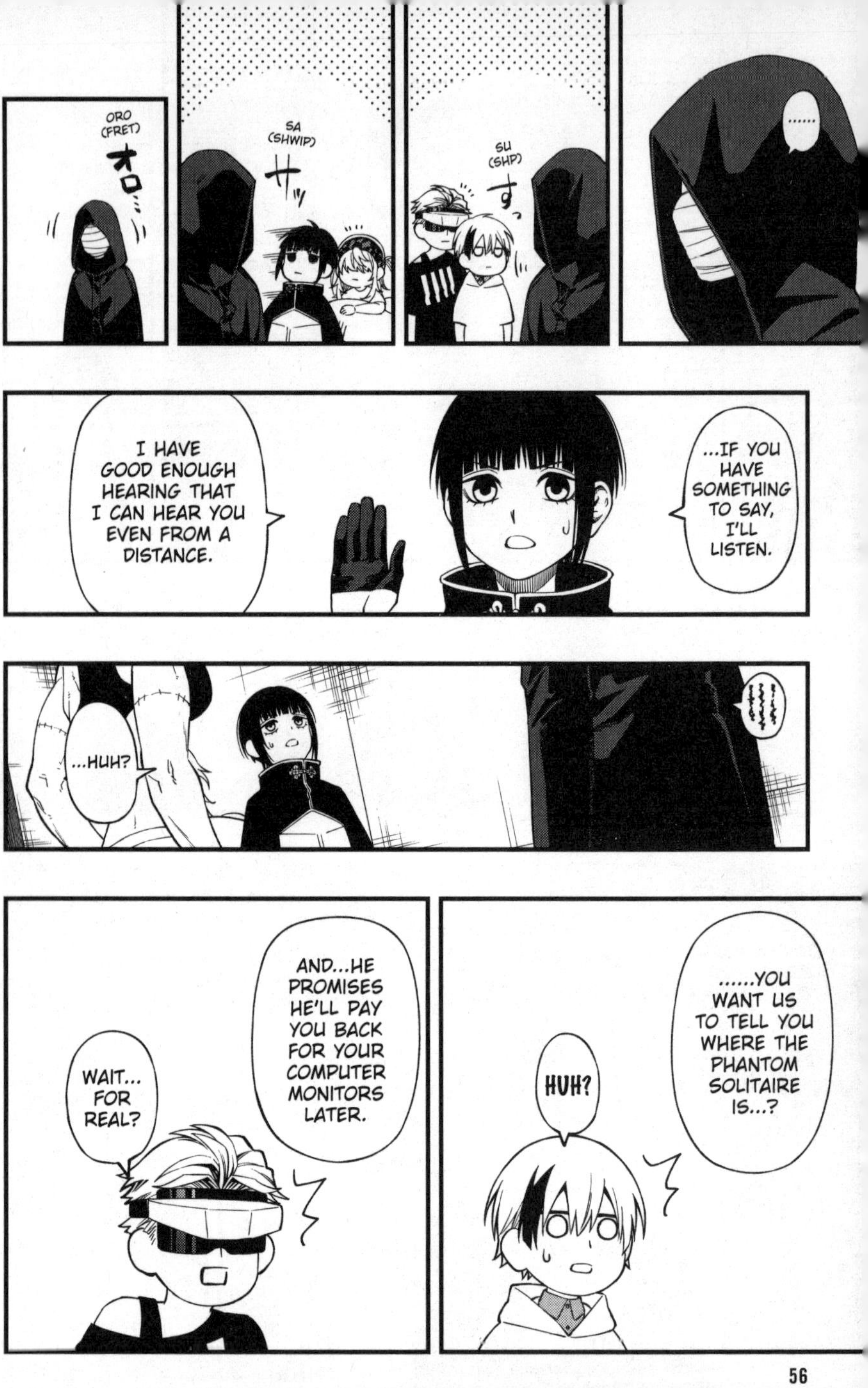
......
SU (SHP)
すっ
SA (SHWIP)
サッ
ORO (FRET)
オロ
...IF YOU HAVE SOMETHING TO SAY, I'LL LISTEN.
I HAVE GOOD ENOUGH HEARING THAT I CAN HEAR YOU EVEN FROM A DISTANCE.
...HUH?
......YOU WANT US TO TELL YOU WHERE THE PHANTOM SOLITAIRE IS...?
HUH?
AND...HE PROMISES HE'LL PAY YOU BACK FOR YOUR COMPUTER MONITORS LATER.
WAIT... FOR REAL?

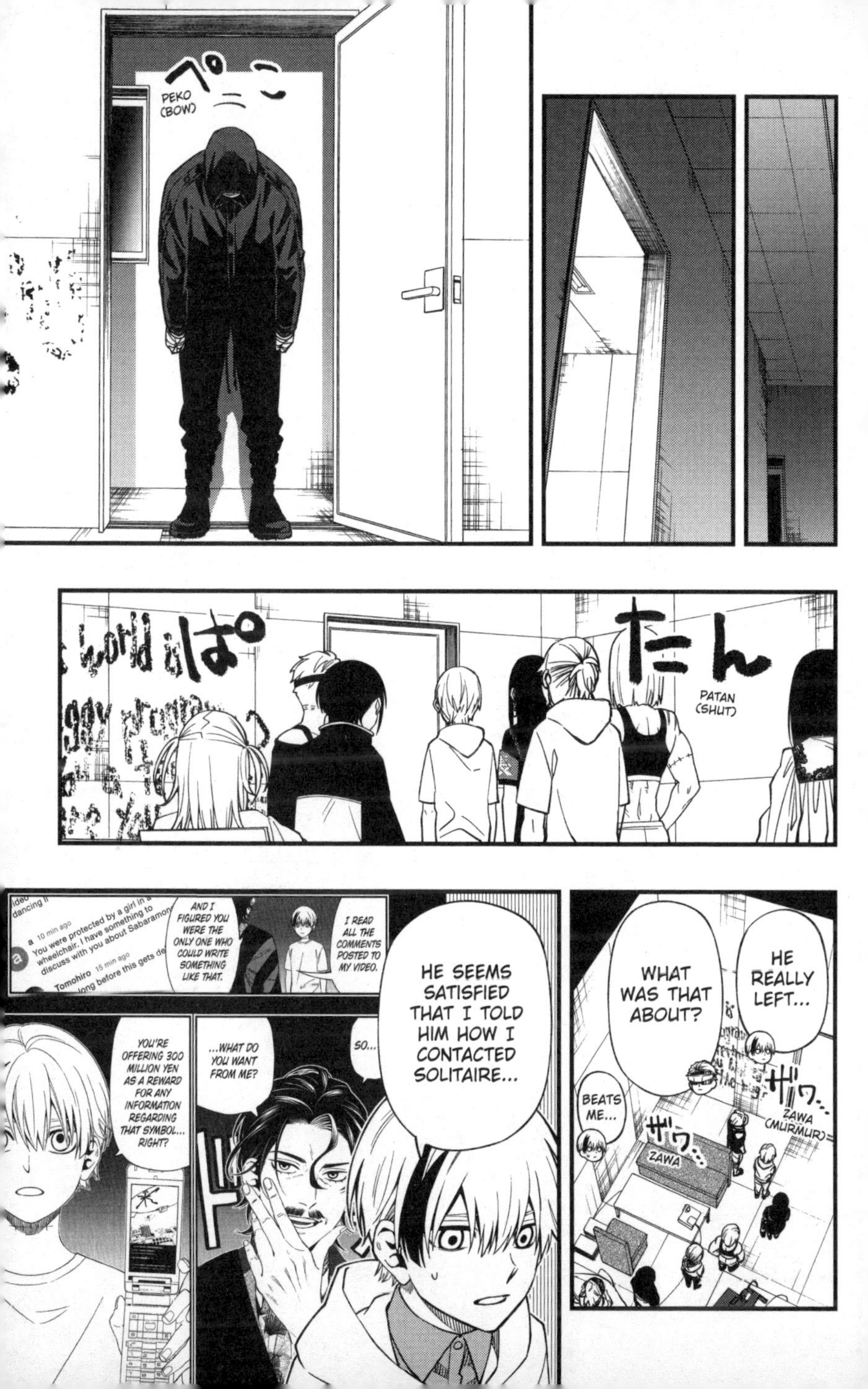

PEKO (BOW)
PATAN (SHUT)
HE REALLY LEFT...
WHAT WAS THAT ABOUT?
BEATS ME...
ZAWA (MURMUR)
ZAWA
I READ ALL THE COMMENTS POSTED TO MY VIDEO.
AND I FIGURED YOU WERE THE ONLY ONE WHO COULD WRITE SOMETHING LIKE THAT.
a 10 min ago
You were protected by a girl in a wheelchair. I have something to discuss with you about Sabaramon
Tomohiro 15 min ago
HE SEEMS SATISFIED THAT I TOLD HIM HOW I CONTACTED SOLITAIRE...
SO...
...WHAT DO YOU WANT FROM ME?
YOU'RE OFFERING 300 MILLION YEN AS A REWARD FOR ANY INFORMATION REGARDING THAT SYMBOL... RIGHT?

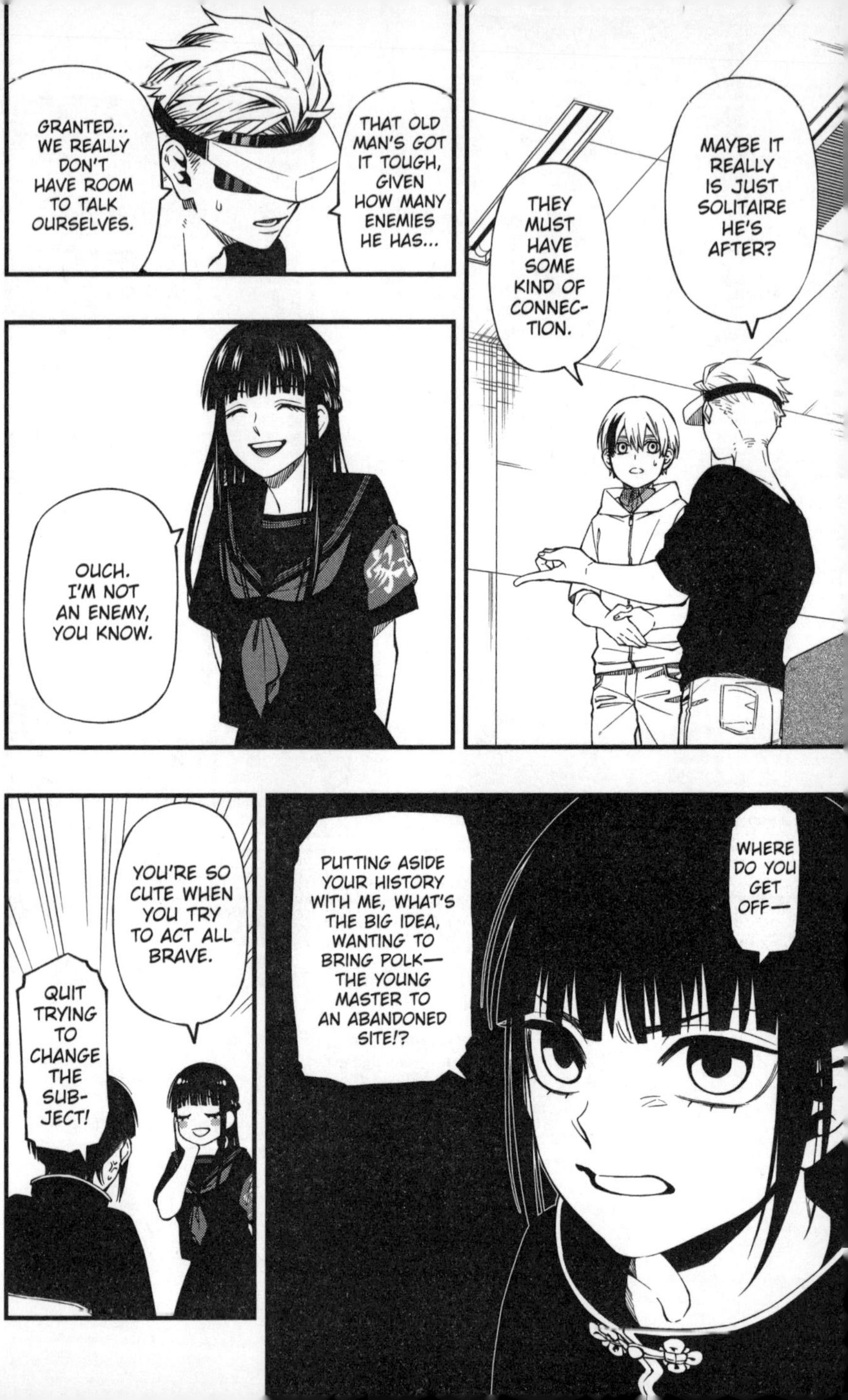
MAYBE IT REALLY IS JUST SOLITAIRE HE'S AFTER?
THEY MUST HAVE SOME KIND OF CONNEC-TION.
THAT OLD MAN'S GOT IT TOUGH, GIVEN HOW MANY ENEMIES HE HAS...
GRANTED... WE REALLY DON'T HAVE ROOM TO TALK OURSELVES.
OUCH. I'M NOT AN ENEMY, YOU KNOW.
WHERE DO YOU GET OFF—
PUTTING ASIDE YOUR HISTORY WITH ME, WHAT'S THE BIG IDEA, WANTING TO BRING POLK—THE YOUNG MASTER TO AN ABANDONED SITE!?
YOU'RE SO CUTE WHEN YOU TRY TO ACT ALL BRAVE.
QUIT TRYING TO CHANGE THE SUB-JECT!

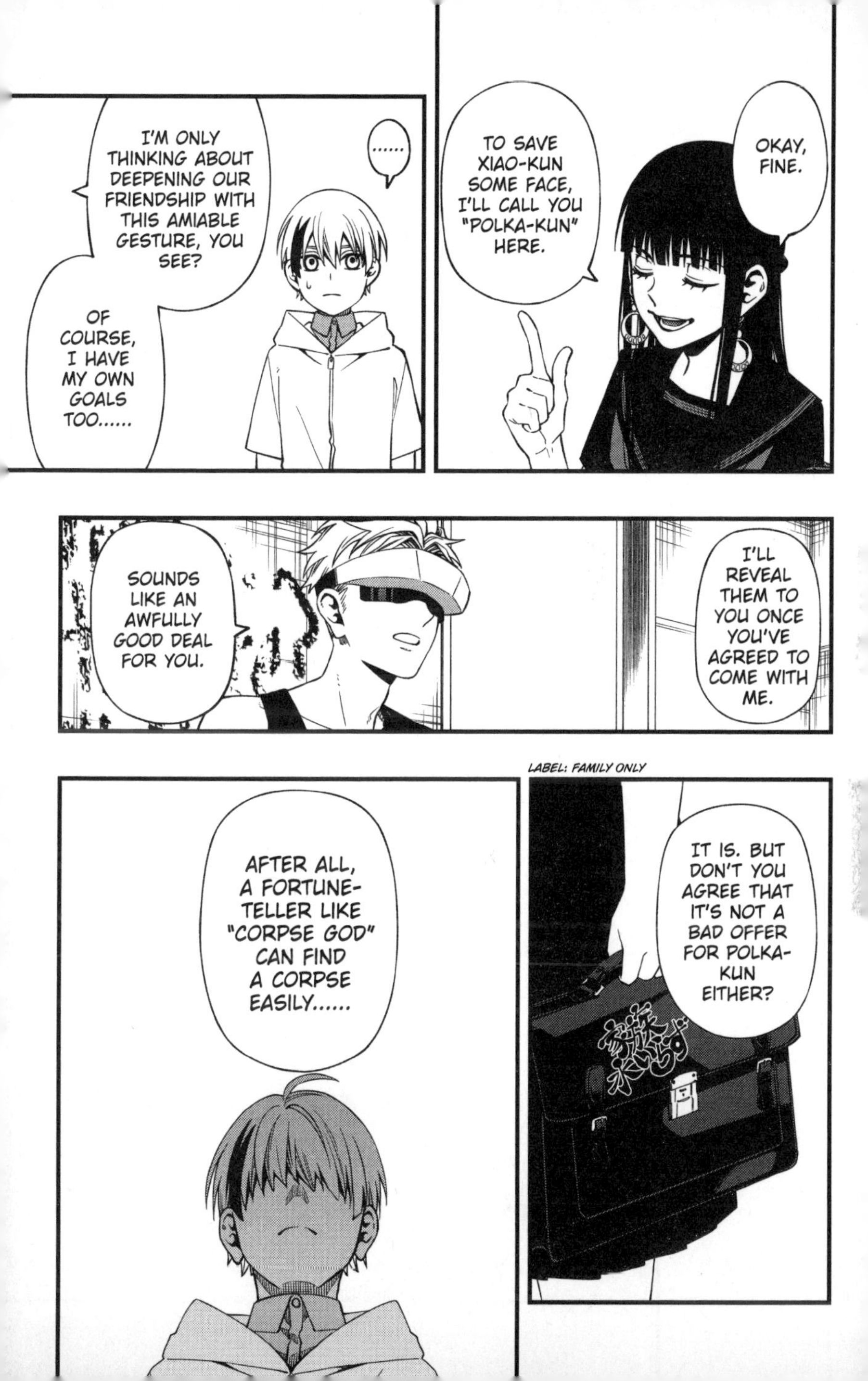
OKAY, FINE.
TO SAVE XIAO-KUN SOME FACE, I'LL CALL YOU "POLKA-KUN" HERE.
......
I'M ONLY THINKING ABOUT DEEPENING OUR FRIENDSHIP WITH THIS AMIABLE GESTURE, YOU SEE?
OF COURSE, I HAVE MY OWN GOALS TOO......
I'LL REVEAL THEM TO YOU ONCE YOU'VE AGREED TO COME WITH ME.
SOUNDS LIKE AN AWFULLY GOOD DEAL FOR YOU.
LABEL: FAMILY ONLY
IT IS. BUT DON'T YOU AGREE THAT IT'S NOT A BAD OFFER FOR POLKA-KUN EITHER?
AFTER ALL, A FORTUNE-TELLER LIKE "CORPSE GOD" CAN FIND A CORPSE EASILY......

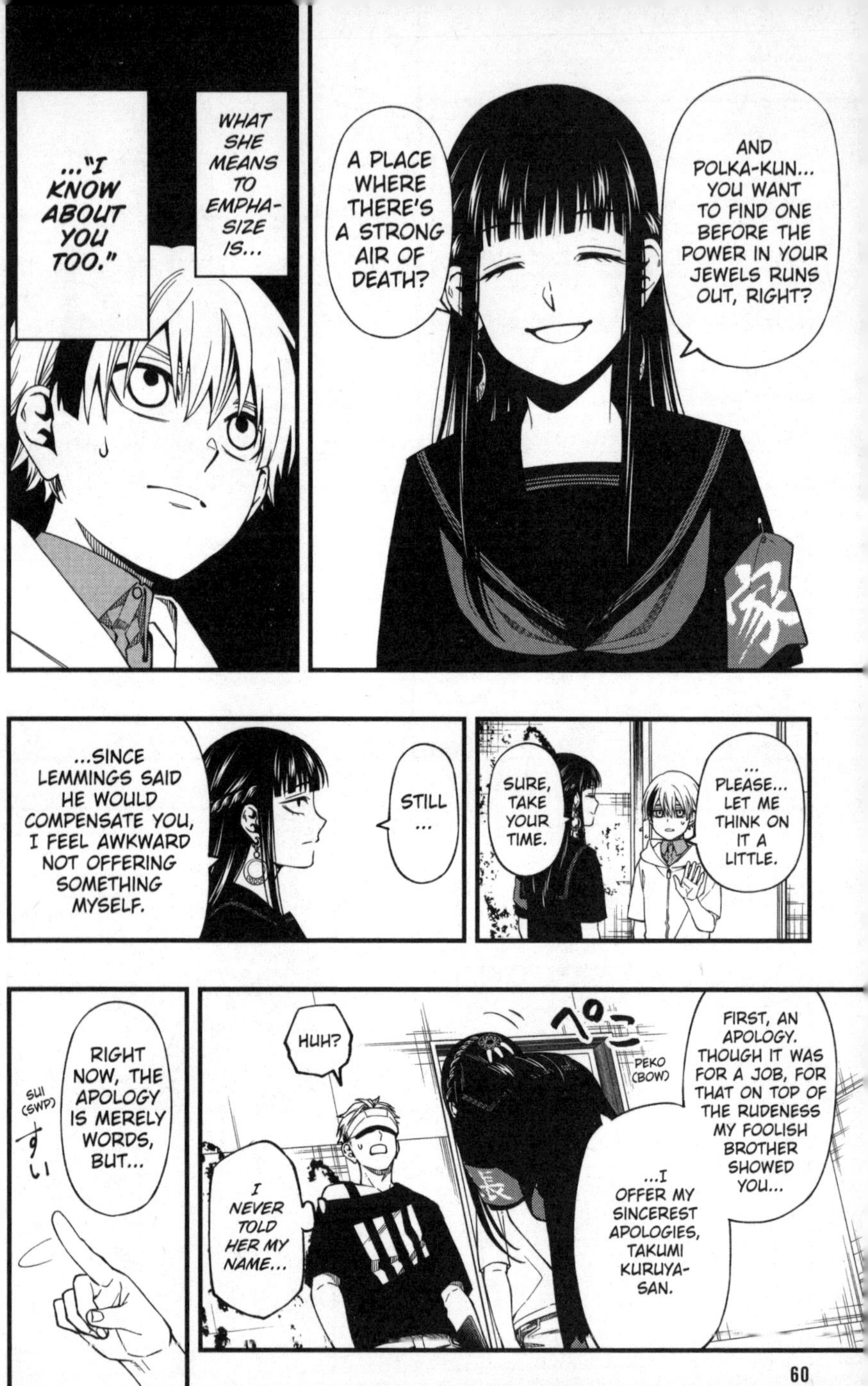
AND POLKA-KUN... YOU WANT TO FIND ONE BEFORE THE POWER IN YOUR JEWELS RUNS OUT, RIGHT?
A PLACE WHERE THERE'S A STRONG AIR OF DEATH?
WHAT SHE MEANS TO EMPHA-SIZE IS...
..."I KNOW ABOUT YOU TOO."
... PLEASE... LET ME THINK ON IT A LITTLE.
SURE, TAKE YOUR TIME.
STILL ...
...SINCE LEMMINGS SAID HE WOULD COMPENSATE YOU, I FEEL AWKWARD NOT OFFERING SOMETHING MYSELF.
FIRST, AN APOLOGY. THOUGH IT WAS FOR A JOB, FOR THAT ON TOP OF THE RUDENESS MY FOOLISH BROTHER SHOWED YOU...
...I OFFER MY SINCEREST APOLOGIES, TAKUMI KURUYA-SAN.
ぺこ
PEKO (BOW)
HUH?
I NEVER TOLD HER MY NAME...
RIGHT NOW, THE APOLOGY IS MERELY WORDS, BUT...
すい
SUI (SWP)

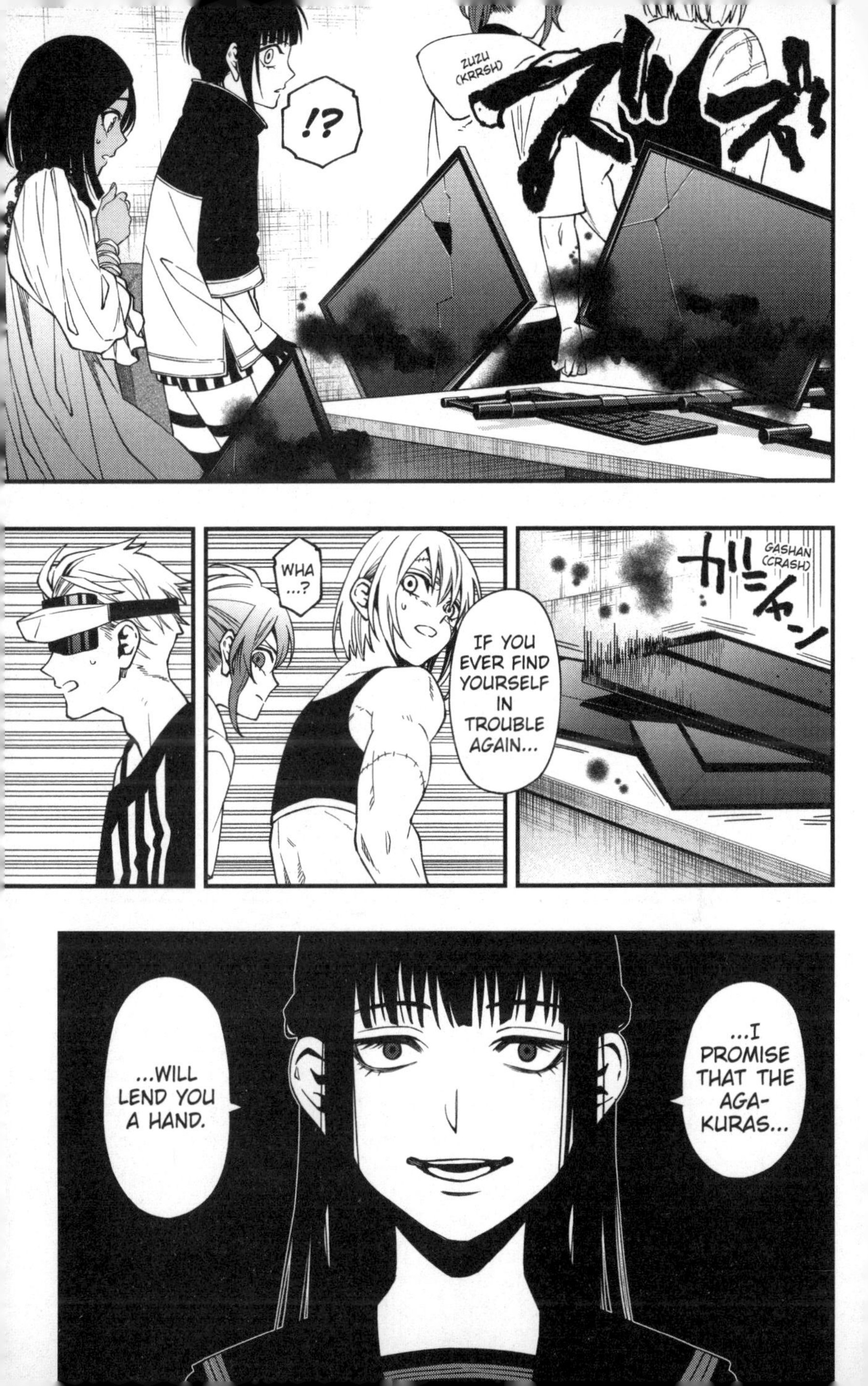
ZUZU (KRRSH)
!?
GASHAN (CRASH)
IF YOU EVER FIND YOURSELF IN TROUBLE AGAIN...
WHA ...?
...I PROMISE THAT THE AGA-KURAS...
...WILL LEND YOU A HAND.

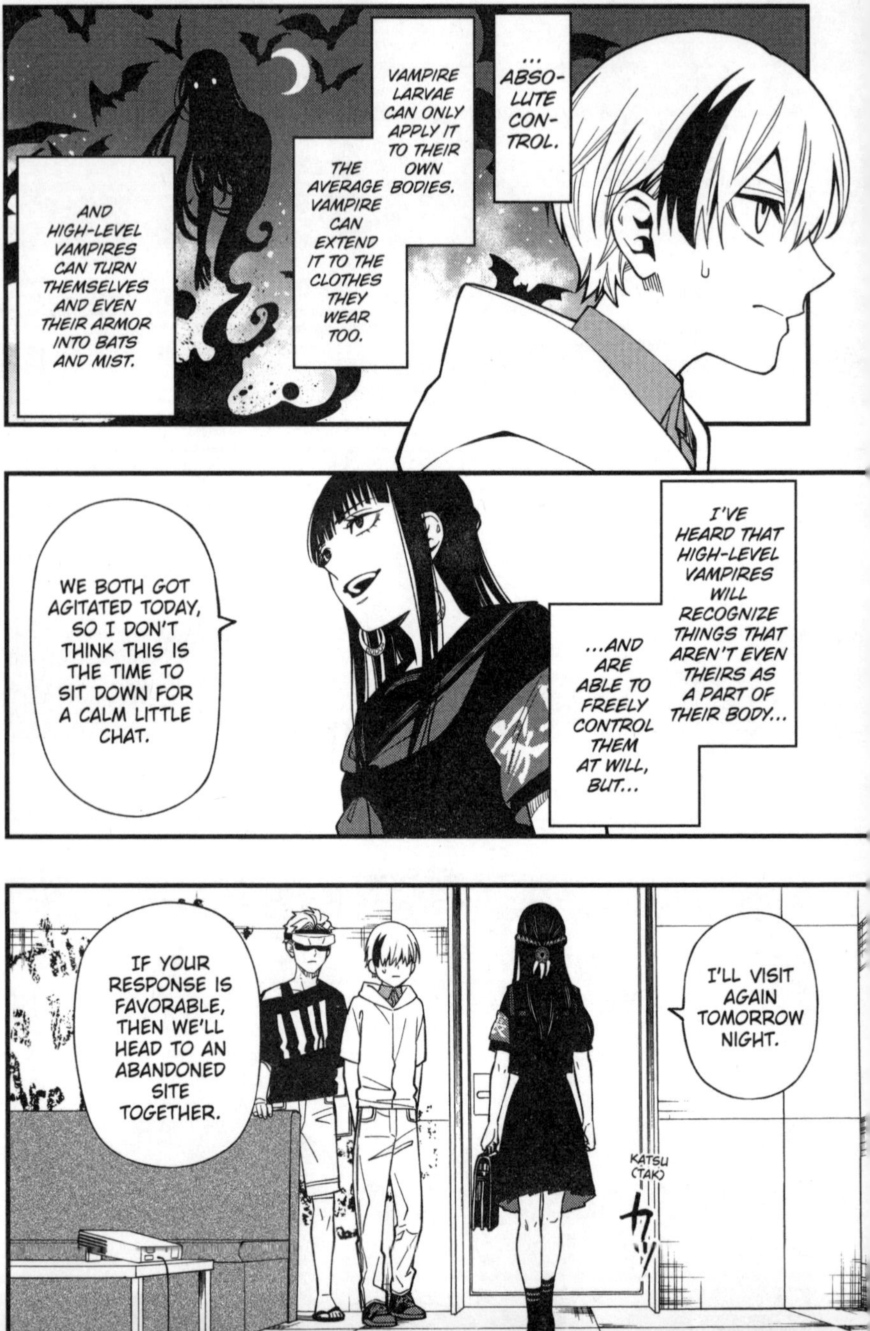
...ABSOLUTE CONTROL.
VAMPIRE LARVAE CAN ONLY APPLY IT TO THEIR OWN BODIES.
THE AVERAGE VAMPIRE CAN EXTEND IT TO THE CLOTHES THEY WEAR TOO.
AND HIGH-LEVEL VAMPIRES CAN TURN THEMSELVES AND EVEN THEIR ARMOR INTO BATS AND MIST.
I'VE HEARD THAT HIGH-LEVEL VAMPIRES WILL RECOGNIZE THINGS THAT AREN'T EVEN THEIRS AS A PART OF THEIR BODY...
...AND ARE ABLE TO FREELY CONTROL THEM AT WILL, BUT...
WE BOTH GOT AGITATED TODAY, SO I DON'T THINK THIS IS THE TIME TO SIT DOWN FOR A CALM LITTLE CHAT.
I'LL VISIT AGAIN TOMORROW NIGHT.
KATSU (TAK)
カッ
IF YOUR RESPONSE IS FAVORABLE, THEN WE'LL HEAD TO AN ABANDONED SITE TOGETHER.

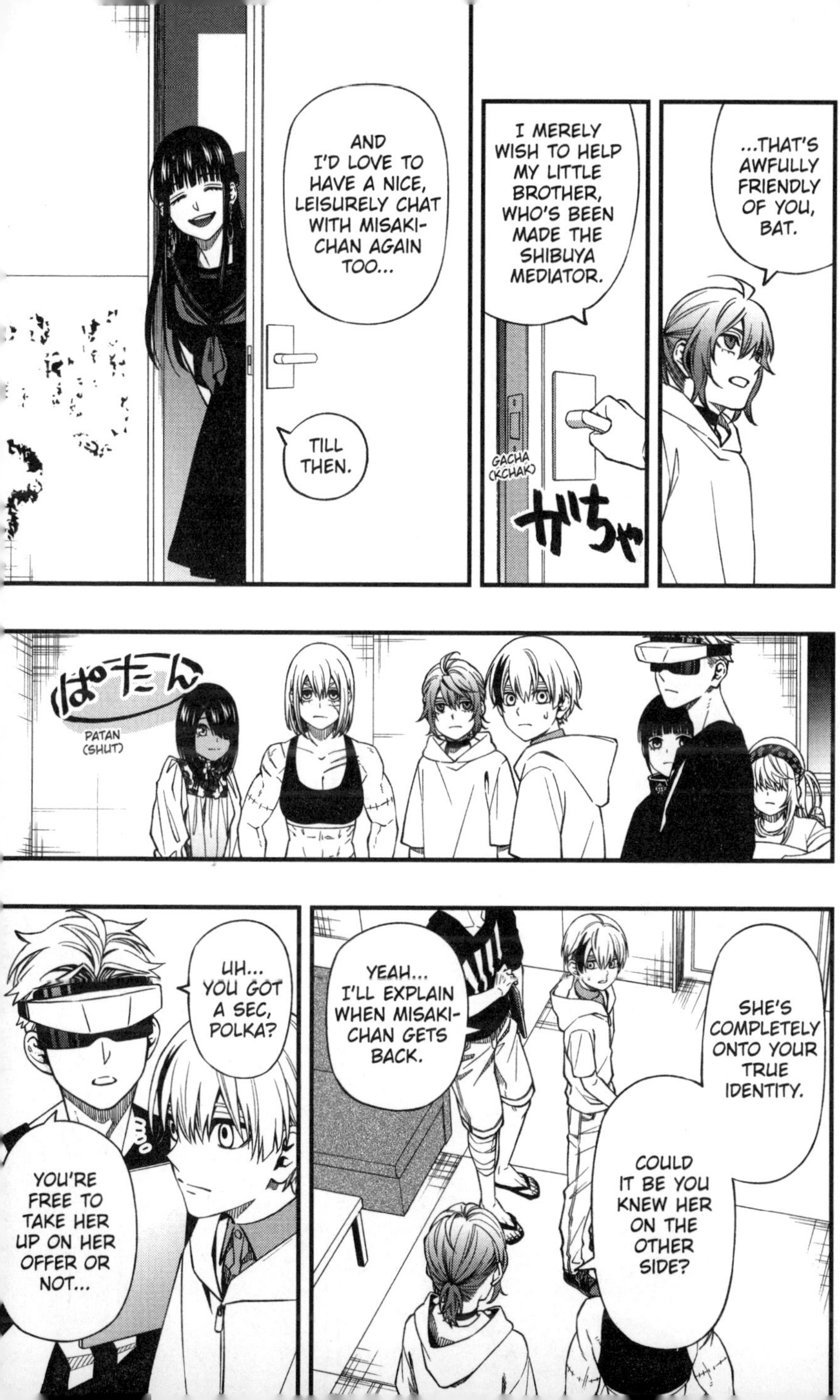
...THAT'S AWFULLY FRIENDLY OF YOU, BAT.
I MERELY WISH TO HELP MY LITTLE BROTHER, WHO'S BEEN MADE THE SHIBUYA MEDIATOR.
がちゃ
GACHA (KCHAK)
AND I'D LOVE TO HAVE A NICE, LEISURELY CHAT WITH MISAKI-CHAN AGAIN TOO...
TILL THEN.
ぱたん
PATAN (SHUT)
SHE'S COMPLETELY ONTO YOUR TRUE IDENTITY.
COULD IT BE YOU KNEW HER ON THE OTHER SIDE?
YEAH... I'LL EXPLAIN WHEN MISAKI-CHAN GETS BACK.
UH... YOU GOT A SEC, POLKA?
YOU'RE FREE TO TAKE HER UP ON HER OFFER OR NOT...

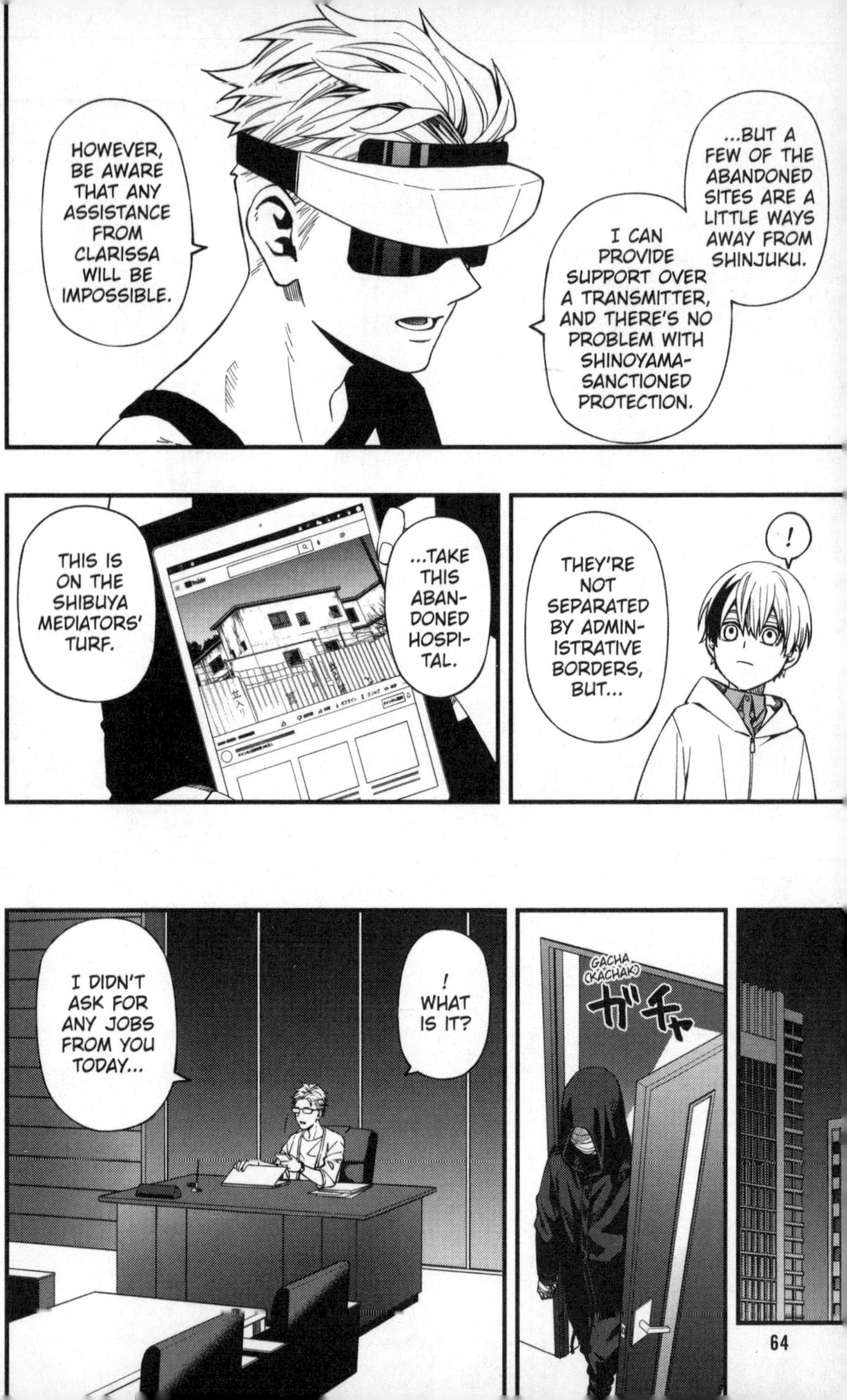

...BUT A FEW OF THE ABANDONED SITES ARE A LITTLE WAYS AWAY FROM SHINJUKU.
I CAN PROVIDE SUPPORT OVER A TRANSMITTER, AND THERE'S NO PROBLEM WITH SHINOYAMA-SANCTIONED PROTECTION.
HOWEVER, BE AWARE THAT ANY ASSISTANCE FROM CLARISSA WILL BE IMPOSSIBLE.
!
THEY'RE NOT SEPARATED BY ADMIN-ISTRATIVE BORDERS, BUT...
...TAKE THIS ABAN-DONED HOSPI-TAL.
THIS IS ON THE SHIBUYA MEDIATORS' TURF.
GACHA (KACHAK)
ガチャ
! WHAT IS IT?
I DIDN'T ASK FOR ANY JOBS FROM YOU TODAY...

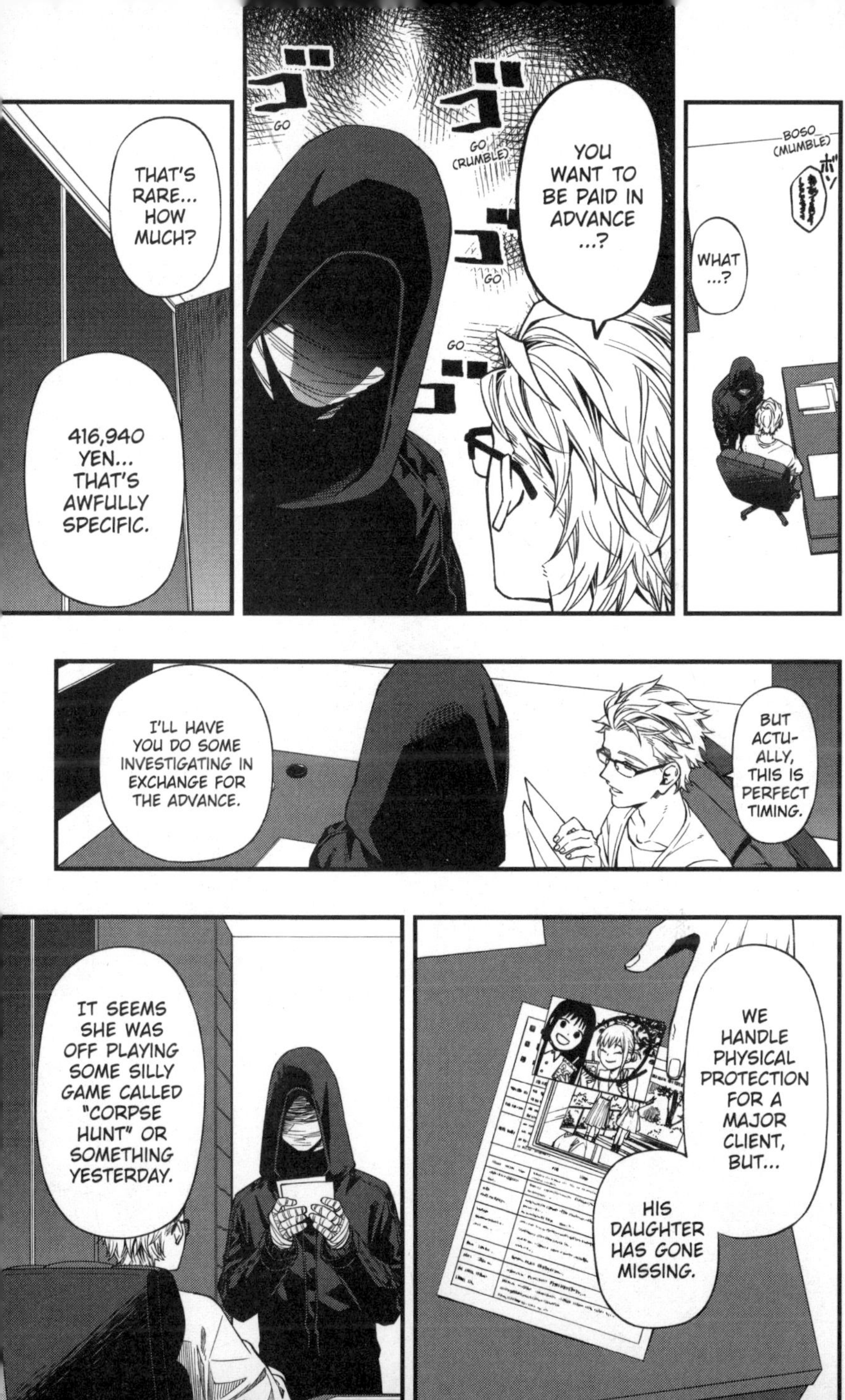
BOSO (MUMBLE)
WHAT ...?
GO
GO (RUMBLE)
GO
GO
YOU WANT TO BE PAID IN ADVANCE ...?
THAT'S RARE... HOW MUCH?
416,940 YEN... THAT'S AWFULLY SPECIFIC.
BUT ACTU-ALLY, THIS IS PERFECT TIMING.
I'LL HAVE YOU DO SOME INVESTIGATING IN EXCHANGE FOR THE ADVANCE.
WE HANDLE PHYSICAL PROTECTION FOR A MAJOR CLIENT, BUT...
HIS DAUGHTER HAS GONE MISSING.
IT SEEMS SHE WAS OFF PLAYING SOME SILLY GAME CALLED "CORPSE HUNT" OR SOMETHING YESTERDAY.

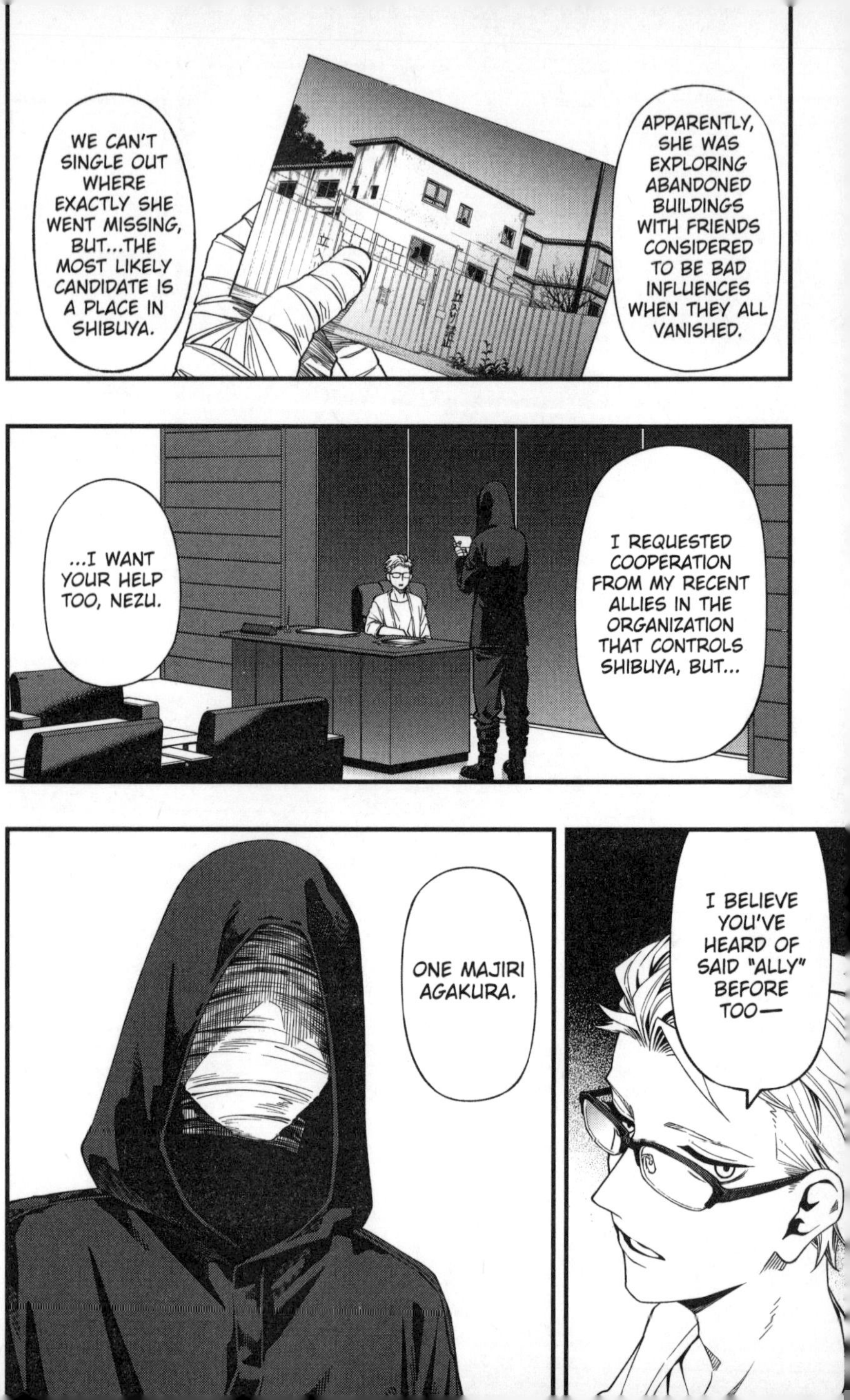
APPARENTLY, SHE WAS EXPLORING ABANDONED BUILDINGS WITH FRIENDS CONSIDERED TO BE BAD INFLUENCES WHEN THEY ALL VANISHED.
WE CAN'T SINGLE OUT WHERE EXACTLY SHE WENT MISSING, BUT...THE MOST LIKELY CANDIDATE IS A PLACE IN SHIBUYA.
I REQUESTED COOPERATION FROM MY RECENT ALLIES IN THE ORGANIZATION THAT CONTROLS SHIBUYA, BUT...
...I WANT YOUR HELP TOO, NEZU.
I BELIEVE YOU'VE HEARD OF SAID "ALLY" BEFORE TOO—
ONE MAJIRI AGAKURA.

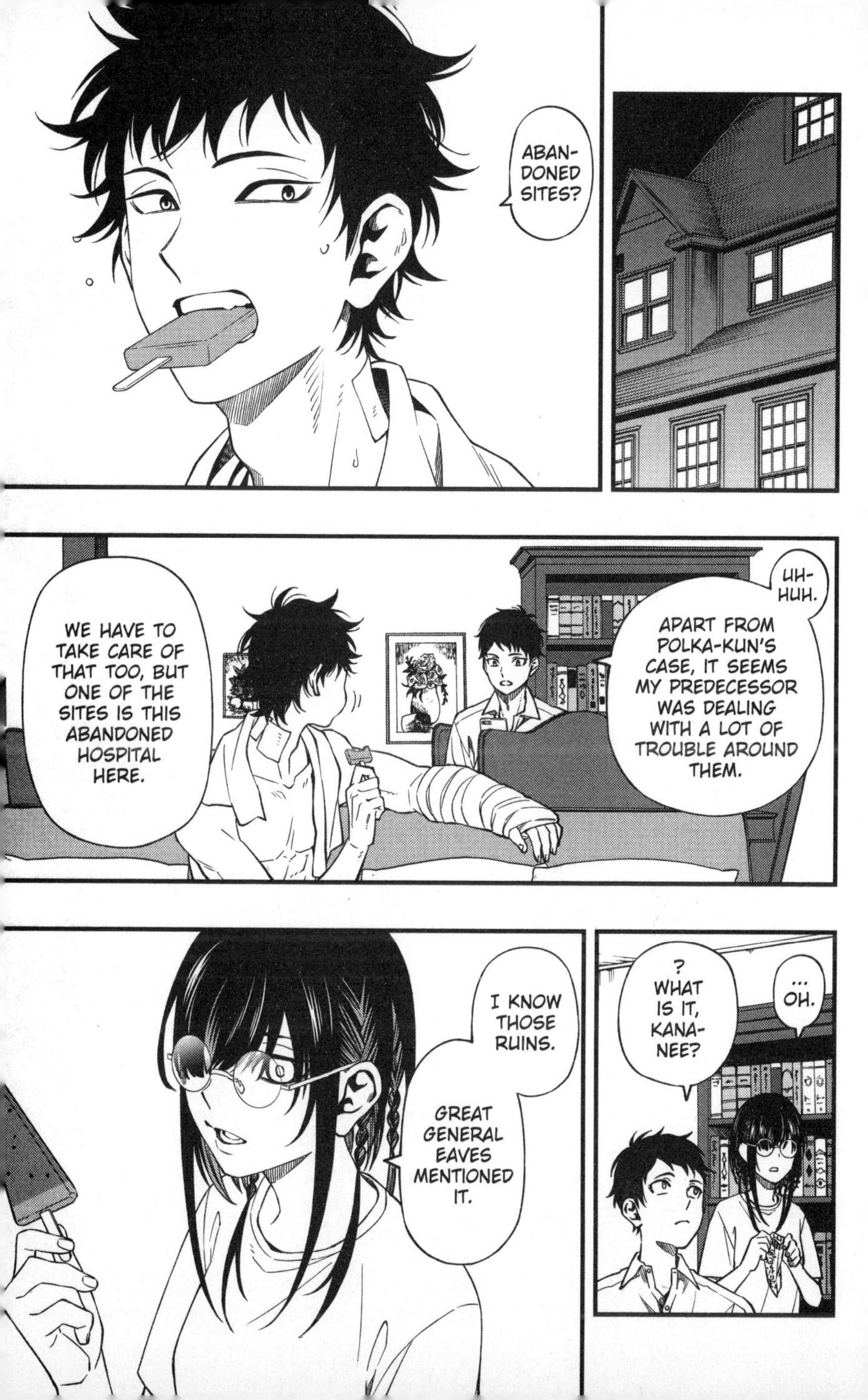
ABAN-DONED SITES?
UH-HUH.
APART FROM POLKA-KUN'S CASE, IT SEEMS MY PREDECESSOR WAS DEALING WITH A LOT OF TROUBLE AROUND THEM.
WE HAVE TO TAKE CARE OF THAT TOO, BUT ONE OF THE SITES IS THIS ABANDONED HOSPITAL HERE.
... OH.
? WHAT IS IT, KANA-NEE?
I KNOW THOSE RUINS.
GREAT GENERAL EAVES MENTIONED IT.

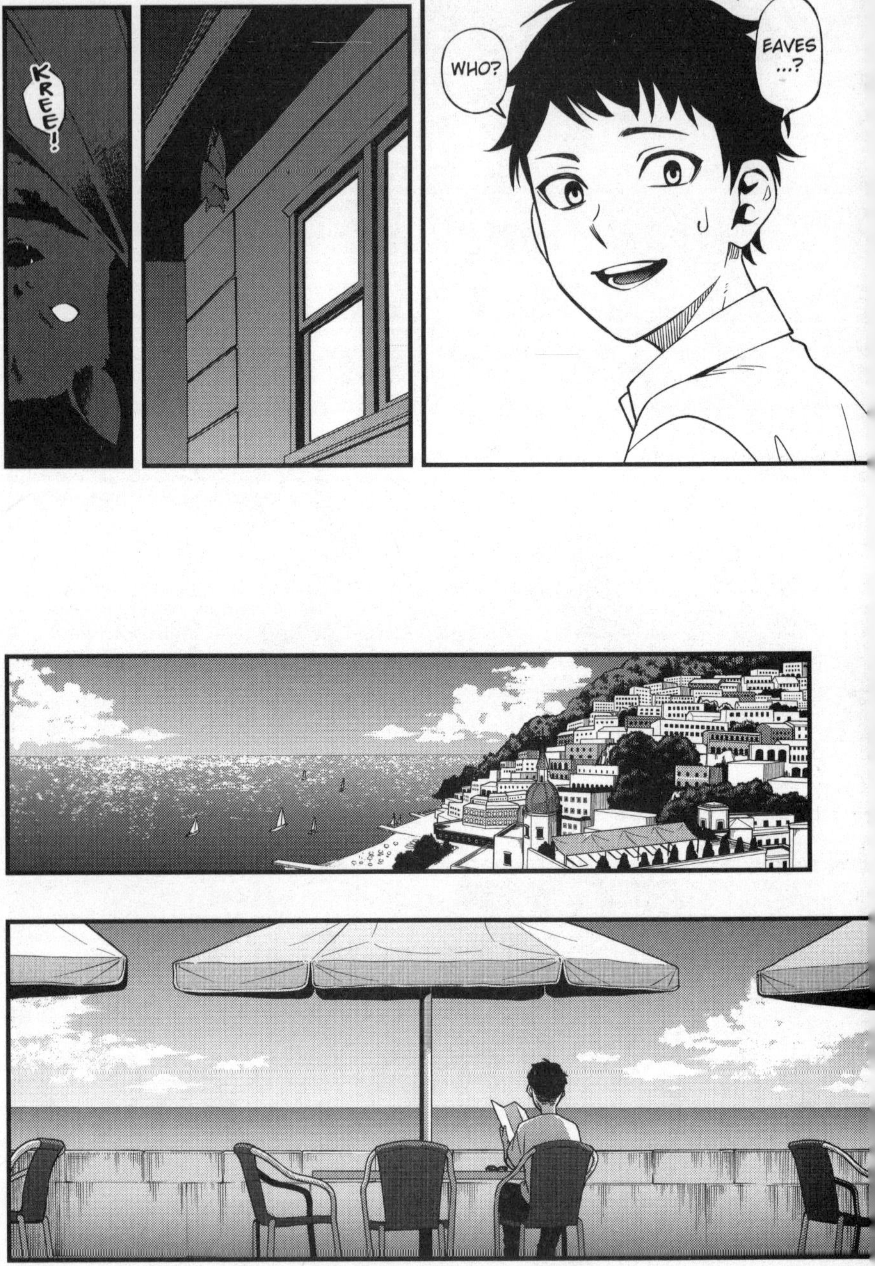
EAVES
...?
WHO?
KREE!

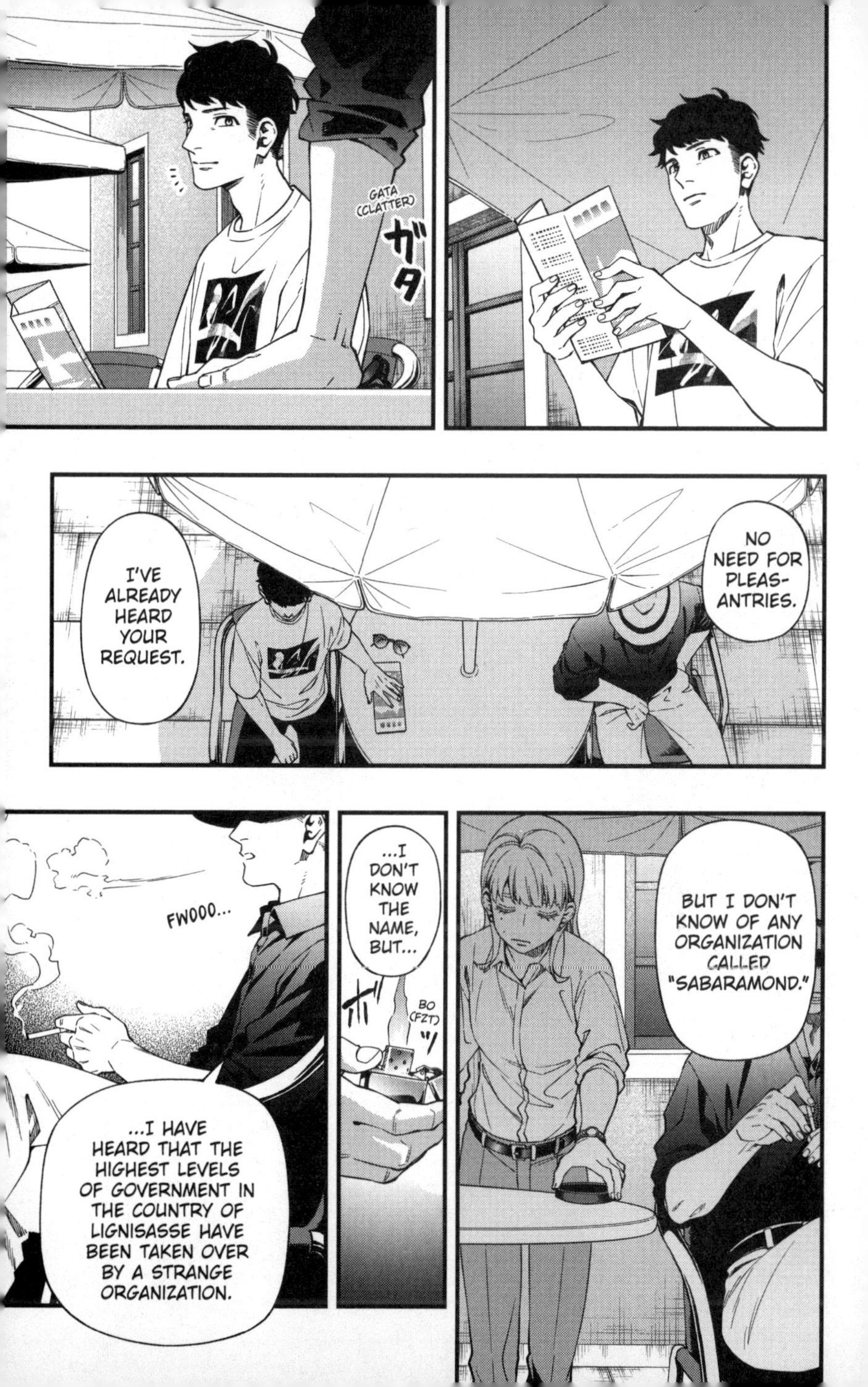
...
GATA (CLATTER)
ガタ
NO NEED FOR PLEAS-ANTRIES.
I'VE ALREADY HEARD YOUR REQUEST.
BUT I DON'T KNOW OF ANY ORGANIZATION CALLED "SABARAMOND."
...I DON'T KNOW THE NAME, BUT...
BO (FZT)
ボッ
FWOOO...
...I HAVE HEARD THAT THE HIGHEST LEVELS OF GOVERNMENT IN THE COUNTRY OF LIGNISASSE HAVE BEEN TAKEN OVER BY A STRANGE ORGANIZATION.

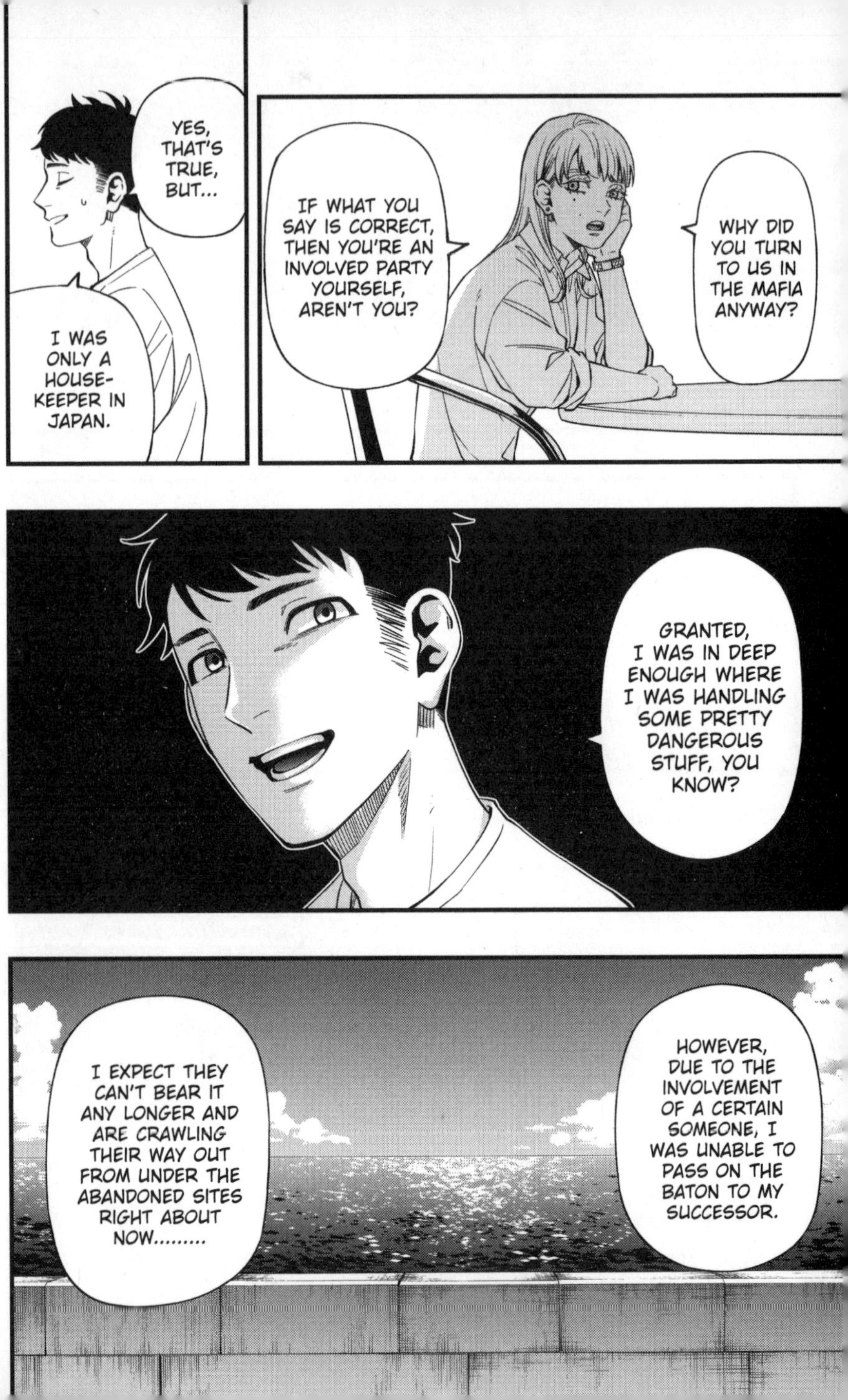
WHY DID YOU TURN TO US IN THE MAFIA ANYWAY?
IF WHAT YOU SAY IS CORRECT, THEN YOU'RE AN INVOLVED PARTY YOURSELF, AREN'T YOU?
YES, THAT'S TRUE, BUT...
I WAS ONLY A HOUSE-KEEPER IN JAPAN.
GRANTED, I WAS IN DEEP ENOUGH WHERE I WAS HANDLING SOME PRETTY DANGEROUS STUFF, YOU KNOW?
HOWEVER, DUE TO THE INVOLVEMENT OF A CERTAIN SOMEONE, I WAS UNABLE TO PASS ON THE BATON TO MY SUCCESSOR.
I EXPECT THEY CAN'T BEAR IT ANY LONGER AND ARE CRAWLING THEIR WAY OUT FROM UNDER THE ABANDONED SITES RIGHT ABOUT NOW.........

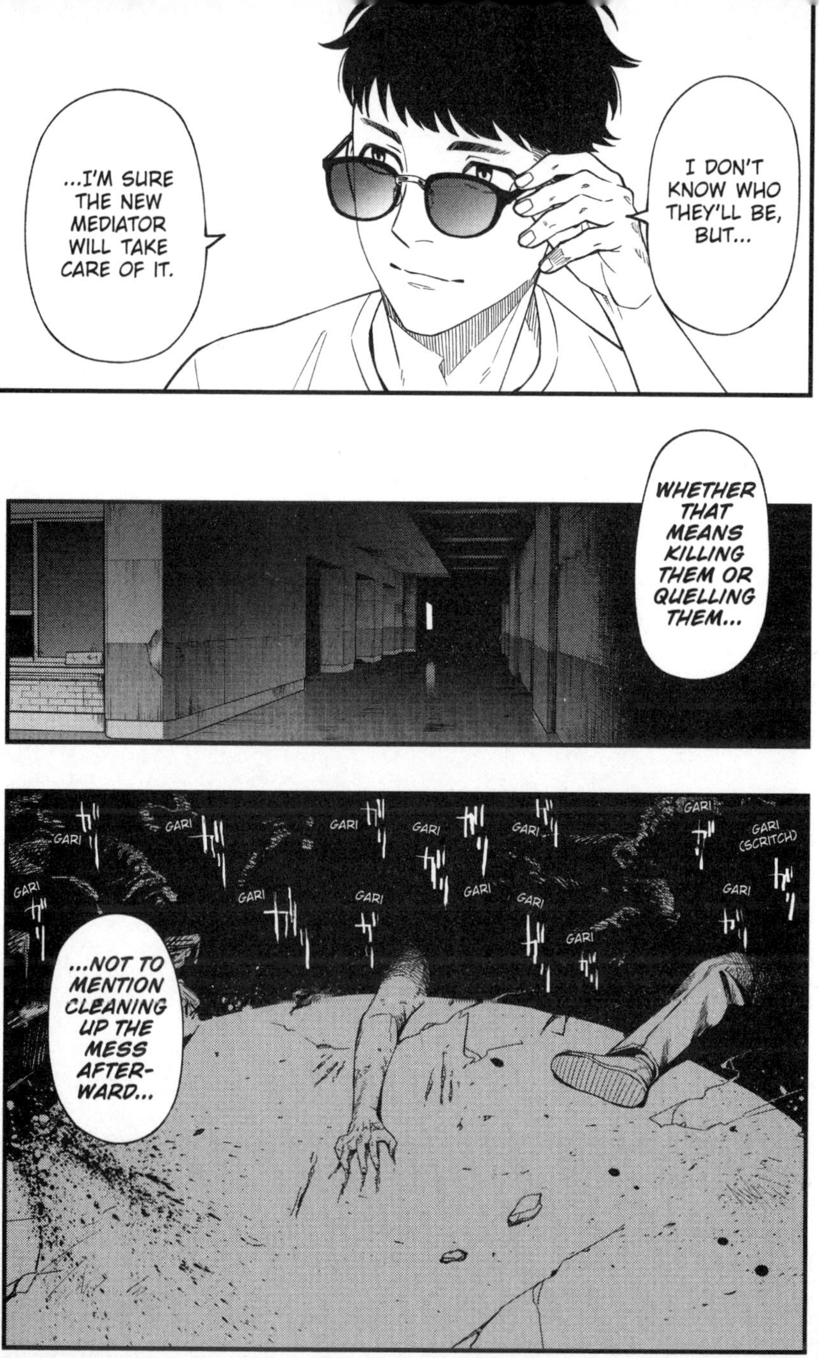
I DON'T KNOW WHO THEY'LL BE, BUT...
...I'M SURE THE NEW MEDIATOR WILL TAKE CARE OF IT.
WHETHER THAT MEANS KILLING THEM OR QUELLING THEM...
GARI
GARI (SCRITCH)
GARI
GARI
GARI
GARI
GARI
GARI
GARI
GARI
GARI
GARI
GARI
GARI
...NOT TO MENTION CLEANING UP THE MESS AFTER-WARD...

DEAD MOUNT
DEATH PLAY

# #91

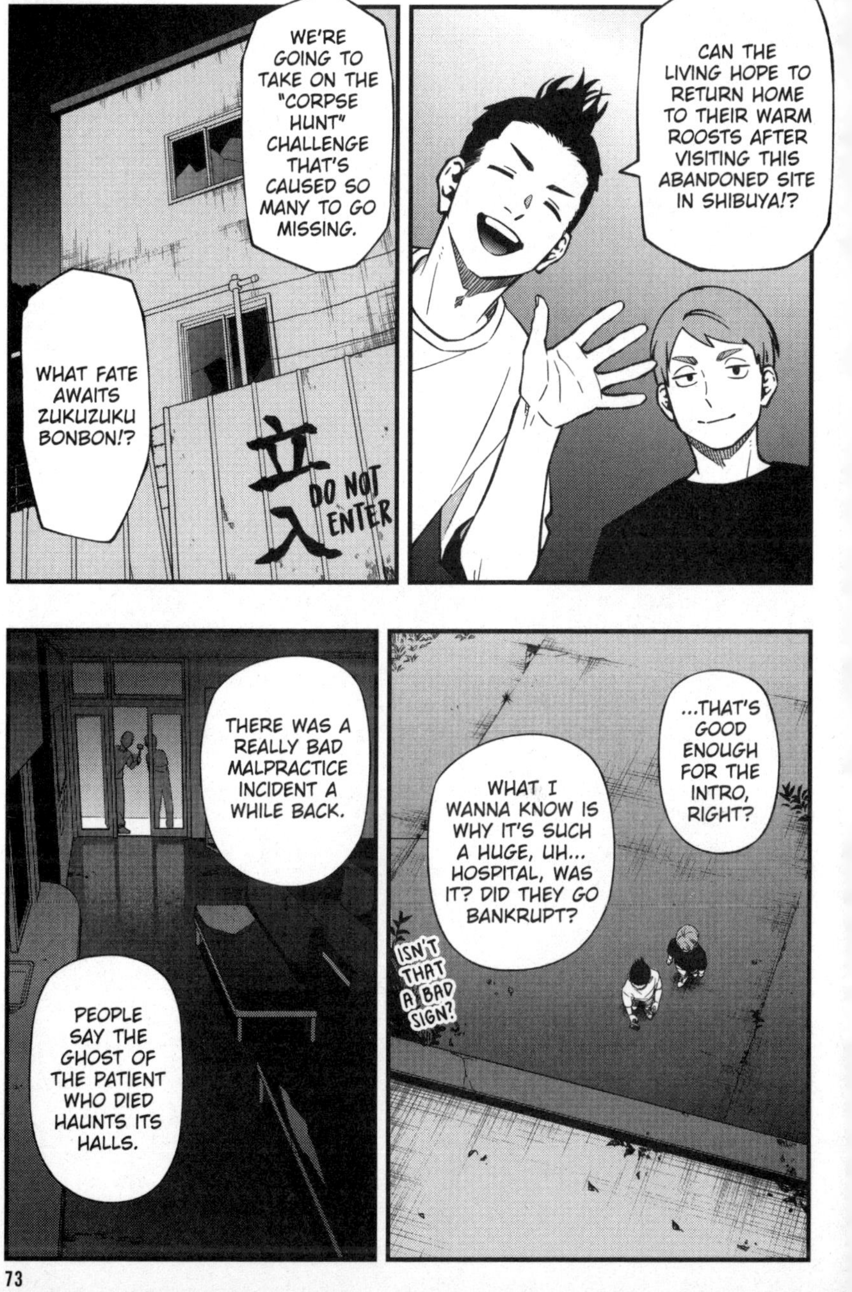
CAN THE LIVING HOPE TO RETURN HOME TO THEIR WARM ROOSTS AFTER VISITING THIS ABANDONED SITE IN SHIBUYA!?
WE'RE GOING TO TAKE ON THE "CORPSE HUNT" CHALLENGE THAT'S CAUSED SO MANY TO GO MISSING.
WHAT FATE AWAITS ZUKUZUKU BONBON!?
DO NOT ENTER
...THAT'S GOOD ENOUGH FOR THE INTRO, RIGHT?
WHAT I WANNA KNOW IS WHY IT'S SUCH A HUGE, UH... HOSPITAL, WAS IT? DID THEY GO BANKRUPT?
ISN'T THAT A BAD SIGN?
THERE WAS A REALLY BAD MALPRACTICE INCIDENT A WHILE BACK.
PEOPLE SAY THE GHOST OF THE PATIENT WHO DIED HAUNTS ITS HALLS.

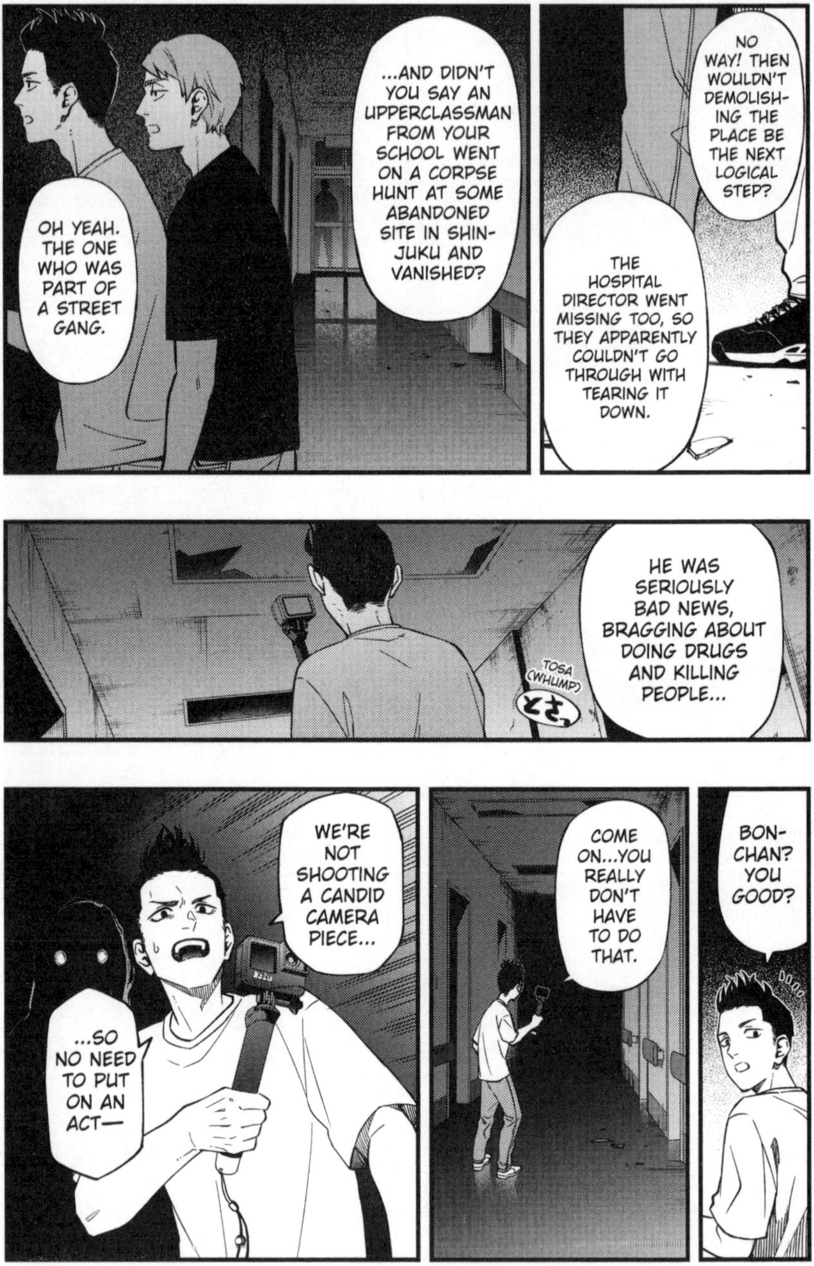
NO WAY! THEN WOULDN'T DEMOLISHING THE PLACE BE THE NEXT LOGICAL STEP?
THE HOSPITAL DIRECTOR WENT MISSING TOO, SO THEY APPARENTLY COULDN'T GO THROUGH WITH TEARING IT DOWN.
...AND DIDN'T YOU SAY AN UPPERCLASSMAN FROM YOUR SCHOOL WENT ON A CORPSE HUNT AT SOME ABANDONED SITE IN SHINJUKU AND VANISHED?
OH YEAH. THE ONE WHO WAS PART OF A STREET GANG.
HE WAS SERIOUSLY BAD NEWS, BRAGGING ABOUT DOING DRUGS AND KILLING PEOPLE...
TOSA (WHUMP)
とさっ
BON-CHAN? YOU GOOD?
COME ON...YOU REALLY DON'T HAVE TO DO THAT.
WE'RE NOT SHOOTING A CANDID CAMERA PIECE...
...SO NO NEED TO PUT ON AN ACT—

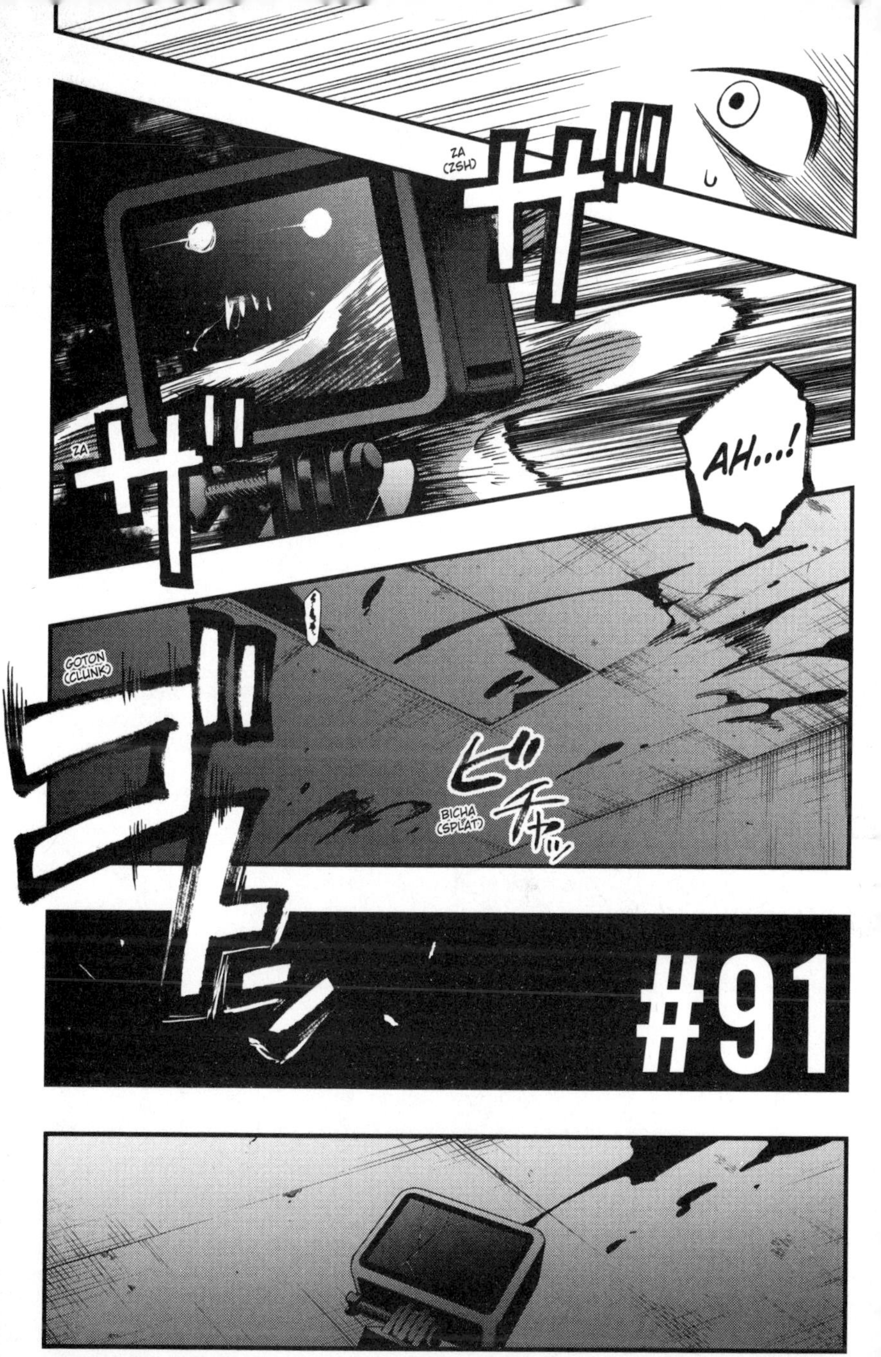
ZA (ZSH)
ZA
AH...!
GOTON (CLUNK)
BICHA (SPLAT)
#91

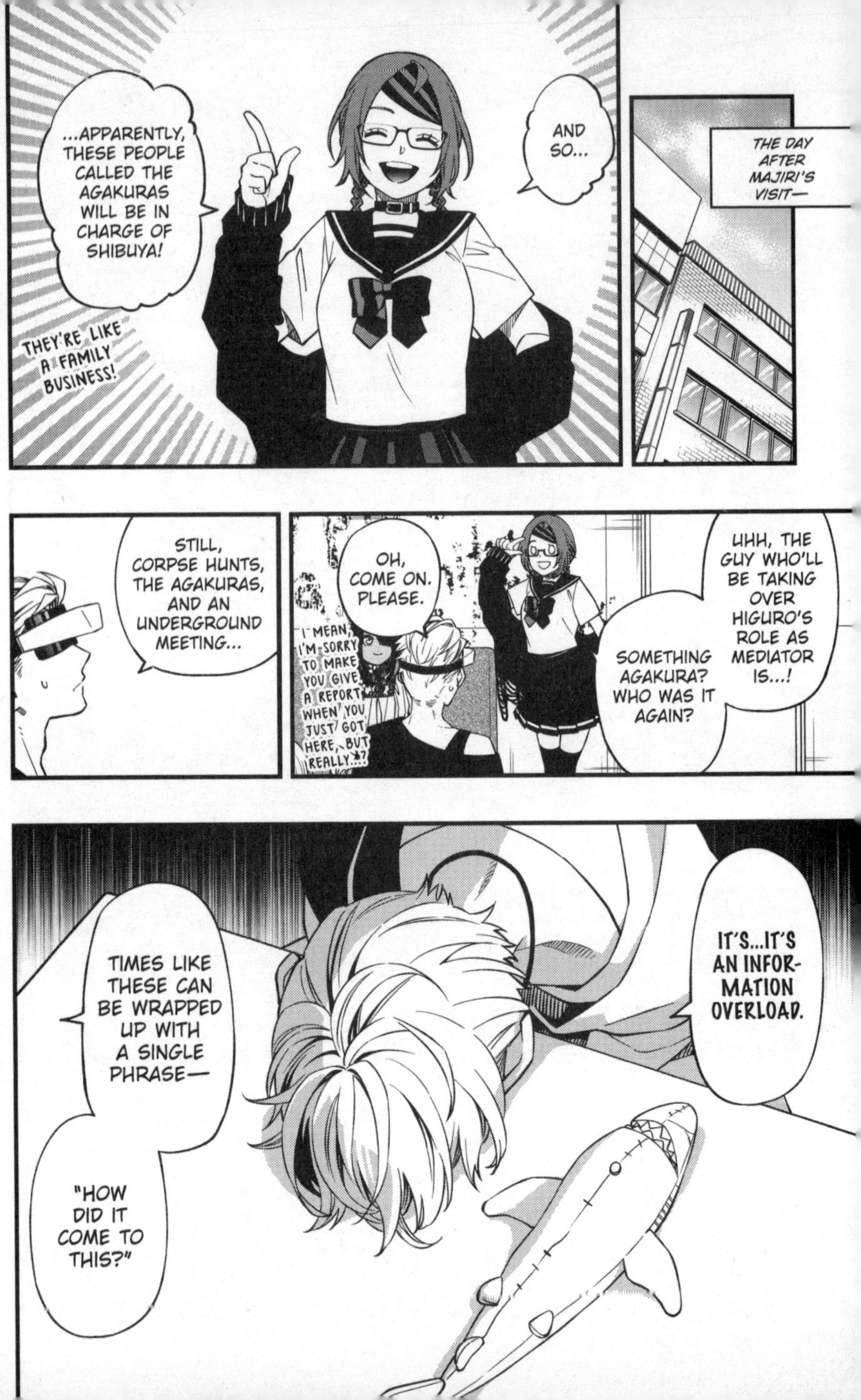
THE DAY AFTER MAJIRI'S VISIT—
AND SO...
...APPARENTLY, THESE PEOPLE CALLED THE AGAKURAS WILL BE IN CHARGE OF SHIBUYA!
THEY'RE LIKE A FAMILY BUSINESS!
UHH, THE GUY WHO'LL BE TAKING OVER HIGURO'S ROLE AS MEDIATOR IS...!
SOMETHING AGAKURA? WHO WAS IT AGAIN?
OH, COME ON. PLEASE.
I MEAN, I'M SORRY TO MAKE YOU GIVE A REPORT WHEN YOU JUST GOT HERE, BUT REALLY...?
STILL, CORPSE HUNTS, THE AGAKURAS, AND AN UNDERGROUND MEETING...
IT'S...IT'S AN INFORMATION OVERLOAD.
TIMES LIKE THESE CAN BE WRAPPED UP WITH A SINGLE PHRASE—
"HOW DID IT COME TO THIS?"

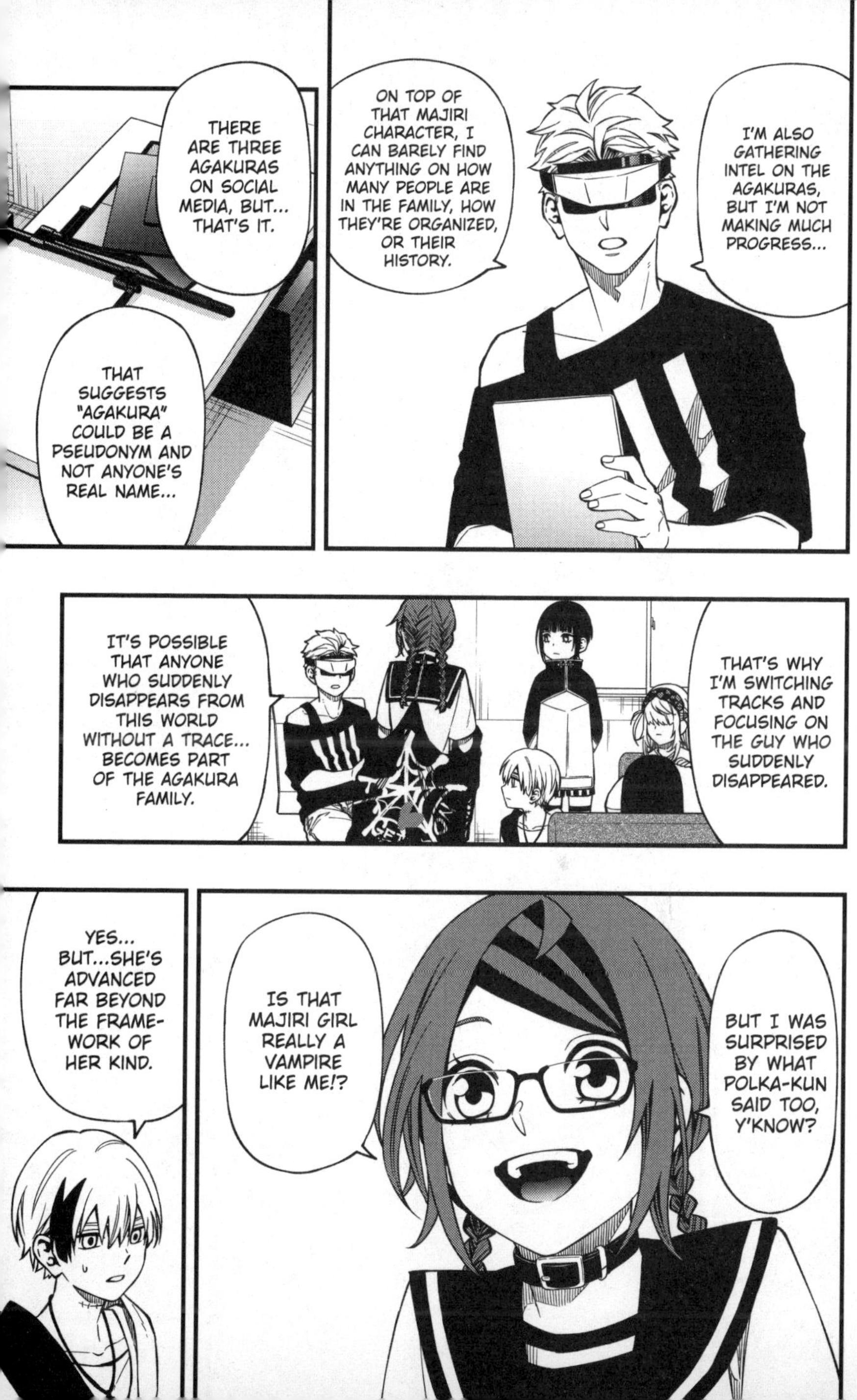

I'M ALSO GATHERING INTEL ON THE AGAKURAS, BUT I'M NOT MAKING MUCH PROGRESS...
ON TOP OF THAT MAJIRI CHARACTER, I CAN BARELY FIND ANYTHING ON HOW MANY PEOPLE ARE IN THE FAMILY, HOW THEY'RE ORGANIZED, OR THEIR HISTORY.
THERE ARE THREE AGAKURAS ON SOCIAL MEDIA, BUT... THAT'S IT.
THAT SUGGESTS "AGAKURA" COULD BE A PSEUDONYM AND NOT ANYONE'S REAL NAME...
THAT'S WHY I'M SWITCHING TRACKS AND FOCUSING ON THE GUY WHO SUDDENLY DISAPPEARED.
IT'S POSSIBLE THAT ANYONE WHO SUDDENLY DISAPPEARS FROM THIS WORLD WITHOUT A TRACE... BECOMES PART OF THE AGAKURA FAMILY.
BUT I WAS SURPRISED BY WHAT POLKA-KUN SAID TOO, Y'KNOW?
IS THAT MAJIRI GIRL REALLY A VAMPIRE LIKE ME!?
YES... BUT...SHE'S ADVANCED FAR BEYOND THE FRAME-WORK OF HER KIND.

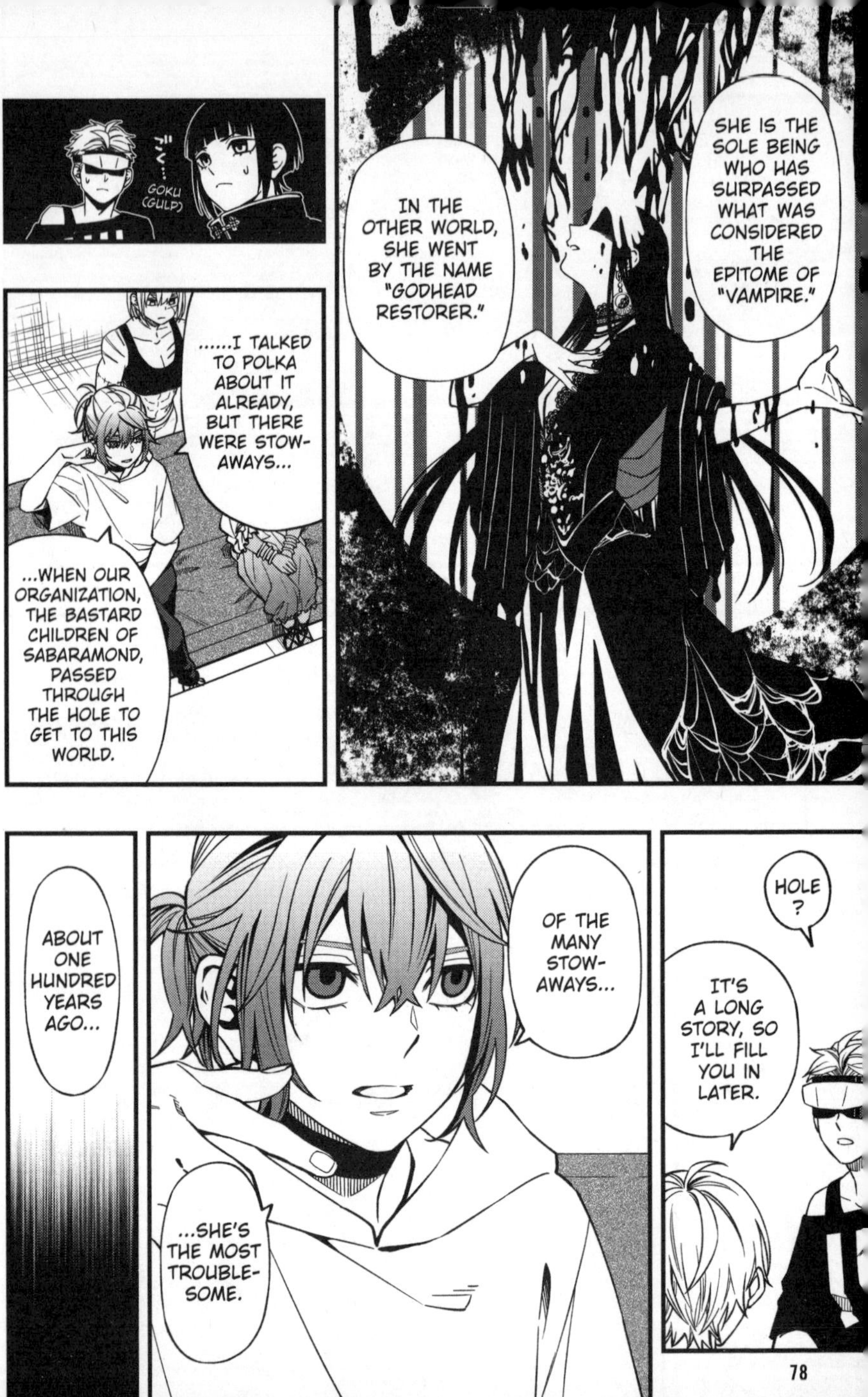
SHE IS THE SOLE BEING WHO HAS SURPASSED WHAT WAS CONSIDERED THE EPITOME OF "VAMPIRE."
IN THE OTHER WORLD, SHE WENT BY THE NAME "GODHEAD RESTORER."
GOKU (GULP)
......I TALKED TO POLKA ABOUT IT ALREADY, BUT THERE WERE STOW-AWAYS...
...WHEN OUR ORGANIZATION, THE BASTARD CHILDREN OF SABARAMOND, PASSED THROUGH THE HOLE TO GET TO THIS WORLD.
HOLE?
IT'S A LONG STORY, SO I'LL FILL YOU IN LATER.
OF THE MANY STOW-AWAYS...
...SHE'S THE MOST TROUBLE-SOME.
ABOUT ONE HUNDRED YEARS AGO...

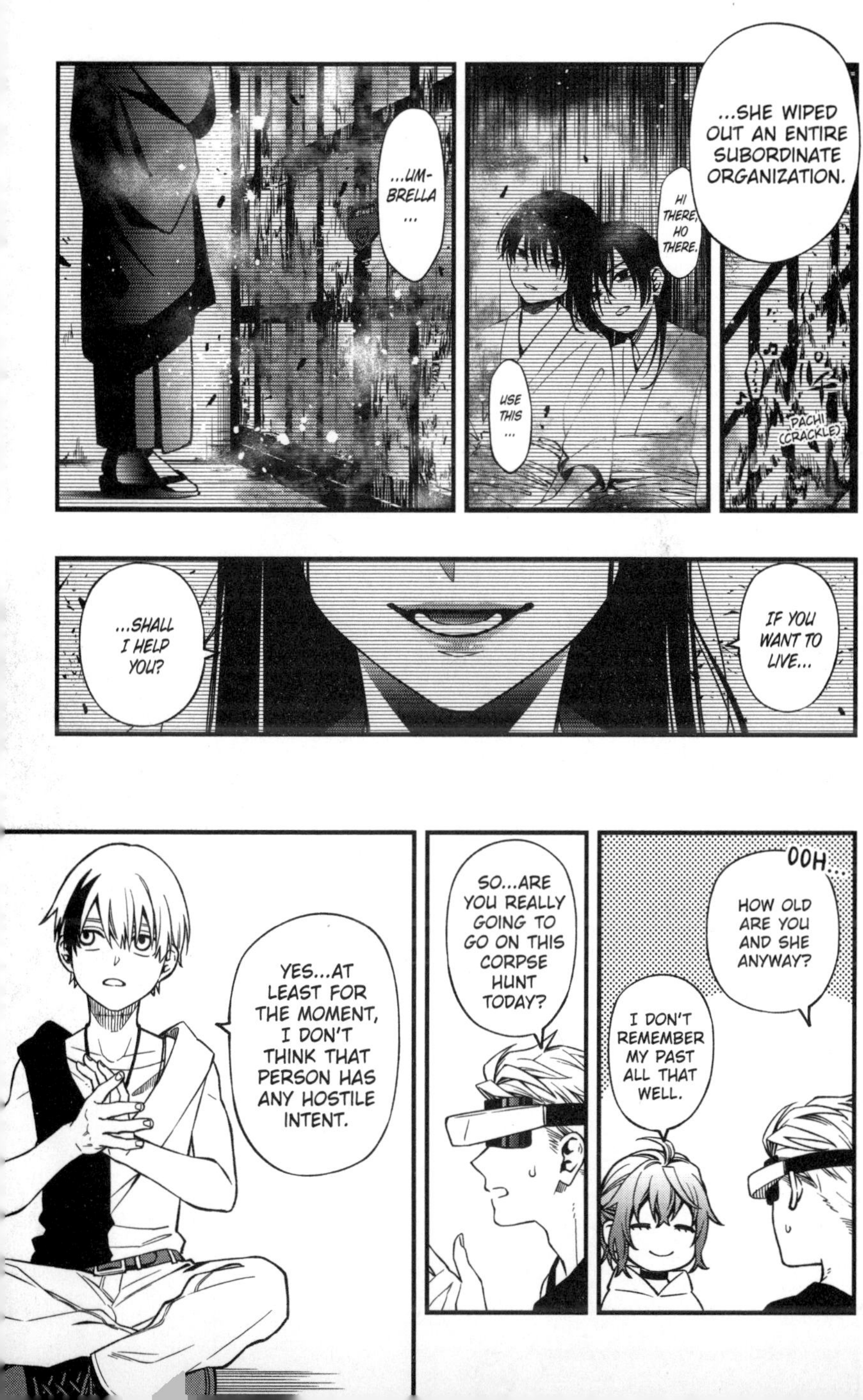
...SHE WIPED OUT AN ENTIRE SUBORDINATE ORGANIZATION.
PACHI (CRACKLE)
HI THERE, HO THERE.
USE THIS ...
...UM-BRELLA ...
IF YOU WANT TO LIVE...
...SHALL I HELP YOU?
OOH...
HOW OLD ARE YOU AND SHE ANYWAY?
I DON'T REMEMBER MY PAST ALL THAT WELL.
SO...ARE YOU REALLY GOING TO GO ON THIS CORPSE HUNT TODAY?
YES...AT LEAST FOR THE MOMENT, I DON'T THINK THAT PERSON HAS ANY HOSTILE INTENT.

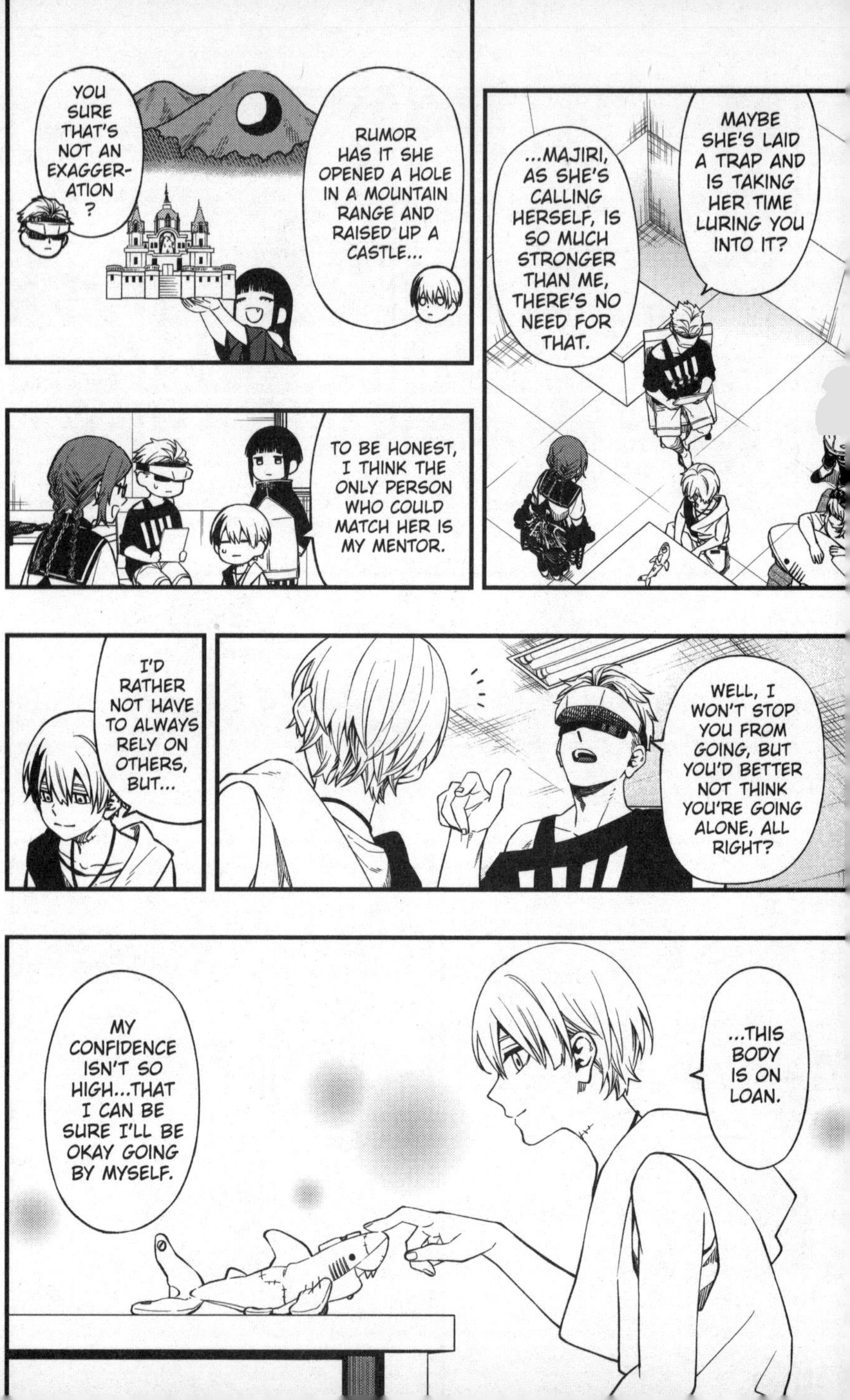

MAYBE SHE'S LAID A TRAP AND IS TAKING HER TIME LURING YOU INTO IT?
...MAJIRI, AS SHE'S CALLING HERSELF, IS SO MUCH STRONGER THAN ME, THERE'S NO NEED FOR THAT.
RUMOR HAS IT SHE OPENED A HOLE IN A MOUNTAIN RANGE AND RAISED UP A CASTLE...
YOU SURE THAT'S NOT AN EXAGGER-ATION ?
TO BE HONEST, I THINK THE ONLY PERSON WHO COULD MATCH HER IS MY MENTOR.
WELL, I WON'T STOP YOU FROM GOING, BUT YOU'D BETTER NOT THINK YOU'RE GOING ALONE, ALL RIGHT?
I'D RATHER NOT HAVE TO ALWAYS RELY ON OTHERS, BUT...
...THIS BODY IS ON LOAN.
MY CONFIDENCE ISN'T SO HIGH...THAT I CAN BE SURE I'LL BE OKAY GOING BY MYSELF.

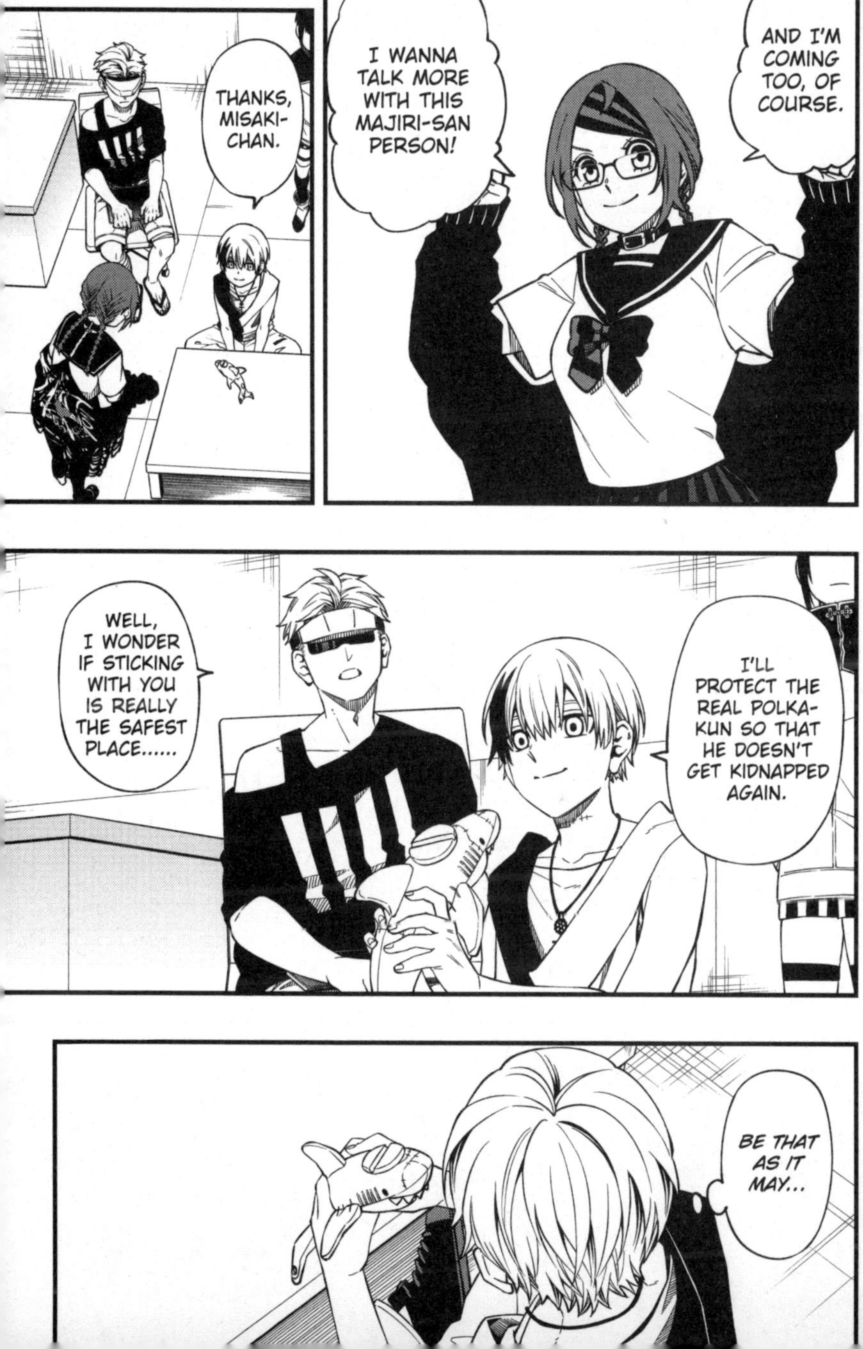
AND I'M COMING TOO, OF COURSE.
I WANNA TALK MORE WITH THIS MAJIRI-SAN PERSON!
THANKS, MISAKI-CHAN.
I'LL PROTECT THE REAL POLKA-KUN SO THAT HE DOESN'T GET KIDNAPPED AGAIN.
WELL, I WONDER IF STICKING WITH YOU IS REALLY THE SAFEST PLACE......
BE THAT AS IT MAY...

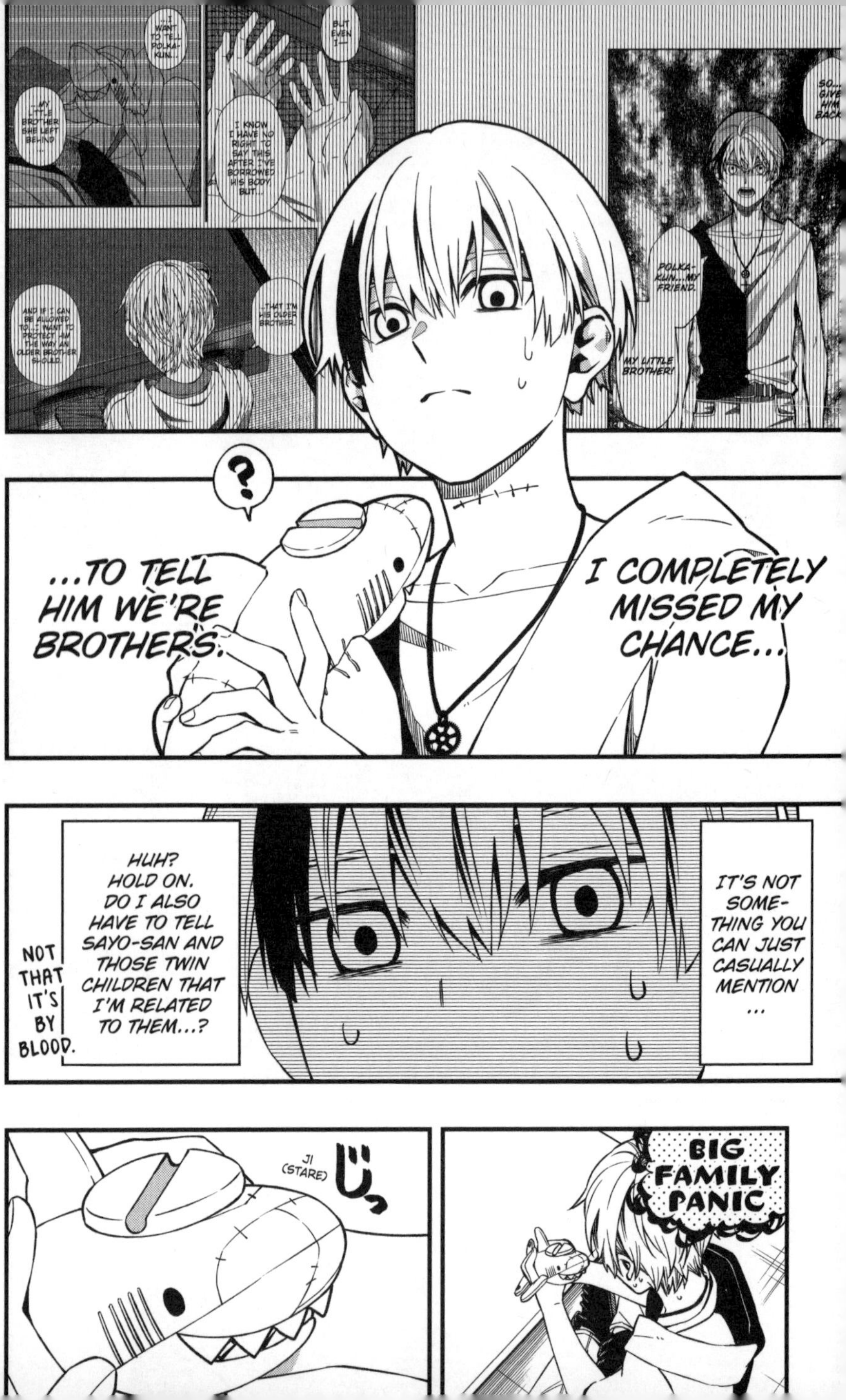
SO... GIVE HIM BACK
POLKA-KUN... MY FRIEND.
MY LITTLE BROTHER!
BUT EVEN I—
...I WANT TO TELL POLKA-KUN...
I KNOW I HAVE NO RIGHT TO SAY THIS AFTER I'VE BORROWED HIS BODY, BUT...
...MY LITTLE BROTHER SHE LEFT BEHIND...
...THAT I'M HIS OLDER BROTHER.
AND IF I CAN BE ALLOWED TO...I WANT TO PROTECT HIM THE WAY AN OLDER BROTHER SHOULD.
?
I COMPLETELY MISSED MY CHANCE...
...TO TELL HIM WE'RE BROTHERS.
IT'S NOT SOME-THING YOU CAN JUST CASUALLY MENTION...
HUH? HOLD ON. DO I ALSO HAVE TO TELL SAYO-SAN AND THOSE TWIN CHILDREN THAT I'M RELATED TO THEM...?
NOT THAT IT'S BY BLOOD.
BIG FAMILY PANIC
JI (STARE)
じっ

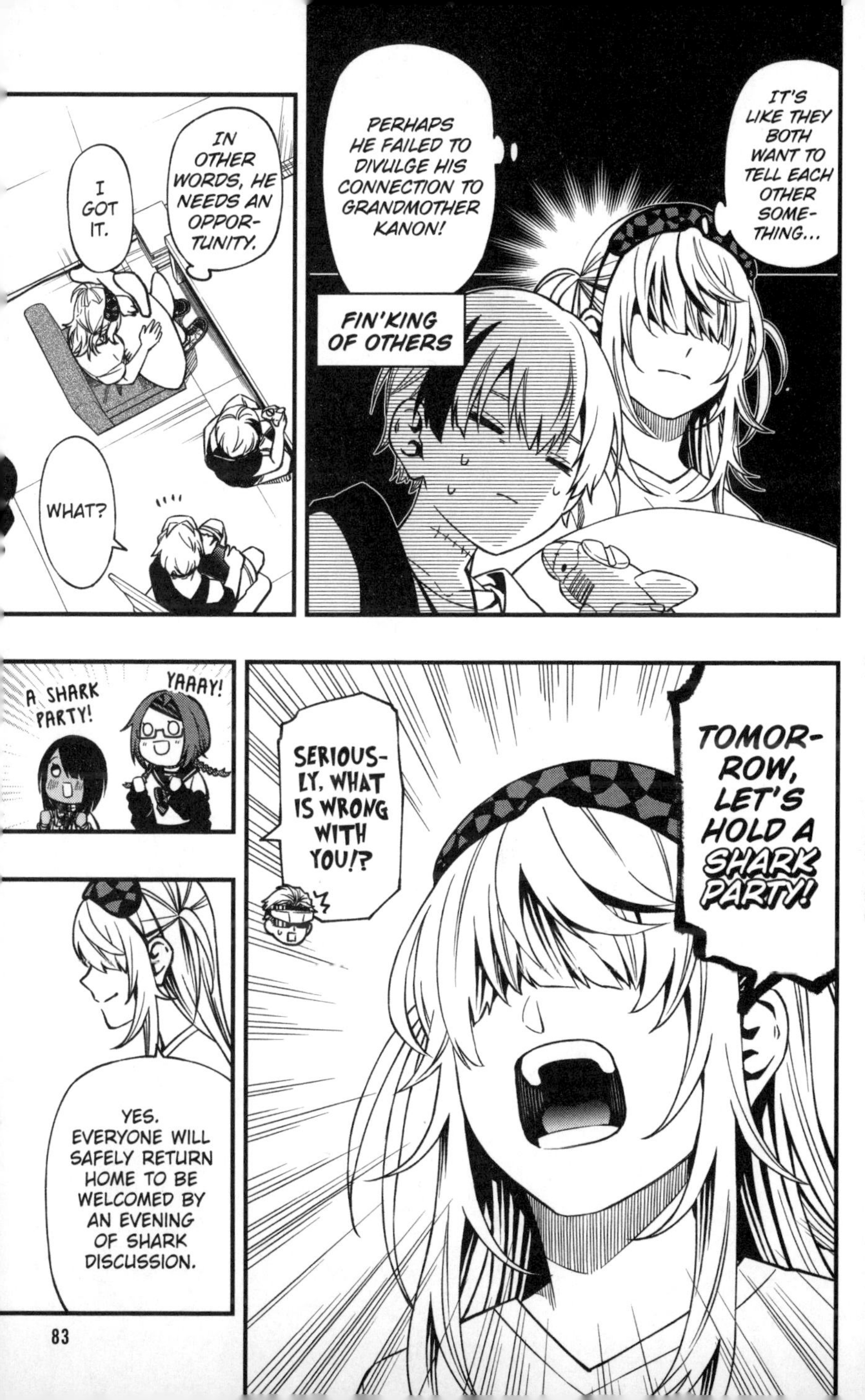
IT'S LIKE THEY BOTH WANT TO TELL EACH OTHER SOMETHING...
PERHAPS HE FAILED TO DIVULGE HIS CONNECTION TO GRANDMOTHER KANON!
FIN'KING OF OTHERS
IN OTHER WORDS, HE NEEDS AN OPPORTUNITY.
I GOT IT.
WHAT?
TOMORROW, LET'S HOLD A SHARK PARTY!
SERIOUSLY, WHAT IS WRONG WITH YOU!?
YAAAY!
A SHARK PARTY!
YES. EVERYONE WILL SAFELY RETURN HOME TO BE WELCOMED BY AN EVENING OF SHARK DISCUSSION.

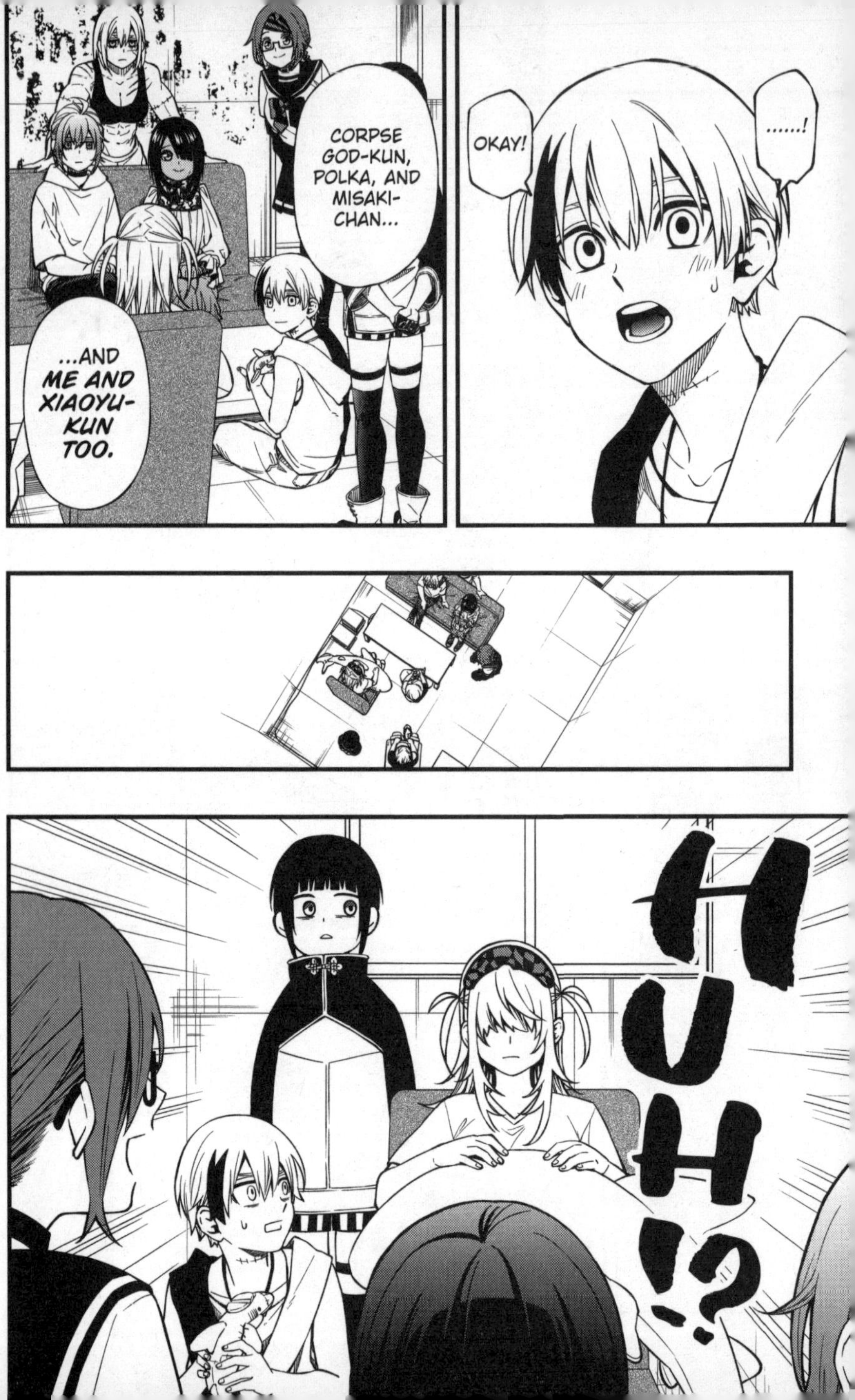
......!
OKAY!
CORPSE GOD-KUN, POLKA, AND MISAKI-CHAN...
...AND ME AND XIAOYU-KUN TOO.
HUH!?

# #92

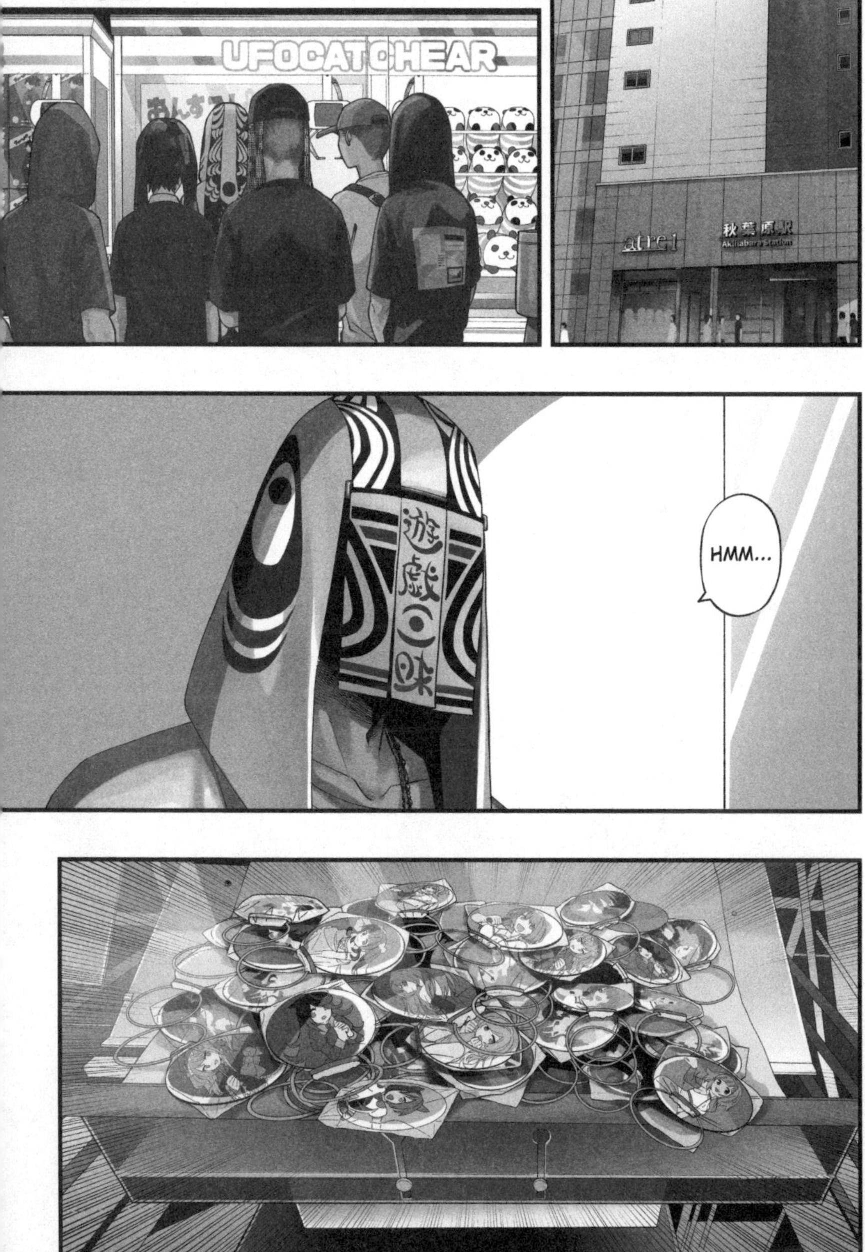
UFOCATCHEAR
atre1
atre1
秋葉原駅
Akihabara Station
遊戯三昧
HMM...

# #92

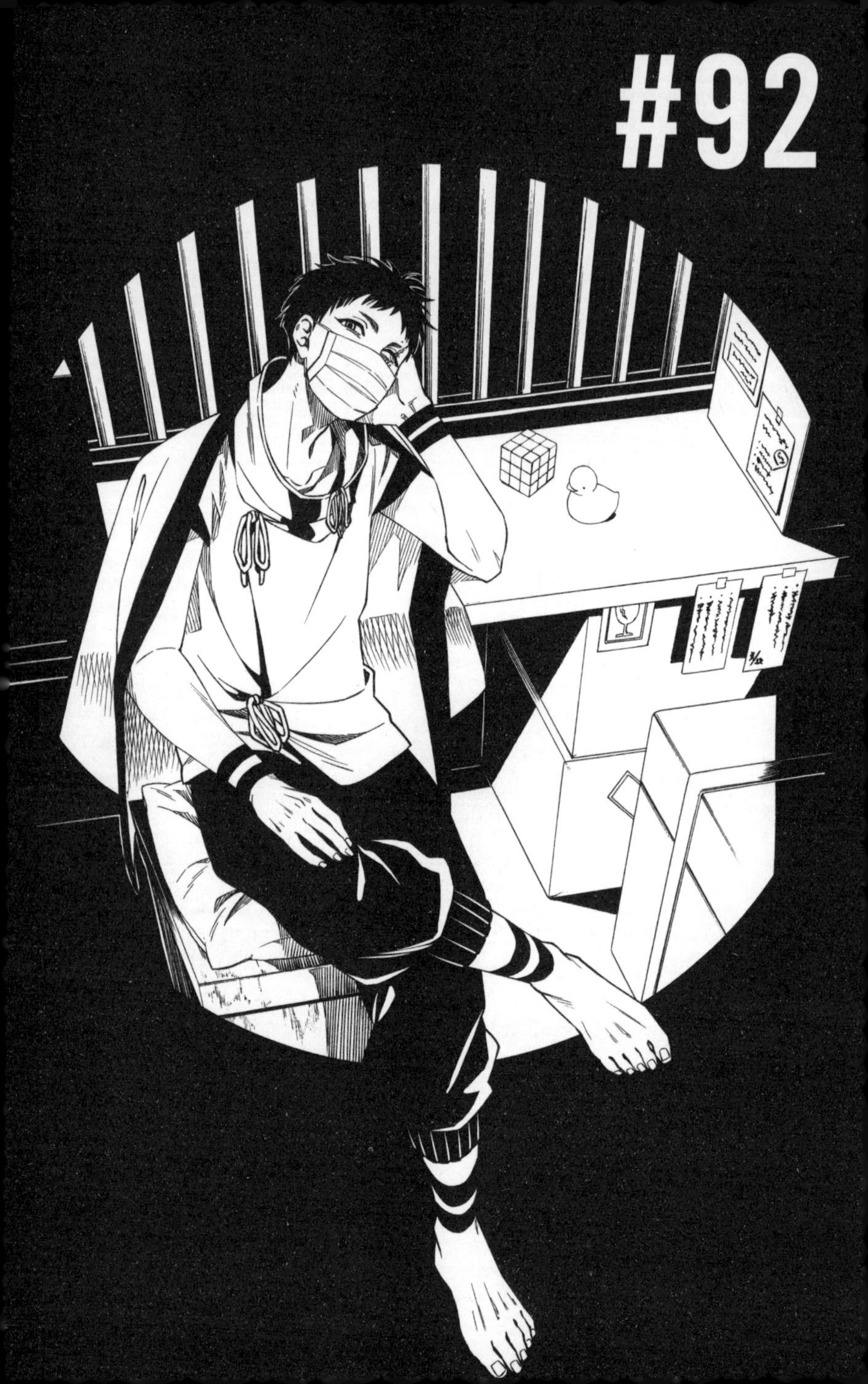

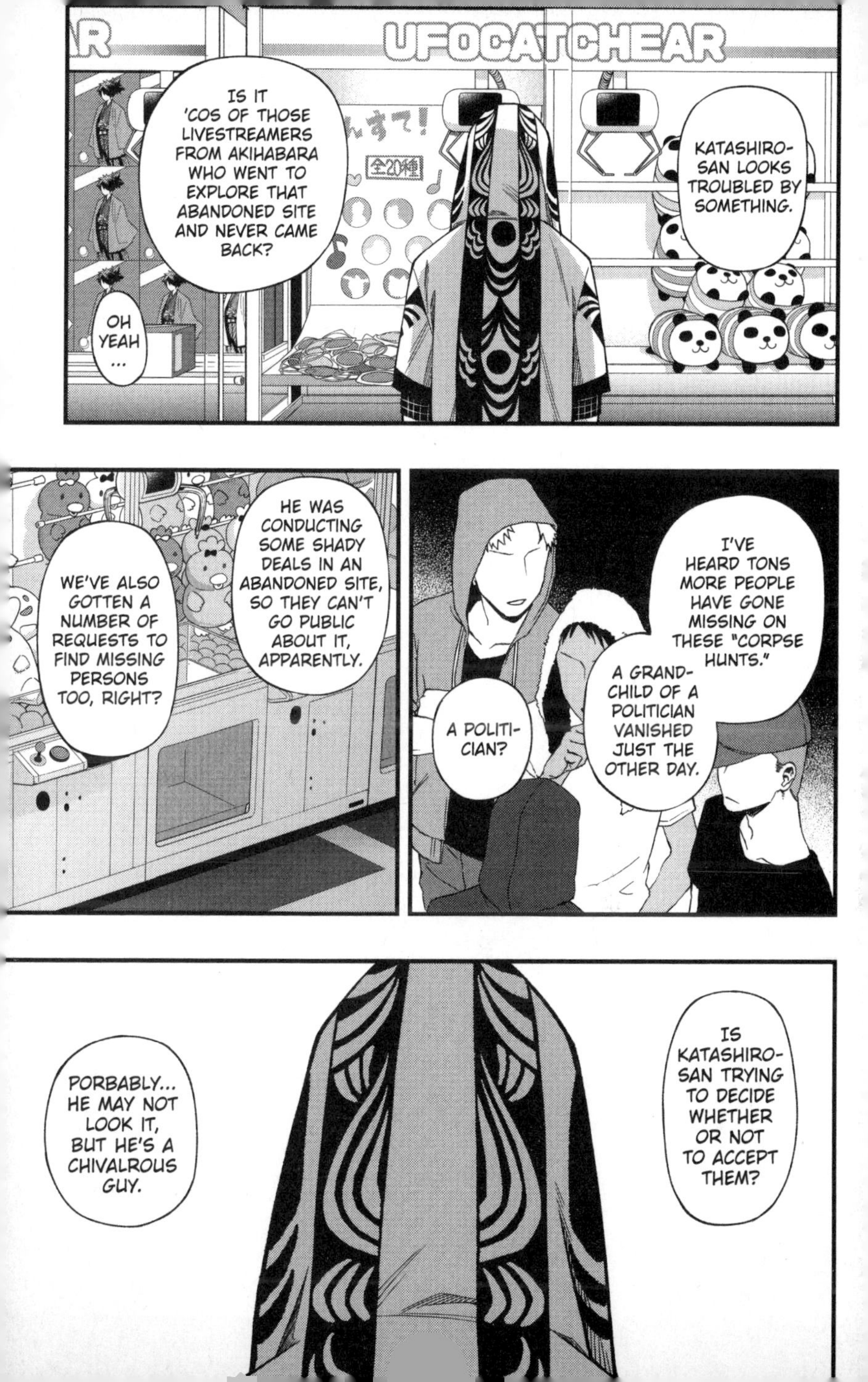
UFOCATCHEAR
KATASHIRO-SAN LOOKS TROUBLED BY SOMETHING.
IS IT 'COS OF THOSE LIVESTREAMERS FROM AKIHABARA WHO WENT TO EXPLORE THAT ABANDONED SITE AND NEVER CAME BACK?
全20種
OH YEAH ...
I'VE HEARD TONS MORE PEOPLE HAVE GONE MISSING ON THESE "CORPSE HUNTS."
A GRAND-CHILD OF A POLITICIAN VANISHED JUST THE OTHER DAY.
A POLITI-CIAN?
HE WAS CONDUCTING SOME SHADY DEALS IN AN ABANDONED SITE, SO THEY CAN'T GO PUBLIC ABOUT IT, APPARENTLY.
WE'VE ALSO GOTTEN A NUMBER OF REQUESTS TO FIND MISSING PERSONS TOO, RIGHT?
IS KATASHIRO-SAN TRYING TO DECIDE WHETHER OR NOT TO ACCEPT THEM?
PORBABLY... HE MAY NOT LOOK IT, BUT HE'S A CHIVALROUS GUY.

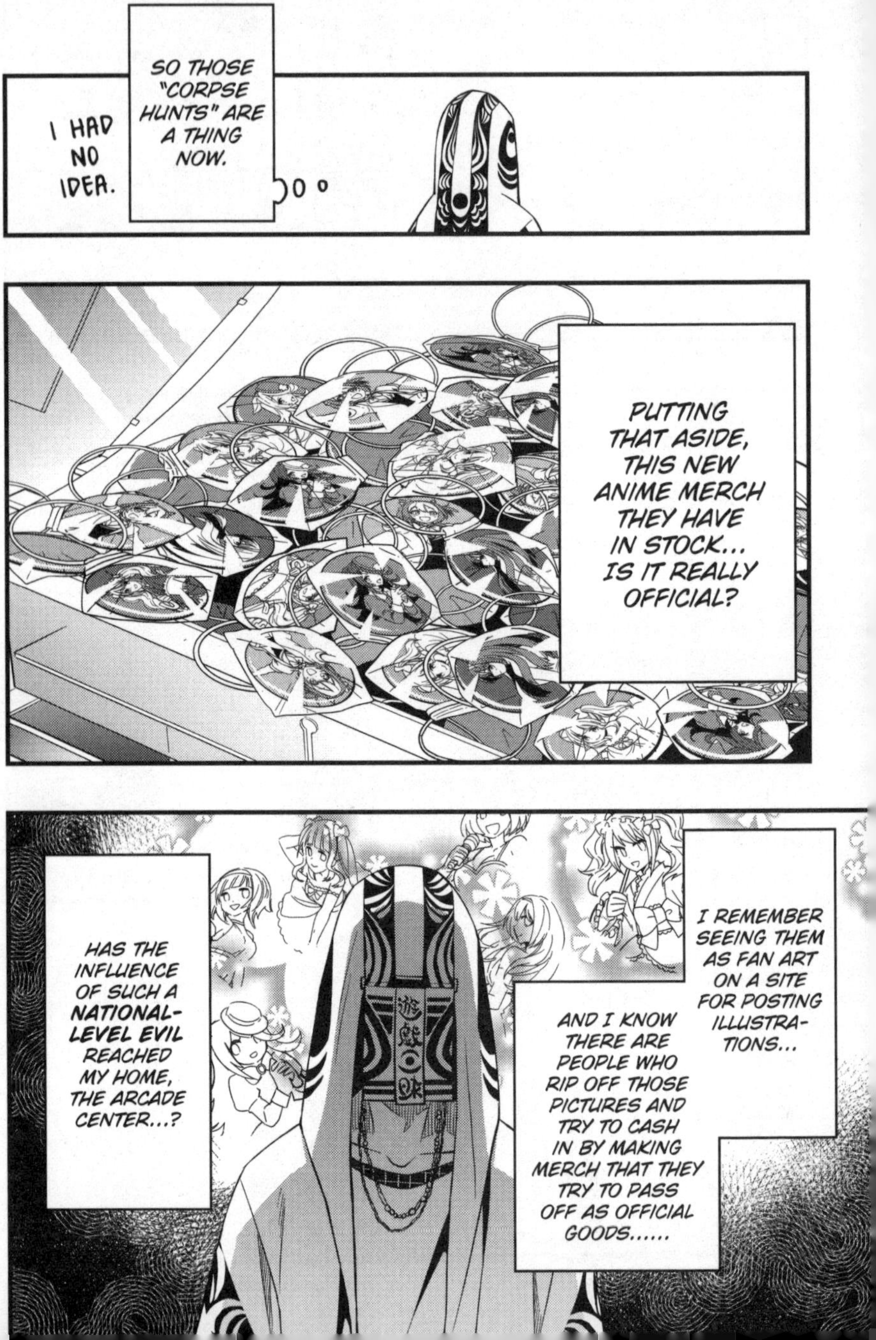
SO THOSE "CORPSE HUNTS" ARE A THING NOW.
I HAD NO IDEA.
PUTTING THAT ASIDE, THIS NEW ANIME MERCH THEY HAVE IN STOCK... IS IT REALLY OFFICIAL?
I REMEMBER SEEING THEM AS FAN ART ON A SITE FOR POSTING ILLUSTRATIONS...
AND I KNOW THERE ARE PEOPLE WHO RIP OFF THOSE PICTURES AND TRY TO CASH IN BY MAKING MERCH THAT THEY TRY TO PASS OFF AS OFFICIAL GOODS......
HAS THE INFLUENCE OF SUCH A **NATIONAL-LEVEL EVIL** REACHED MY HOME, THE ARCADE CENTER...?

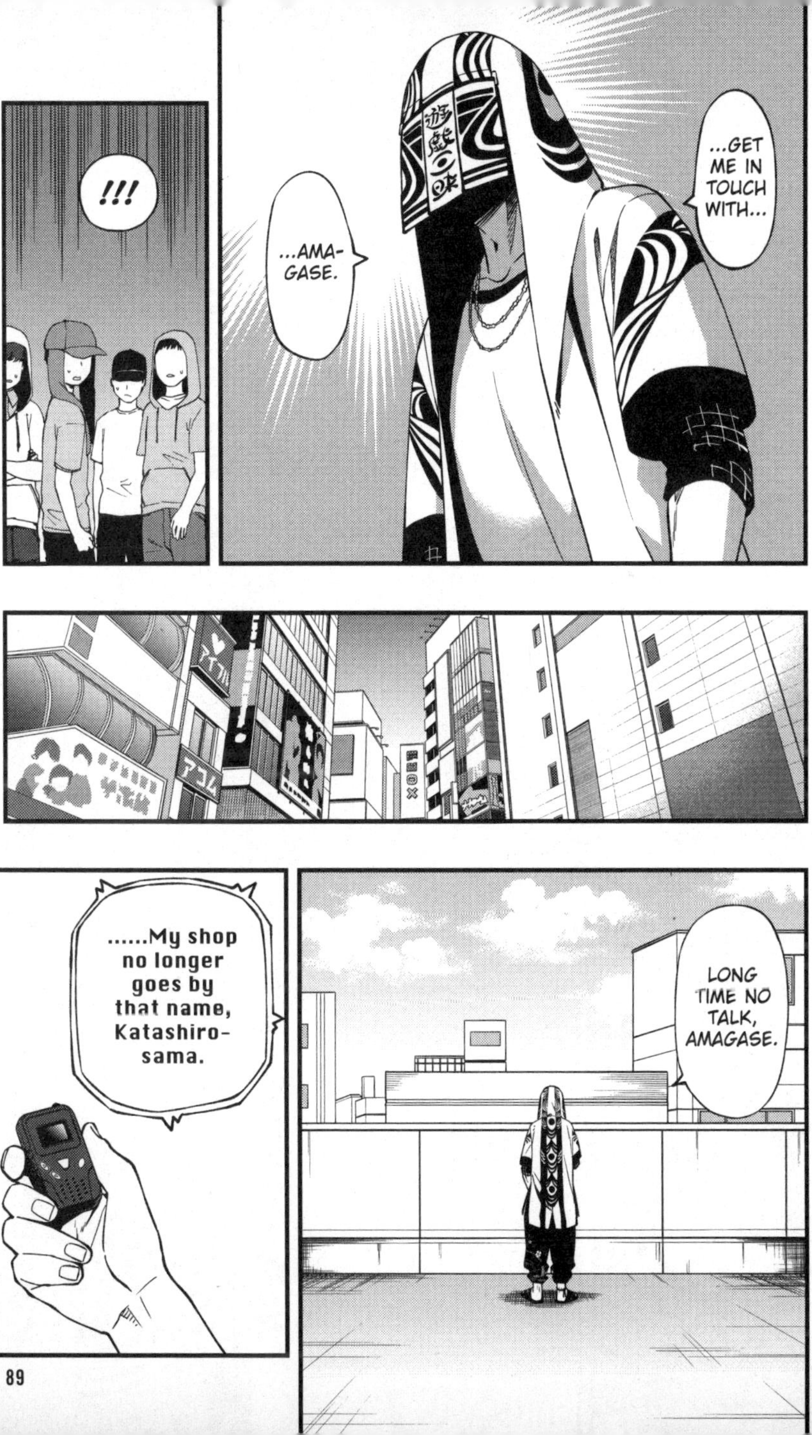
...GET ME IN TOUCH WITH...
...AMAGASE.
!!!
LONG TIME NO TALK, AMAGASE.
......My shop no longer goes by that name, Katashiro-sama.

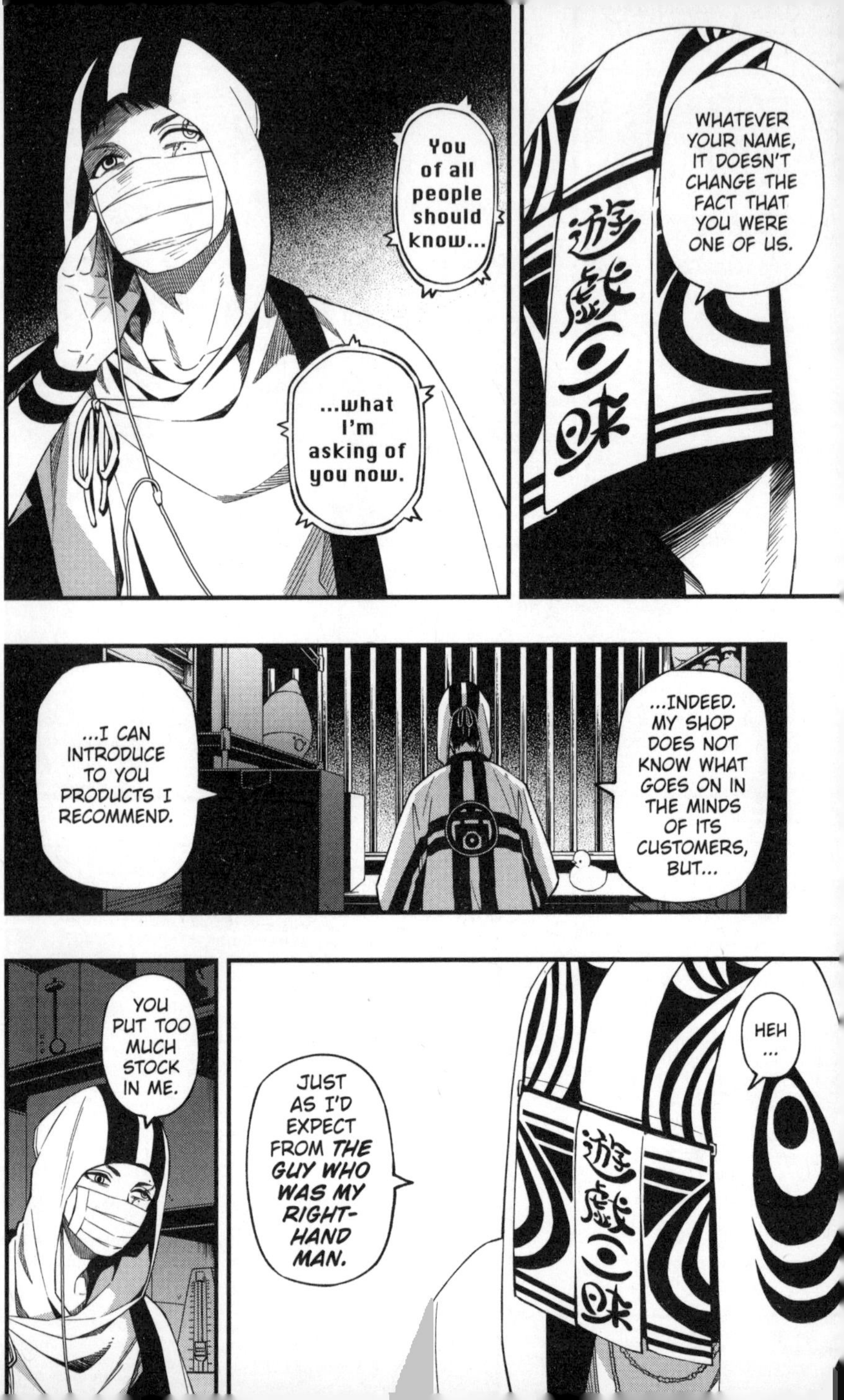

WHATEVER YOUR NAME, IT DOESN'T CHANGE THE FACT THAT YOU WERE ONE OF US.
遊戯三昧
You of all people should know...
...what I'm asking of you now.
...INDEED. MY SHOP DOES NOT KNOW WHAT GOES ON IN THE MINDS OF ITS CUSTOMERS, BUT...
...I CAN INTRODUCE TO YOU PRODUCTS I RECOMMEND.
HEH ...
JUST AS I'D EXPECT FROM *THE GUY WHO WAS MY RIGHT-HAND MAN.*
遊戯三昧
YOU PUT TOO MUCH STOCK IN ME.

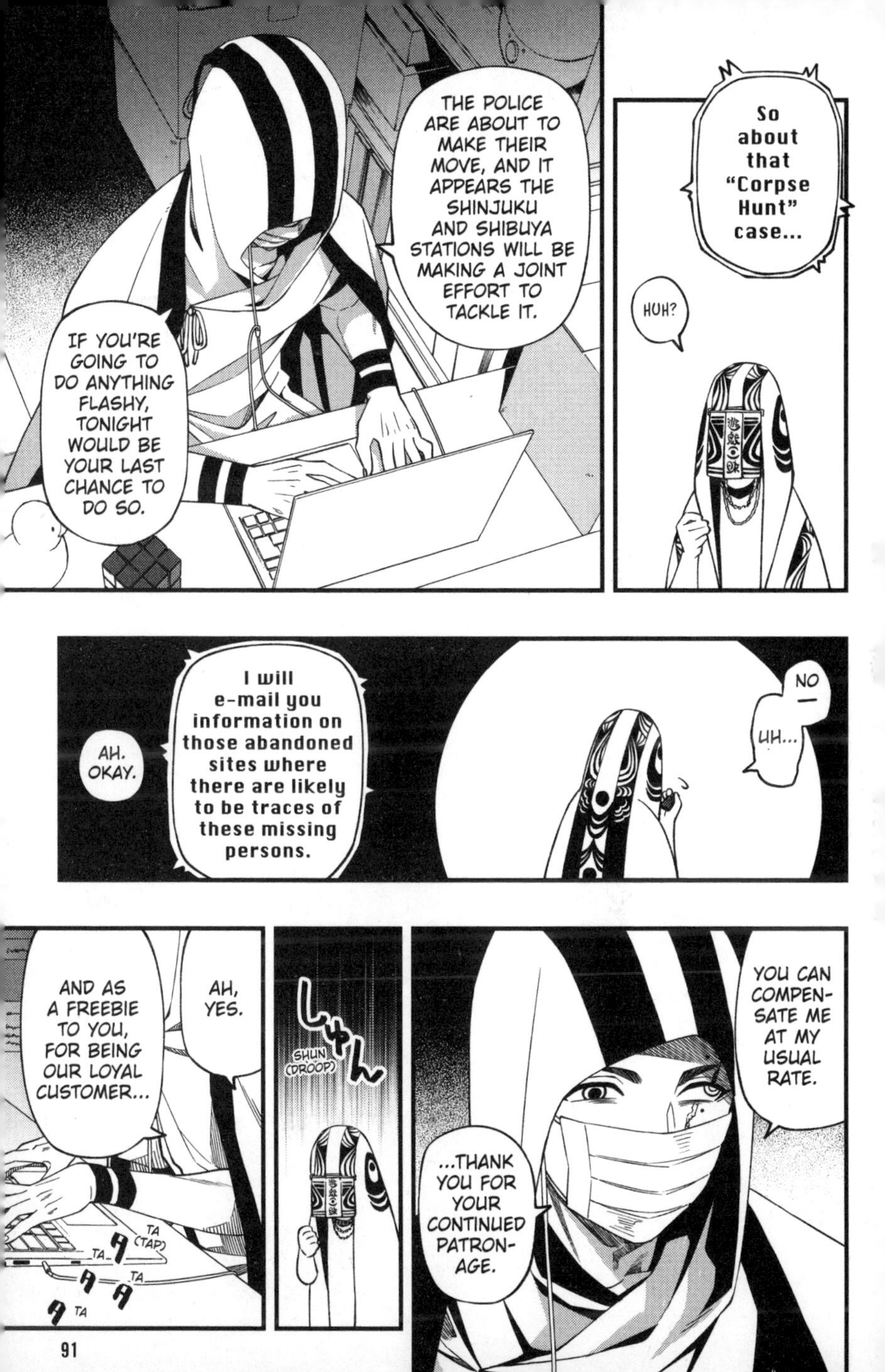
So about that "Corpse Hunt" case...
HUH?
THE POLICE ARE ABOUT TO MAKE THEIR MOVE, AND IT APPEARS THE SHINJUKU AND SHIBUYA STATIONS WILL BE MAKING A JOINT EFFORT TO TACKLE IT.
IF YOU'RE GOING TO DO ANYTHING FLASHY, TONIGHT WOULD BE YOUR LAST CHANCE TO DO SO.
NO — UH...
I will e-mail you information on those abandoned sites where there are likely to be traces of these missing persons.
AH. OKAY.
YOU CAN COMPENSATE ME AT MY USUAL RATE.
...THANK YOU FOR YOUR CONTINUED PATRONAGE.
SHUN (DROOP)
AH, YES.
AND AS A FREEBIE TO YOU, FOR BEING OUR LOYAL CUSTOMER...
TA (TAP) TA TA TA

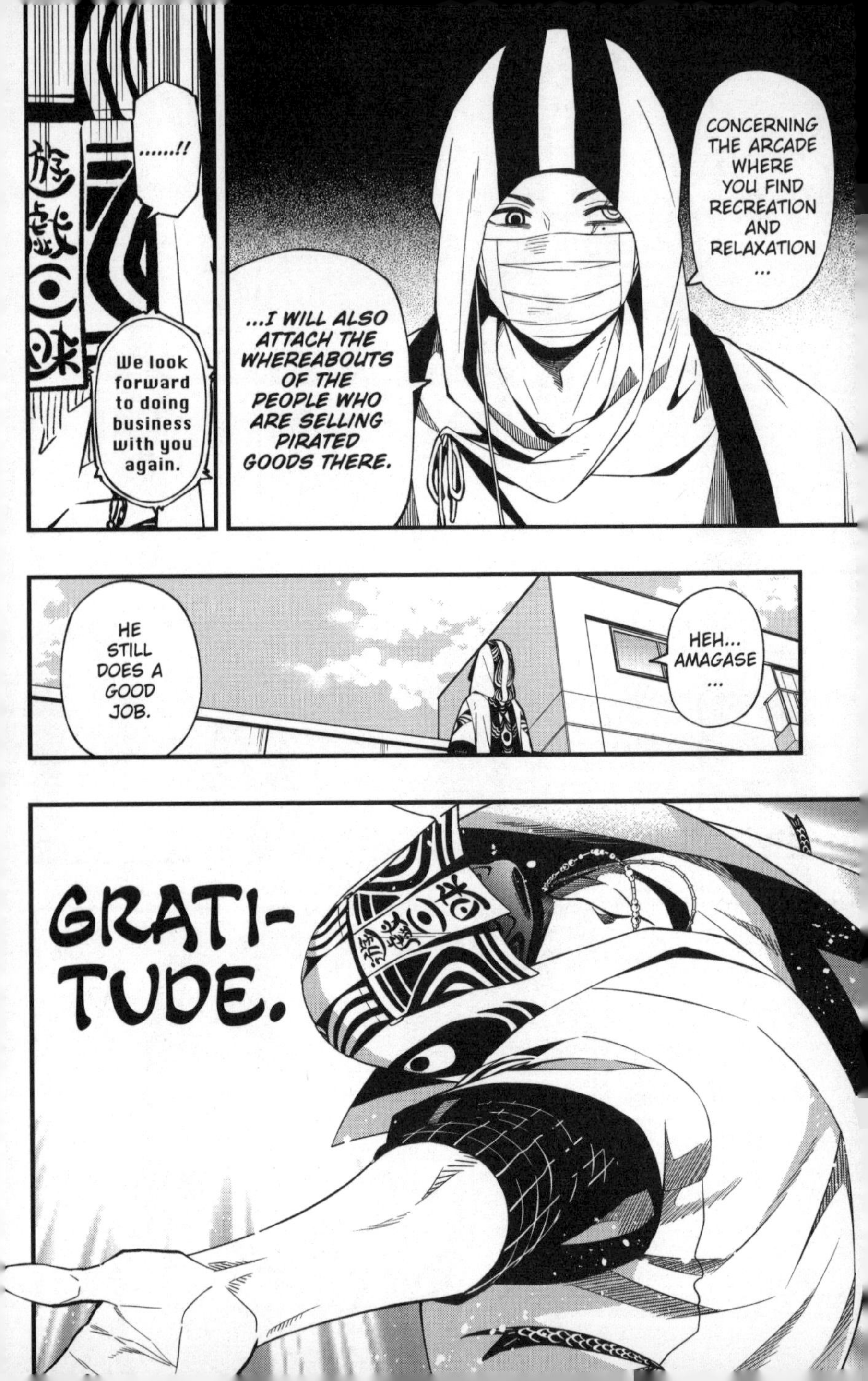
CONCERNING THE ARCADE WHERE YOU FIND RECREATION AND RELAXATION ...
...I WILL ALSO ATTACH THE WHEREABOUTS OF THE PEOPLE WHO ARE SELLING PIRATED GOODS THERE.
......!!
We look forward to doing business with you again.
HEH... AMAGASE ...
HE STILL DOES A GOOD JOB.
GRATI-TUDE.

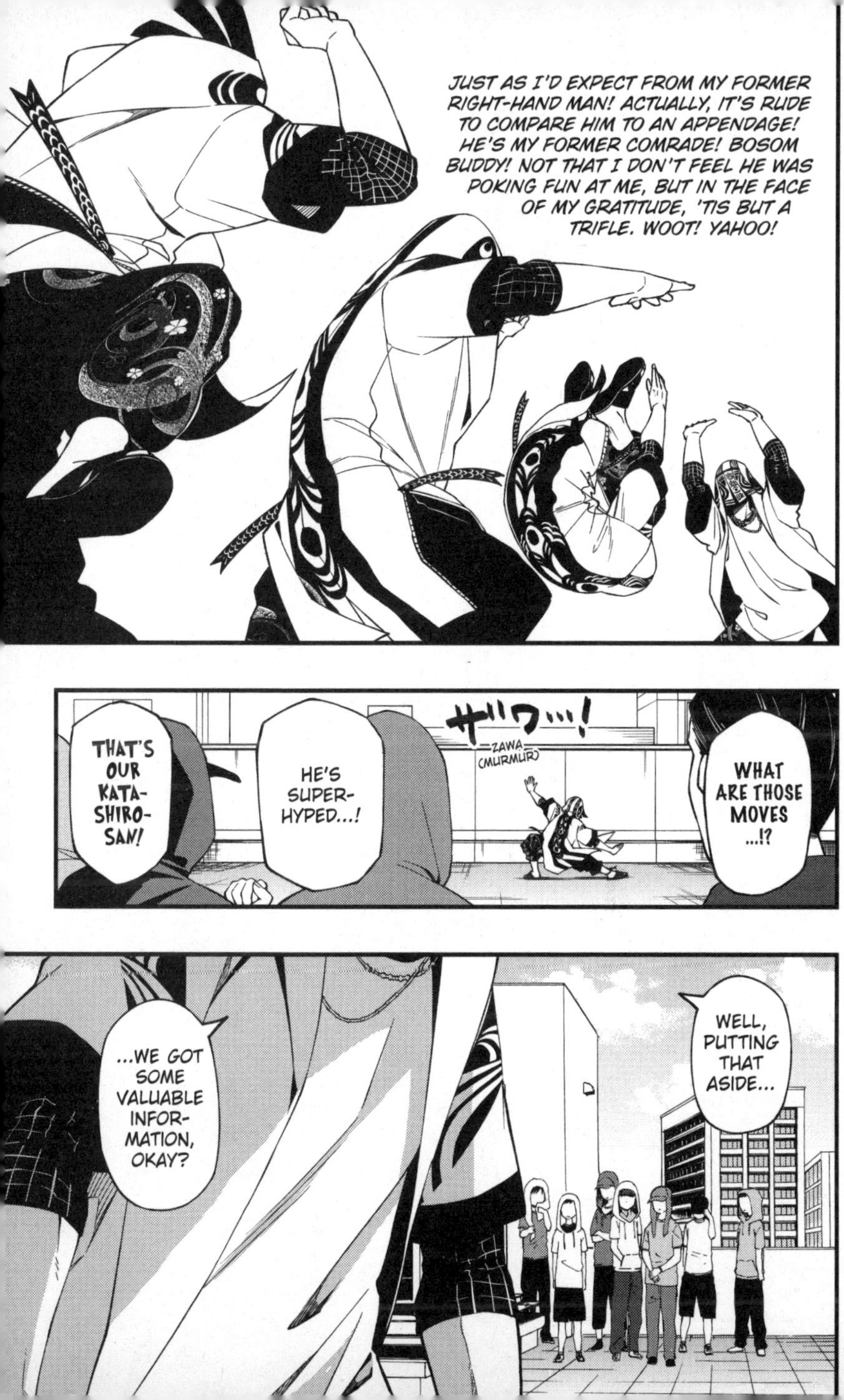
JUST AS I'D EXPECT FROM MY FORMER RIGHT-HAND MAN! ACTUALLY, IT'S RUDE TO COMPARE HIM TO AN APPENDAGE! HE'S MY FORMER COMRADE! BOSOM BUDDY! NOT THAT I DON'T FEEL HE WAS POKING FUN AT ME, BUT IN THE FACE OF MY GRATITUDE, 'TIS BUT A TRIFLE. WOOT! YAHOO!
ZAWA (MURMUR)
WHAT ARE THOSE MOVES ...!?
HE'S SUPER-HYPED...!
THAT'S OUR KATA-SHIRO-SAN!
WELL, PUTTING THAT ASIDE...
...WE GOT SOME VALUABLE INFOR-MATION, OKAY?

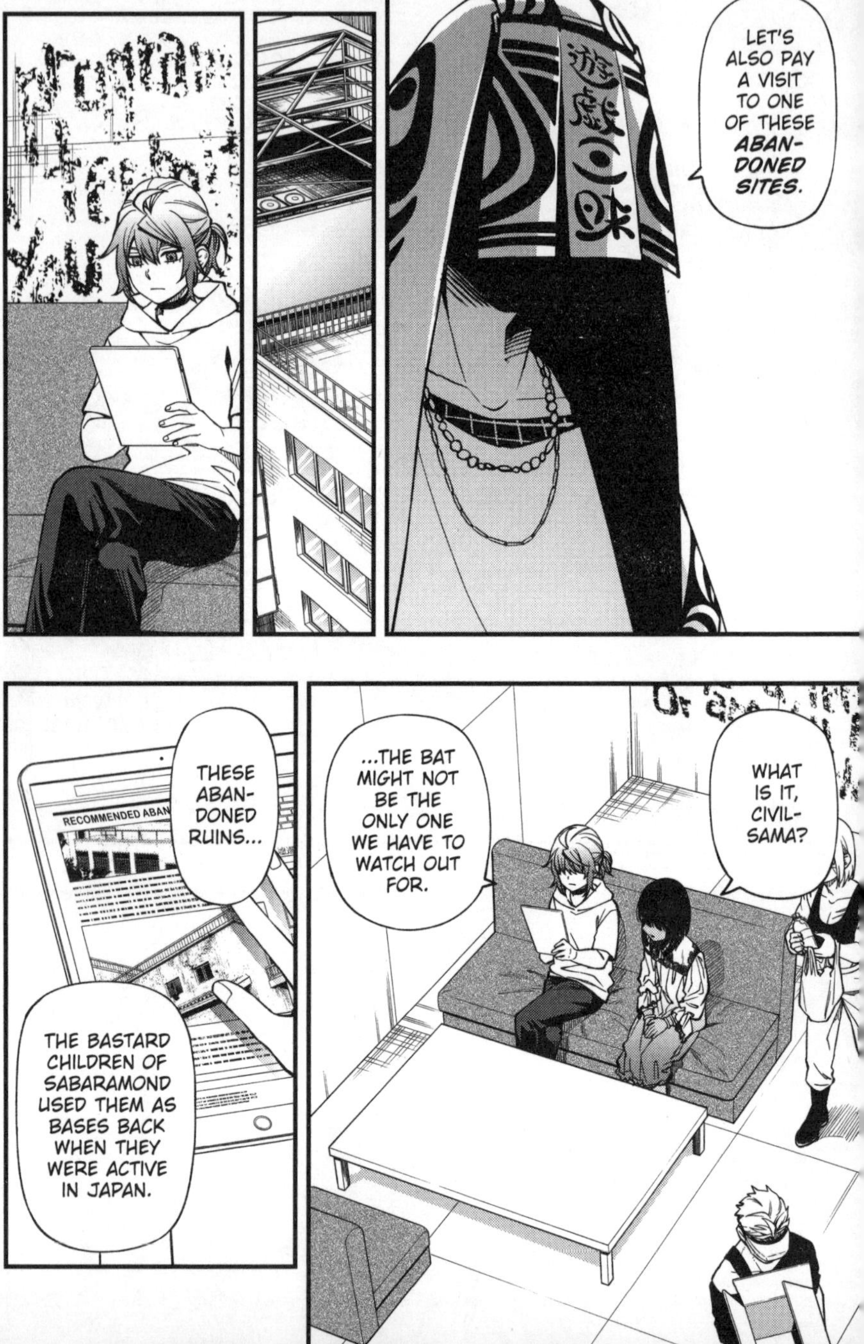
LET'S ALSO PAY A VISIT TO ONE OF THESE ABANDONED SITES.
WHAT IS IT, CIVIL-SAMA?
...THE BAT MIGHT NOT BE THE ONLY ONE WE HAVE TO WATCH OUT FOR.
RECOMMENDED ABAN
THESE ABANDONED RUINS...
THE BASTARD CHILDREN OF SABARAMOND USED THEM AS BASES BACK WHEN THEY WERE ACTIVE IN JAPAN.

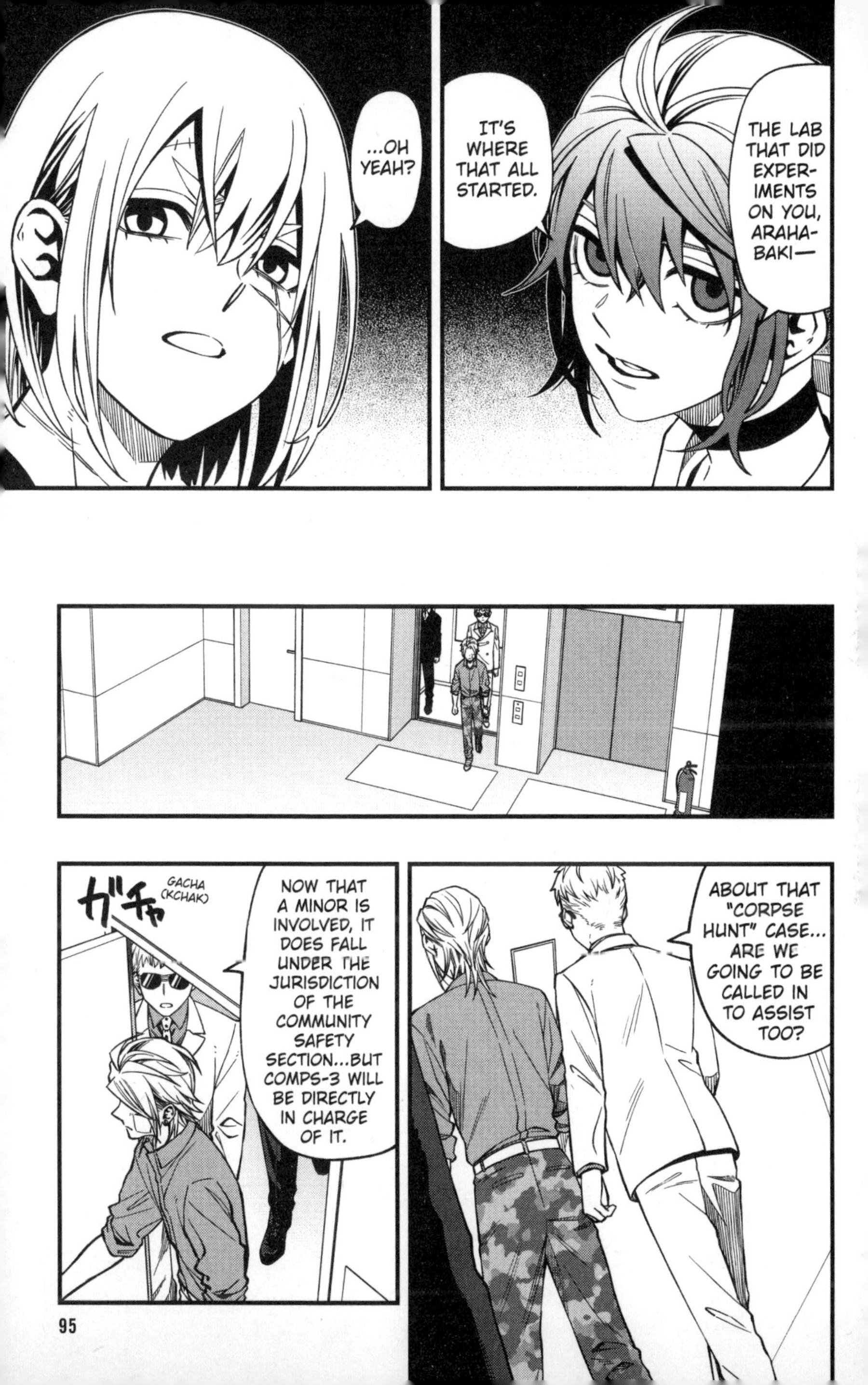
THE LAB THAT DID EXPER-IMENTS ON YOU, ARAHA-BAKI—
IT'S WHERE THAT ALL STARTED.
...OH YEAH?
ABOUT THAT "CORPSE HUNT" CASE... ARE WE GOING TO BE CALLED IN TO ASSIST TOO?
NOW THAT A MINOR IS INVOLVED, IT DOES FALL UNDER THE JURISDICTION OF THE COMMUNITY SAFETY SECTION...BUT COMPS-3 WILL BE DIRECTLY IN CHARGE OF IT.
ガチャ
GACHA (KCHAK)

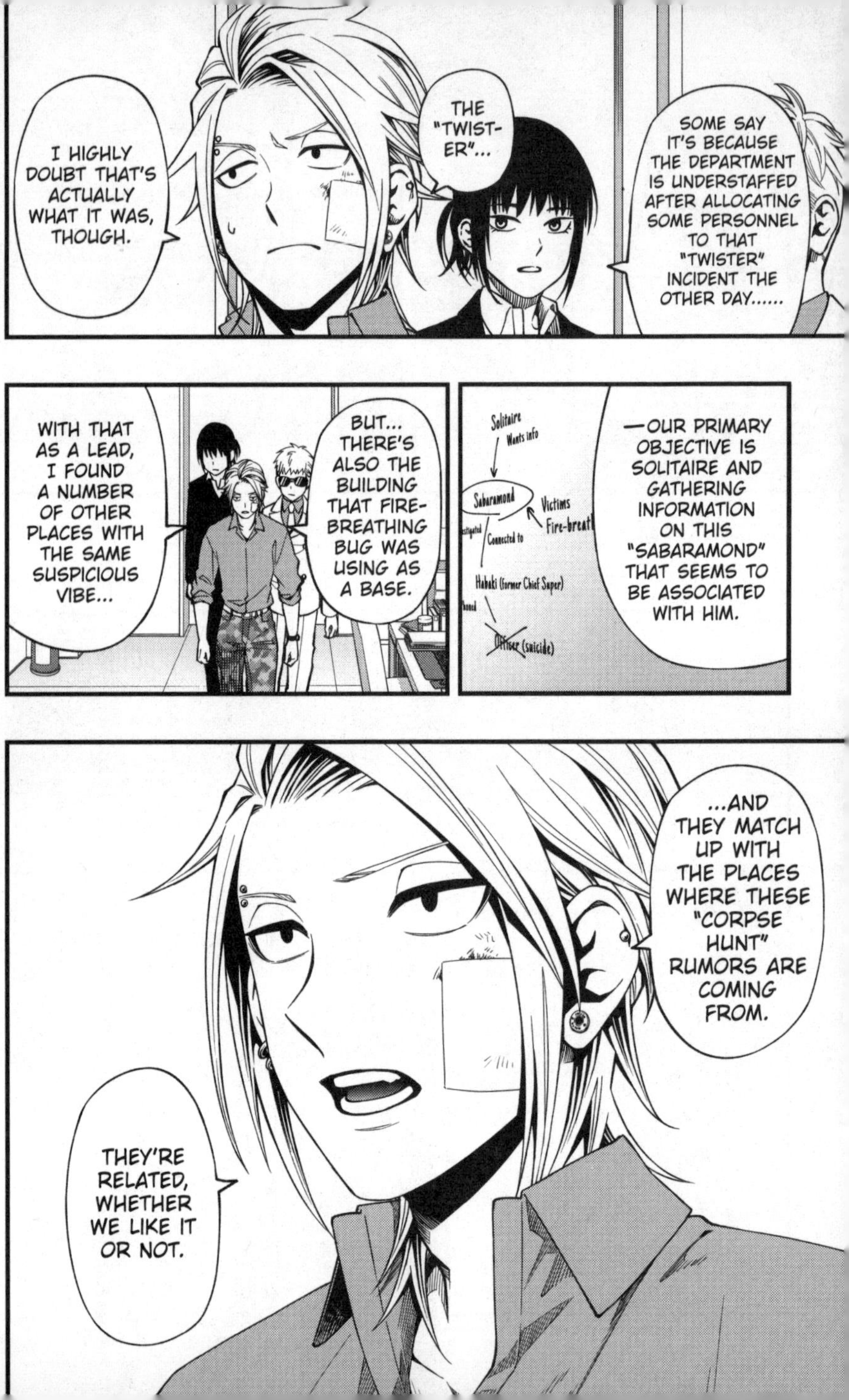
SOME SAY IT'S BECAUSE THE DEPARTMENT IS UNDERSTAFFED AFTER ALLOCATING SOME PERSONNEL TO THAT "TWISTER" INCIDENT THE OTHER DAY......
THE "TWIST-ER"...
I HIGHLY DOUBT THAT'S ACTUALLY WHAT IT WAS, THOUGH.
—OUR PRIMARY OBJECTIVE IS SOLITAIRE AND GATHERING INFORMATION ON THIS "SABARAMOND" THAT SEEMS TO BE ASSOCIATED WITH HIM.
Solitaire
Wants info
Sabaramond
Victims
Connected to
Habaki (former Chief Super)
Officer (suicide)
BUT... THERE'S ALSO THE BUILDING THAT FIRE-BREATHING BUG WAS USING AS A BASE.
WITH THAT AS A LEAD, I FOUND A NUMBER OF OTHER PLACES WITH THE SAME SUSPICIOUS VIBE...
...AND THEY MATCH UP WITH THE PLACES WHERE THESE "CORPSE HUNT" RUMORS ARE COMING FROM.
THEY'RE RELATED, WHETHER WE LIKE IT OR NOT.

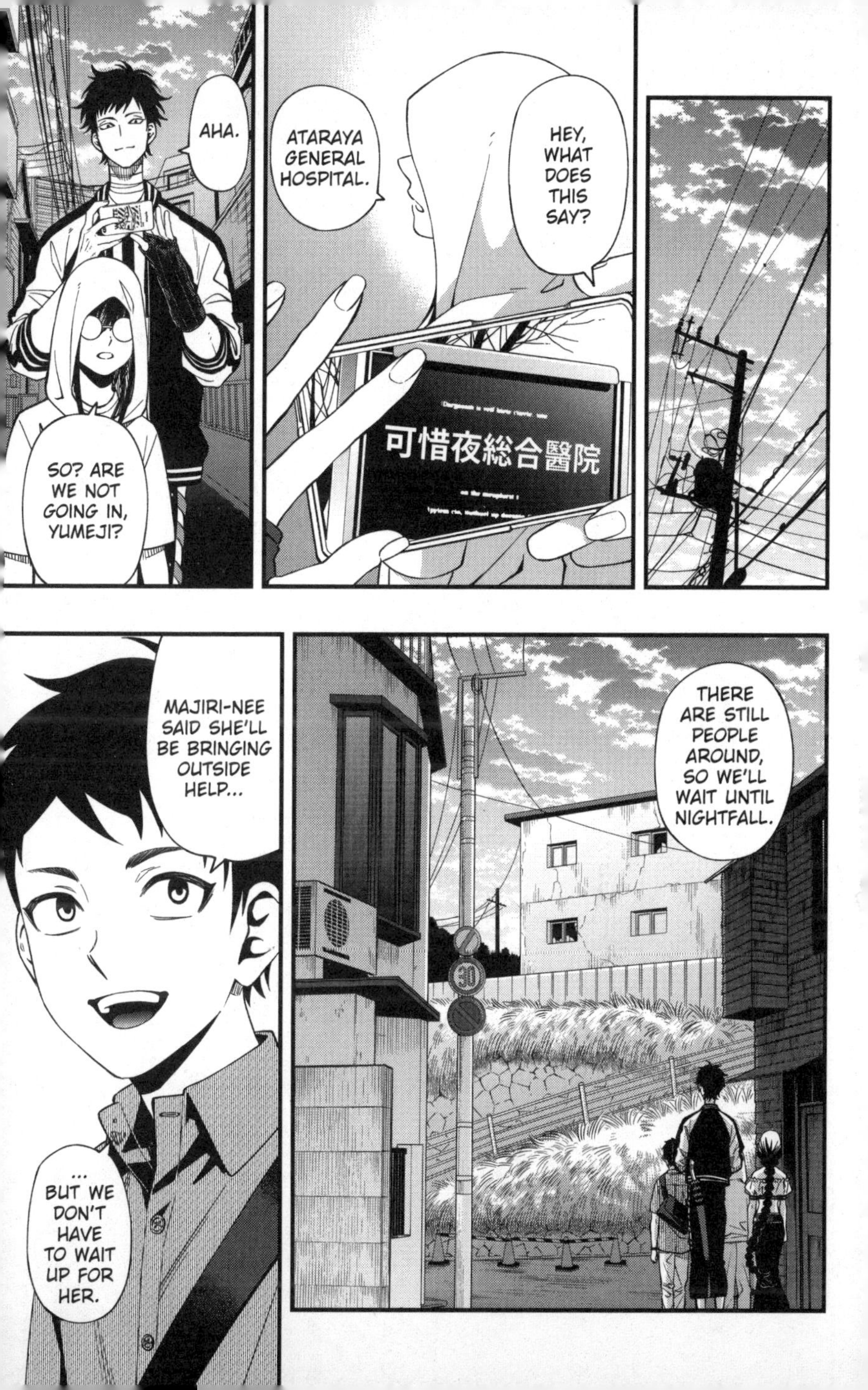
HEY, WHAT DOES THIS SAY?
可惜夜総合醫院
ATARAYA GENERAL HOSPITAL.
AHA.
SO? ARE WE NOT GOING IN, YUMEJI?
THERE ARE STILL PEOPLE AROUND, SO WE'LL WAIT UNTIL NIGHTFALL.
MAJIRI-NEE SAID SHE'LL BE BRINGING OUTSIDE HELP...
...BUT WE DON'T HAVE TO WAIT UP FOR HER.

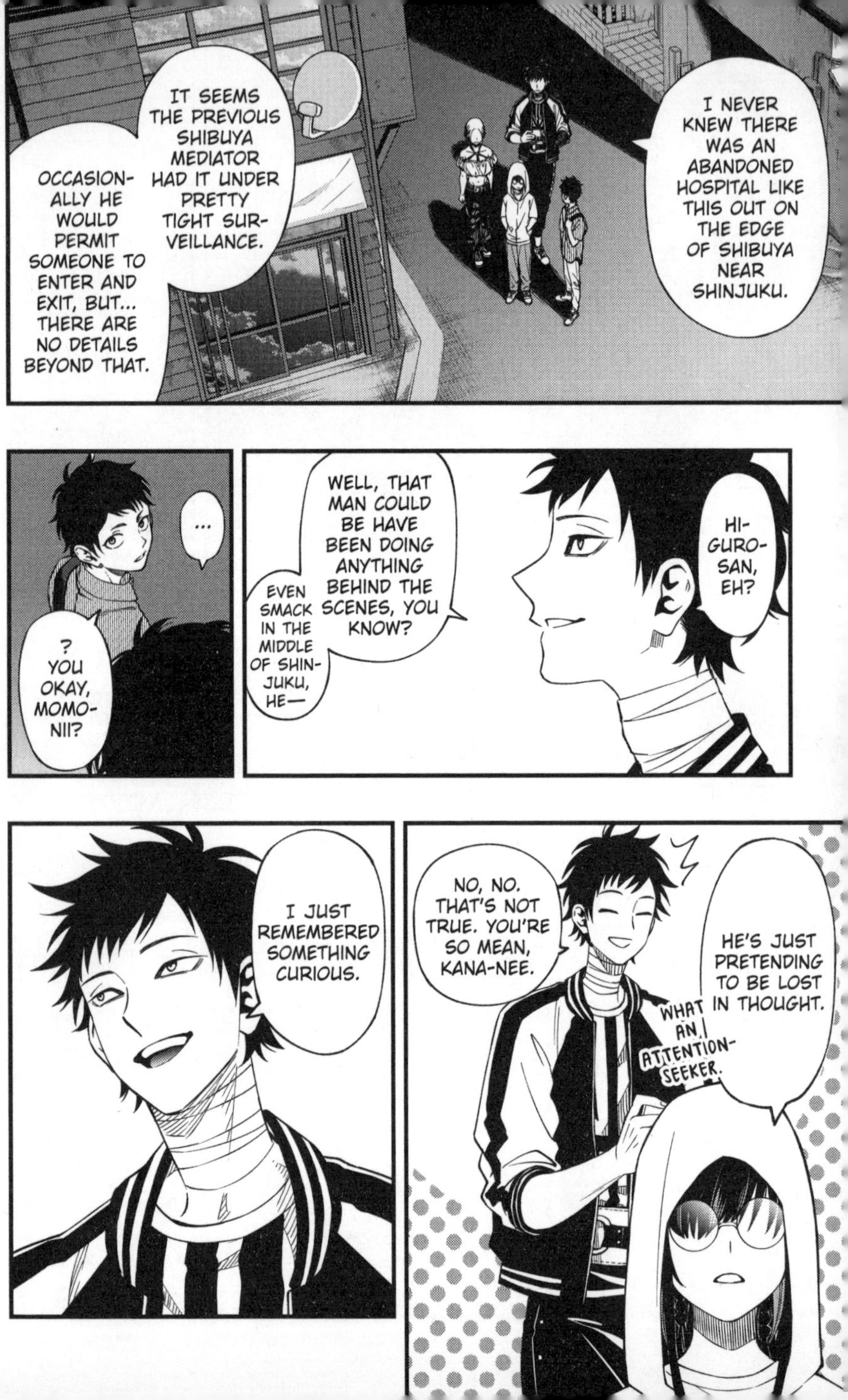
I NEVER KNEW THERE WAS AN ABANDONED HOSPITAL LIKE THIS OUT ON THE EDGE OF SHIBUYA NEAR SHINJUKU.
IT SEEMS THE PREVIOUS SHIBUYA MEDIATOR HAD IT UNDER PRETTY TIGHT SURVEILLANCE.
OCCASIONALLY HE WOULD PERMIT SOMEONE TO ENTER AND EXIT, BUT... THERE ARE NO DETAILS BEYOND THAT.
HIGURO-SAN, EH?
WELL, THAT MAN COULD BE HAVE BEEN DOING ANYTHING BEHIND THE SCENES, YOU KNOW?
EVEN SMACK IN THE MIDDLE OF SHINJUKU, HE—
...
? YOU OKAY, MOMONII?
I JUST REMEMBERED SOMETHING CURIOUS.
HE'S JUST PRETENDING TO BE LOST IN THOUGHT.
WHAT AN ATTENTION-SEEKER.
NO, NO. THAT'S NOT TRUE. YOU'RE SO MEAN, KANA-NEE.

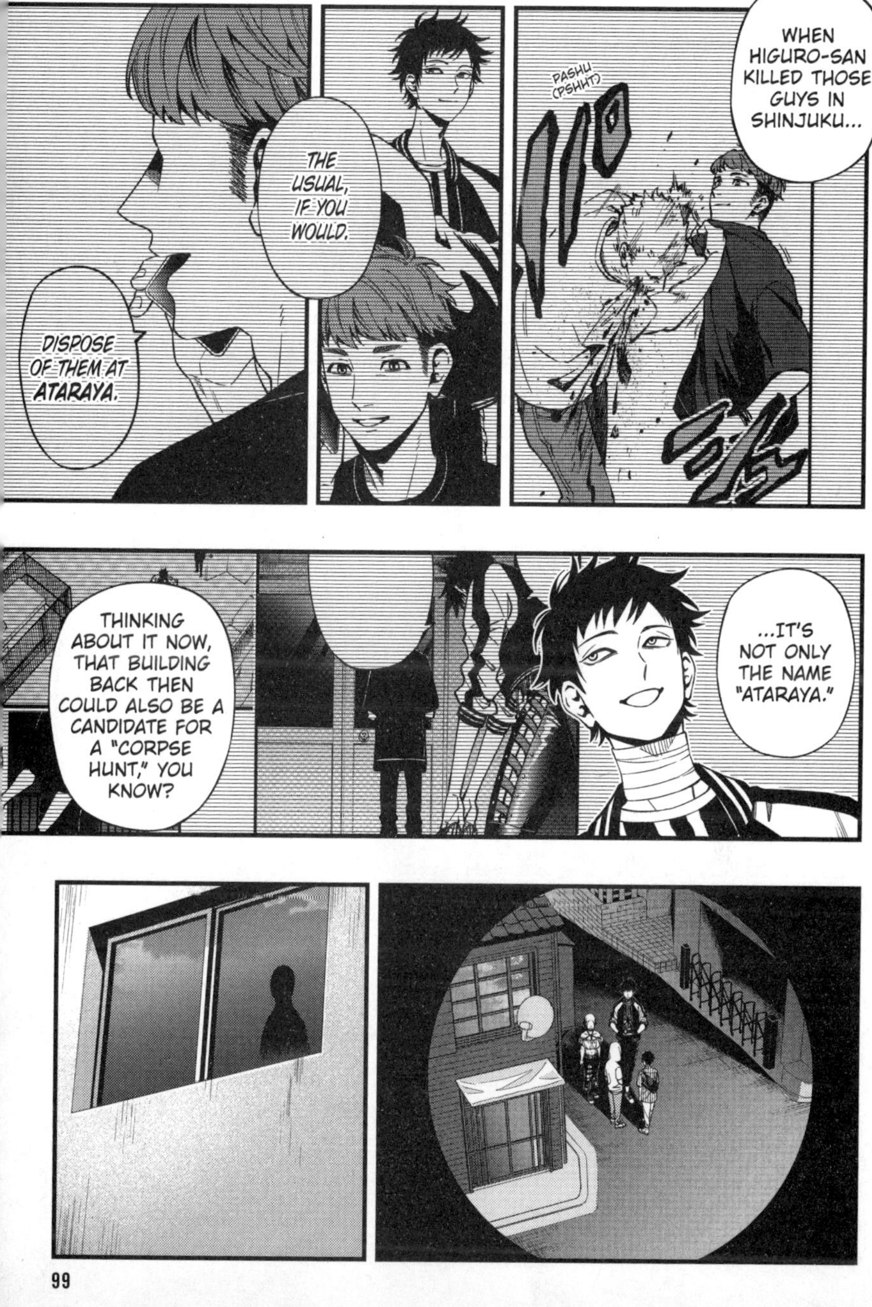
WHEN HIGURO-SAN KILLED THOSE GUYS IN SHINJUKU...
PASHU (PSHHT)
THE USUAL, IF YOU WOULD.
DISPOSE OF THEM AT ATARAYA.
...IT'S NOT ONLY THE NAME "ATARAYA."
THINKING ABOUT IT NOW, THAT BUILDING BACK THEN COULD ALSO BE A CANDIDATE FOR A "CORPSE HUNT," YOU KNOW?

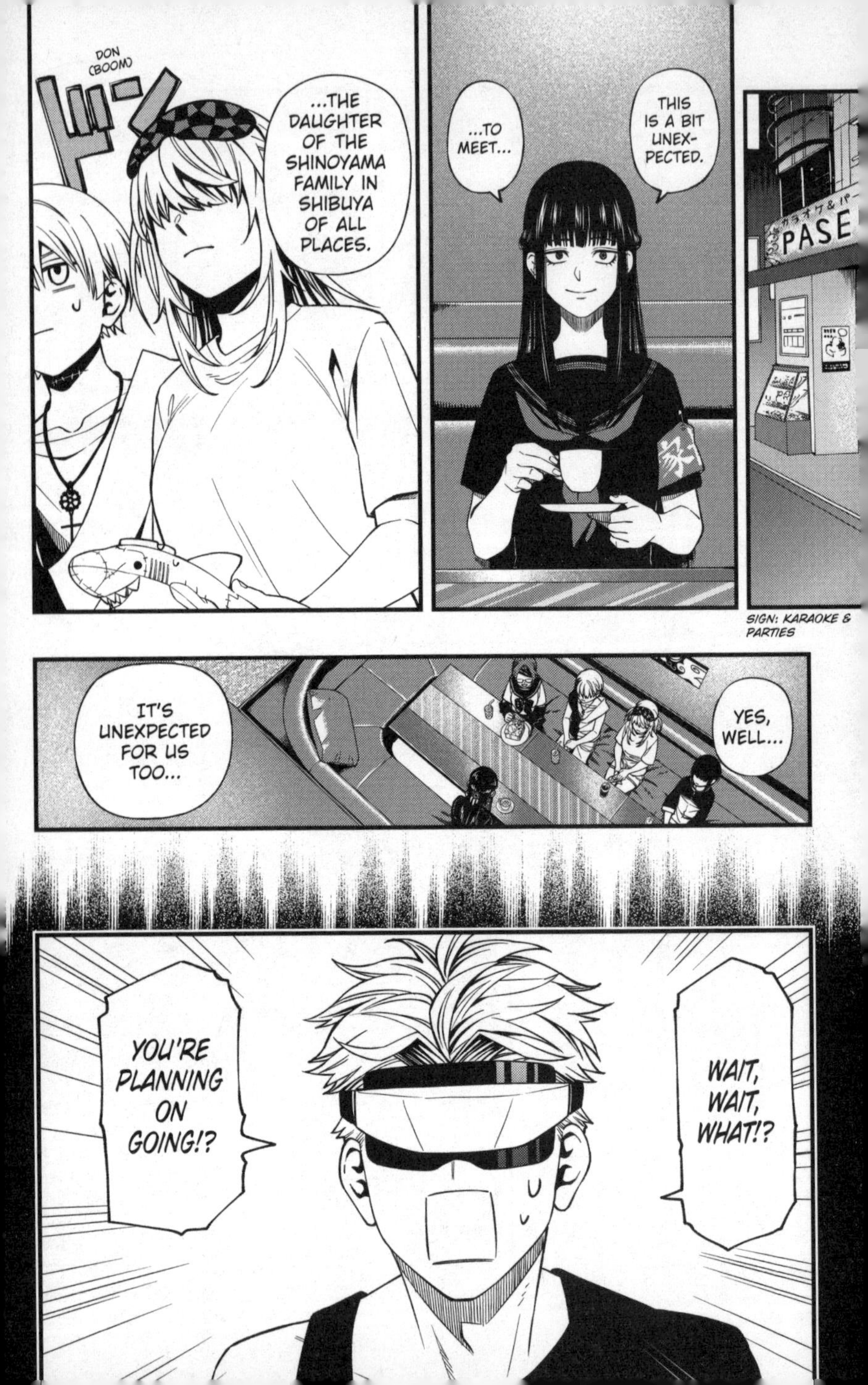
PASE
SIGN: KARAOKE & PARTIES
THIS IS A BIT UNEXPECTED.
...TO MEET...
DON (BOOM)
...THE DAUGHTER OF THE SHINOYAMA FAMILY IN SHIBUYA OF ALL PLACES.
YES, WELL...
IT'S UNEXPECTED FOR US TOO...
WAIT, WAIT, WHAT!?
YOU'RE PLANNING ON GOING!?

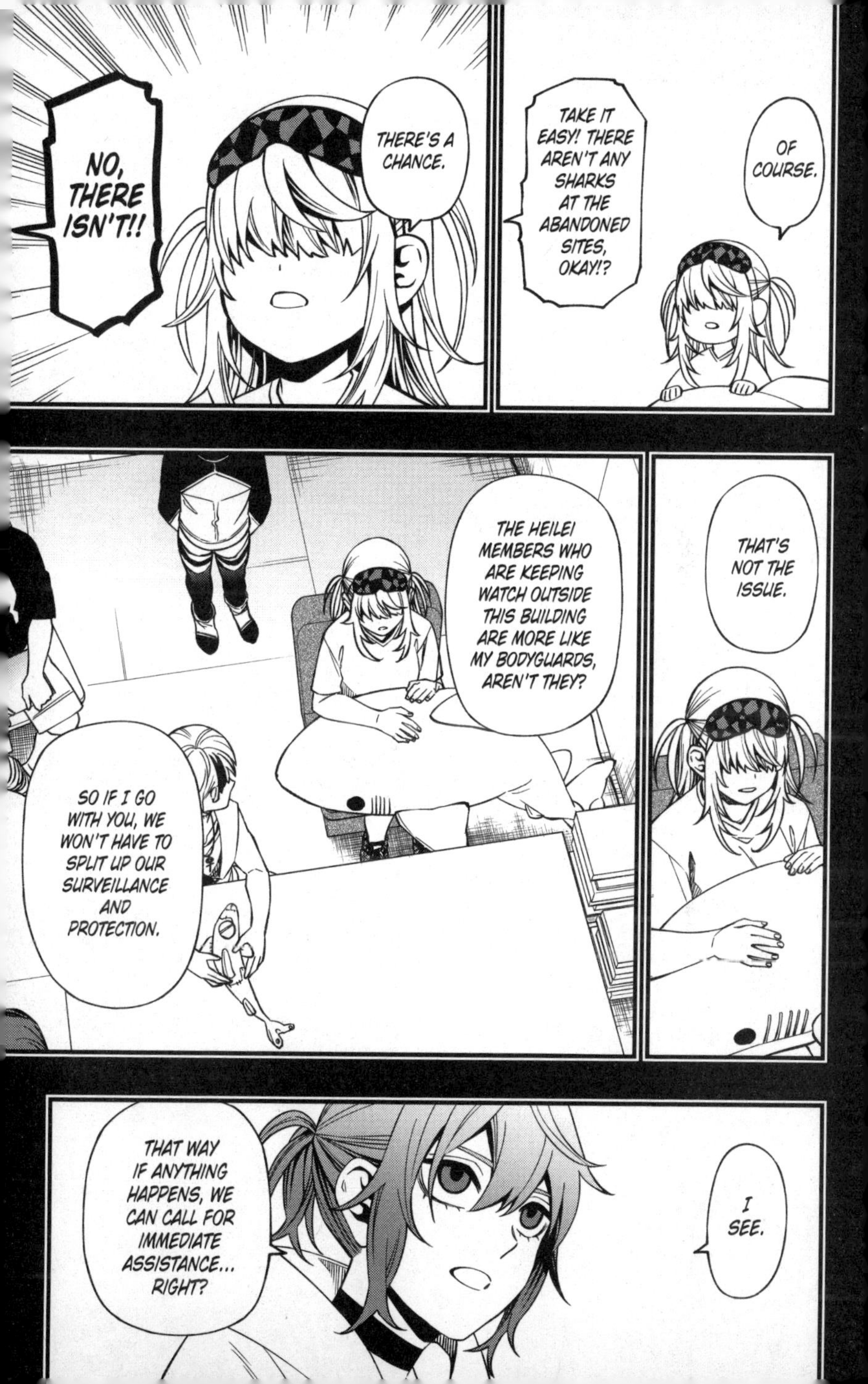

TAKE IT EASY! THERE AREN'T ANY SHARKS AT THE ABANDONED SITES, OKAY!?
OF COURSE.
THERE'S A CHANCE.
NO, THERE ISN'T!!
THAT'S NOT THE ISSUE.
THE HEILEI MEMBERS WHO ARE KEEPING WATCH OUTSIDE THIS BUILDING ARE MORE LIKE MY BODYGUARDS, AREN'T THEY?
SO IF I GO WITH YOU, WE WON'T HAVE TO SPLIT UP OUR SURVEILLANCE AND PROTECTION.
THAT WAY IF ANYTHING HAPPENS, WE CAN CALL FOR IMMEDIATE ASSISTANCE... RIGHT?
I SEE.

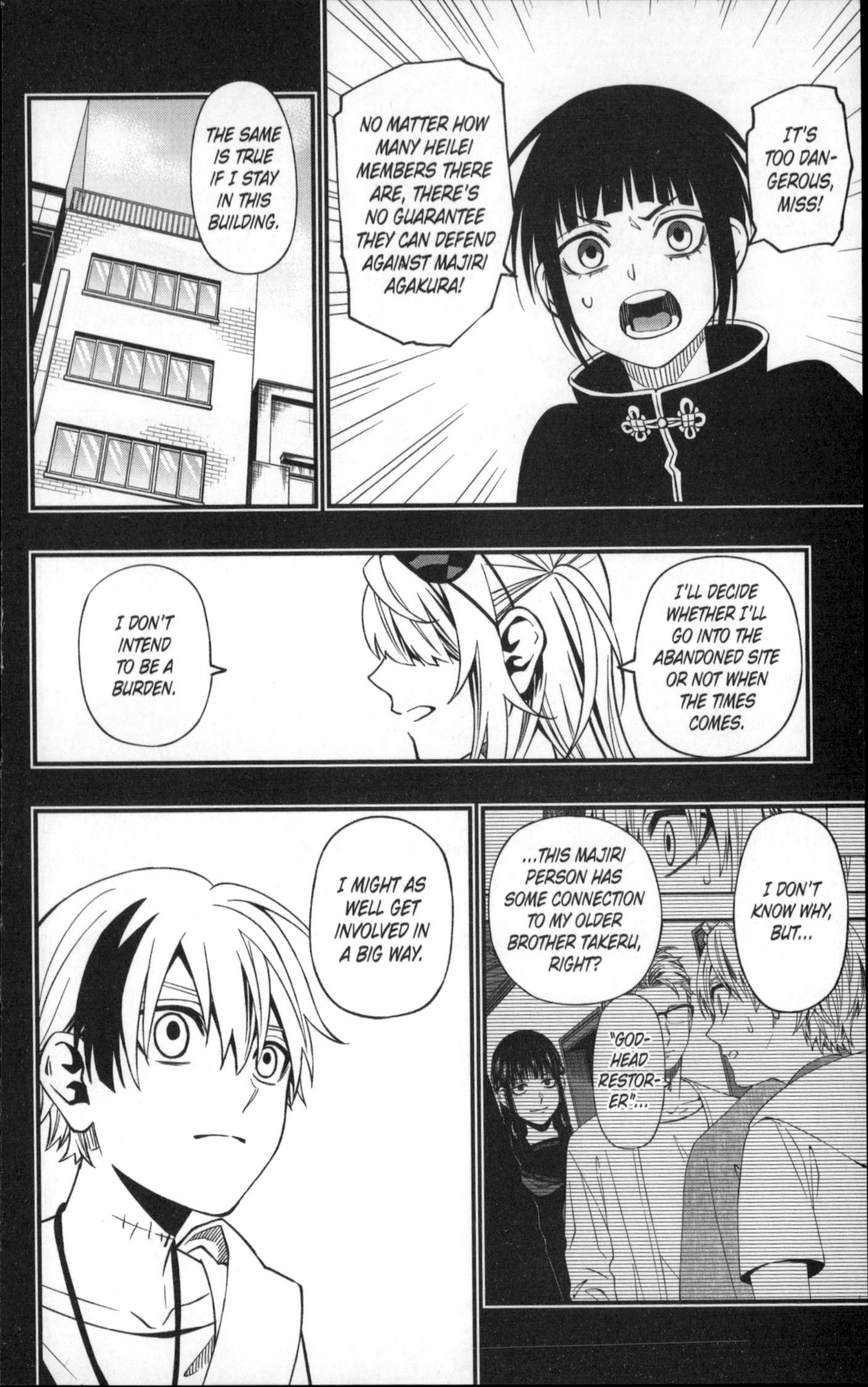
IT'S TOO DAN-GEROUS, MISS!
NO MATTER HOW MANY HEILEI MEMBERS THERE ARE, THERE'S NO GUARANTEE THEY CAN DEFEND AGAINST MAJIRI AGAKURA!
THE SAME IS TRUE IF I STAY IN THIS BUILDING.
I'LL DECIDE WHETHER I'LL GO INTO THE ABANDONED SITE OR NOT WHEN THE TIMES COMES.
I DON'T INTEND TO BE A BURDEN.
I DON'T KNOW WHY, BUT...
...THIS MAJIRI PERSON HAS SOME CONNECTION TO MY OLDER BROTHER TAKERU, RIGHT?
"GOD-HEAD RESTOR-ER"...
I MIGHT AS WELL GET INVOLVED IN A BIG WAY.

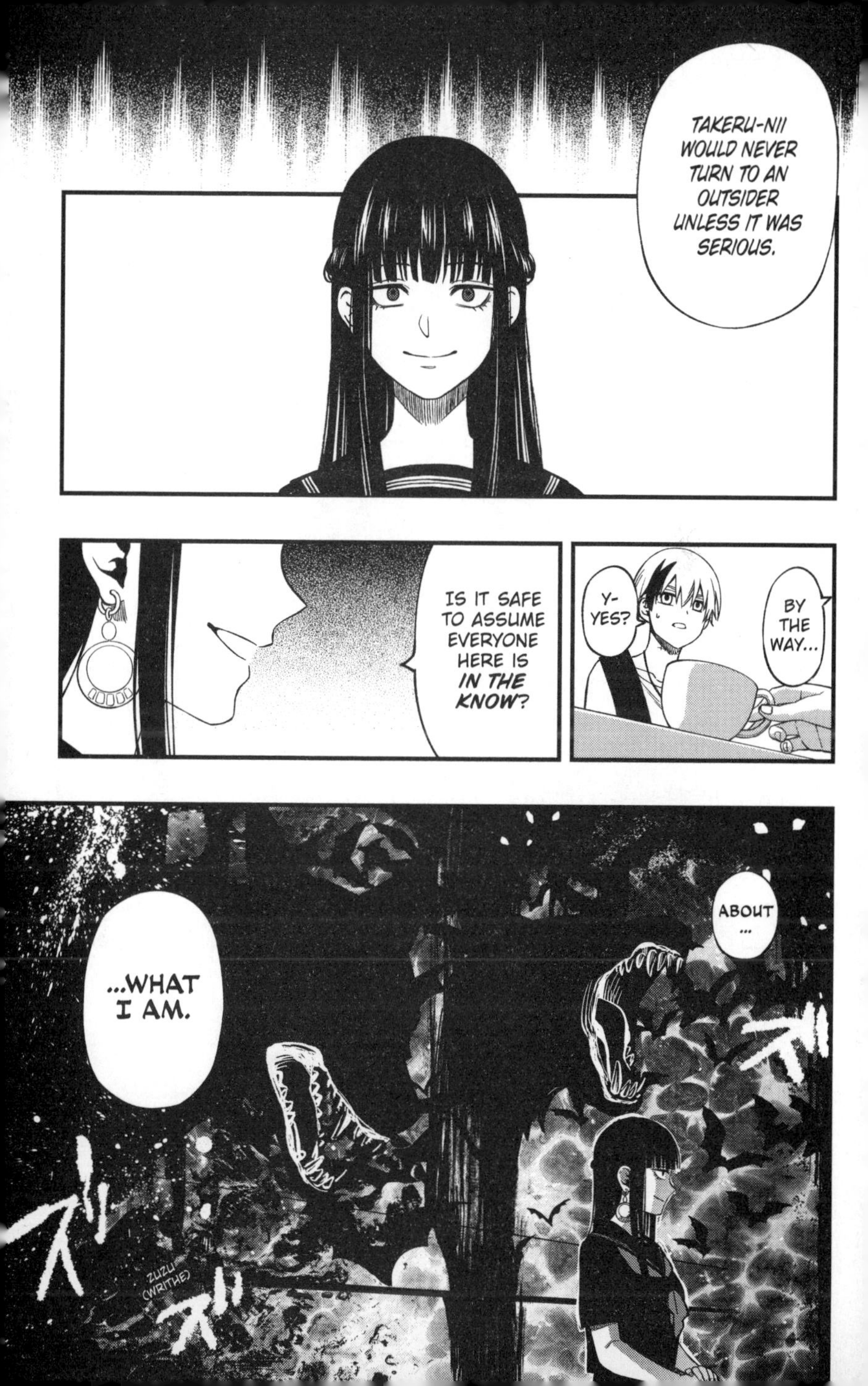
TAKERU-NII WOULD NEVER TURN TO AN OUTSIDER UNLESS IT WAS SERIOUS.
BY THE WAY...
Y- YES?
IS IT SAFE TO ASSUME EVERYONE HERE IS IN THE KNOW?
ABOUT ...
...WHAT I AM.
ZUZU (WRITHE)

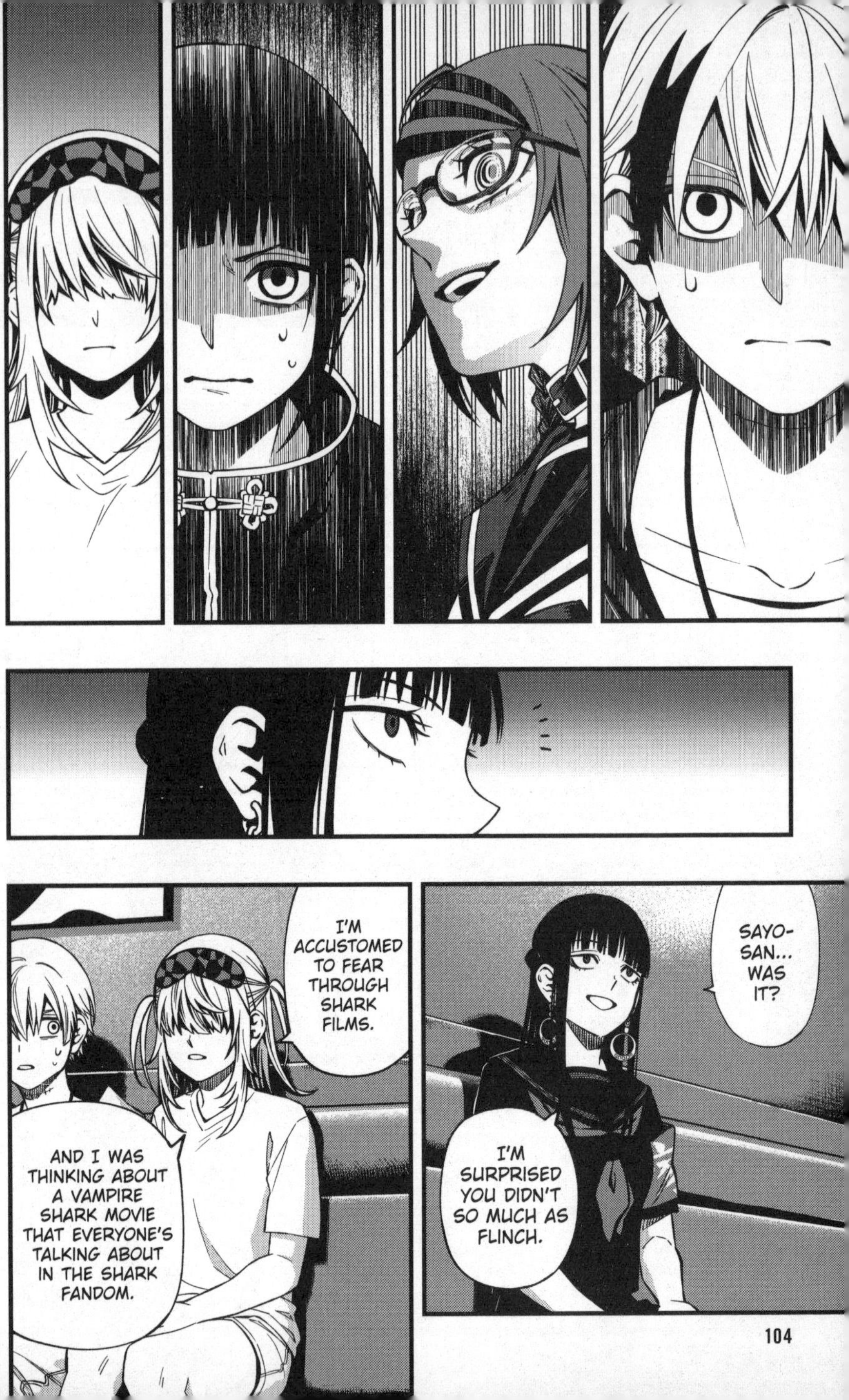
SAYO-SAN... WAS IT?
I'M SURPRISED YOU DIDN'T SO MUCH AS FLINCH.
I'M ACCUSTOMED TO FEAR THROUGH SHARK FILMS.
AND I WAS THINKING ABOUT A VAMPIRE SHARK MOVIE THAT EVERYONE'S TALKING ABOUT IN THE SHARK FANDOM.

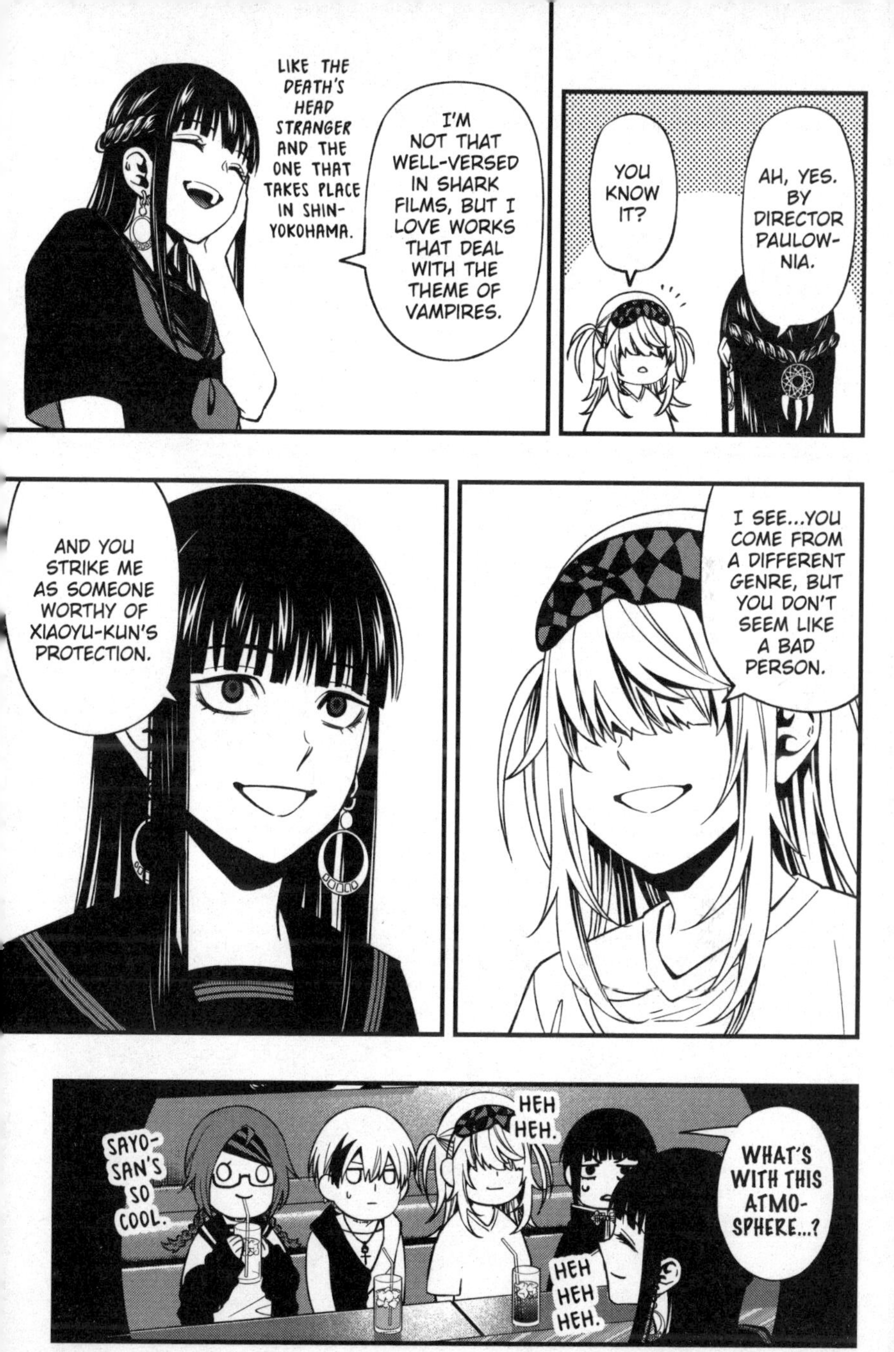
AH, YES. BY DIRECTOR PAULOW-NIA.
YOU KNOW IT?
LIKE THE DEATH'S HEAD STRANGER AND THE ONE THAT TAKES PLACE IN SHIN-YOKOHAMA.
I'M NOT THAT WELL-VERSED IN SHARK FILMS, BUT I LOVE WORKS THAT DEAL WITH THE THEME OF VAMPIRES.
I SEE...YOU COME FROM A DIFFERENT GENRE, BUT YOU DON'T SEEM LIKE A BAD PERSON.
AND YOU STRIKE ME AS SOMEONE WORTHY OF XIAOYU-KUN'S PROTECTION.
WHAT'S WITH THIS ATMO-SPHERE...?
HEH HEH.
HEH HEH HEH.
SAYO-SAN'S SO COOL.

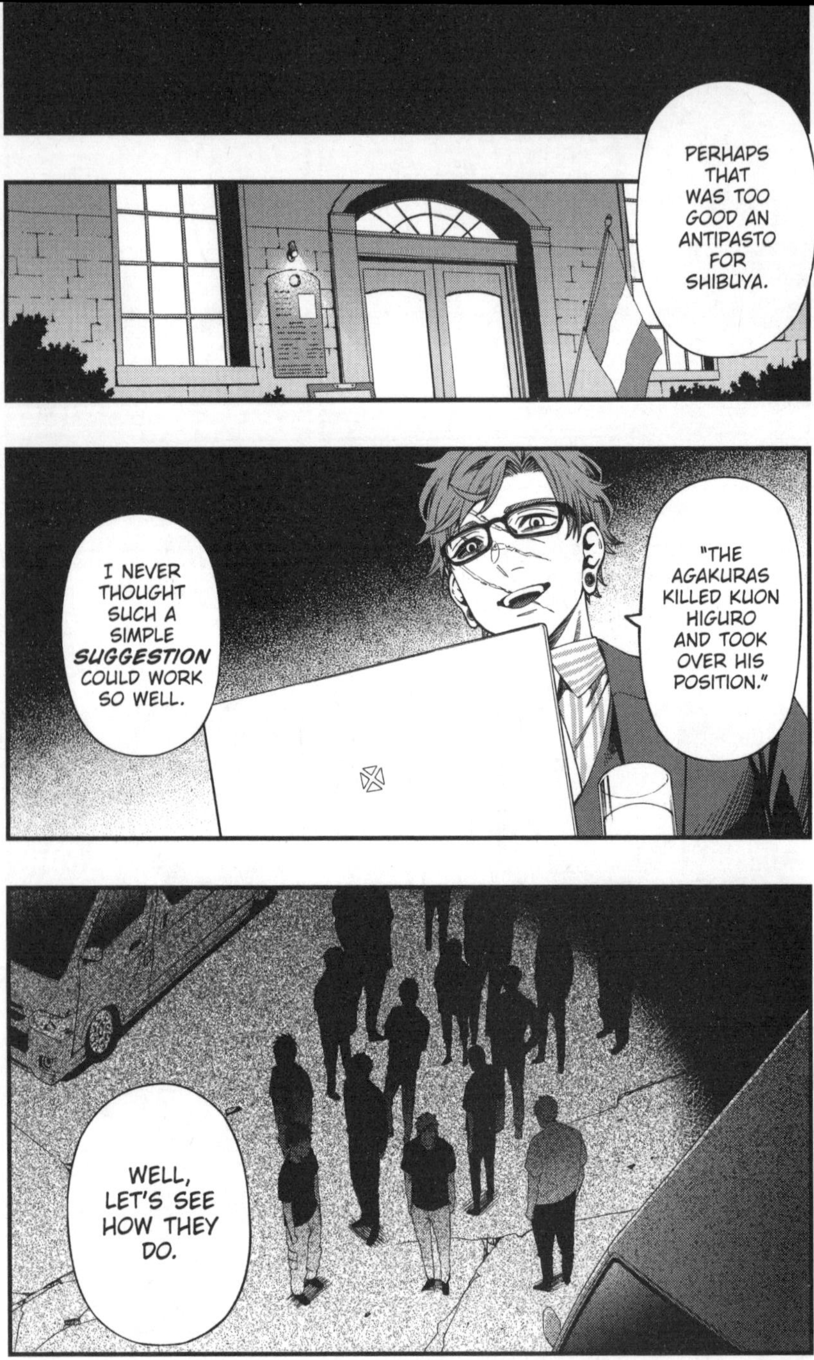
PERHAPS THAT WAS TOO GOOD AN ANTIPASTO FOR SHIBUYA.
"THE AGAKURAS KILLED KUON HIGURO AND TOOK OVER HIS POSITION."
I NEVER THOUGHT SUCH A SIMPLE *SUGGESTION* COULD WORK SO WELL.
WELL, LET'S SEE HOW THEY DO.

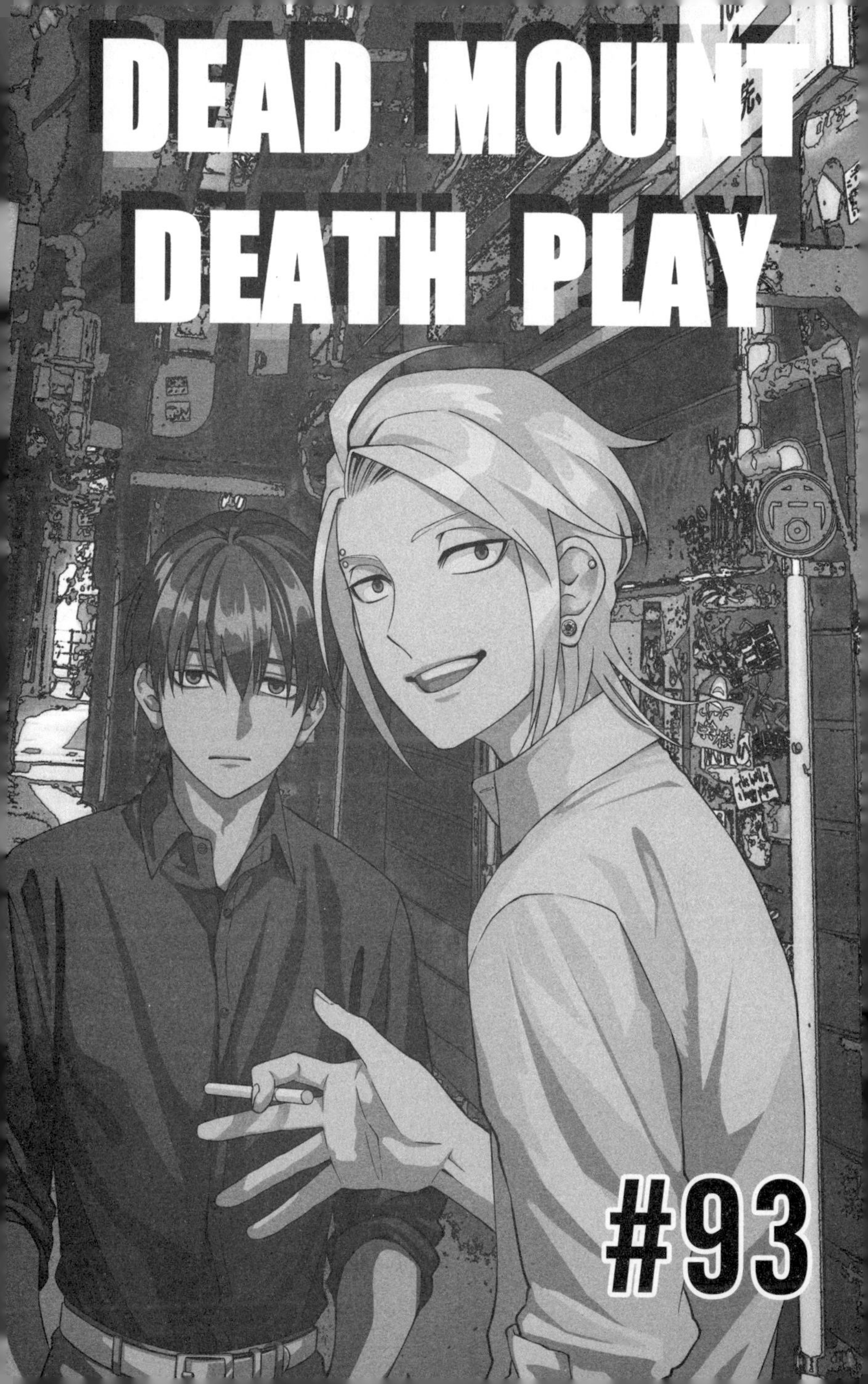
DEAD MOUNT
DEATH PLAY
#93

**DEAD MOUNT DEATH PLAY**

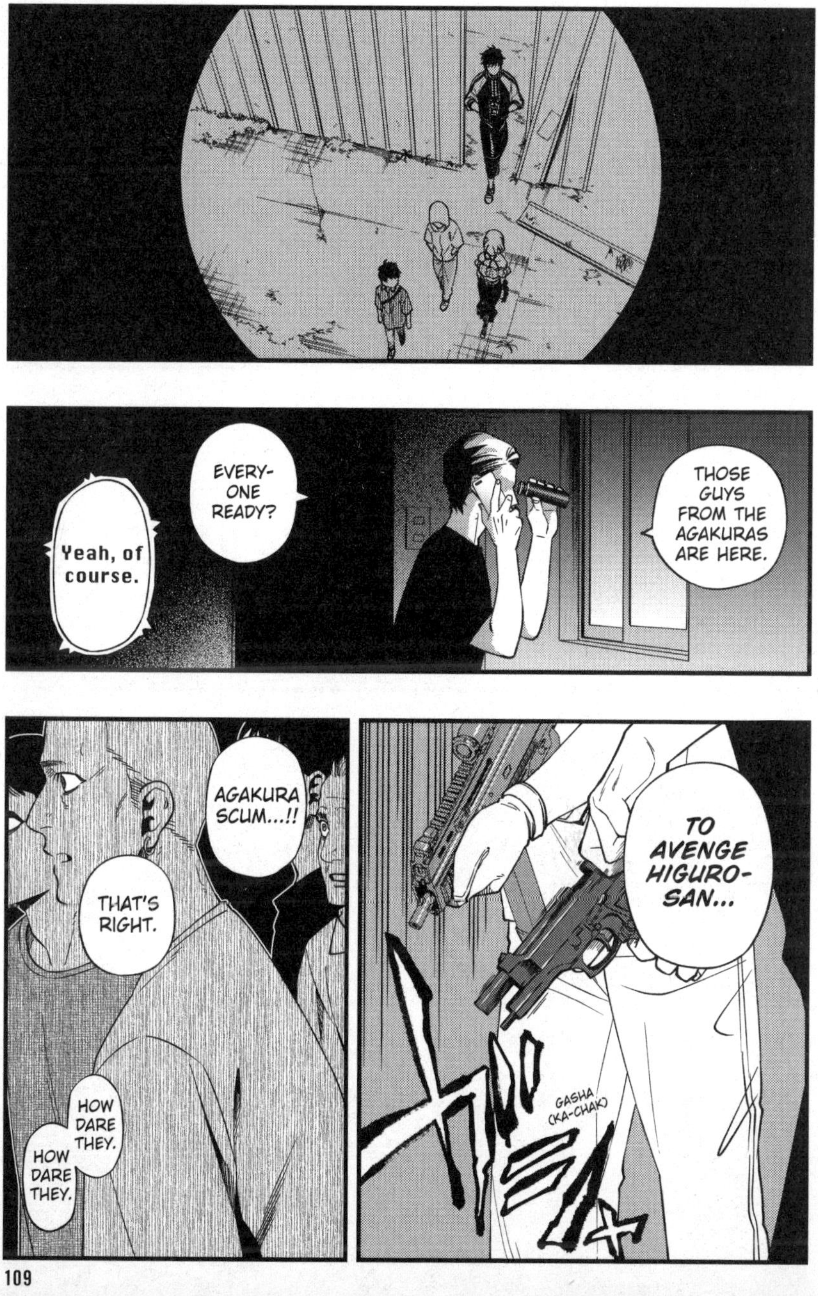
THOSE GUYS FROM THE AGAKURAS ARE HERE.
EVERY-ONE READY?
Yeah, of course.
TO AVENGE HIGURO-SAN...
GASHA (KA-CHAK)
AGAKURA SCUM...!!
THAT'S RIGHT.
HOW DARE THEY.
HOW DARE THEY.

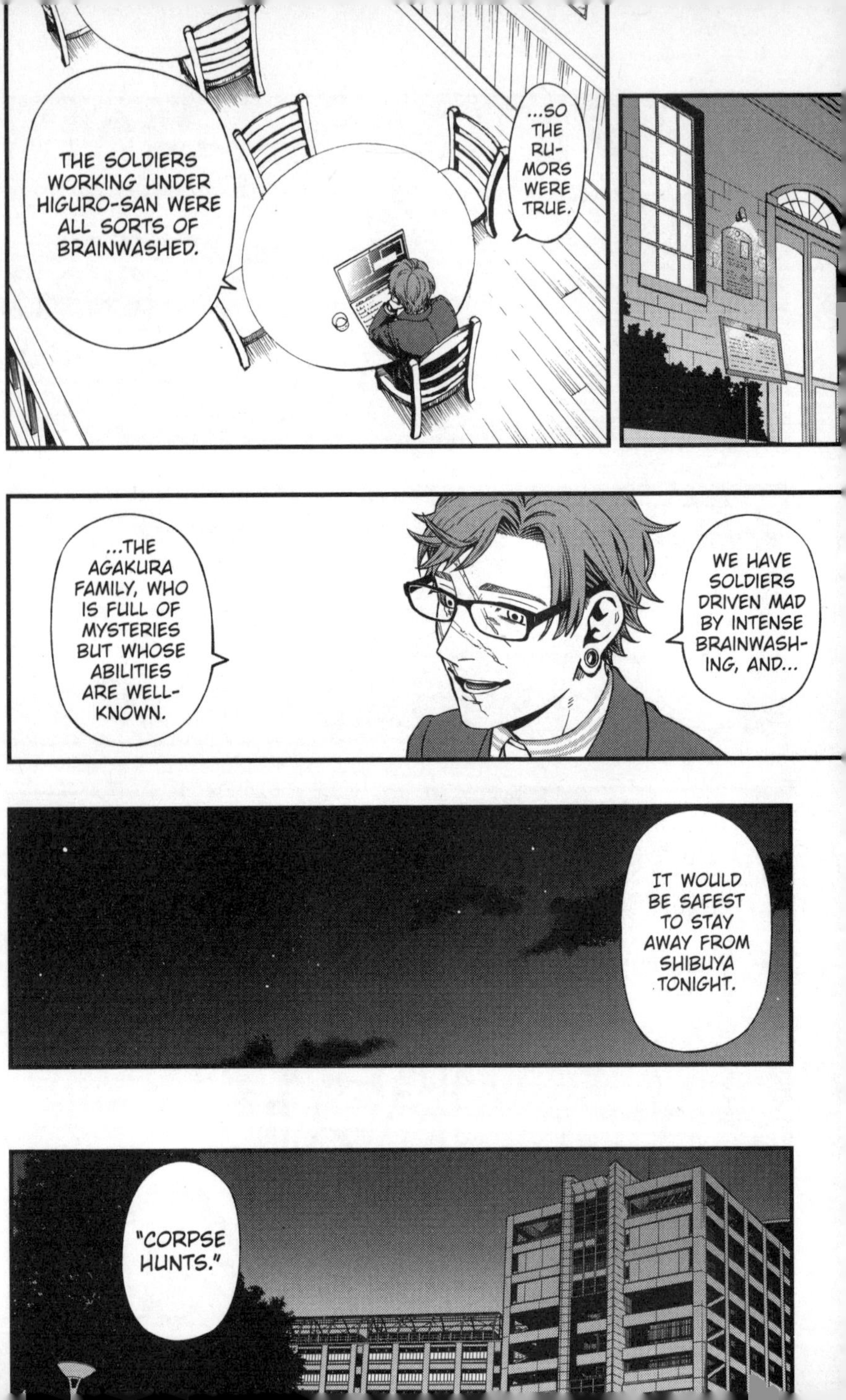
...SO THE RUMORS WERE TRUE.
THE SOLDIERS WORKING UNDER HIGURO-SAN WERE ALL SORTS OF BRAINWASHED.
WE HAVE SOLDIERS DRIVEN MAD BY INTENSE BRAINWASHING, AND...
...THE AGAKURA FAMILY, WHO IS FULL OF MYSTERIES BUT WHOSE ABILITIES ARE WELL-KNOWN.
IT WOULD BE SAFEST TO STAY AWAY FROM SHIBUYA TONIGHT.
"CORPSE HUNTS."

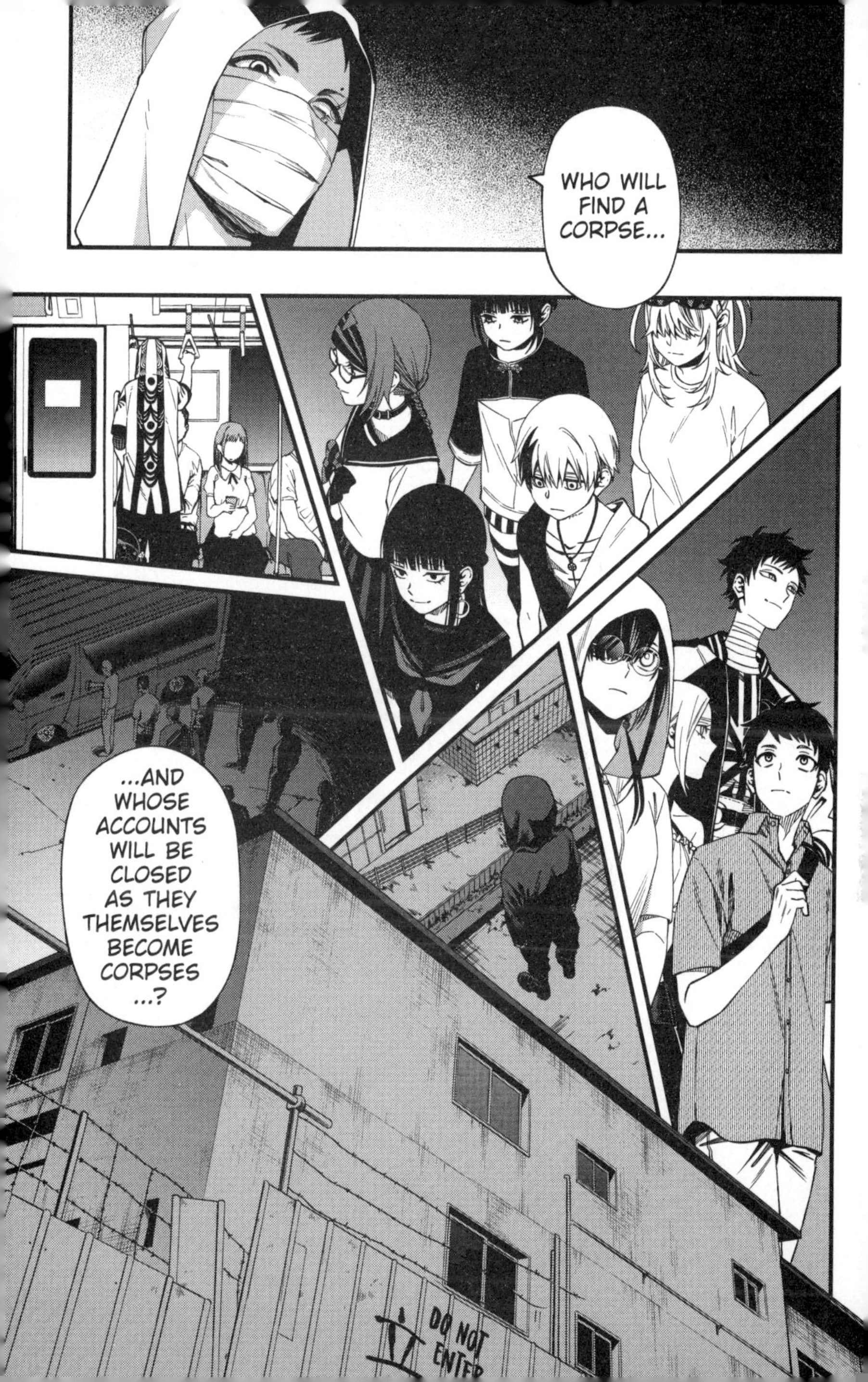
WHO WILL FIND A CORPSE...
...AND WHOSE ACCOUNTS WILL BE CLOSED AS THEY THEMSELVES BECOME CORPSES ...?
DO NOT ENTER

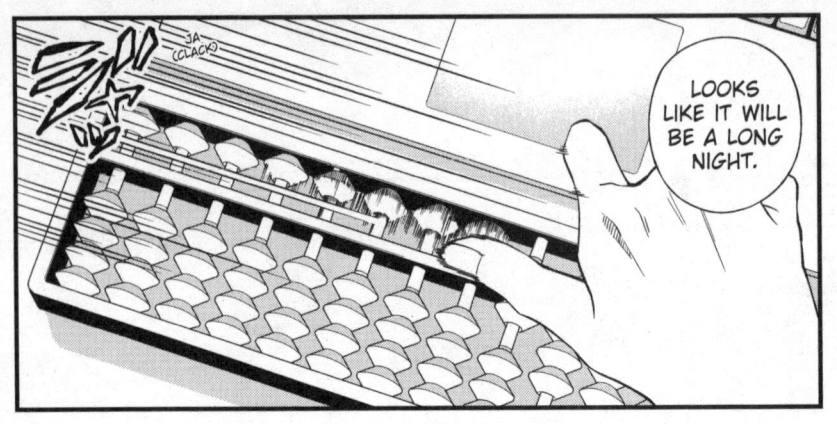

LOOKS LIKE IT WILL BE A LONG NIGHT.

JA (CLACK)

SO THIS IS THE ABANDONED SITE OF THE "CORPSE HUNT"...

YES, ONE OF THEM.

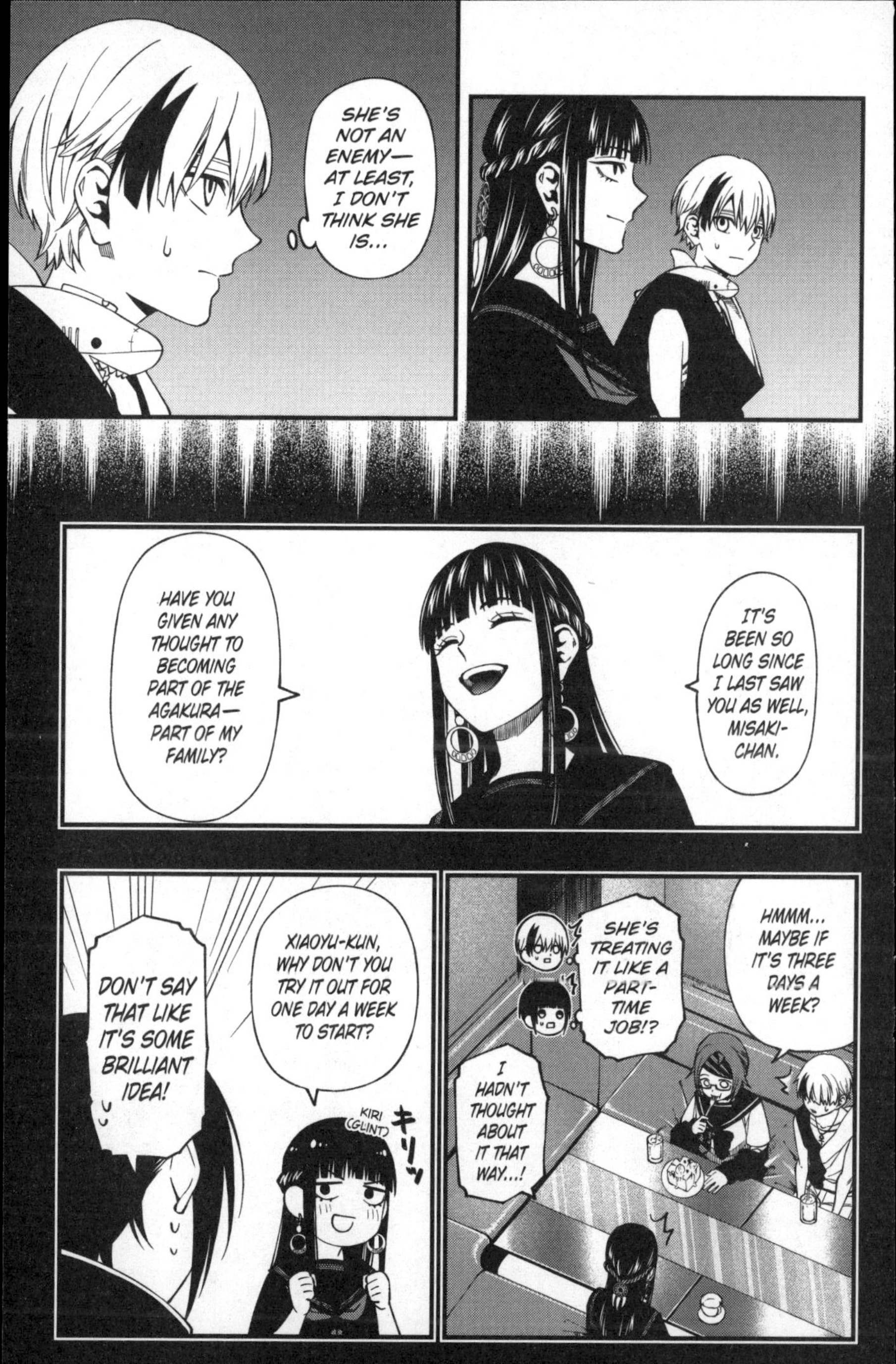
SHE'S NOT AN ENEMY— AT LEAST, I DON'T THINK SHE IS...
IT'S BEEN SO LONG SINCE I LAST SAW YOU AS WELL, MISAKI-CHAN.
HAVE YOU GIVEN ANY THOUGHT TO BECOMING PART OF THE AGAKURA— PART OF MY FAMILY?
HMMM... MAYBE IF IT'S THREE DAYS A WEEK?
SHE'S TREATING IT LIKE A PART-TIME JOB!?
I HADN'T THOUGHT ABOUT IT THAT WAY...!
XIAOYU-KUN, WHY DON'T YOU TRY IT OUT FOR ONE DAY A WEEK TO START?
キリッ
KIRI (GLINT)
DON'T SAY THAT LIKE IT'S SOME BRILLIANT IDEA!

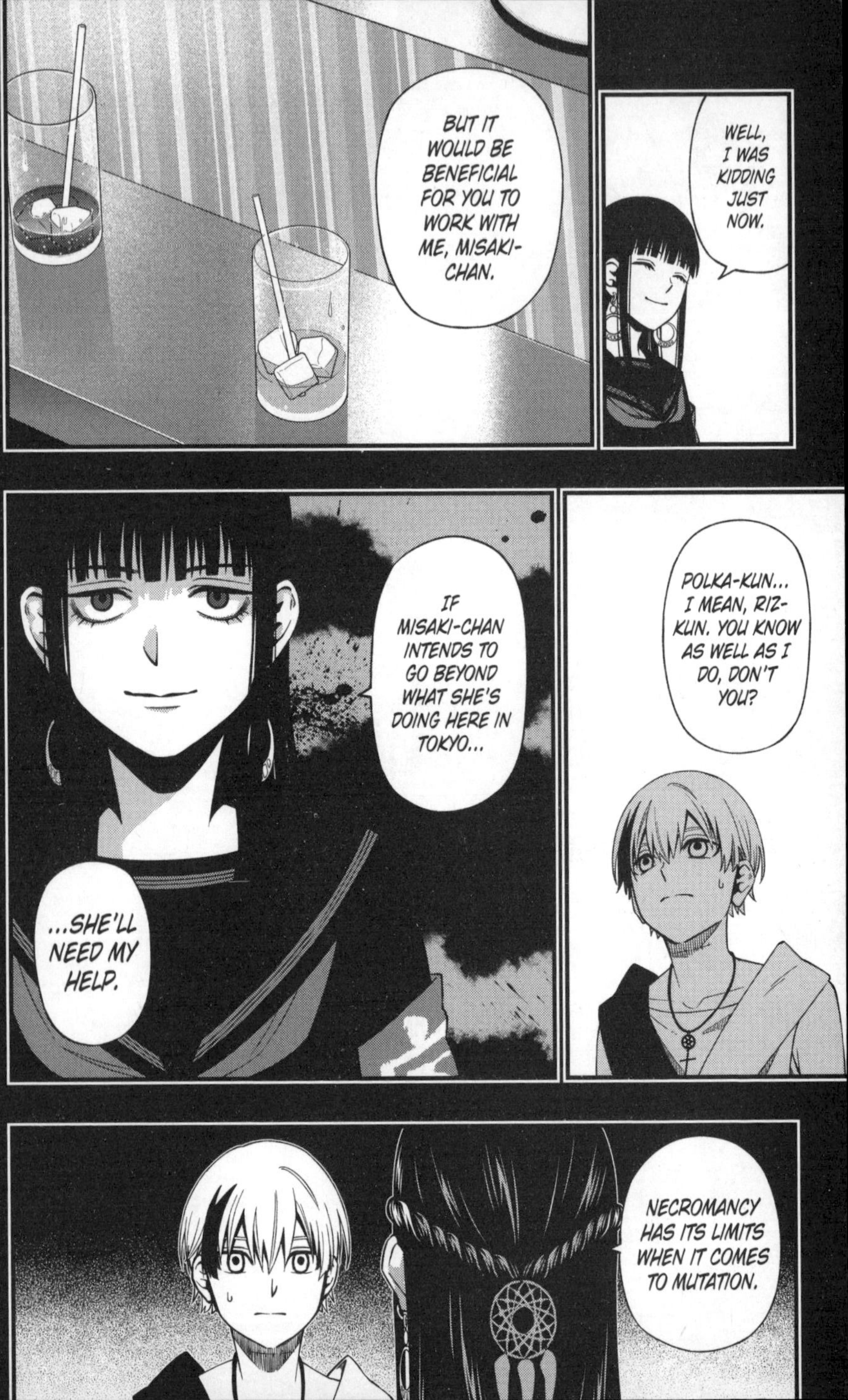
WELL, I WAS KIDDING JUST NOW.
BUT IT WOULD BE BENEFICIAL FOR YOU TO WORK WITH ME, MISAKI-CHAN.
POLKA-KUN... I MEAN, RIZ-KUN. YOU KNOW AS WELL AS I DO, DON'T YOU?
IF MISAKI-CHAN INTENDS TO GO BEYOND WHAT SHE'S DOING HERE IN TOKYO...
...SHE'LL NEED MY HELP.
NECROMANCY HAS ITS LIMITS WHEN IT COMES TO MUTATION.

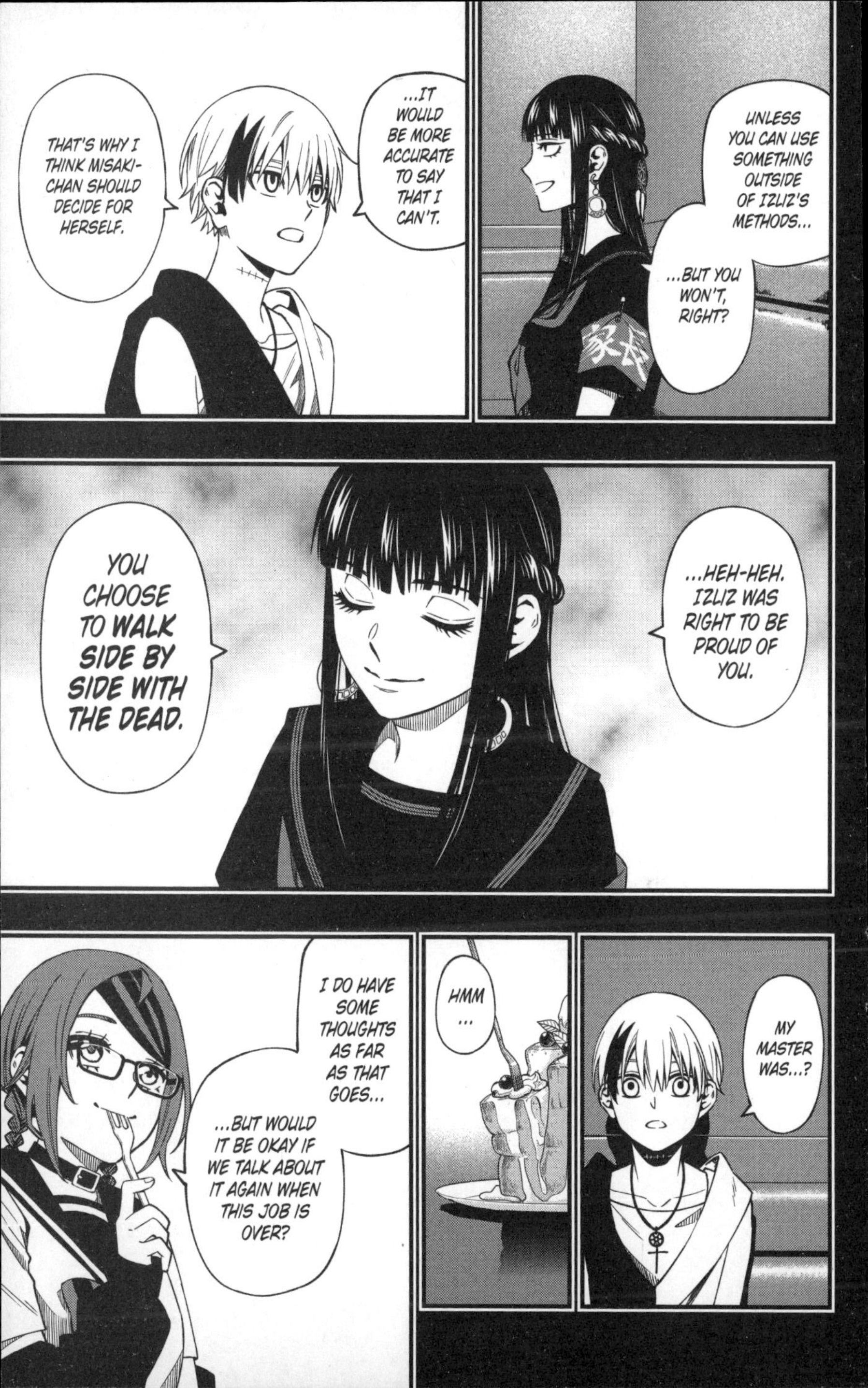
UNLESS YOU CAN USE SOMETHING OUTSIDE OF IZLIZ'S METHODS...
...BUT YOU WON'T, RIGHT?
家長
...IT WOULD BE MORE ACCURATE TO SAY THAT I CAN'T.
THAT'S WHY I THINK MISAKI-CHAN SHOULD DECIDE FOR HERSELF.
...HEH-HEH. IZLIZ WAS RIGHT TO BE PROUD OF YOU.
YOU CHOOSE TO WALK SIDE BY SIDE WITH THE DEAD.
MY MASTER WAS...?
HMM...
I DO HAVE SOME THOUGHTS AS FAR AS THAT GOES...
...BUT WOULD IT BE OKAY IF WE TALK ABOUT IT AGAIN WHEN THIS JOB IS OVER?

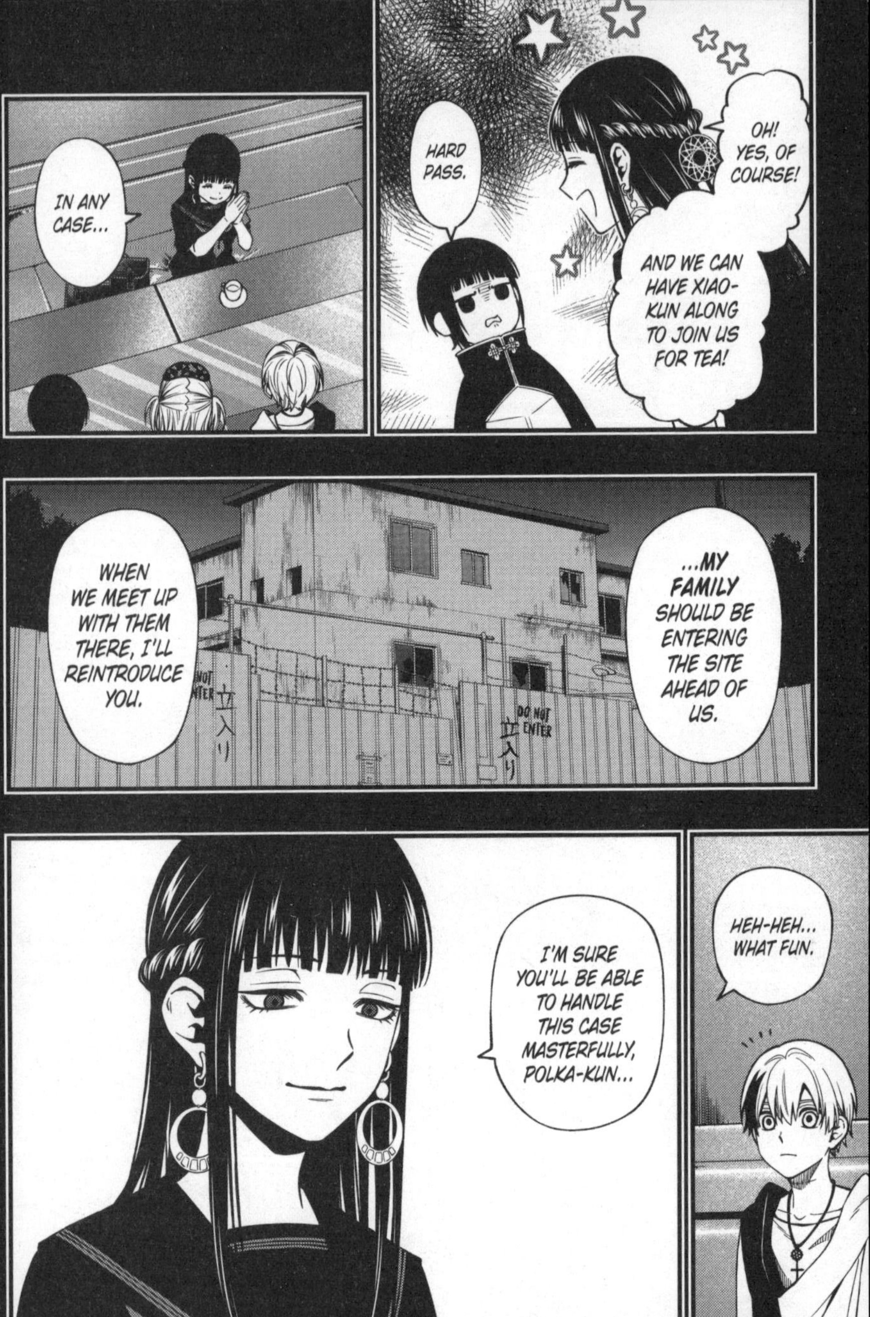
OH! YES, OF COURSE!
AND WE CAN HAVE XIAO-KUN ALONG TO JOIN US FOR TEA!
HARD PASS.
IN ANY CASE...
...MY FAMILY SHOULD BE ENTERING THE SITE AHEAD OF US.
WHEN WE MEET UP WITH THEM THERE, I'LL REINTRODUCE YOU.
DO NOT ENTER
HEH-HEH... WHAT FUN.
I'M SURE YOU'LL BE ABLE TO HANDLE THIS CASE MASTERFULLY, POLKA-KUN...

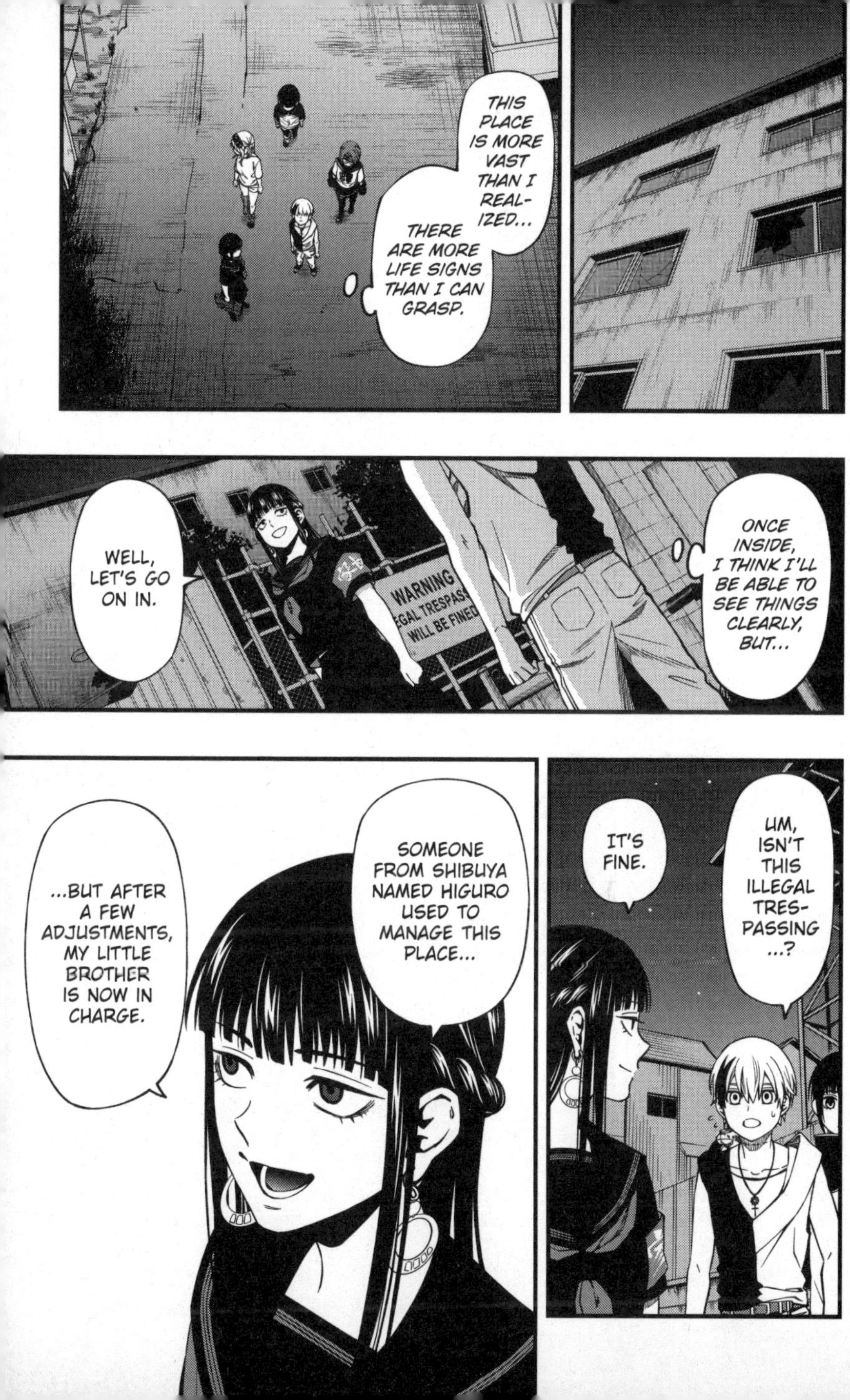
THIS PLACE IS MORE VAST THAN I REAL-IZED...
THERE ARE MORE LIFE SIGNS THAN I CAN GRASP.
ONCE INSIDE, I THINK I'LL BE ABLE TO SEE THINGS CLEARLY, BUT...
WARNING
WILL BE FINED
WELL, LET'S GO ON IN.
UM, ISN'T THIS ILLEGAL TRES-PASSING ...?
IT'S FINE.
SOMEONE FROM SHIBUYA NAMED HIGURO USED TO MANAGE THIS PLACE...
...BUT AFTER A FEW ADJUSTMENTS, MY LITTLE BROTHER IS NOW IN CHARGE.

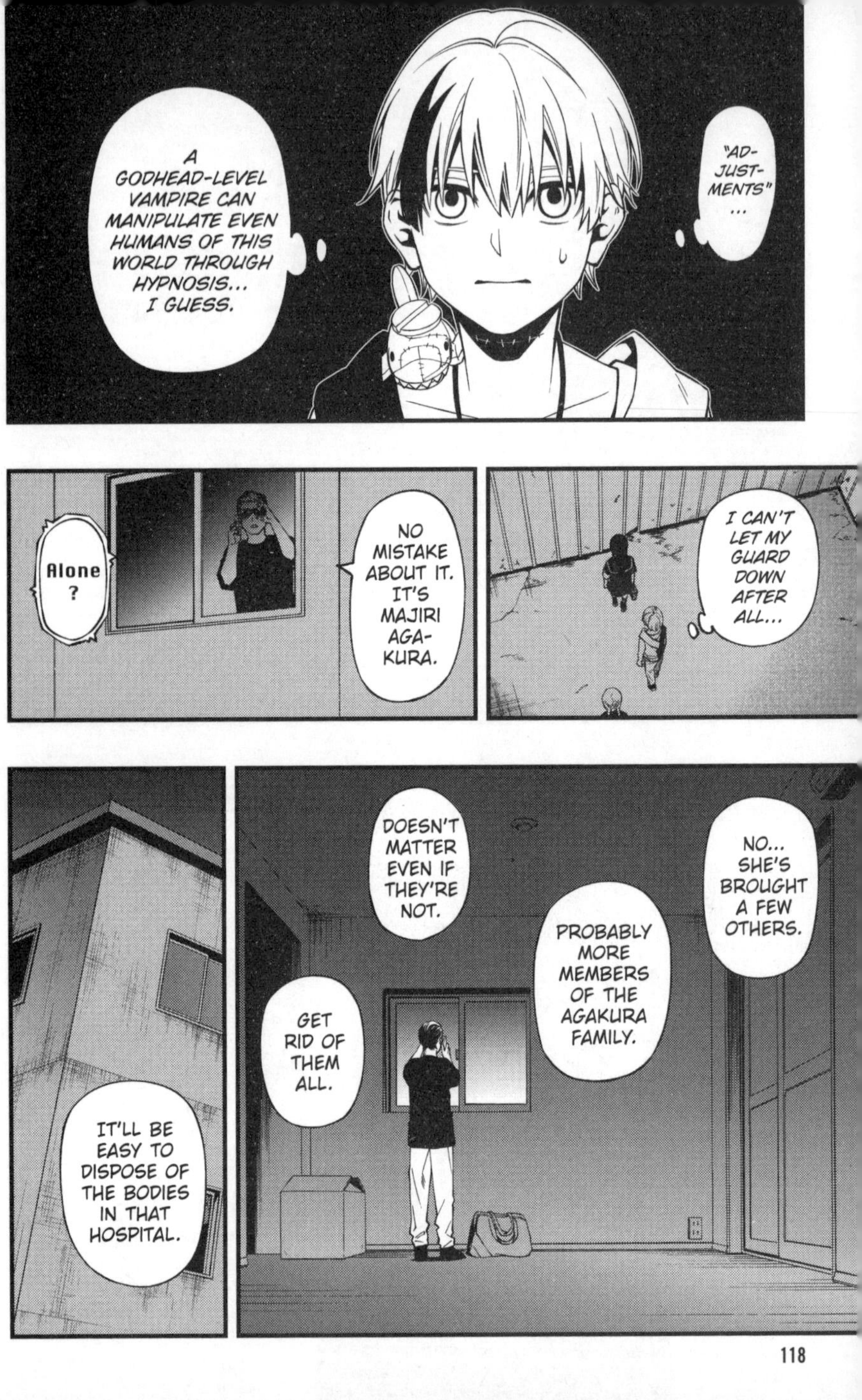
"ADJUSTMENTS"...
A GODHEAD-LEVEL VAMPIRE CAN MANIPULATE EVEN HUMANS OF THIS WORLD THROUGH HYPNOSIS... I GUESS.
I CAN'T LET MY GUARD DOWN AFTER ALL...
NO MISTAKE ABOUT IT. IT'S MAJIRI AGAKURA.
Alone?
NO... SHE'S BROUGHT A FEW OTHERS.
PROBABLY MORE MEMBERS OF THE AGAKURA FAMILY.
DOESN'T MATTER EVEN IF THEY'RE NOT.
GET RID OF THEM ALL.
IT'LL BE EASY TO DISPOSE OF THE BODIES IN THAT HOSPITAL.

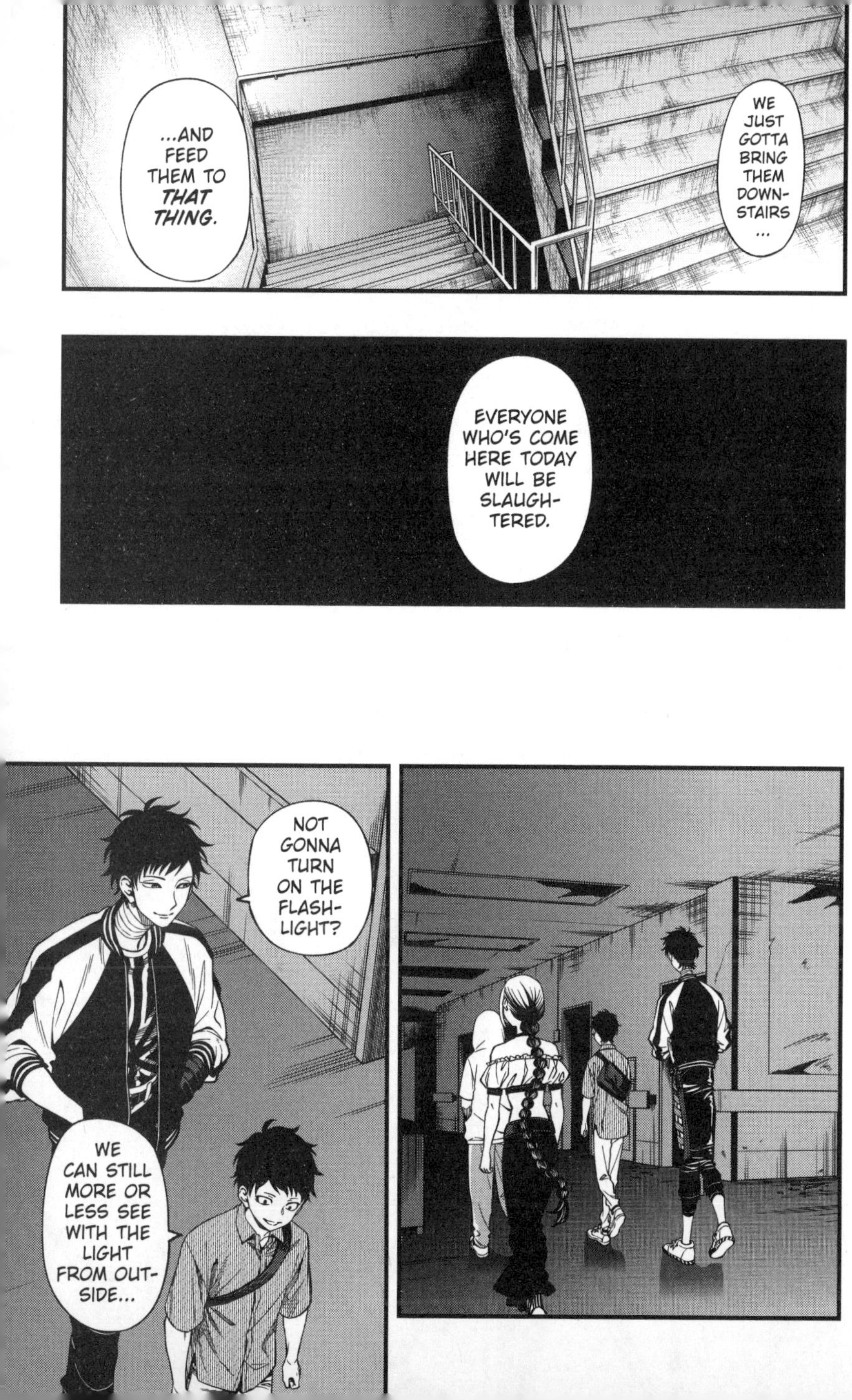
WE JUST GOTTA BRING THEM DOWNSTAIRS...
...AND FEED THEM TO *THAT THING*.
EVERYONE WHO'S COME HERE TODAY WILL BE SLAUGHTERED.
NOT GONNA TURN ON THE FLASHLIGHT?
WE CAN STILL MORE OR LESS SEE WITH THE LIGHT FROM OUTSIDE...

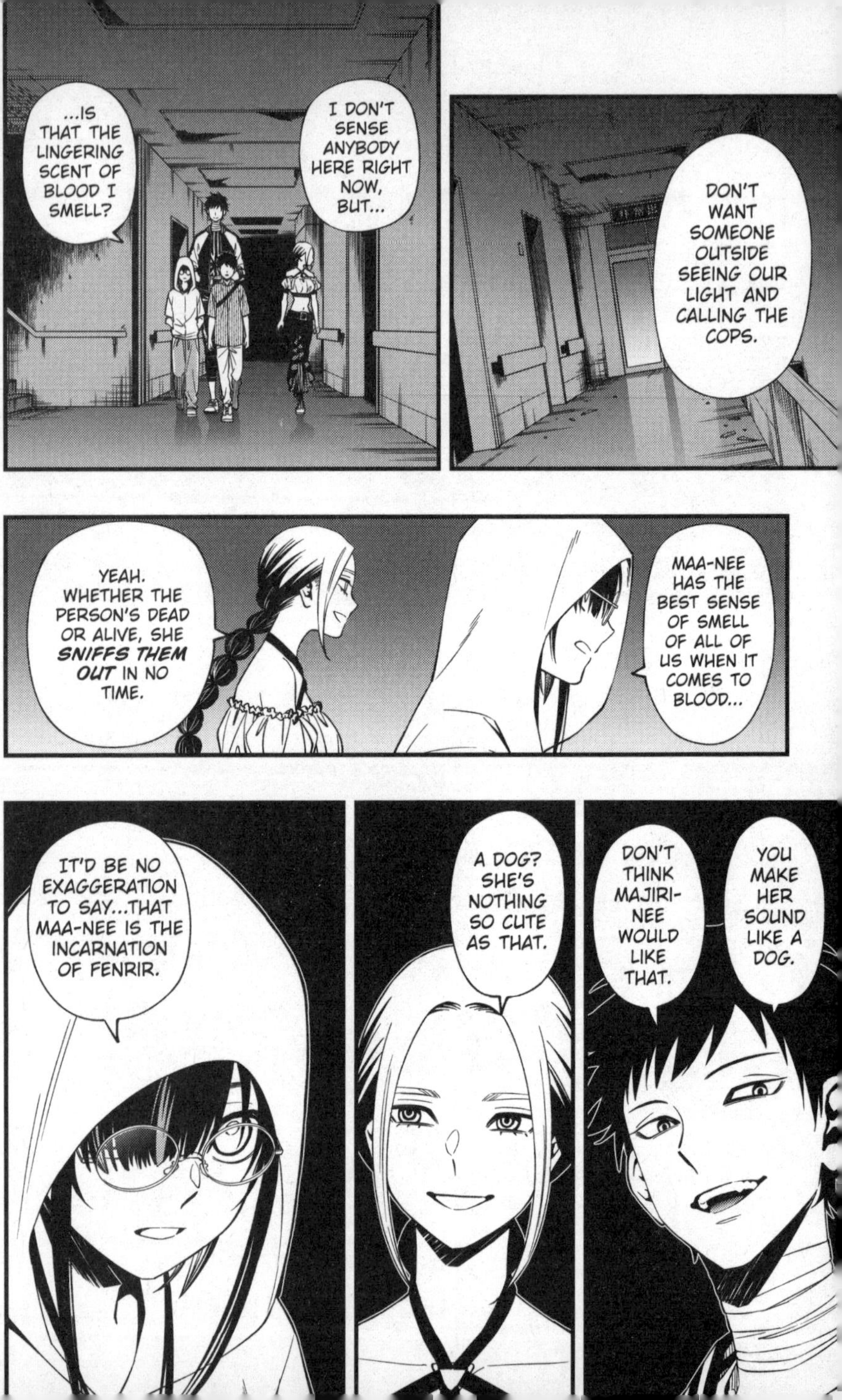
DON'T WANT SOMEONE OUTSIDE SEEING OUR LIGHT AND CALLING THE COPS.
I DON'T SENSE ANYBODY HERE RIGHT NOW, BUT...
...IS THAT THE LINGERING SCENT OF BLOOD I SMELL?
MAA-NEE HAS THE BEST SENSE OF SMELL OF ALL OF US WHEN IT COMES TO BLOOD...
YEAH. WHETHER THE PERSON'S DEAD OR ALIVE, SHE ***SNIFFS THEM OUT*** IN NO TIME.
YOU MAKE HER SOUND LIKE A DOG.
DON'T THINK MAJIRI-NEE WOULD LIKE THAT.
A DOG? SHE'S NOTHING SO CUTE AS THAT.
IT'D BE NO EXAGGERATION TO SAY...THAT MAA-NEE IS THE INCARNATION OF FENRIR.

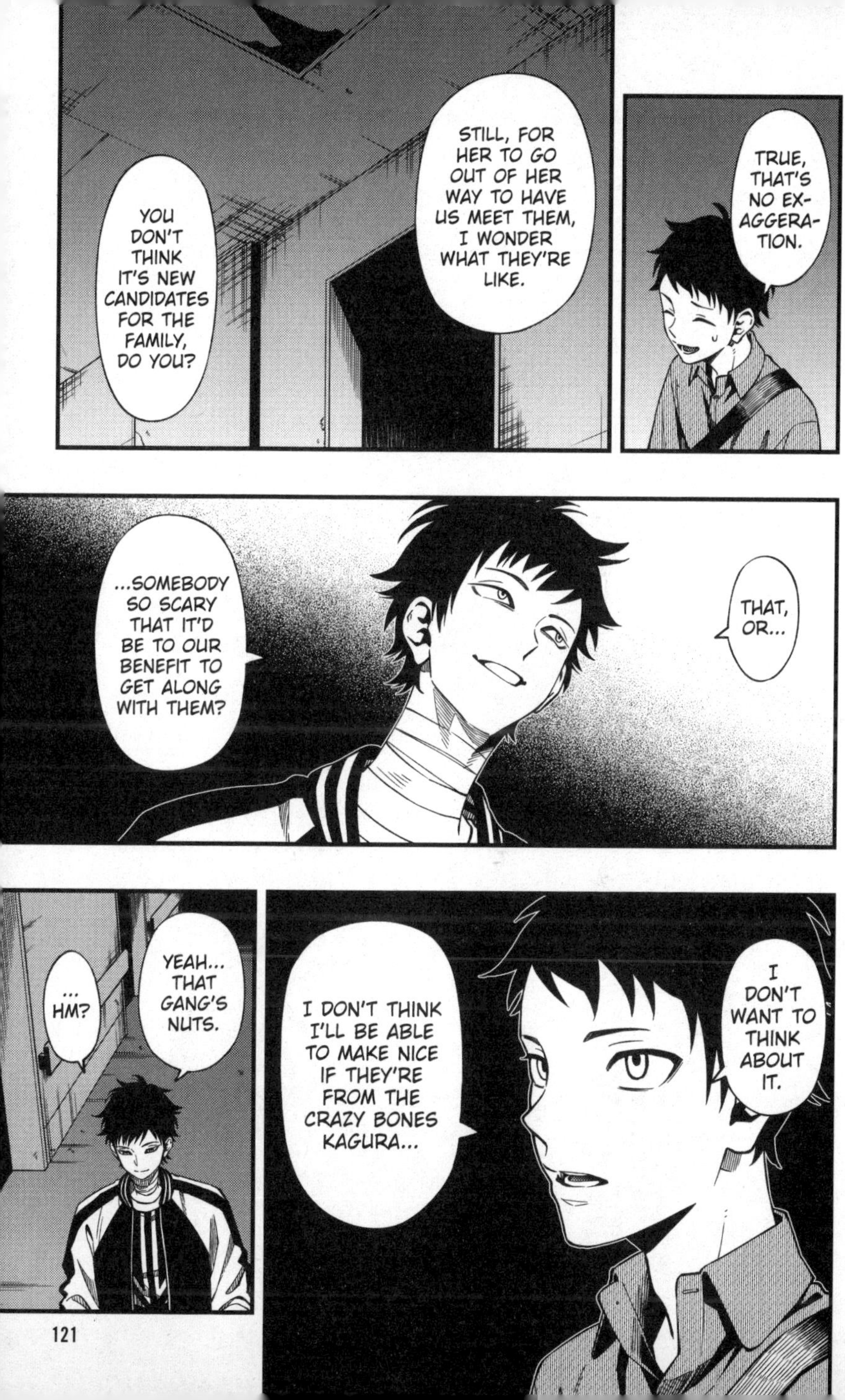
TRUE, THAT'S NO EX-AGGERA-TION.
STILL, FOR HER TO GO OUT OF HER WAY TO HAVE US MEET THEM, I WONDER WHAT THEY'RE LIKE.
YOU DON'T THINK IT'S NEW CANDIDATES FOR THE FAMILY, DO YOU?
THAT, OR...
...SOMEBODY SO SCARY THAT IT'D BE TO OUR BENEFIT TO GET ALONG WITH THEM?
I DON'T WANT TO THINK ABOUT IT.
I DON'T THINK I'LL BE ABLE TO MAKE NICE IF THEY'RE FROM THE CRAZY BONES KAGURA...
YEAH... THAT GANG'S NUTS.
... HM?

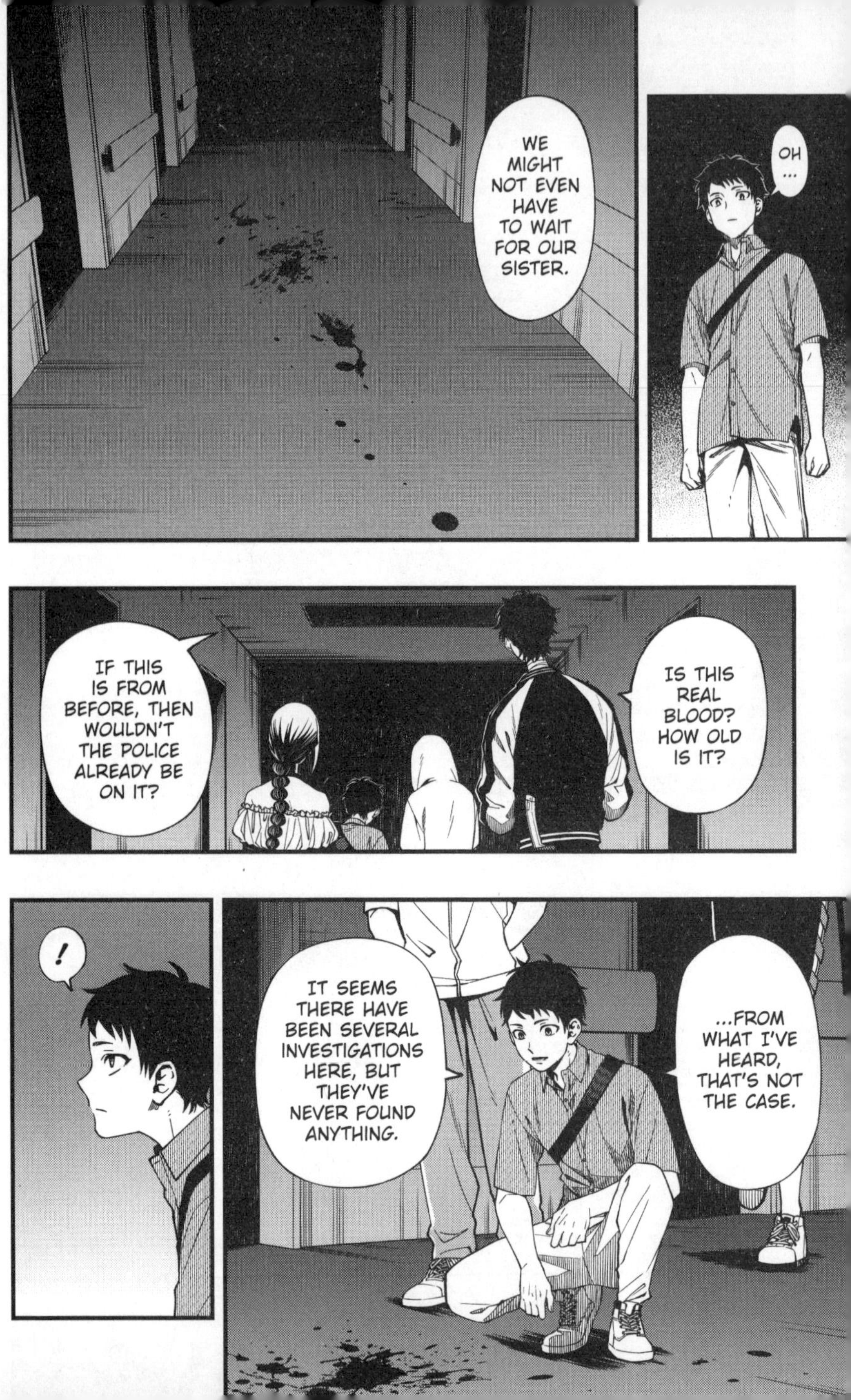

OH ...
WE MIGHT NOT EVEN HAVE TO WAIT FOR OUR SISTER.
IS THIS REAL BLOOD? HOW OLD IS IT?
IF THIS IS FROM BEFORE, THEN WOULDN'T THE POLICE ALREADY BE ON IT?
...FROM WHAT I'VE HEARD, THAT'S NOT THE CASE.
IT SEEMS THERE HAVE BEEN SEVERAL INVESTIGATIONS HERE, BUT THEY'VE NEVER FOUND ANYTHING.
!

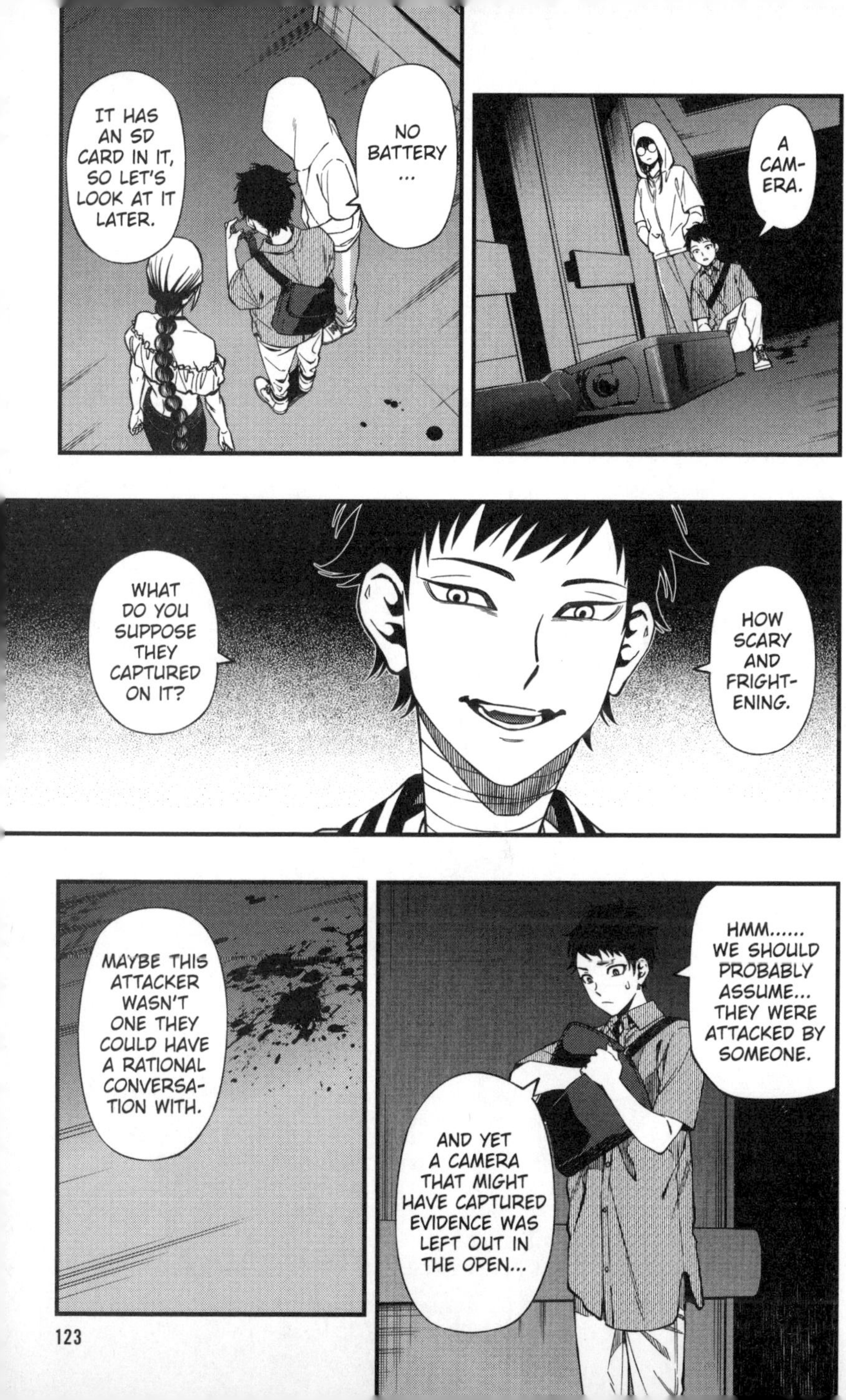
A CAM-ERA.
NO BATTERY ...
IT HAS AN SD CARD IN IT, SO LET'S LOOK AT IT LATER.
HOW SCARY AND FRIGHT-ENING.
WHAT DO YOU SUPPOSE THEY CAPTURED ON IT?
HMM...... WE SHOULD PROBABLY ASSUME... THEY WERE ATTACKED BY SOMEONE.
AND YET A CAMERA THAT MIGHT HAVE CAPTURED EVIDENCE WAS LEFT OUT IN THE OPEN...
MAYBE THIS ATTACKER WASN'T ONE THEY COULD HAVE A RATIONAL CONVERSA-TION WITH.

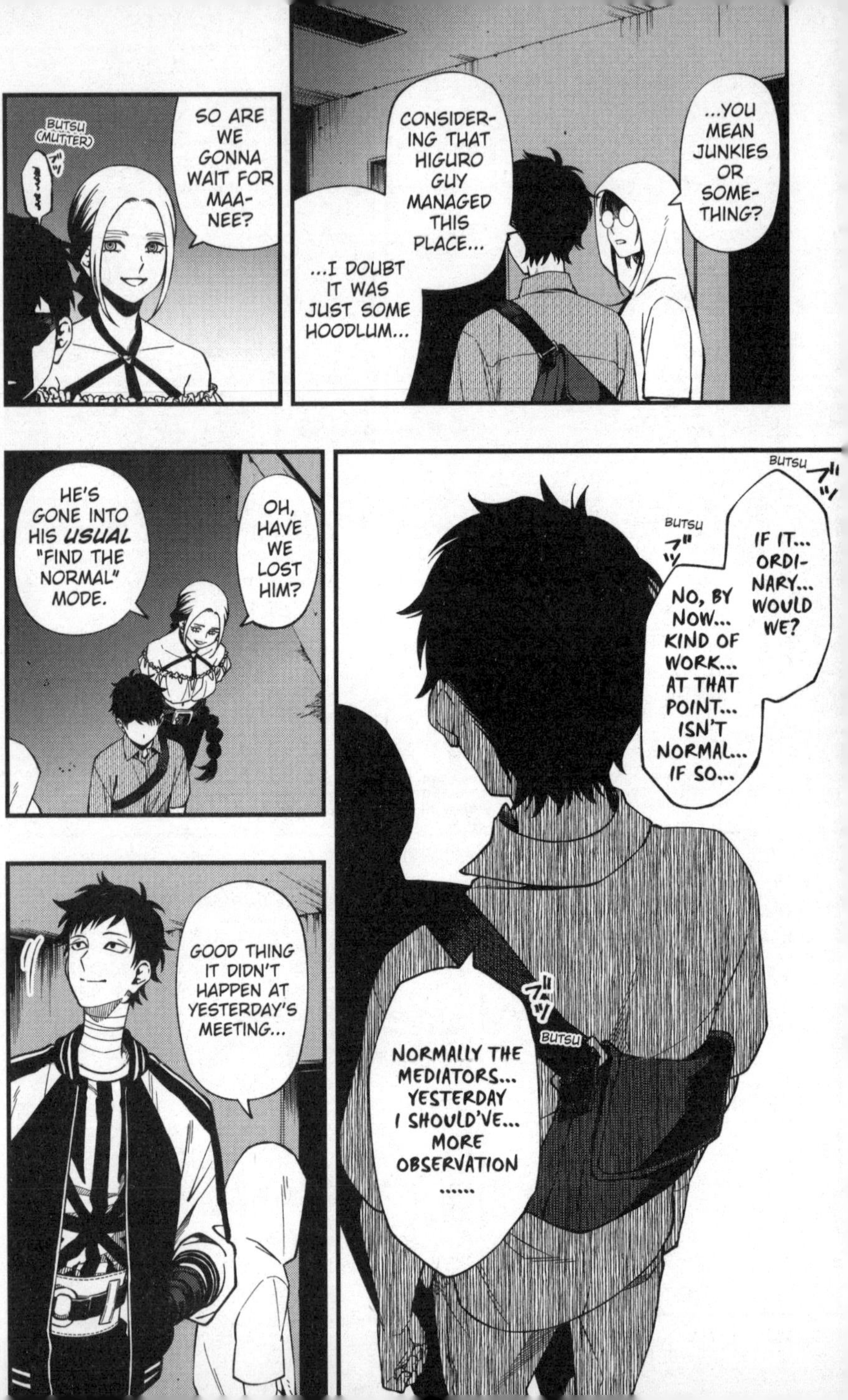
...YOU MEAN JUNKIES OR SOME-THING?
CONSIDER-ING THAT HIGURO GUY MANAGED THIS PLACE...
...I DOUBT IT WAS JUST SOME HOODLUM...
SO ARE WE GONNA WAIT FOR MAA-NEE?
BUTSU (MUTTER)
BUTSU
BUTSU
IF IT... ORDI-NARY... WOULD WE?
NO, BY NOW... KIND OF WORK... AT THAT POINT... ISN'T NORMAL... IF SO...
OH, HAVE WE LOST HIM?
HE'S GONE INTO HIS *USUAL* "FIND THE NORMAL" MODE.
BUTSU
NORMALLY THE MEDIATORS... YESTERDAY I SHOULD'VE... MORE OBSERVATION ......
GOOD THING IT DIDN'T HAPPEN AT YESTERDAY'S MEETING...

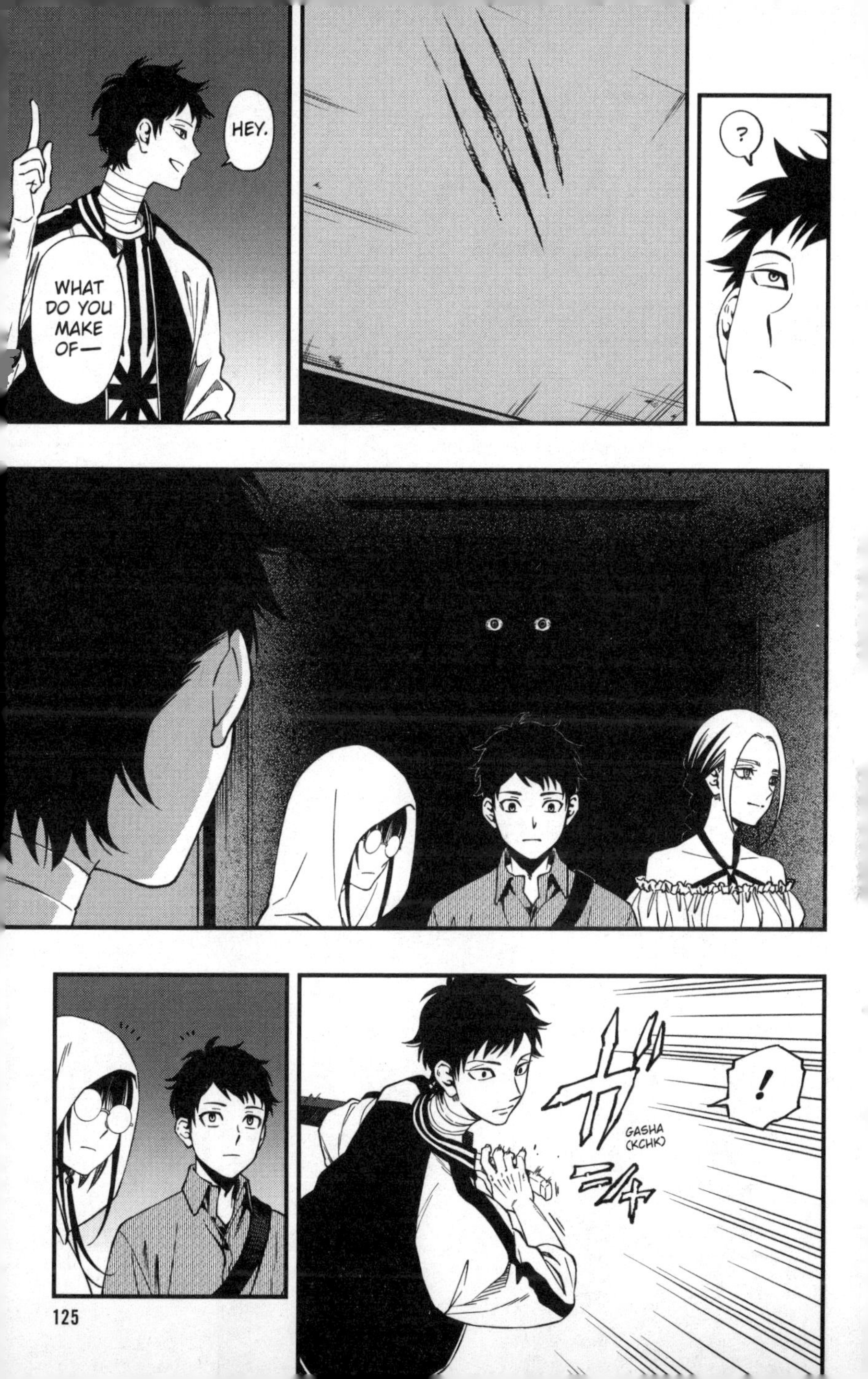
HEY.
WHAT DO YOU MAKE OF—
?
!
GASHA (KCHK)

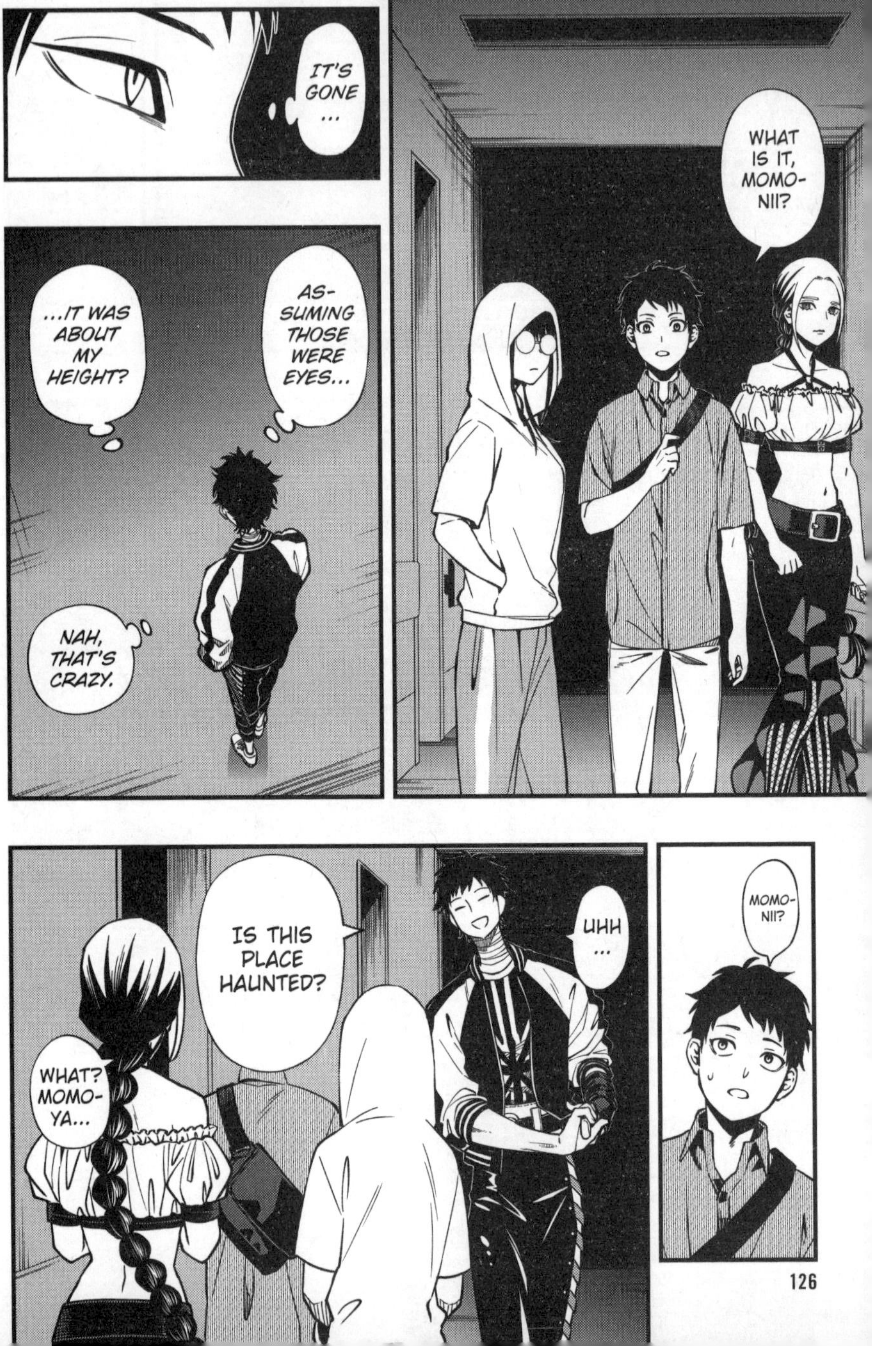
IT'S GONE ...
AS-SUMING THOSE WERE EYES...
...IT WAS ABOUT MY HEIGHT?
NAH, THAT'S CRAZY.
WHAT IS IT, MOMO-NII?
MOMO-NII?
UHH ...
IS THIS PLACE HAUNTED?
WHAT? MOMO-YA...

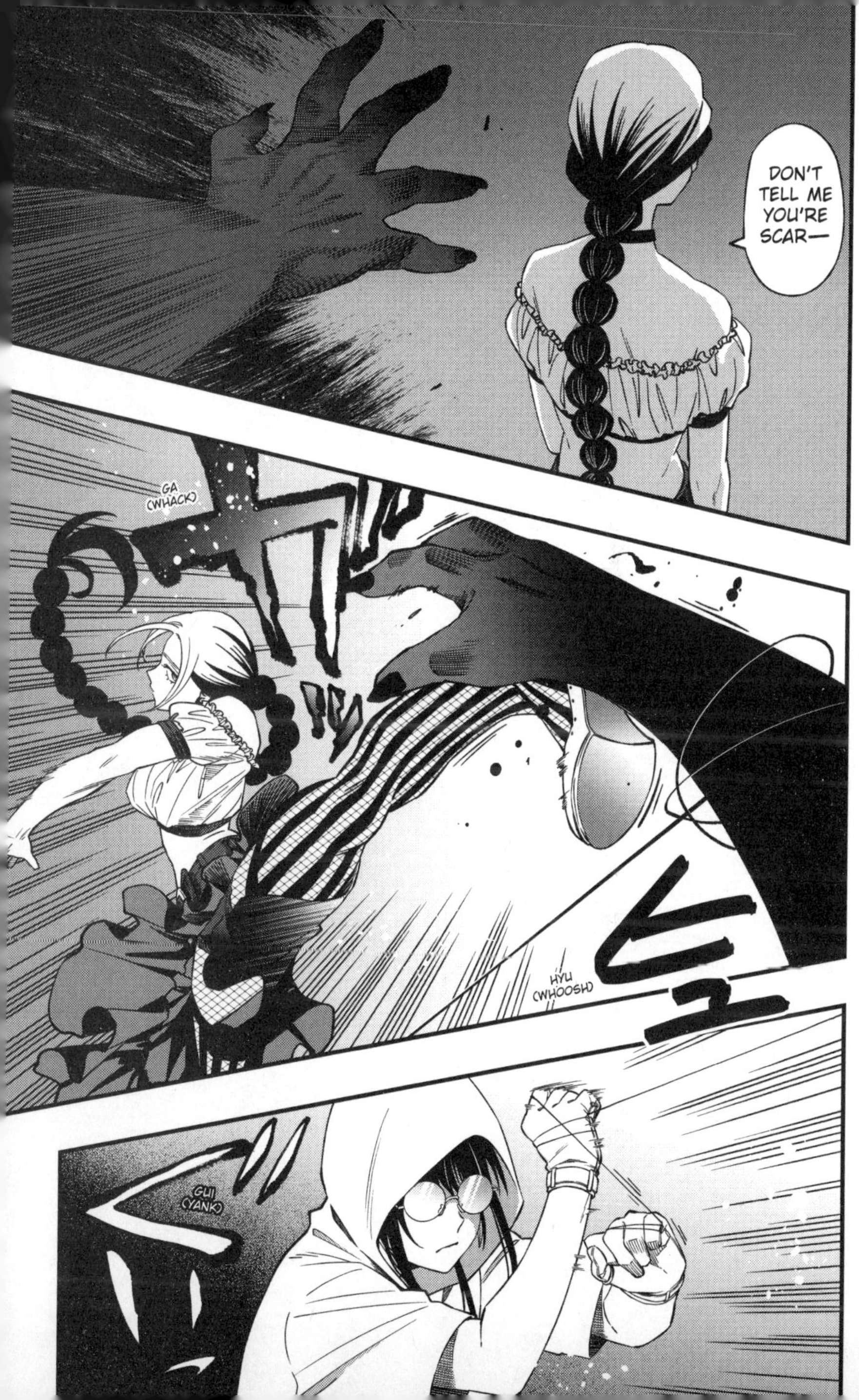
DON'T TELL ME YOU'RE SCAR—
GA (WHACK)
HYU (WHOOSH)
GUI (YANK)

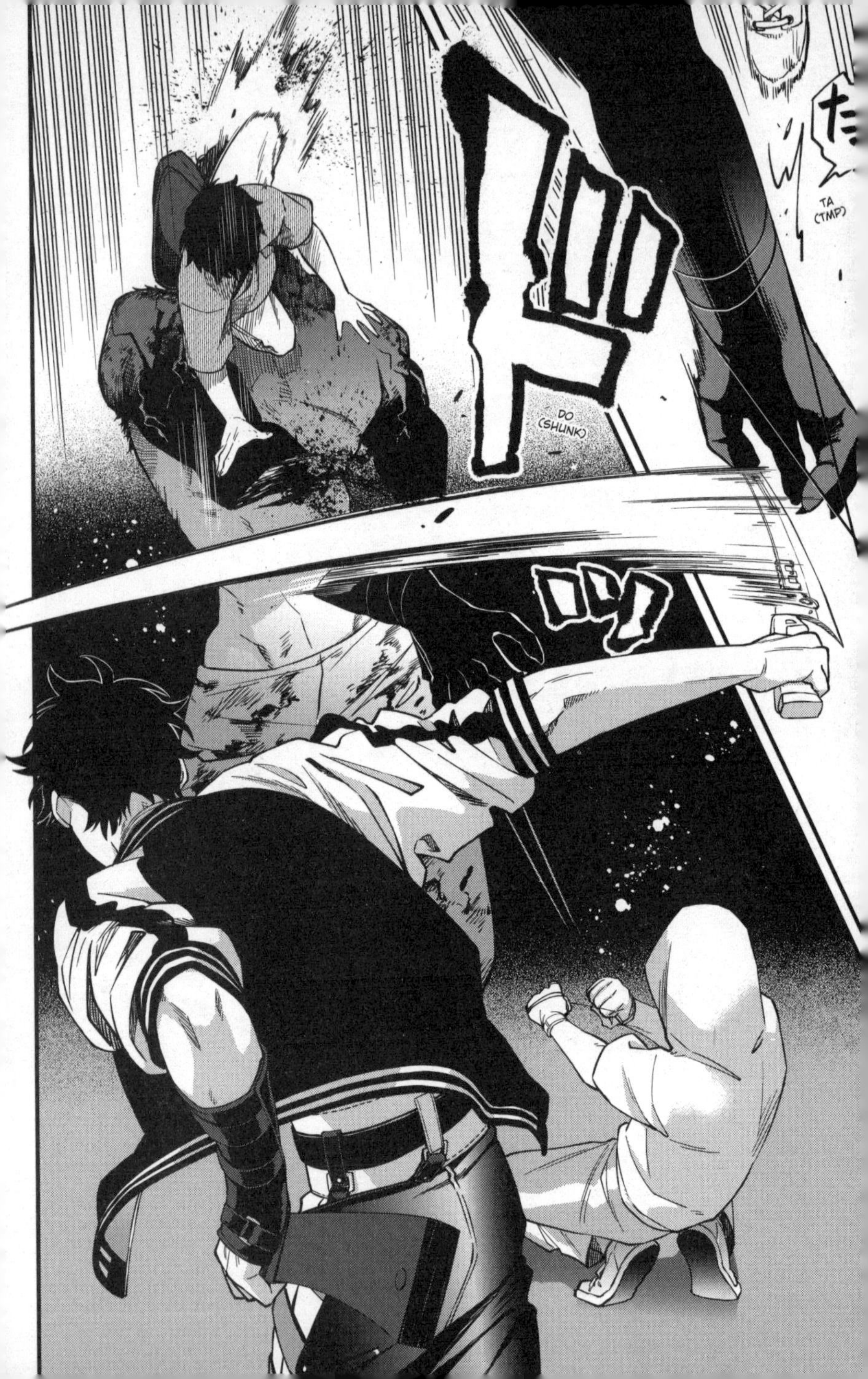

TA
(TMP)
DO
(SHUNK)

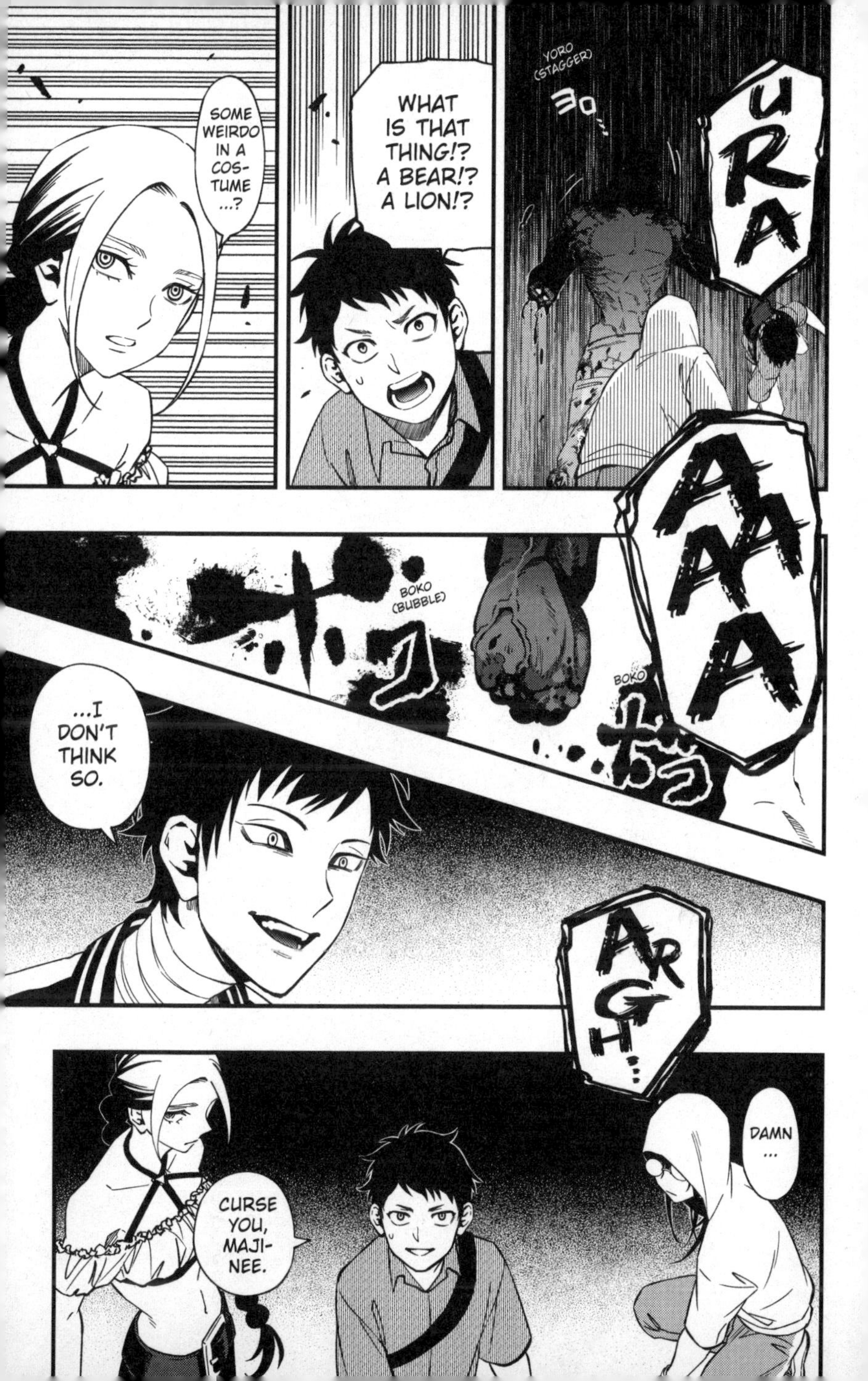

URA
AAAA
YORO (STAGGER)
WHAT IS THAT THING!? A BEAR!? A LION!?
SOME WEIRDO IN A COS-TUME ...?
BOKO (BUBBLE)
BOKO
...I DON'T THINK SO.
ARGH...
DAMN ...
CURSE YOU, MAJI-NEE.

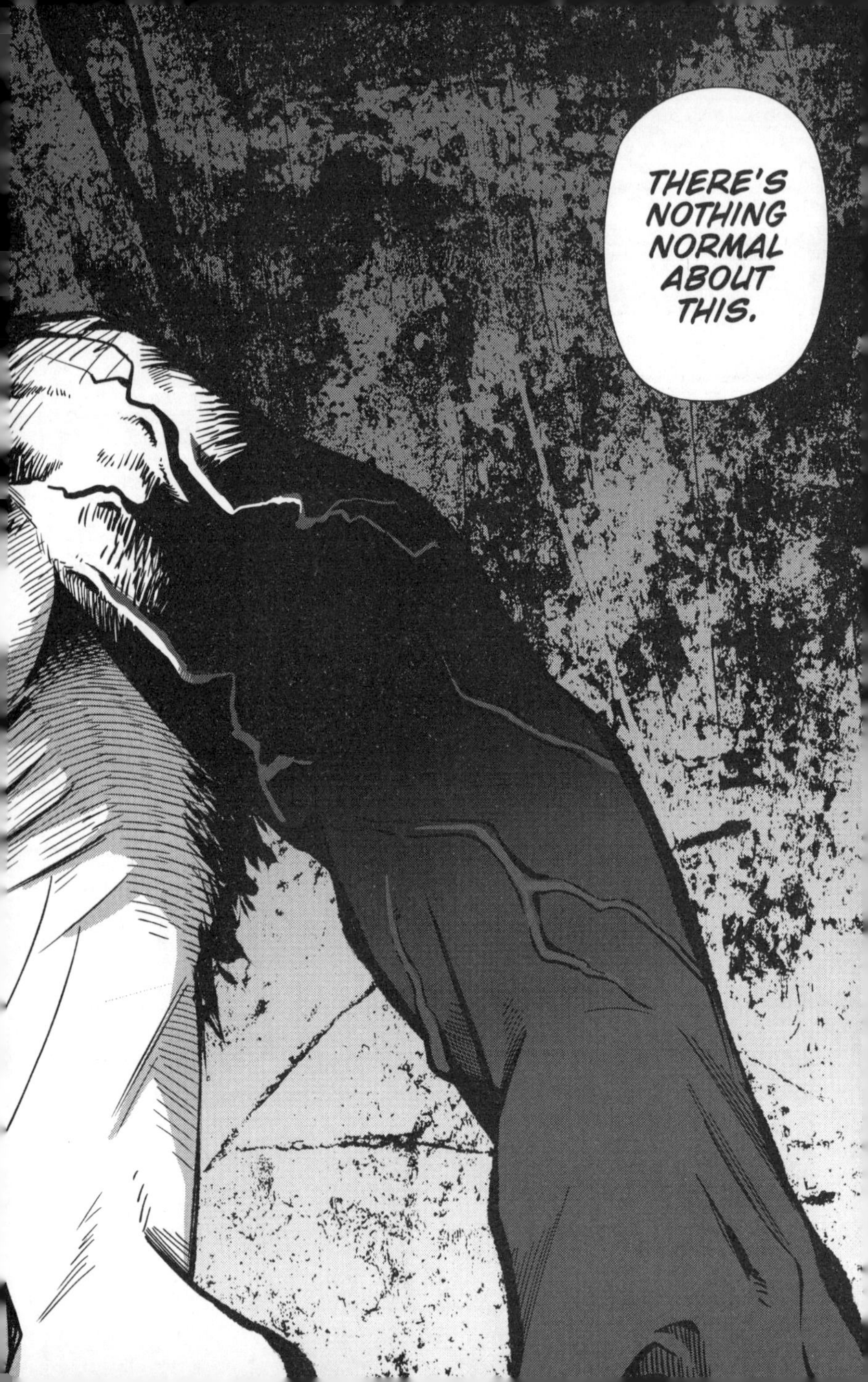
THERE'S NOTHING NORMAL ABOUT THIS.

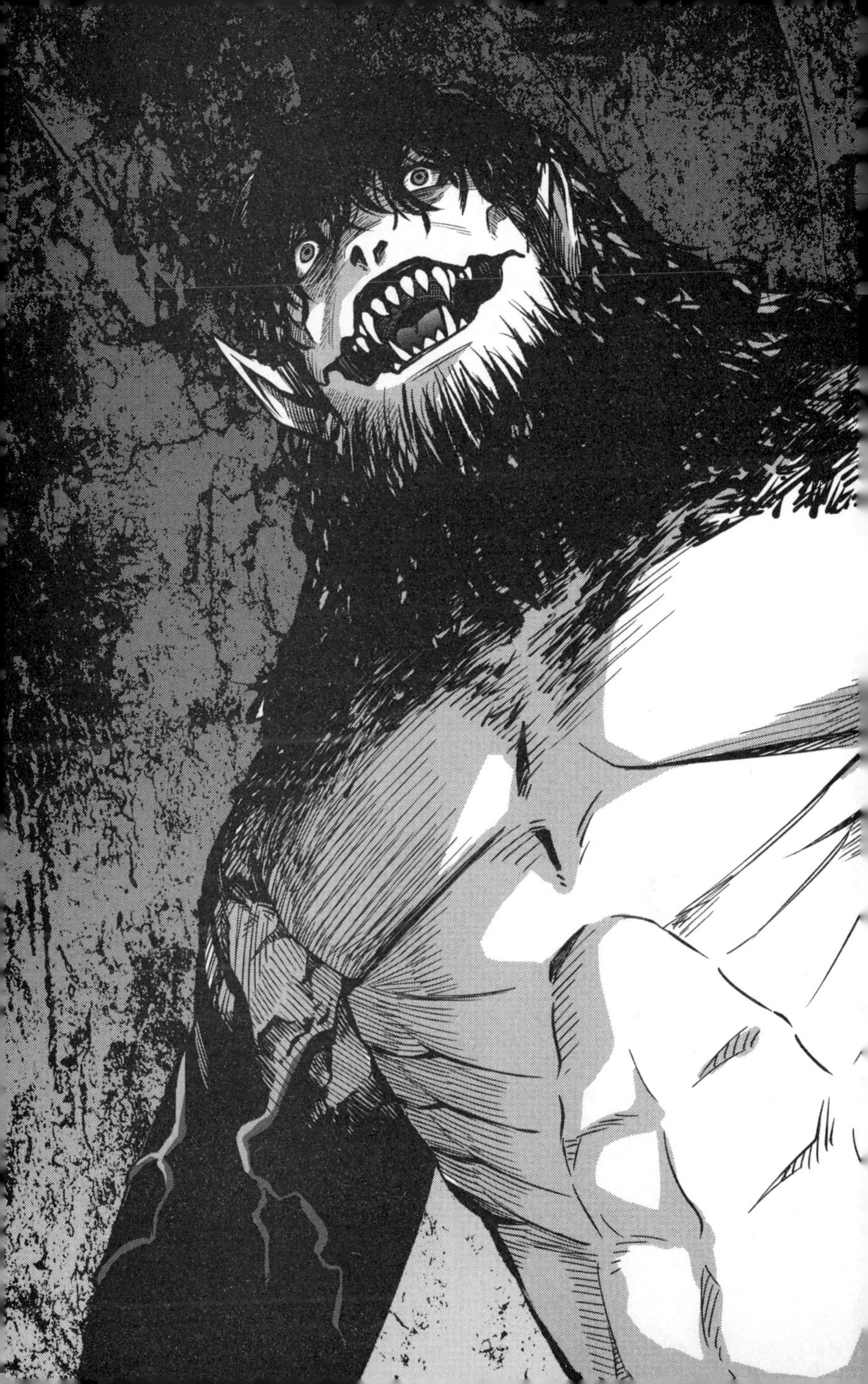

DEAD MOUNT
DEATH PLAY

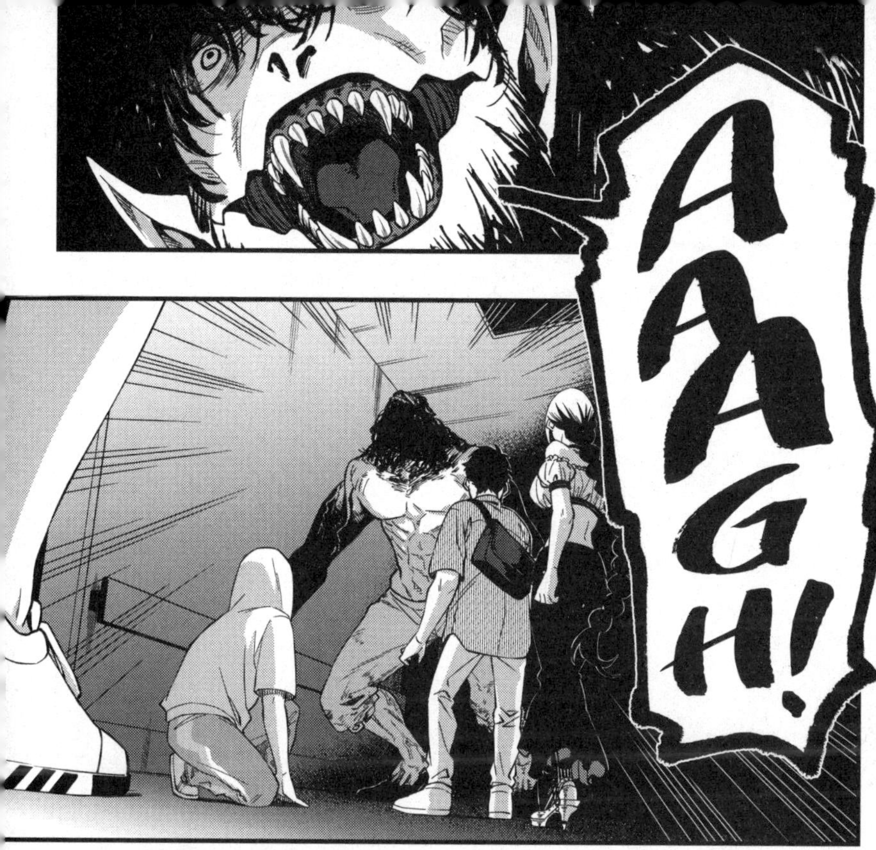
AAAGH!

# #94

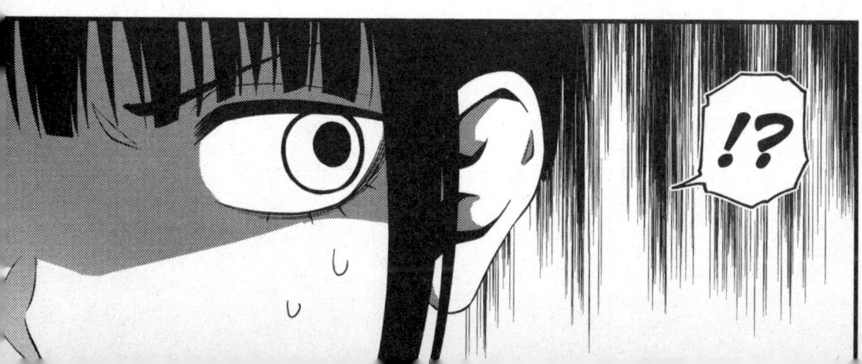
!?

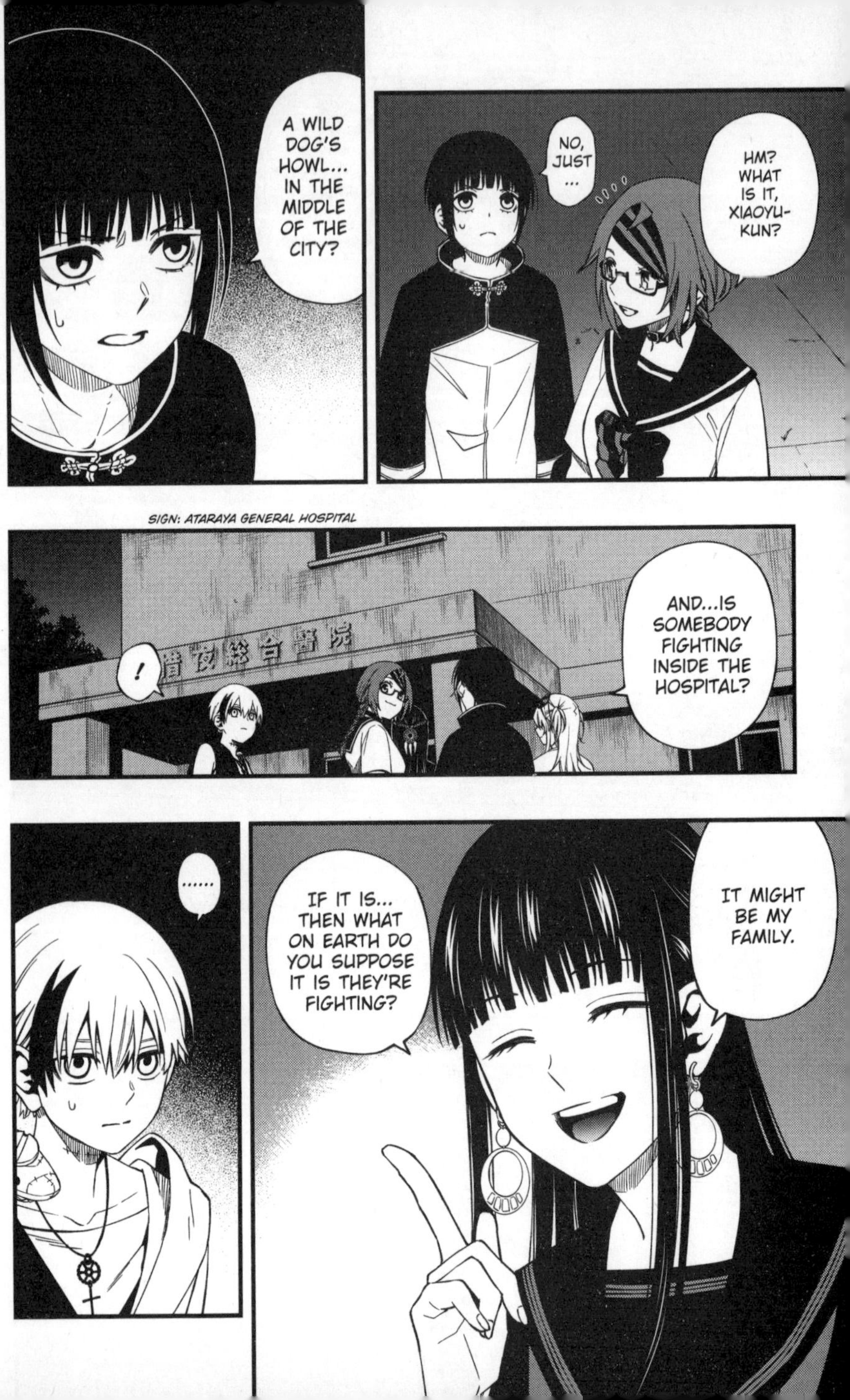
HM? WHAT IS IT, XIAOYU-KUN?
NO, JUST ...
A WILD DOG'S HOWL... IN THE MIDDLE OF THE CITY?
SIGN: ATARAYA GENERAL HOSPITAL
AND...IS SOMEBODY FIGHTING INSIDE THE HOSPITAL?
!
IT MIGHT BE MY FAMILY.
IF IT IS... THEN WHAT ON EARTH DO YOU SUPPOSE IT IS THEY'RE FIGHTING?
......

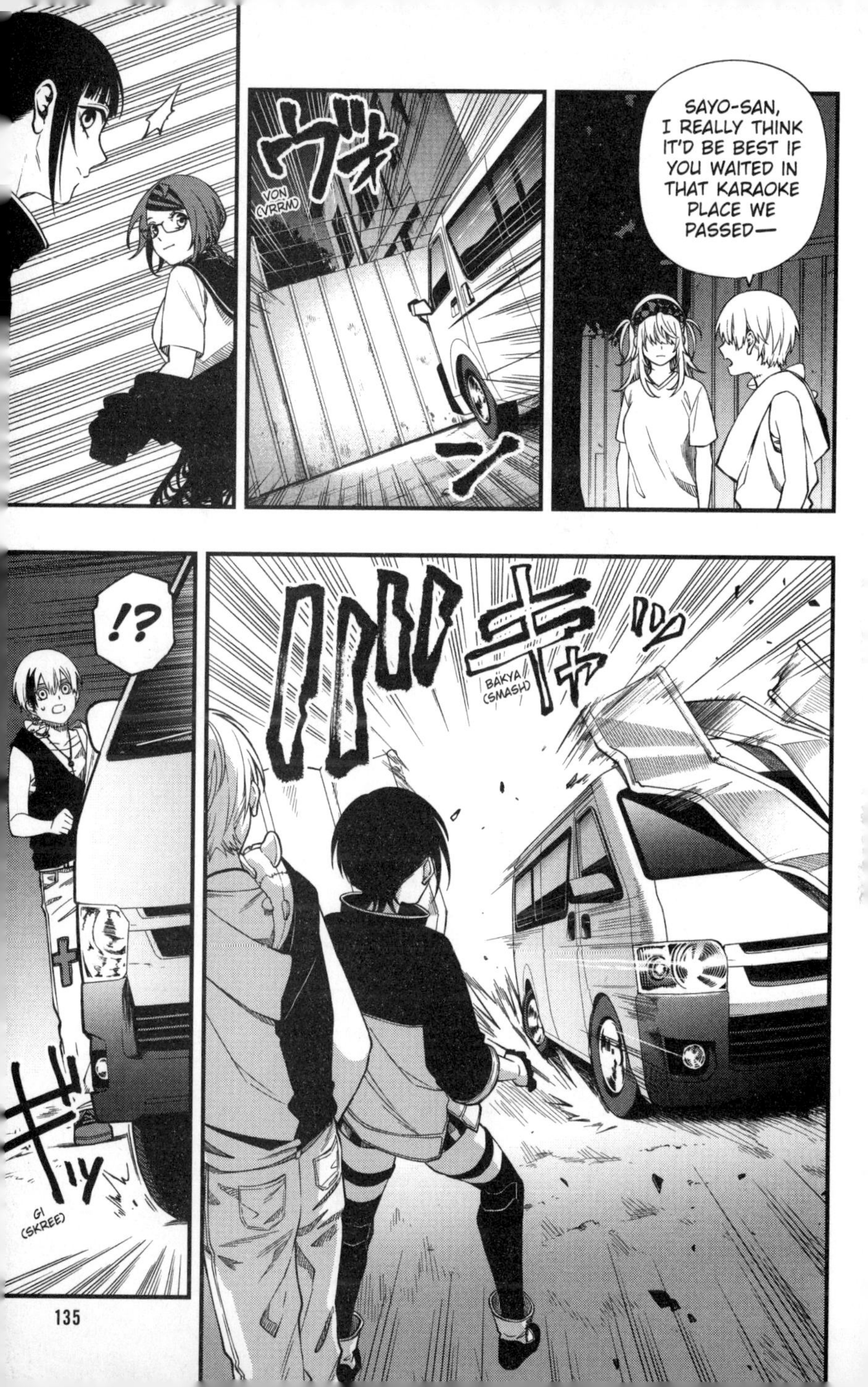

VON (VRRM)
SAYO-SAN, I REALLY THINK IT'D BE BEST IF YOU WAITED IN THAT KARAOKE PLACE WE PASSED—
!?
BAKYA (SMASH)
GI (SKREE)

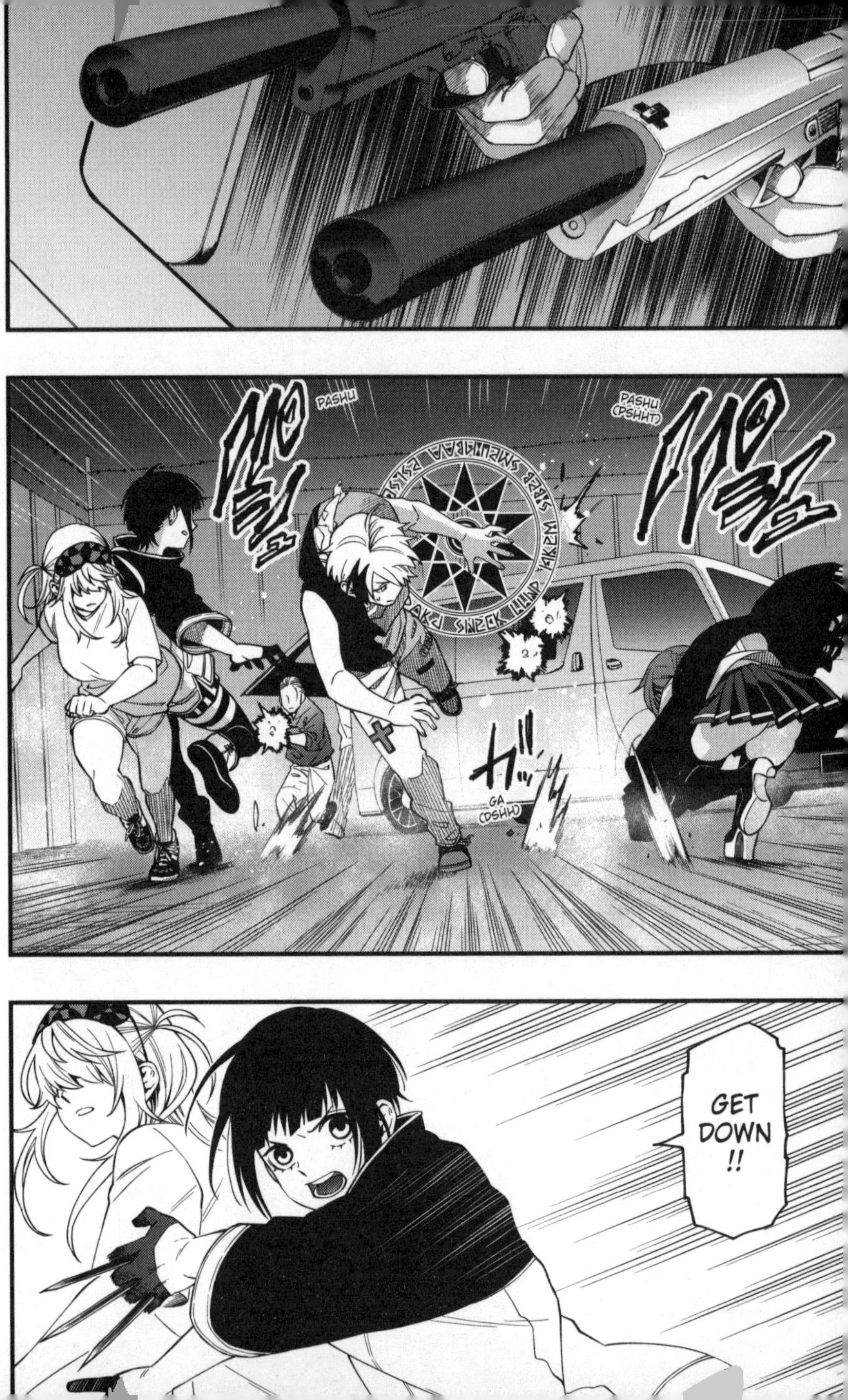
PASHU (PSHHT)
PASHU
GA (DSHH)
GET DOWN!!

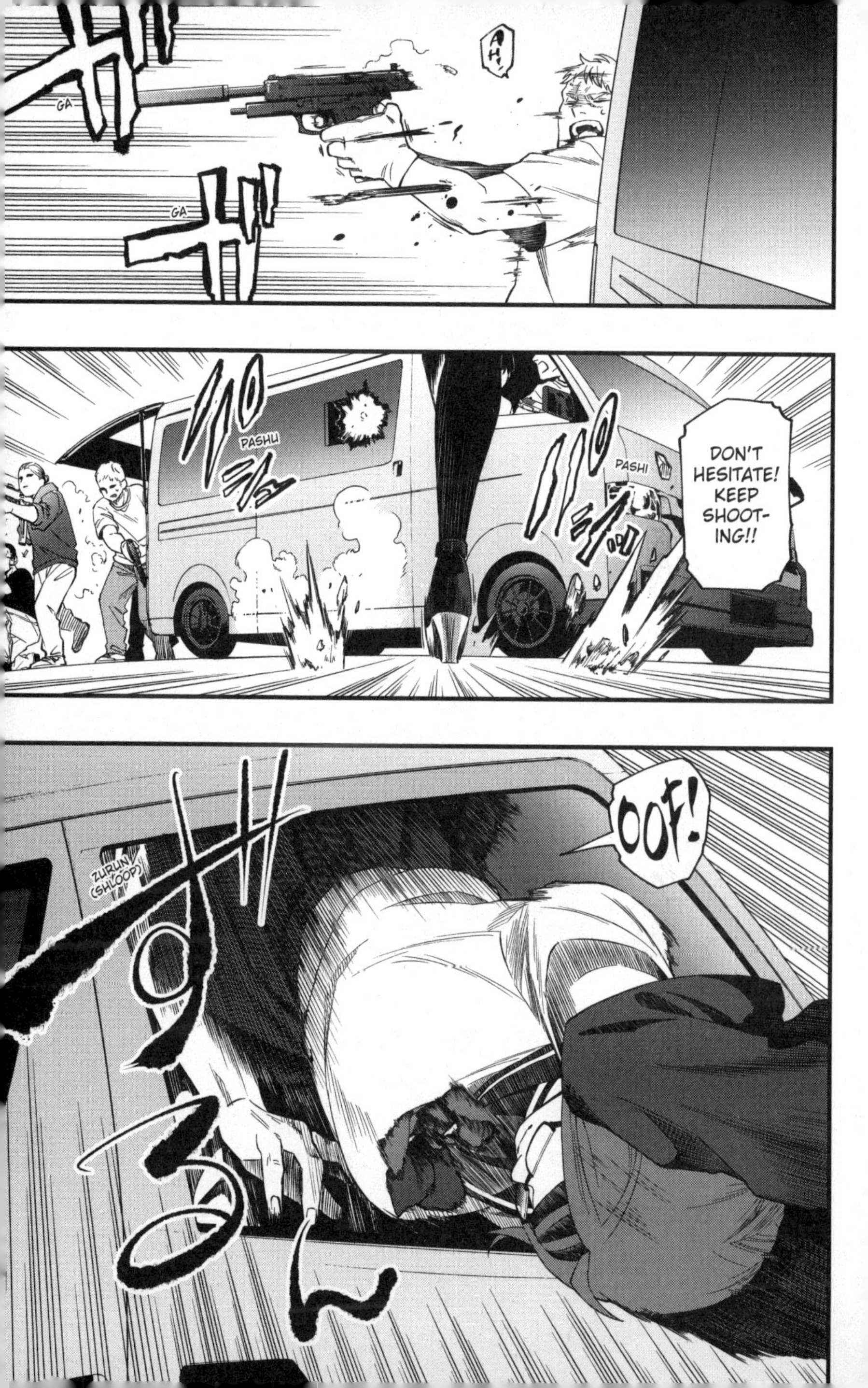
AH!
GA
GA
DON'T HESITATE! KEEP SHOOTING!!
PASHI
PASHU
OOF!
ZURUN (SHLOOP)

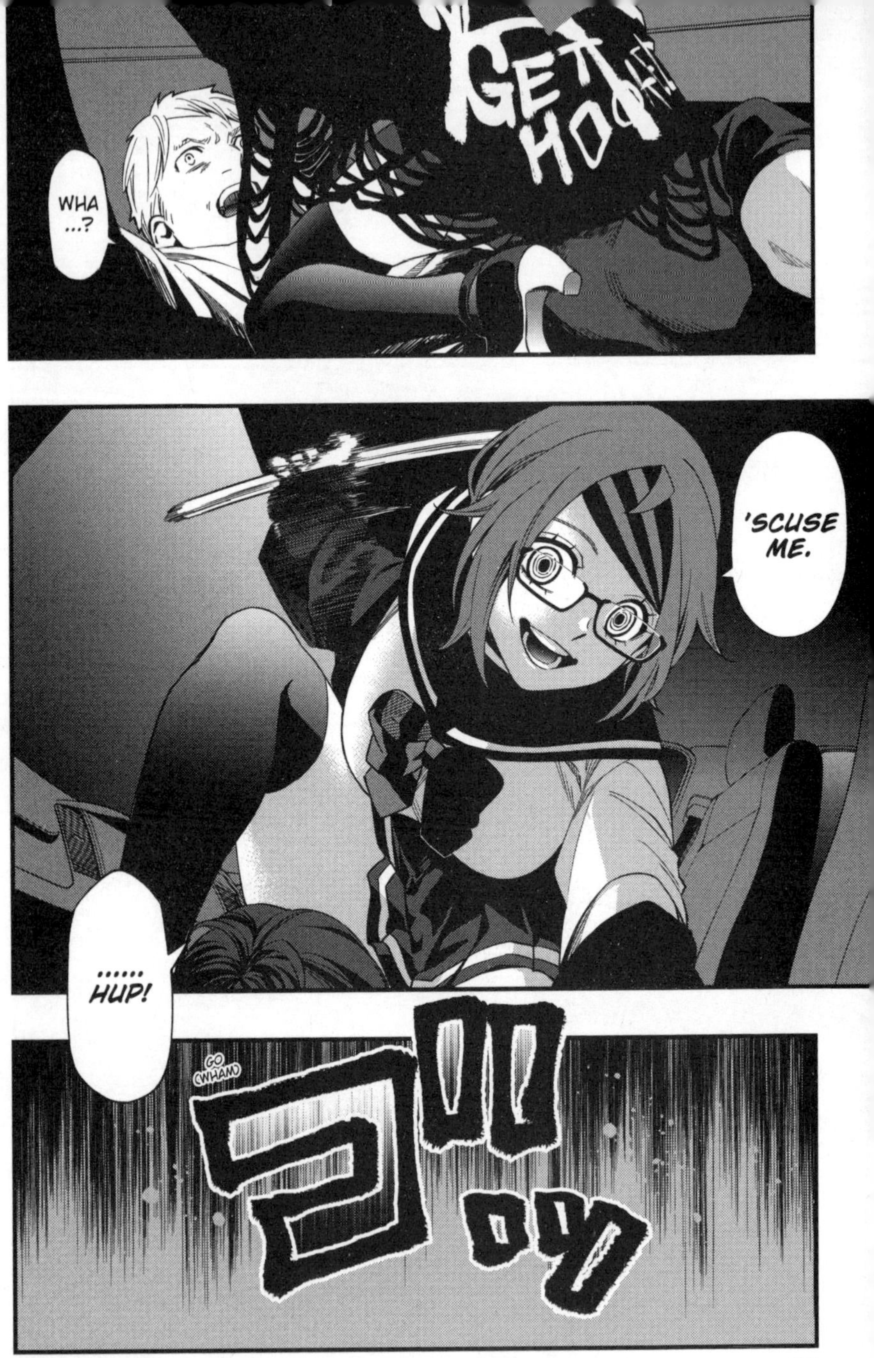
WHA ...?
'SCUSE ME.
...... HUP!
GO (WHAM)

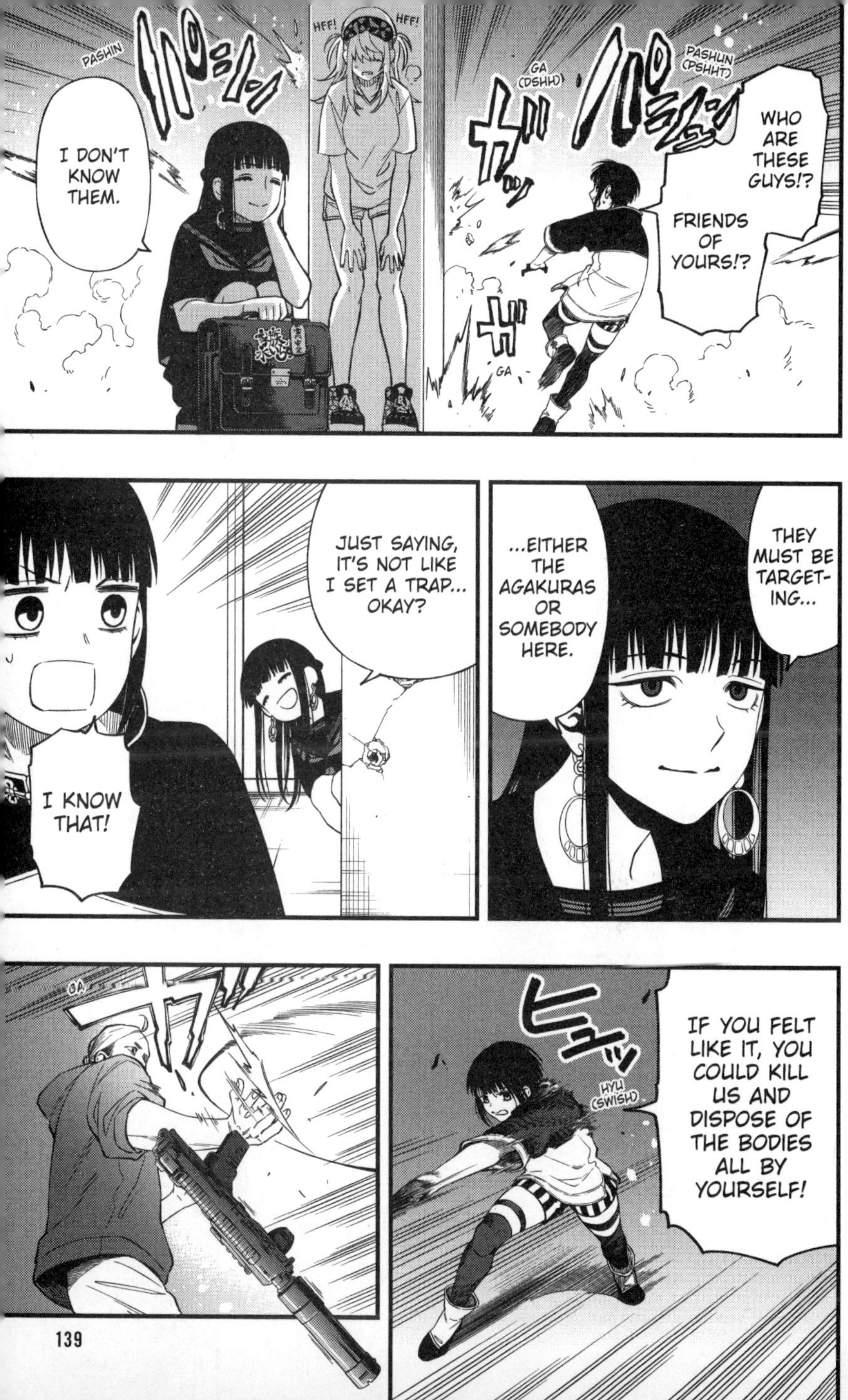
PASHUN (PSHHT)
GA (DSHH)
WHO ARE THESE GUYS!?
FRIENDS OF YOURS!?
GA
HFF! HFF!
PASHIN
I DON'T KNOW THEM.
THEY MUST BE TARGET-ING...
...EITHER THE AGAKURAS OR SOMEBODY HERE.
JUST SAYING, IT'S NOT LIKE I SET A TRAP... OKAY?
I KNOW THAT!
HYU (SWISH)
IF YOU FELT LIKE IT, YOU COULD KILL US AND DISPOSE OF THE BODIES ALL BY YOURSELF!
GA

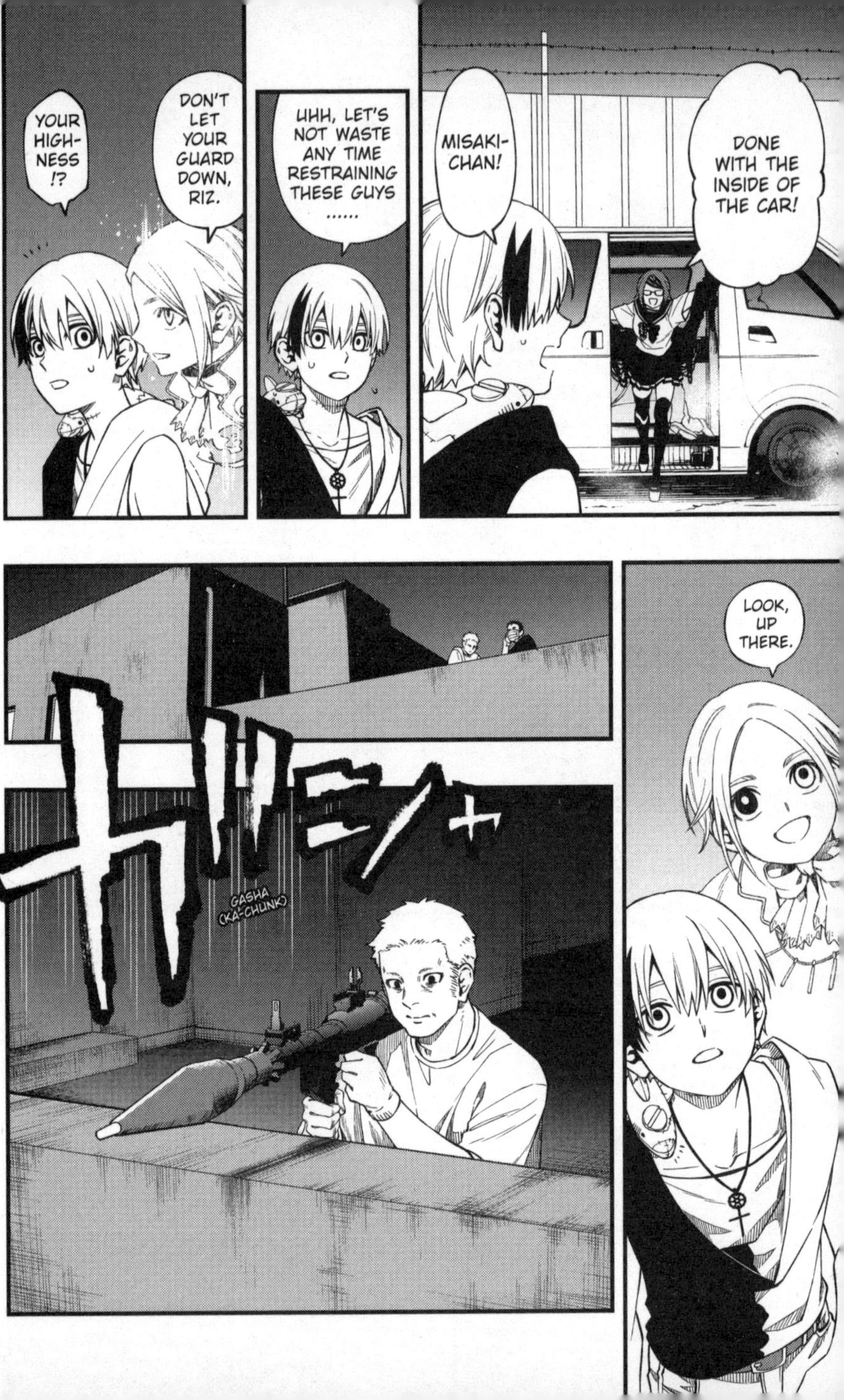
DONE WITH THE INSIDE OF THE CAR!
MISAKI-CHAN!
UHH, LET'S NOT WASTE ANY TIME RESTRAINING THESE GUYS ......
DON'T LET YOUR GUARD DOWN, RIZ.
YOUR HIGHNESS !?
LOOK, UP THERE.
GASHA (KA-CHUNK)

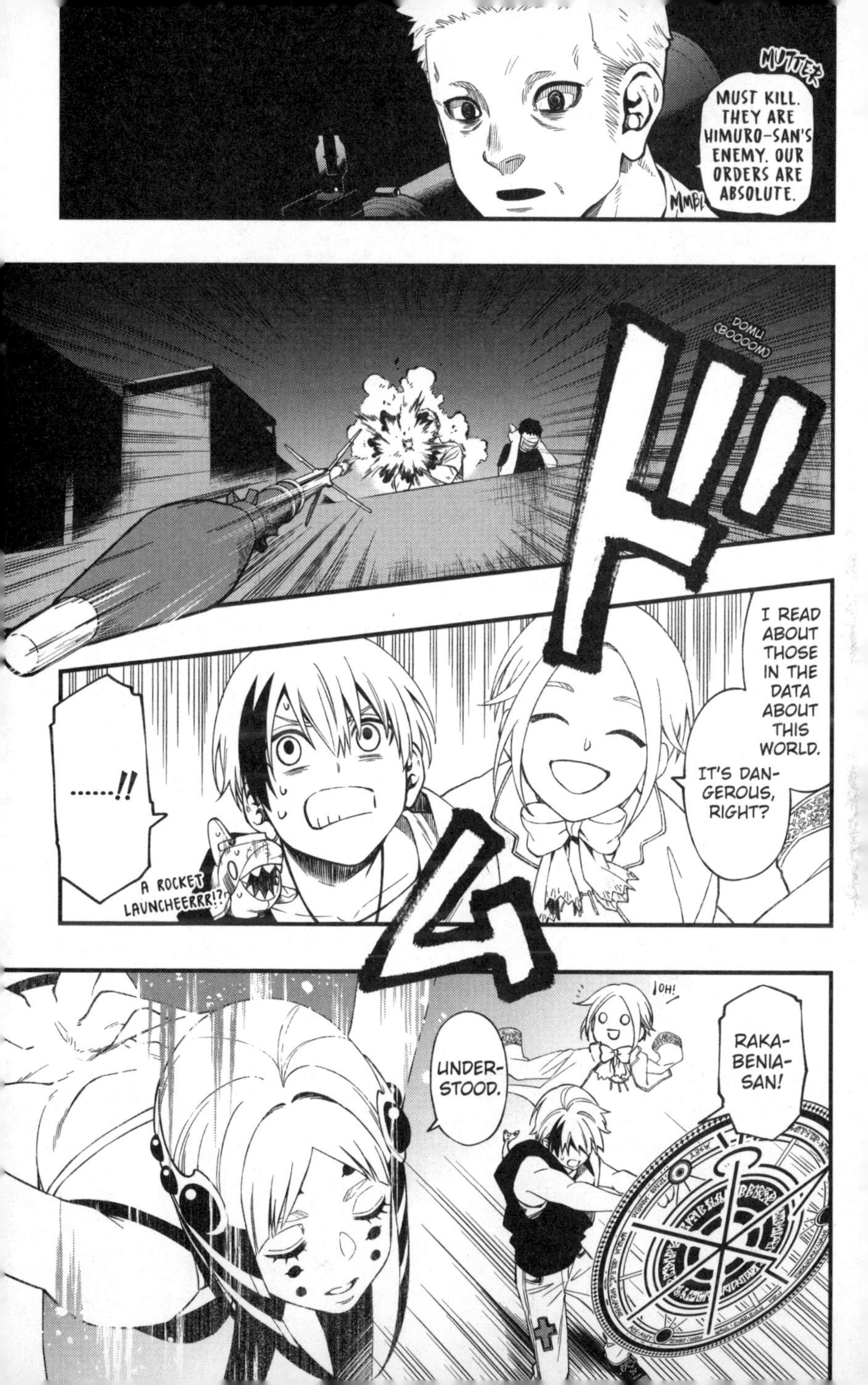
MUTTER
MUST KILL. THEY ARE HIMURO-SAN'S ENEMY. OUR ORDERS ARE ABSOLUTE.
MMBL
DOMU (BOOOOM)
I READ ABOUT THOSE IN THE DATA ABOUT THIS WORLD.
IT'S DANGEROUS, RIGHT?
......!!
A ROCKET LAUNCHEERRR!?
RAKA-BENIA-SAN!
OH!
UNDER-STOOD.

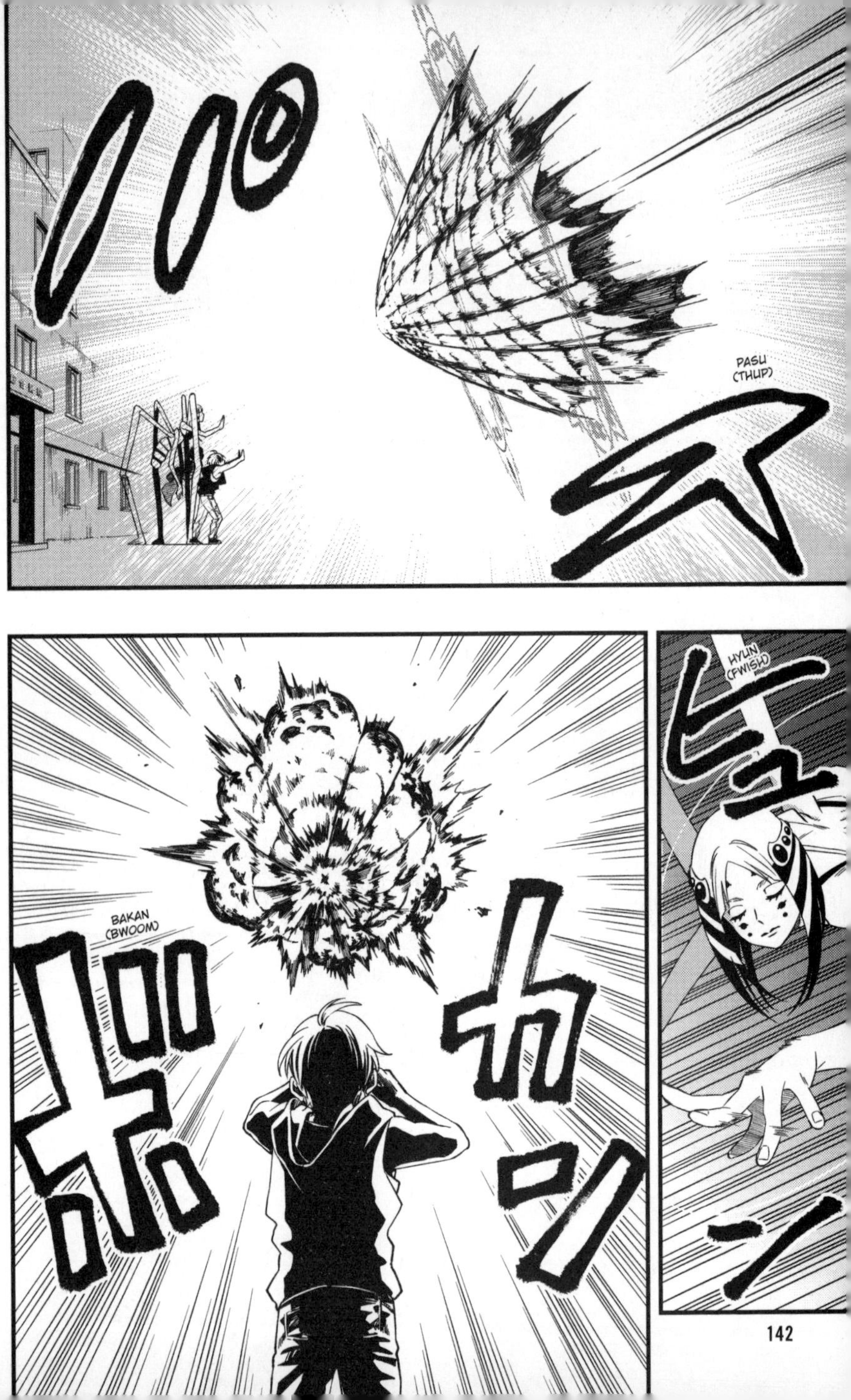
PASU
(THUP)
HYUN
(FWISH)
BAKAN
(BWOOM)

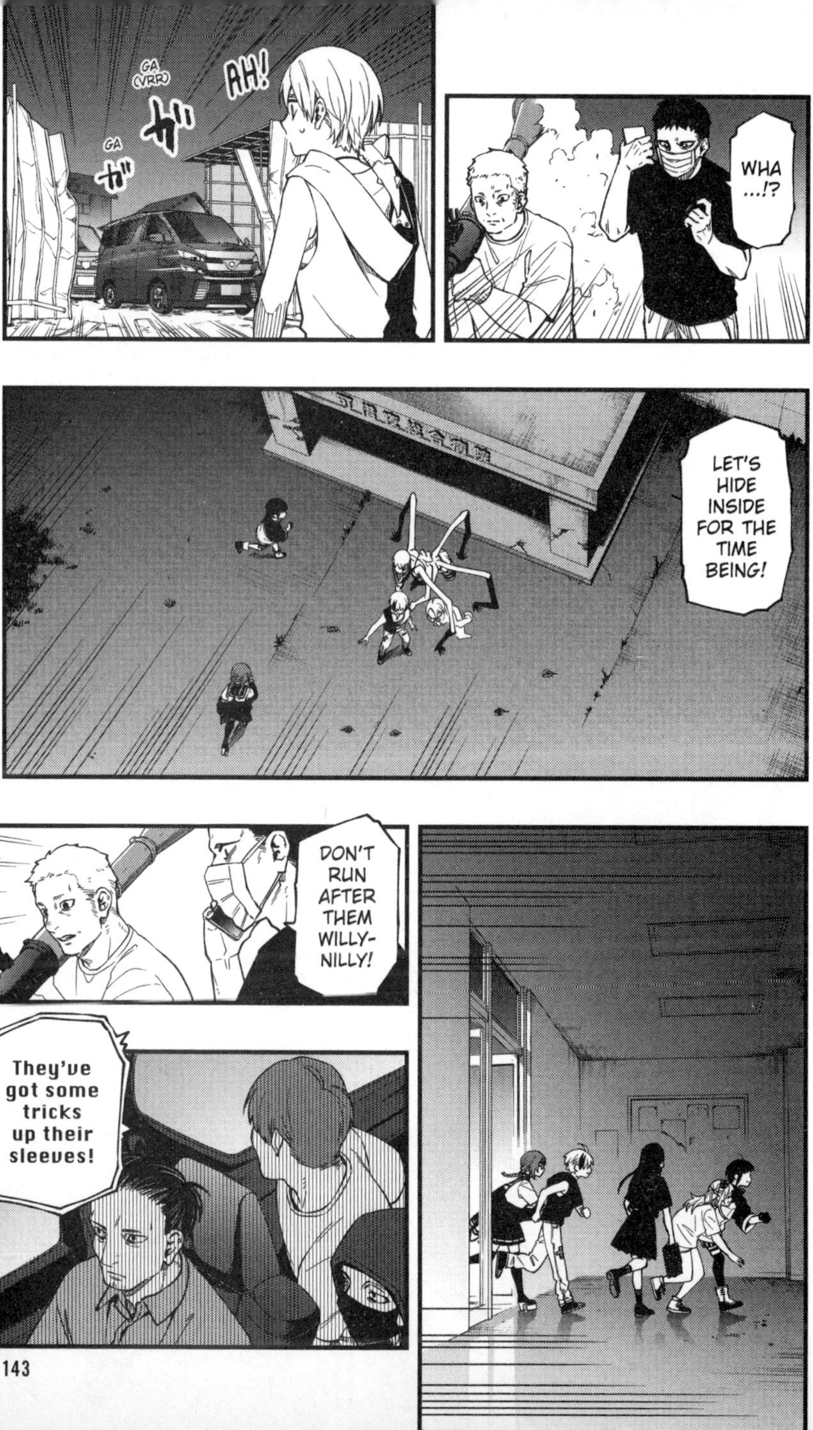
WHA ...!?
AH!
GA (VRR) ガ
GA ガ
LET'S HIDE INSIDE FOR THE TIME BEING!
DON'T RUN AFTER THEM WILLY-NILLY!
They've got some tricks up their sleeves!

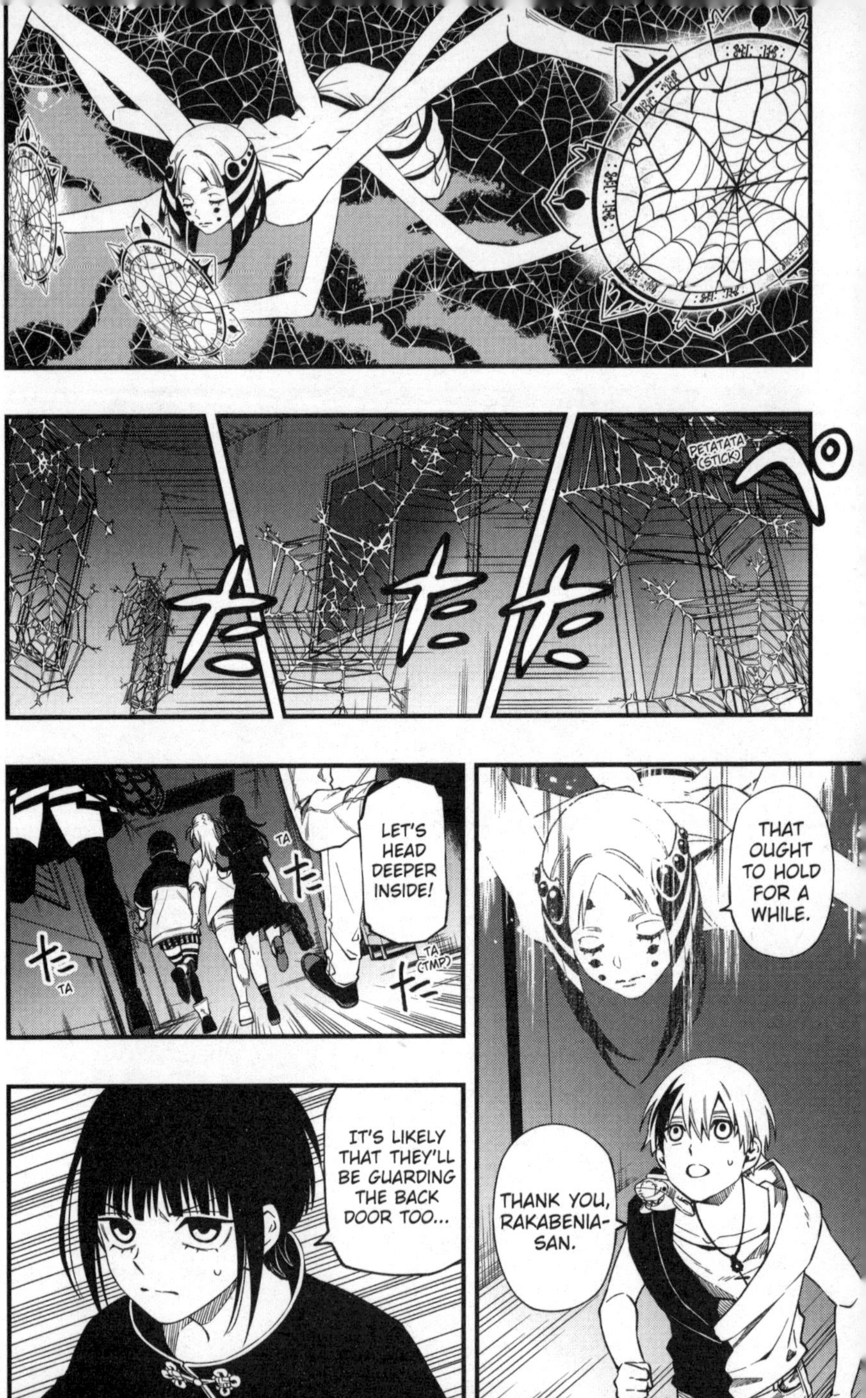
PETATATA (STICK)
THAT OUGHT TO HOLD FOR A WHILE.
THANK YOU, RAKABENIA-SAN.
LET'S HEAD DEEPER INSIDE!
TA
TA (TMP)
TA
IT'S LIKELY THAT THEY'LL BE GUARDING THE BACK DOOR TOO...

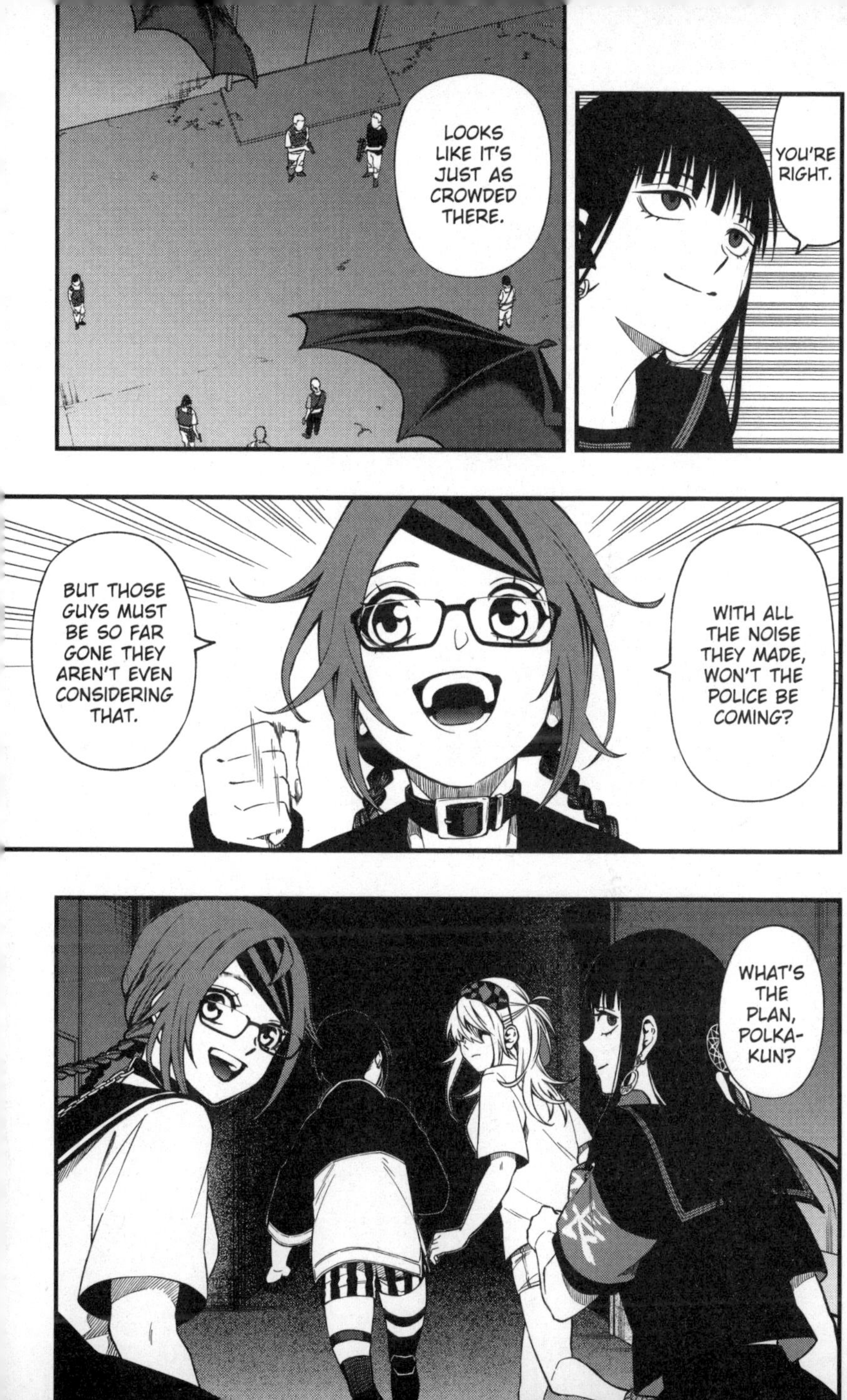
LOOKS LIKE IT'S JUST AS CROWDED THERE.
YOU'RE RIGHT.
WITH ALL THE NOISE THEY MADE, WON'T THE POLICE BE COMING?
BUT THOSE GUYS MUST BE SO FAR GONE THEY AREN'T EVEN CONSIDERING THAT.
WHAT'S THE PLAN, POLKA-KUN?

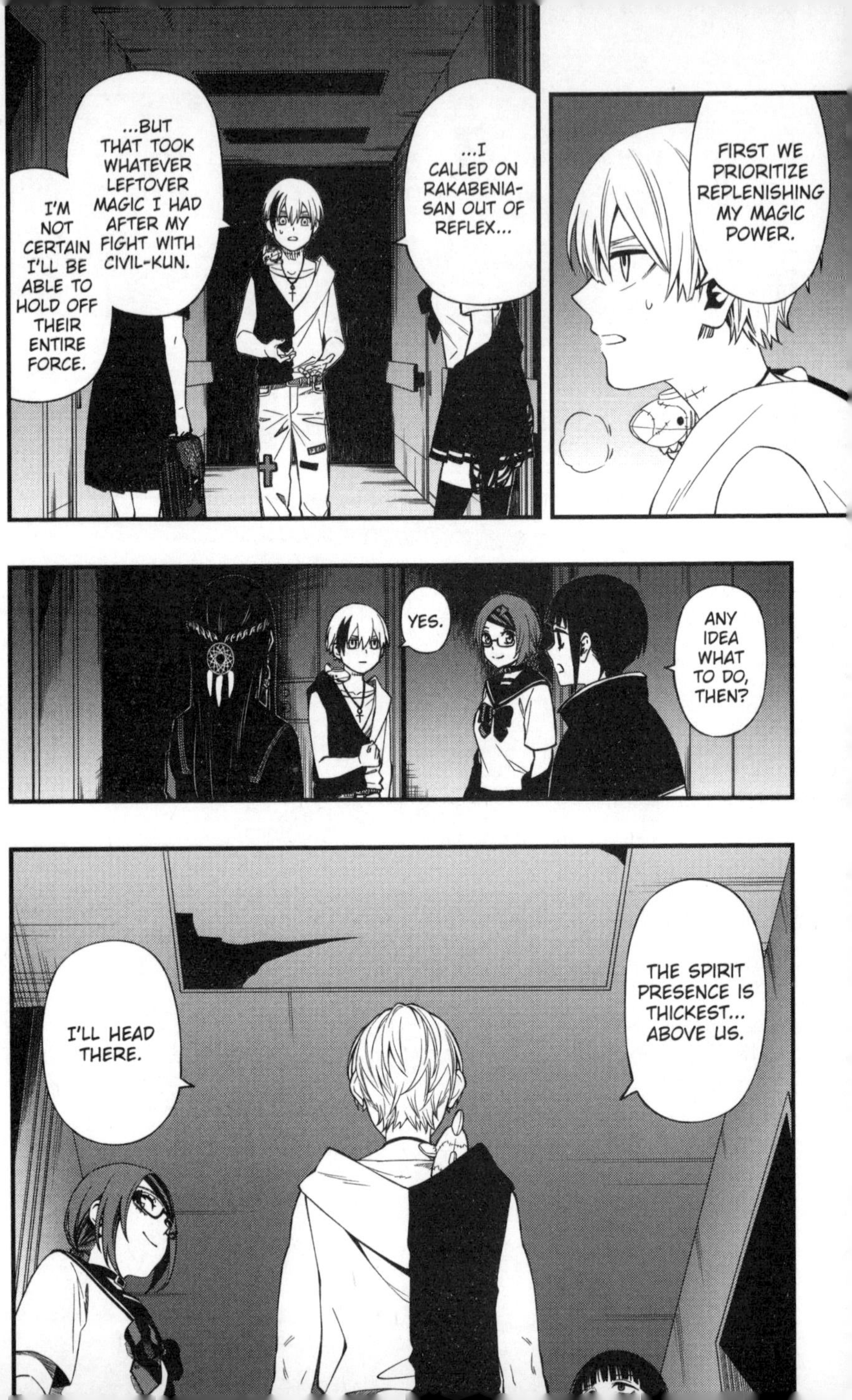
FIRST WE PRIORITIZE REPLENISHING MY MAGIC POWER.
...I CALLED ON RAKABENIA-SAN OUT OF REFLEX...
...BUT THAT TOOK WHATEVER LEFTOVER MAGIC I HAD AFTER MY FIGHT WITH CIVIL-KUN.
I'M NOT CERTAIN I'LL BE ABLE TO HOLD OFF THEIR ENTIRE FORCE.
ANY IDEA WHAT TO DO, THEN?
YES.
THE SPIRIT PRESENCE IS THICKEST... ABOVE US.
I'LL HEAD THERE.

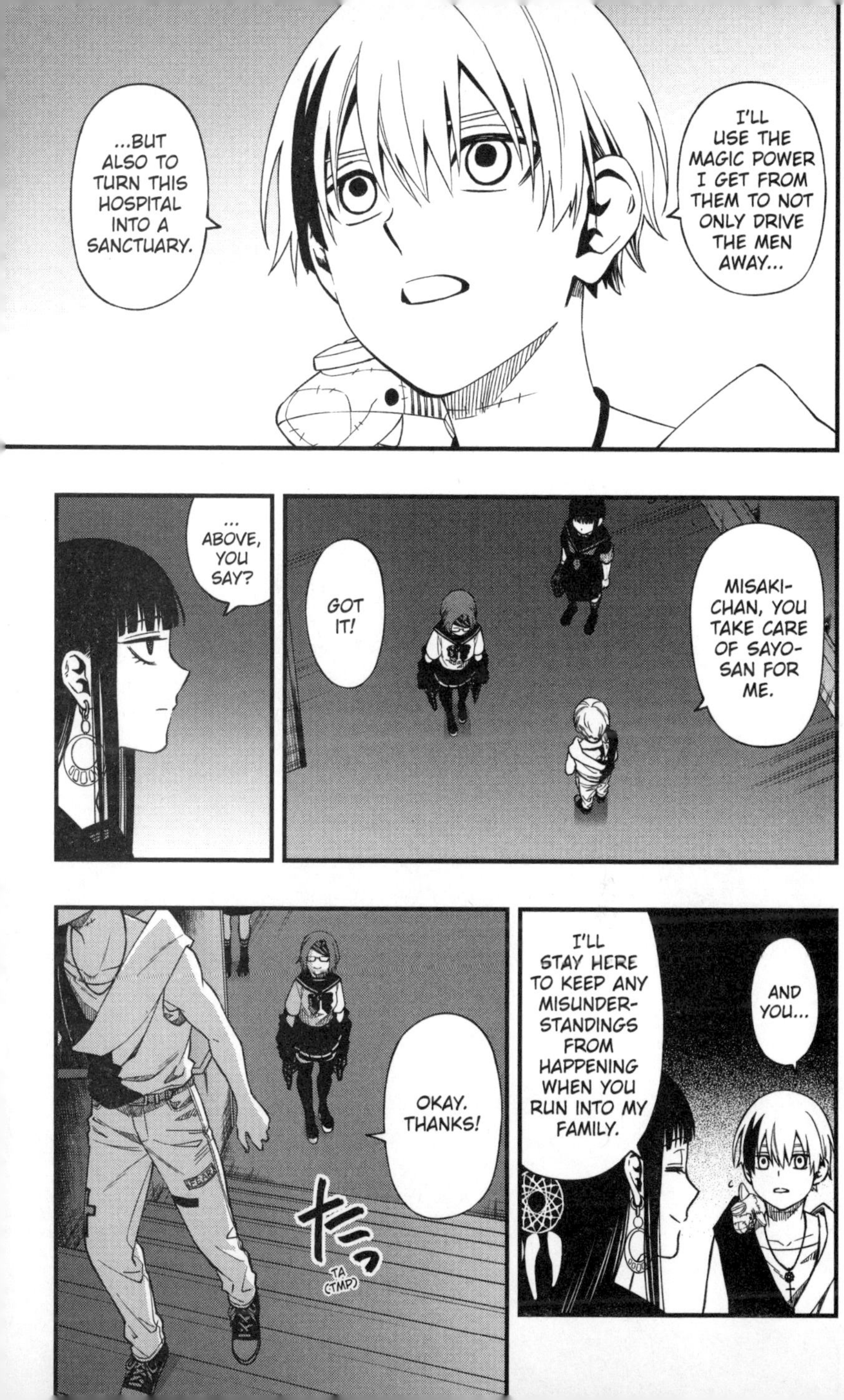
I'LL USE THE MAGIC POWER I GET FROM THEM TO NOT ONLY DRIVE THE MEN AWAY...
...BUT ALSO TO TURN THIS HOSPITAL INTO A SANCTUARY.
MISAKI-CHAN, YOU TAKE CARE OF SAYO-SAN FOR ME.
GOT IT!
... ABOVE, YOU SAY?
AND YOU...
I'LL STAY HERE TO KEEP ANY MISUNDER-STANDINGS FROM HAPPENING WHEN YOU RUN INTO MY FAMILY.
OKAY. THANKS!
TA (TMP)

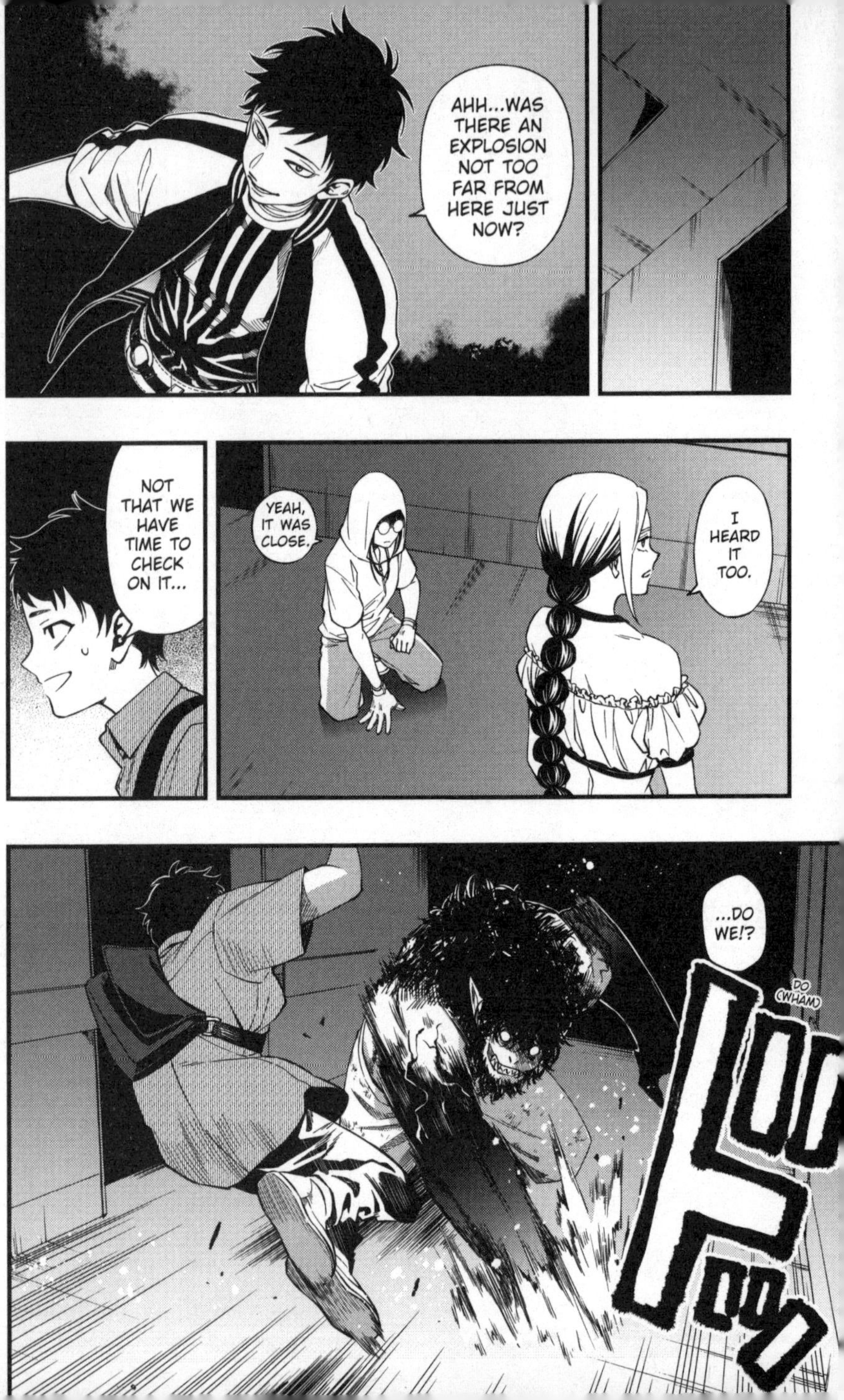
AHH...WAS THERE AN EXPLOSION NOT TOO FAR FROM HERE JUST NOW?
I HEARD IT TOO.
YEAH, IT WAS CLOSE.
NOT THAT WE HAVE TIME TO CHECK ON IT...
...DO WE!?
DO (WHAM)

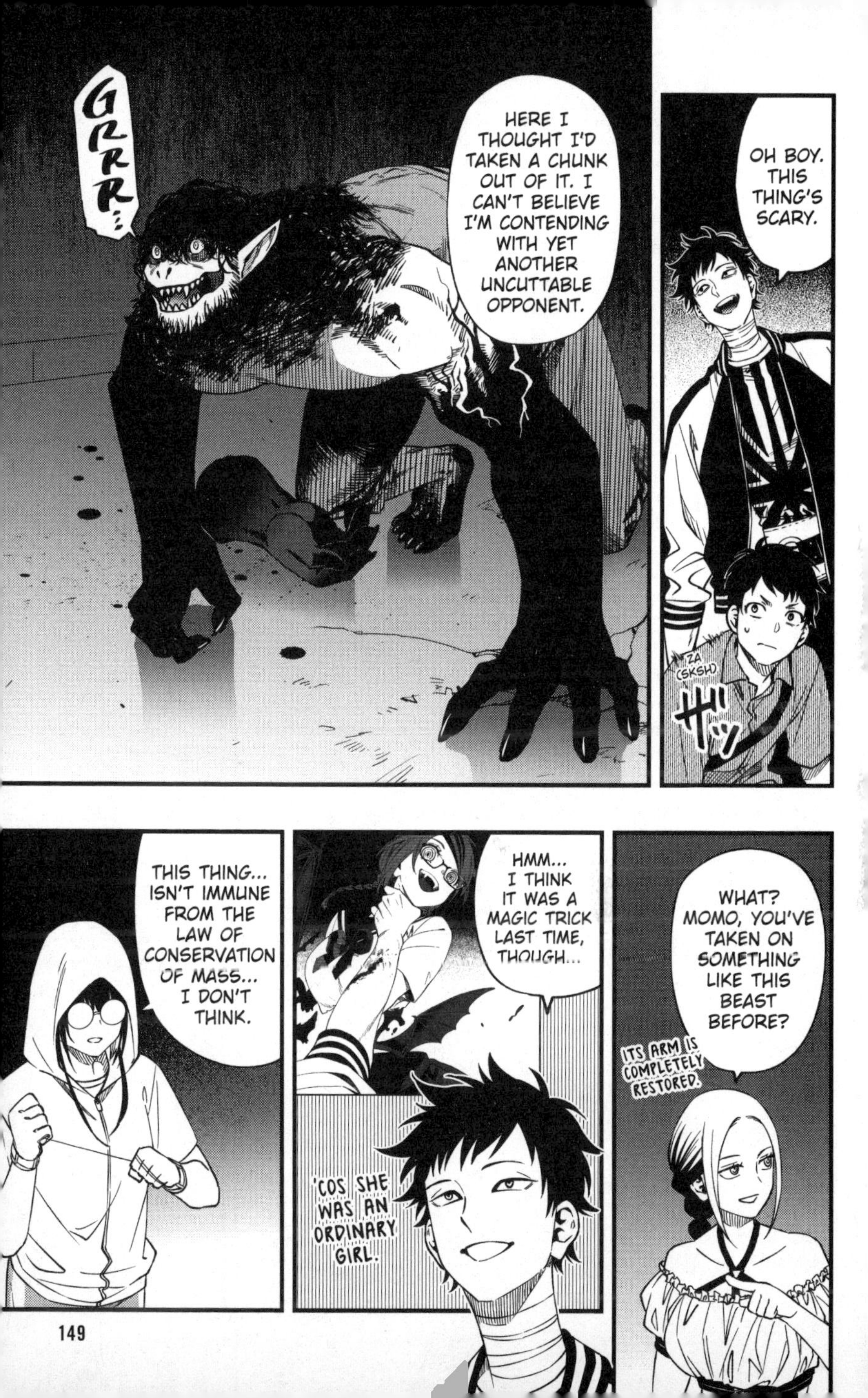
OH BOY. THIS THING'S SCARY.
ZA (SKSH)
GRRR...
HERE I THOUGHT I'D TAKEN A CHUNK OUT OF IT. I CAN'T BELIEVE I'M CONTENDING WITH YET ANOTHER UNCUTTABLE OPPONENT.
WHAT? MOMO, YOU'VE TAKEN ON SOMETHING LIKE THIS BEAST BEFORE?
ITS ARM IS COMPLETELY RESTORED.
HMM... I THINK IT WAS A MAGIC TRICK LAST TIME, THOUGH...
'COS SHE WAS AN ORDINARY GIRL.
THIS THING... ISN'T IMMUNE FROM THE LAW OF CONSERVATION OF MASS... I DON'T THINK.

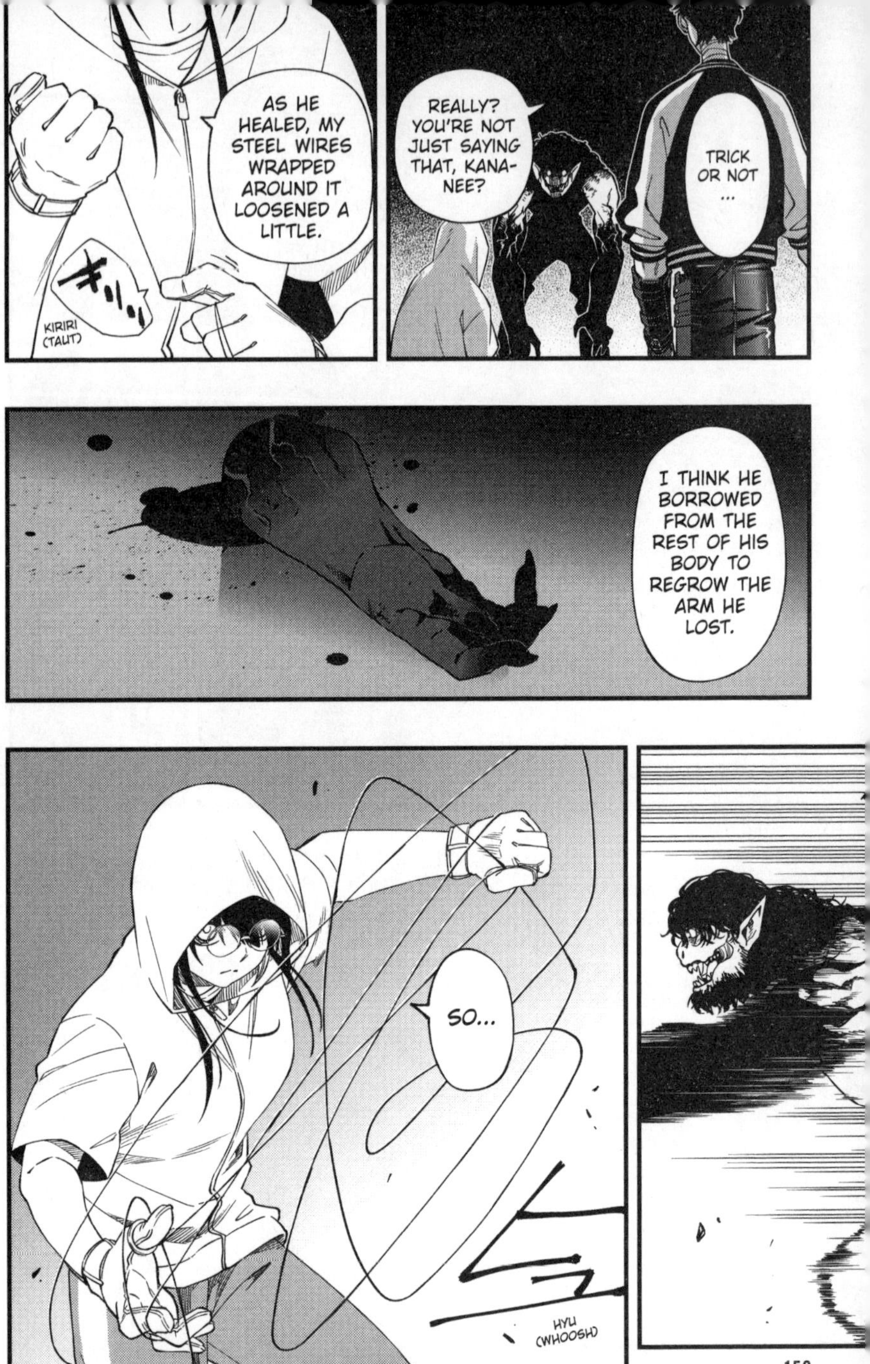
TRICK OR NOT ...
REALLY? YOU'RE NOT JUST SAYING THAT, KANA-NEE?
AS HE HEALED, MY STEEL WIRES WRAPPED AROUND IT LOOSENED A LITTLE.
KIRIRI (TAUT)
I THINK HE BORROWED FROM THE REST OF HIS BODY TO REGROW THE ARM HE LOST.
SO...
HYU (WHOOSH)

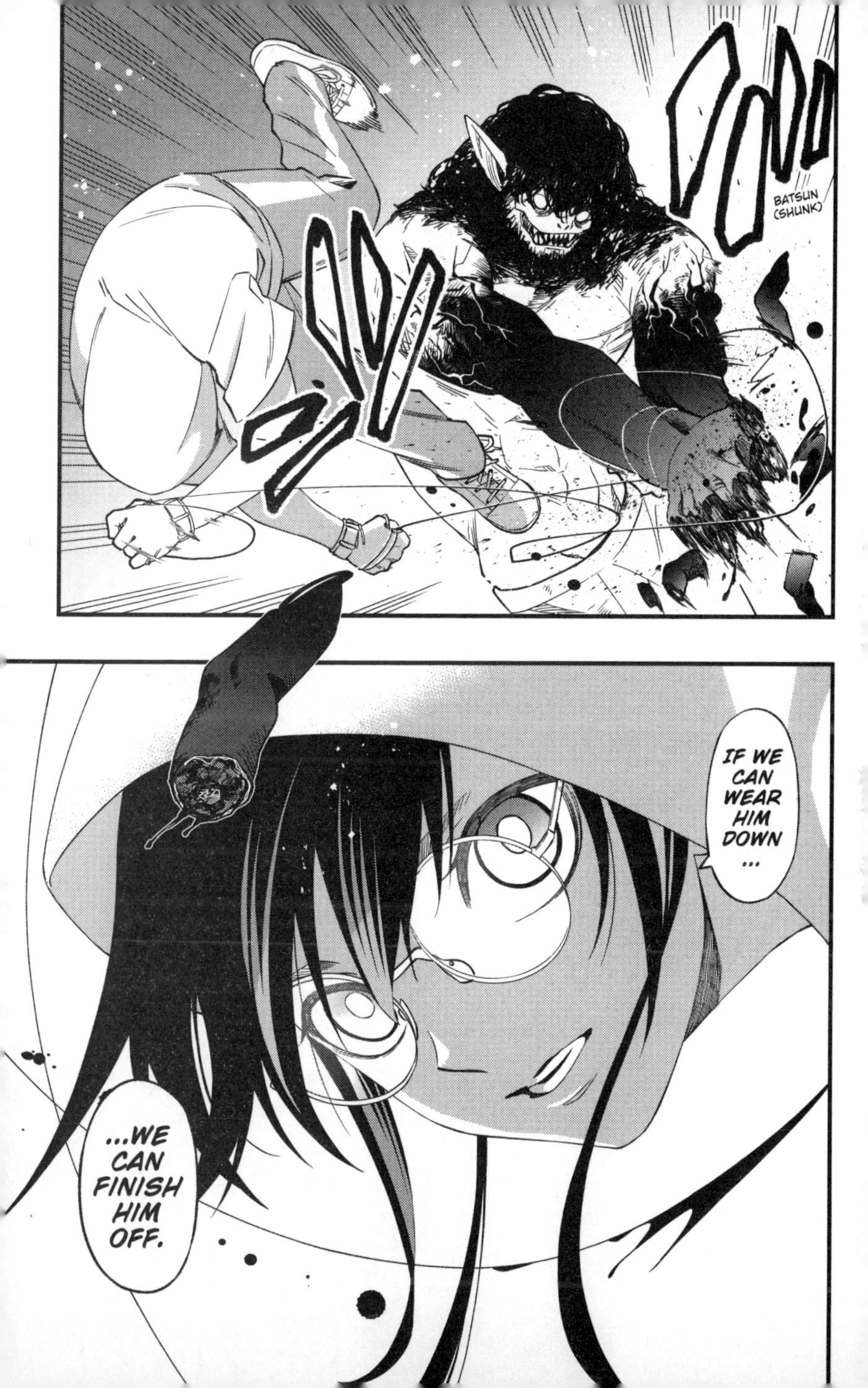
BATSUN (SHUNK)
IF WE CAN WEAR HIM DOWN...
...WE CAN FINISH HIM OFF.

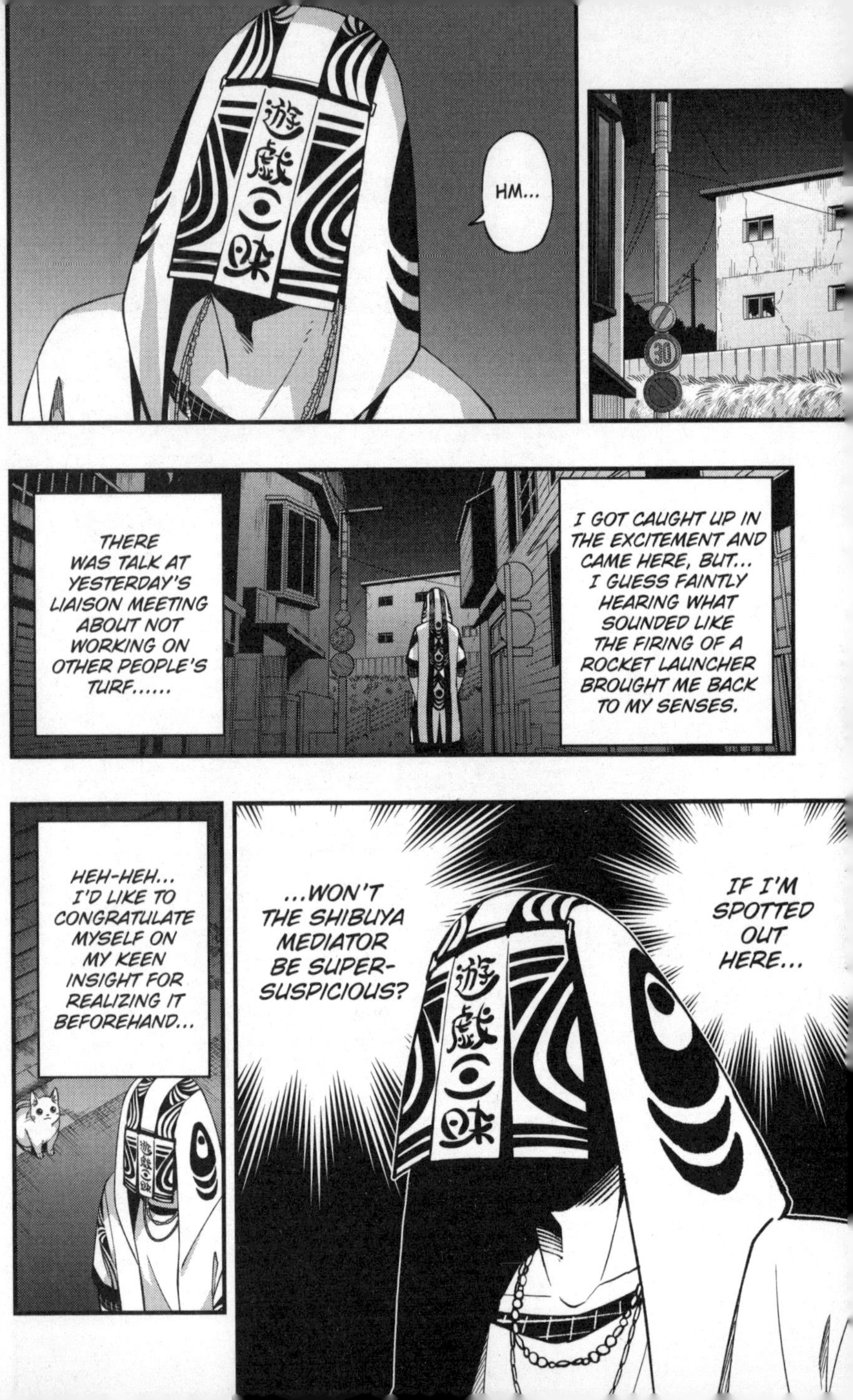
HM...
I GOT CAUGHT UP IN THE EXCITEMENT AND CAME HERE, BUT... I GUESS FAINTLY HEARING WHAT SOUNDED LIKE THE FIRING OF A ROCKET LAUNCHER BROUGHT ME BACK TO MY SENSES.
THERE WAS TALK AT YESTERDAY'S LIAISON MEETING ABOUT NOT WORKING ON OTHER PEOPLE'S TURF......
IF I'M SPOTTED OUT HERE...
...WON'T THE SHIBUYA MEDIATOR BE SUPER-SUSPICIOUS?
HEH-HEH... I'D LIKE TO CONGRATULATE MYSELF ON MY KEEN INSIGHT FOR REALIZING IT BEFOREHAND...

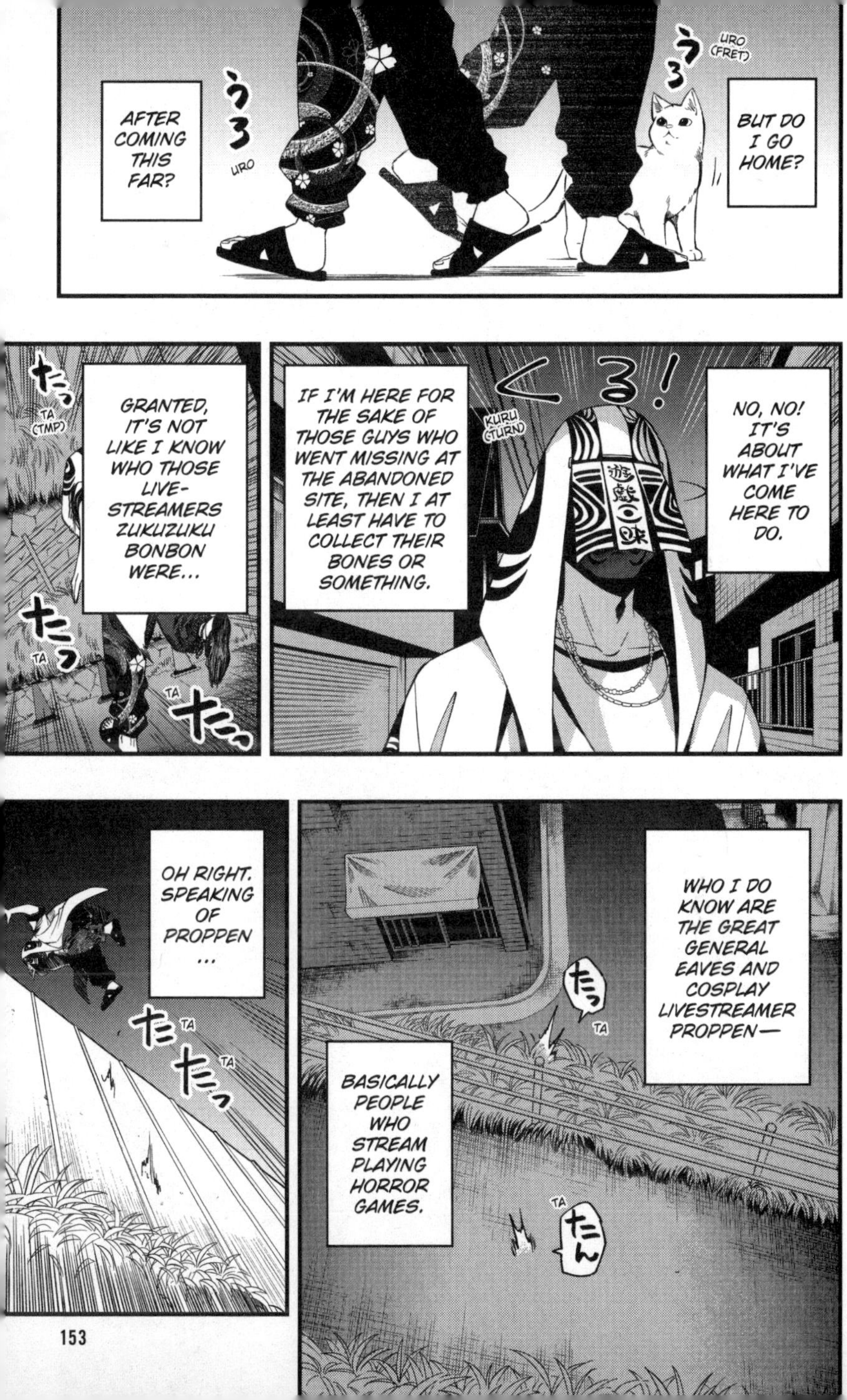
BUT DO I GO HOME?
うろ
URO (FRET)
うろ
URO
AFTER COMING THIS FAR?
NO, NO! IT'S ABOUT WHAT I'VE COME HERE TO DO.
くる!
KURU (TURN)
IF I'M HERE FOR THE SAKE OF THOSE GUYS WHO WENT MISSING AT THE ABANDONED SITE, THEN I AT LEAST HAVE TO COLLECT THEIR BONES OR SOMETHING.
GRANTED, IT'S NOT LIKE I KNOW WHO THOSE LIVE-STREAMERS ZUKUZUKU BONBON WERE...
たっ
TA (TMP)
たっ
TA
たっ
TA
WHO I DO KNOW ARE THE GREAT GENERAL EAVES AND COSPLAY LIVESTREAMER PROPPEN—
たっ
TA
BASICALLY PEOPLE WHO STREAM PLAYING HORROR GAMES.
たん
TA
OH RIGHT. SPEAKING OF PROPPEN...
たた
TA
たっ
TA

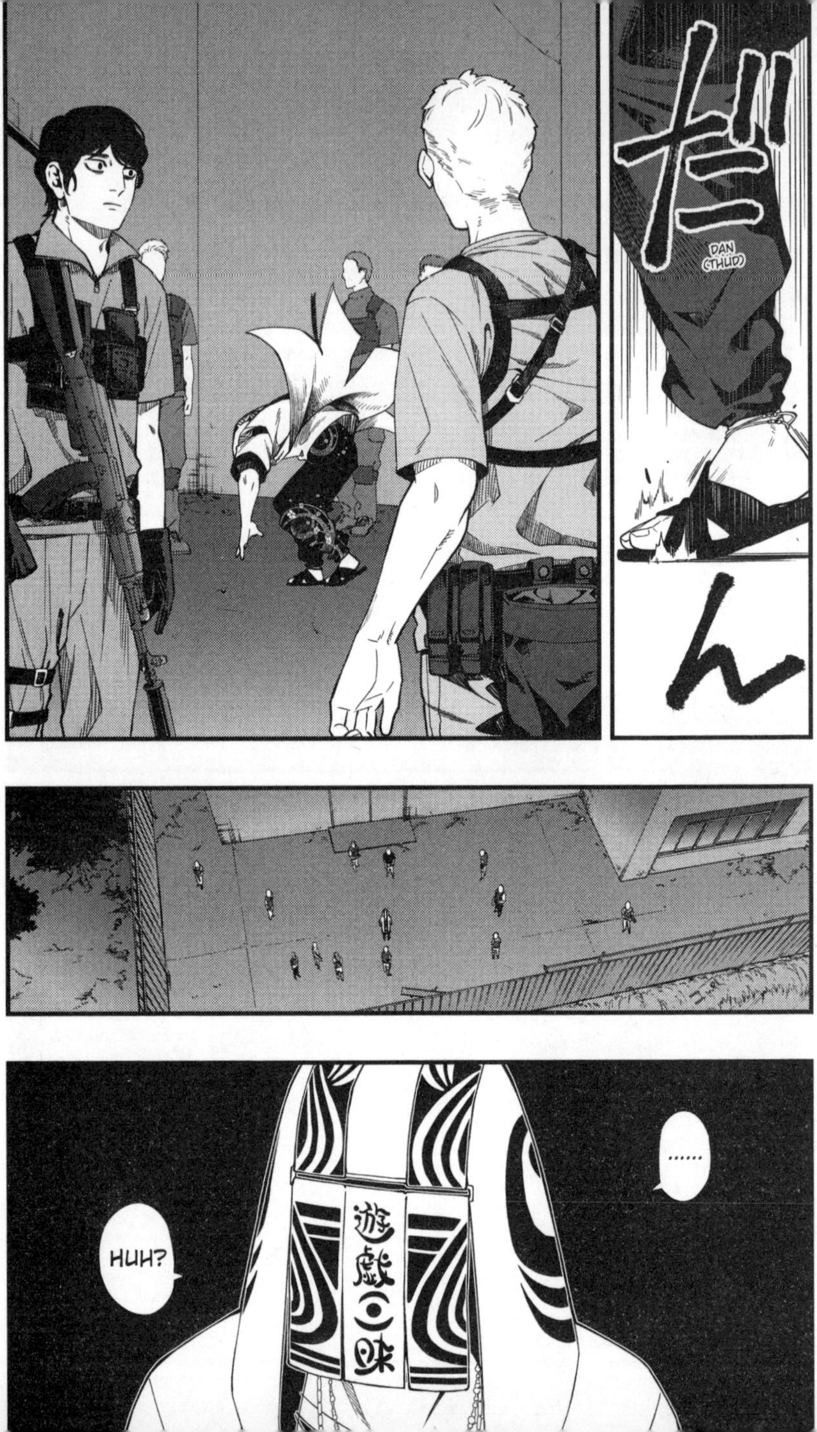

だん
DAN (THUD)
......
HUH?
遊戯三昧

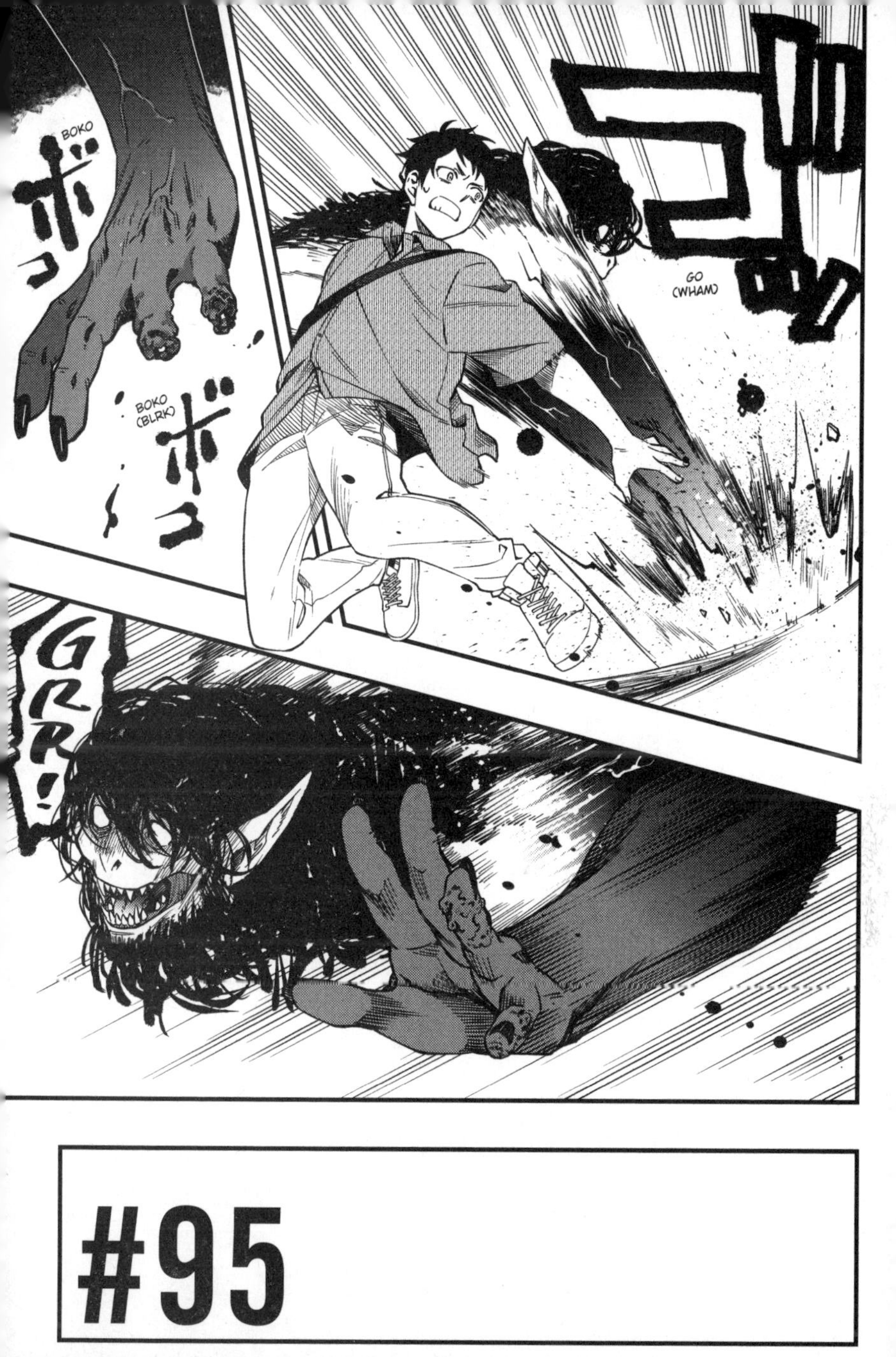
GO
(WHAM)
BOKO
BOKO
(BLRK)
GRR!

# #95

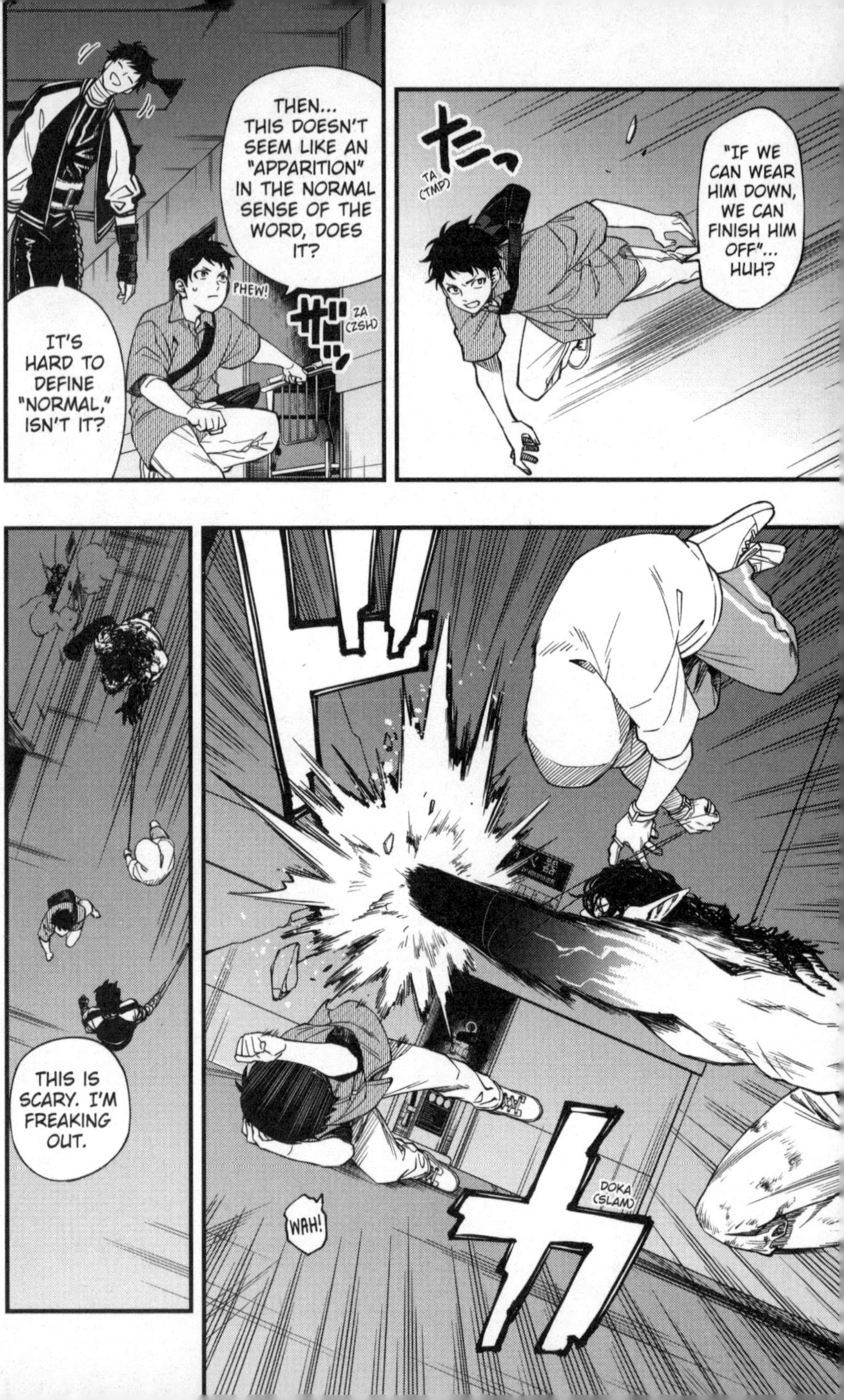
TA (TMP)
"IF WE CAN WEAR HIM DOWN, WE CAN FINISH HIM OFF"... HUH?
THEN... THIS DOESN'T SEEM LIKE AN "APPARITION" IN THE NORMAL SENSE OF THE WORD, DOES IT?
PHEW!
ZA (ZSH)
IT'S HARD TO DEFINE "NORMAL," ISN'T IT?
DOKA (SLAM)
WAH!
THIS IS SCARY. I'M FREAKING OUT.

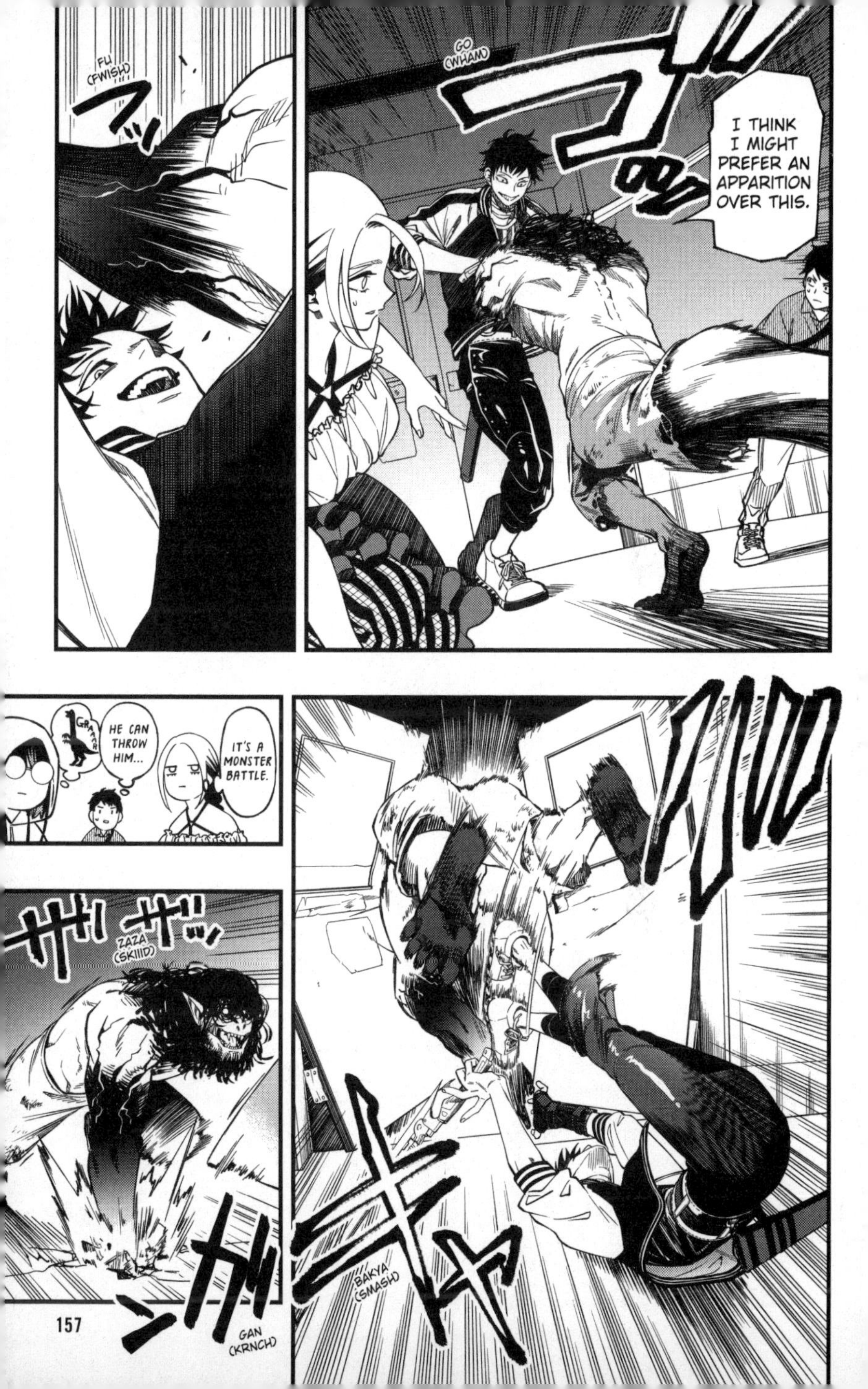
GO (WHAM)
I THINK I MIGHT PREFER AN APPARITION OVER THIS.
FU (FWISH)
IT'S A MONSTER BATTLE.
HE CAN THROW HIM...
GRATTA
ZAZA (SKIIID)
BAKYA (SMASH)
GAN (KRNCH)

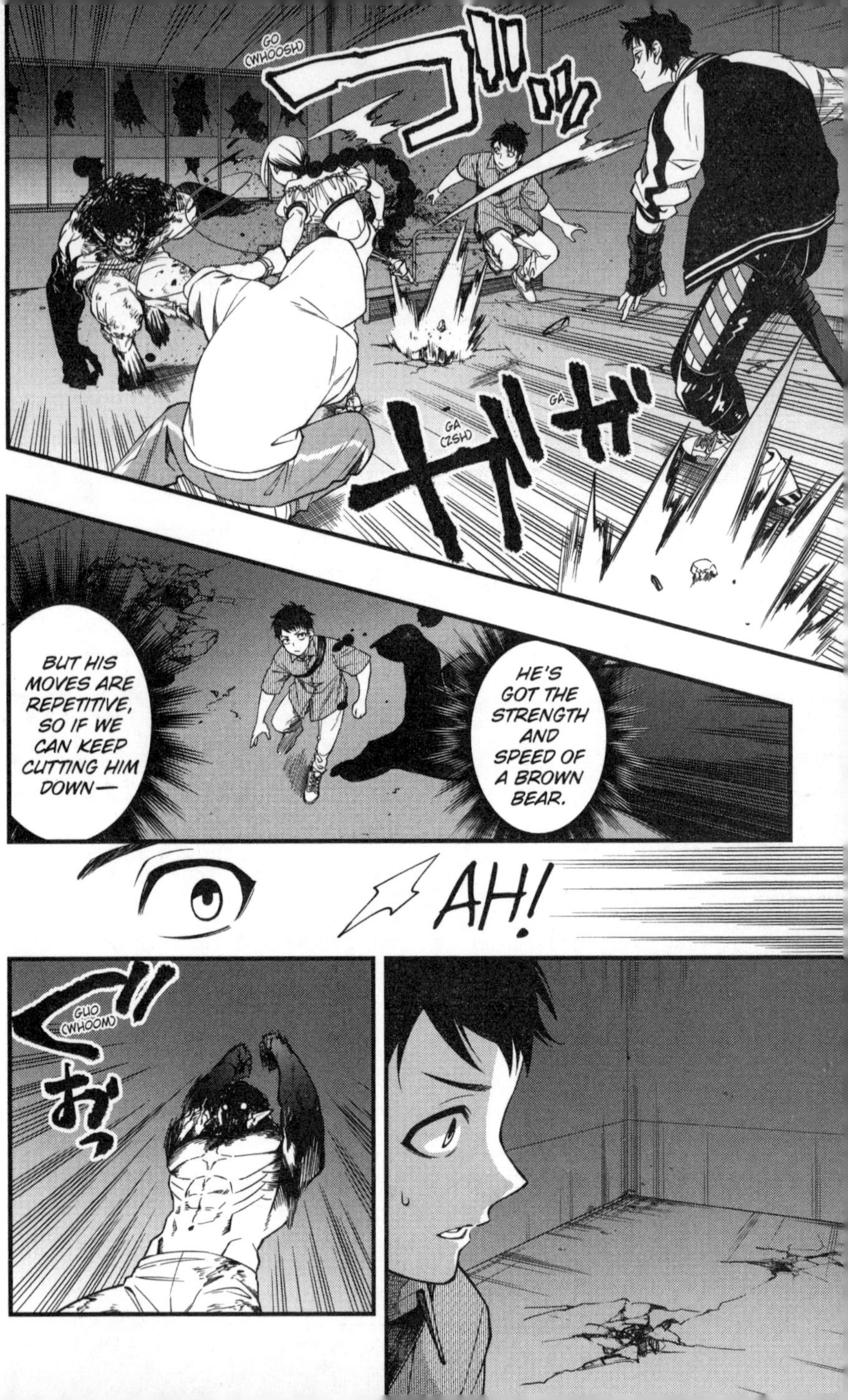
GO (WHOOSH)
GA
GA (ZSH)
HE'S GOT THE STRENGTH AND SPEED OF A BROWN BEAR.
BUT HIS MOVES ARE REPETITIVE, SO IF WE CAN KEEP CUTTING HIM DOWN—
AH!
GUO (WHOOM)

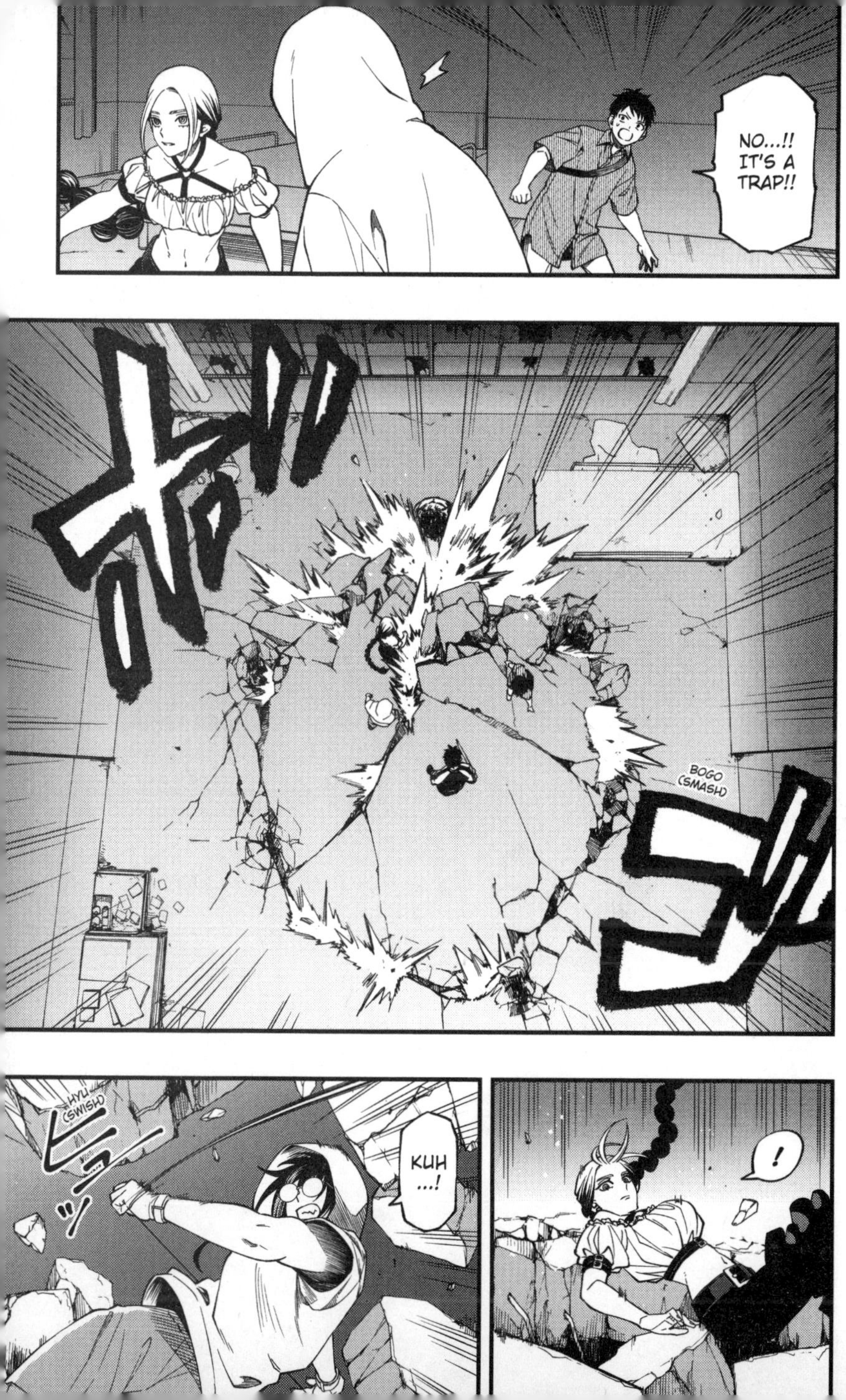
NO...!! IT'S A TRAP!!
BOGO (SMASH)
!
KUH ...!
HYU (SWISH)

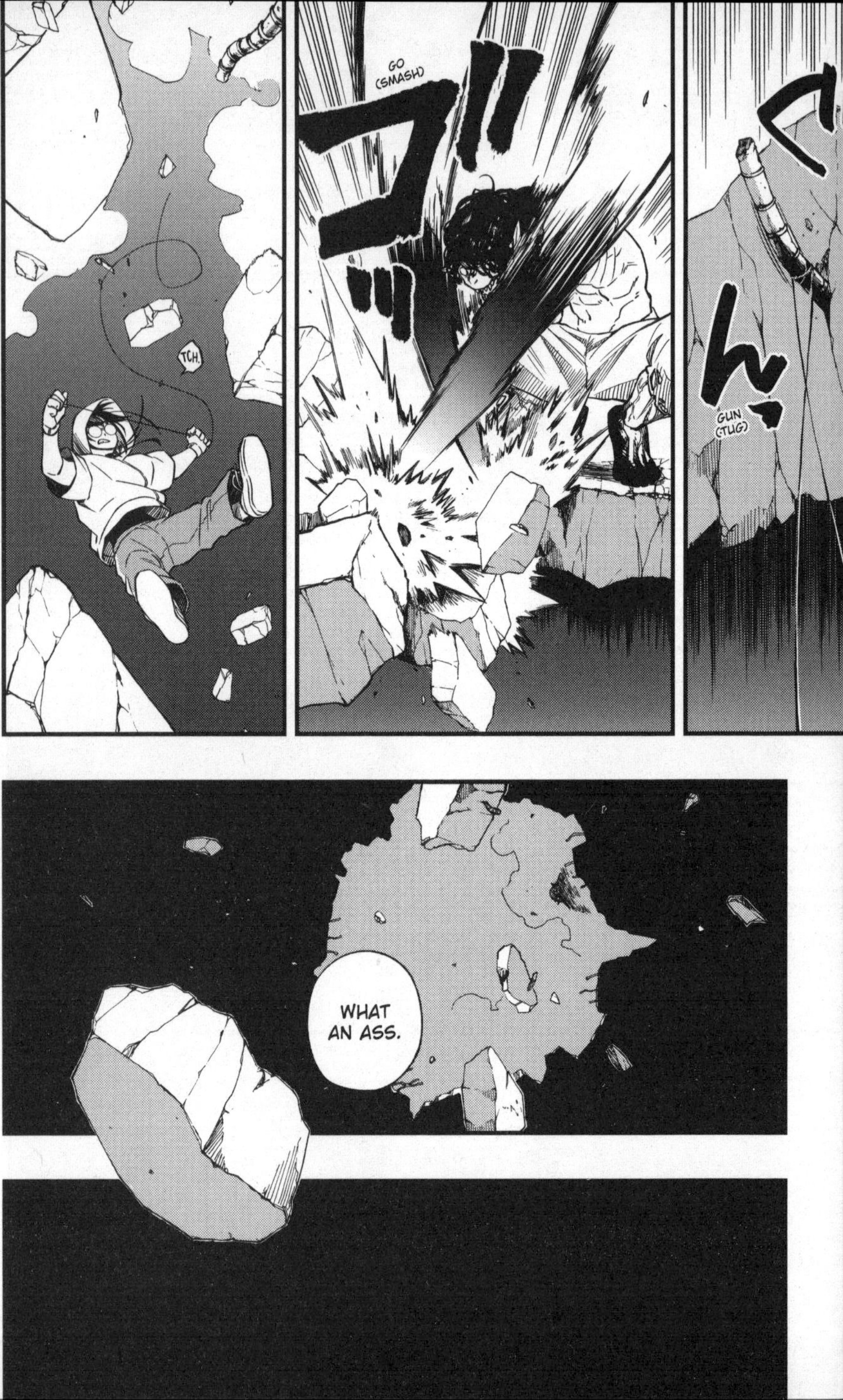
GUN (TUG)
GO (SMASH)
TCH.
WHAT AN ASS.

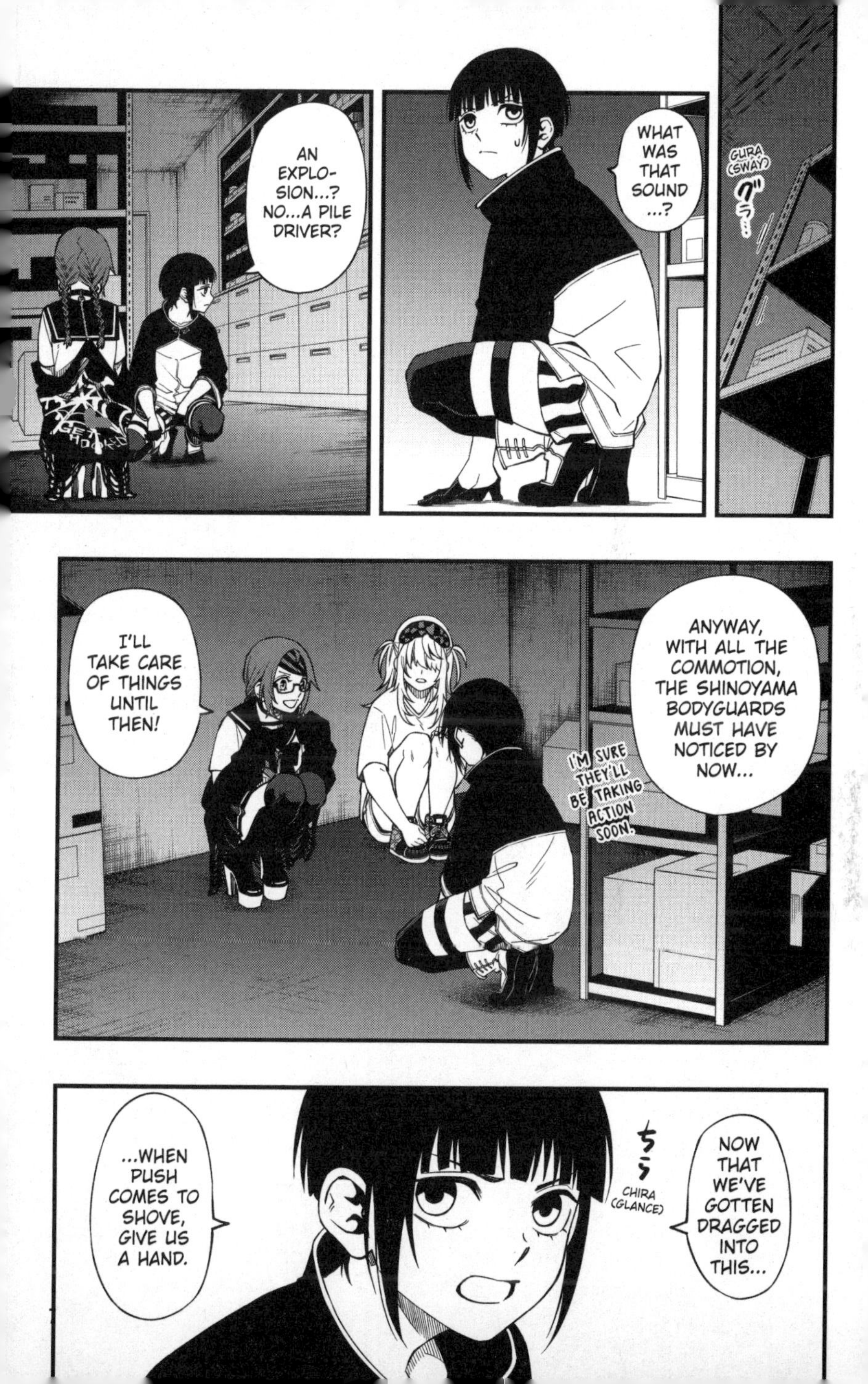
GURA (SWAY) グラ…
WHAT WAS THAT SOUND …?
AN EXPLOSION…? NO…A PILE DRIVER?
ANYWAY, WITH ALL THE COMMOTION, THE SHINOYAMA BODYGUARDS MUST HAVE NOTICED BY NOW…
I'M SURE THEY'LL BE TAKING ACTION SOON.
I'LL TAKE CARE OF THINGS UNTIL THEN!
NOW THAT WE'VE GOTTEN DRAGGED INTO THIS…
ちら CHIRA (GLANCE)
…WHEN PUSH COMES TO SHOVE, GIVE US A HAND.

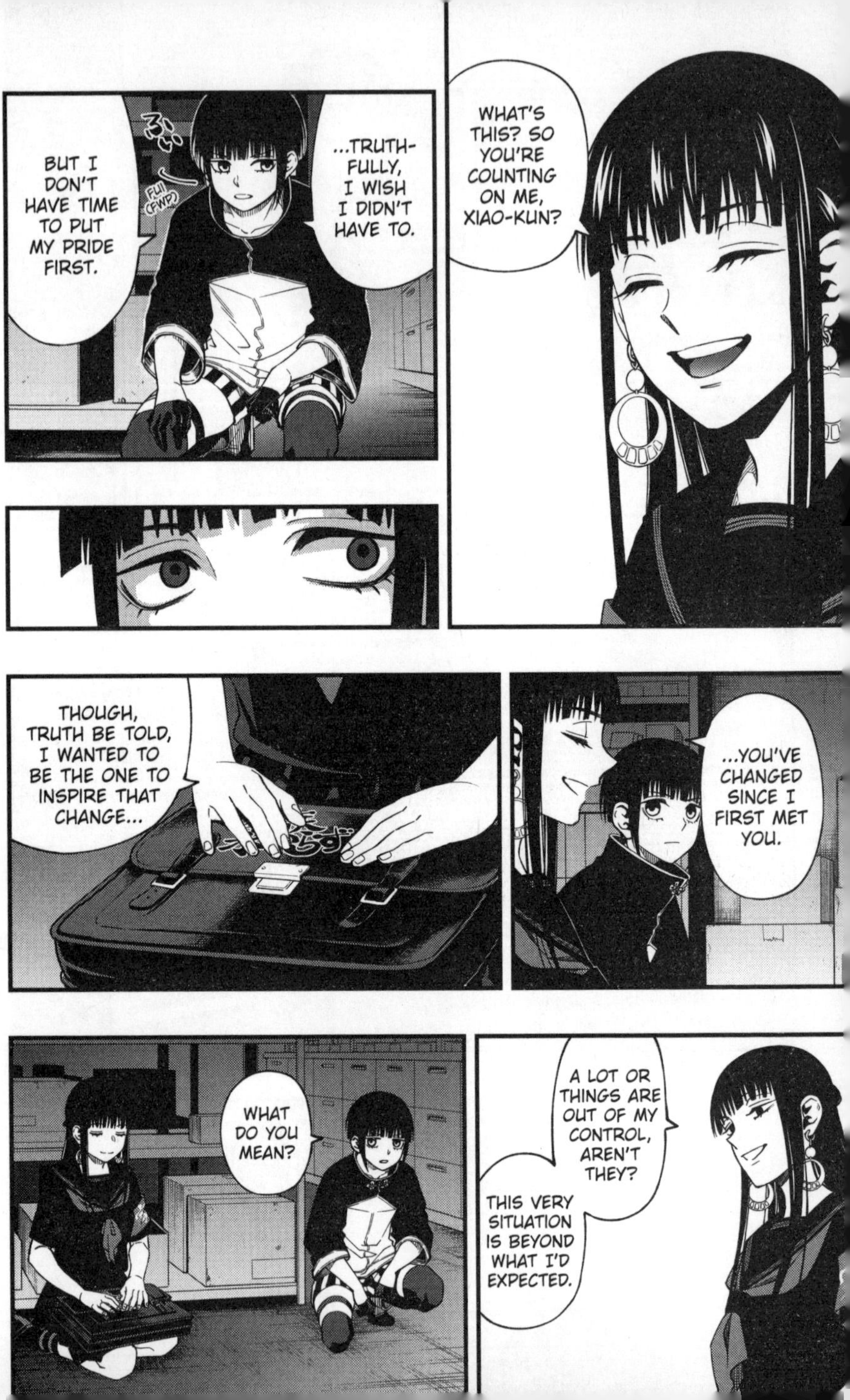
WHAT'S THIS? SO YOU'RE COUNTING ON ME, XIAO-KUN?
...TRUTH-FULLY, I WISH I DIDN'T HAVE TO.
FUI (FWP)
BUT I DON'T HAVE TIME TO PUT MY PRIDE FIRST.
...YOU'VE CHANGED SINCE I FIRST MET YOU.
THOUGH, TRUTH BE TOLD, I WANTED TO BE THE ONE TO INSPIRE THAT CHANGE...
A LOT OR THINGS ARE OUT OF MY CONTROL, AREN'T THEY?
THIS VERY SITUATION IS BEYOND WHAT I'D EXPECTED.
WHAT DO YOU MEAN?

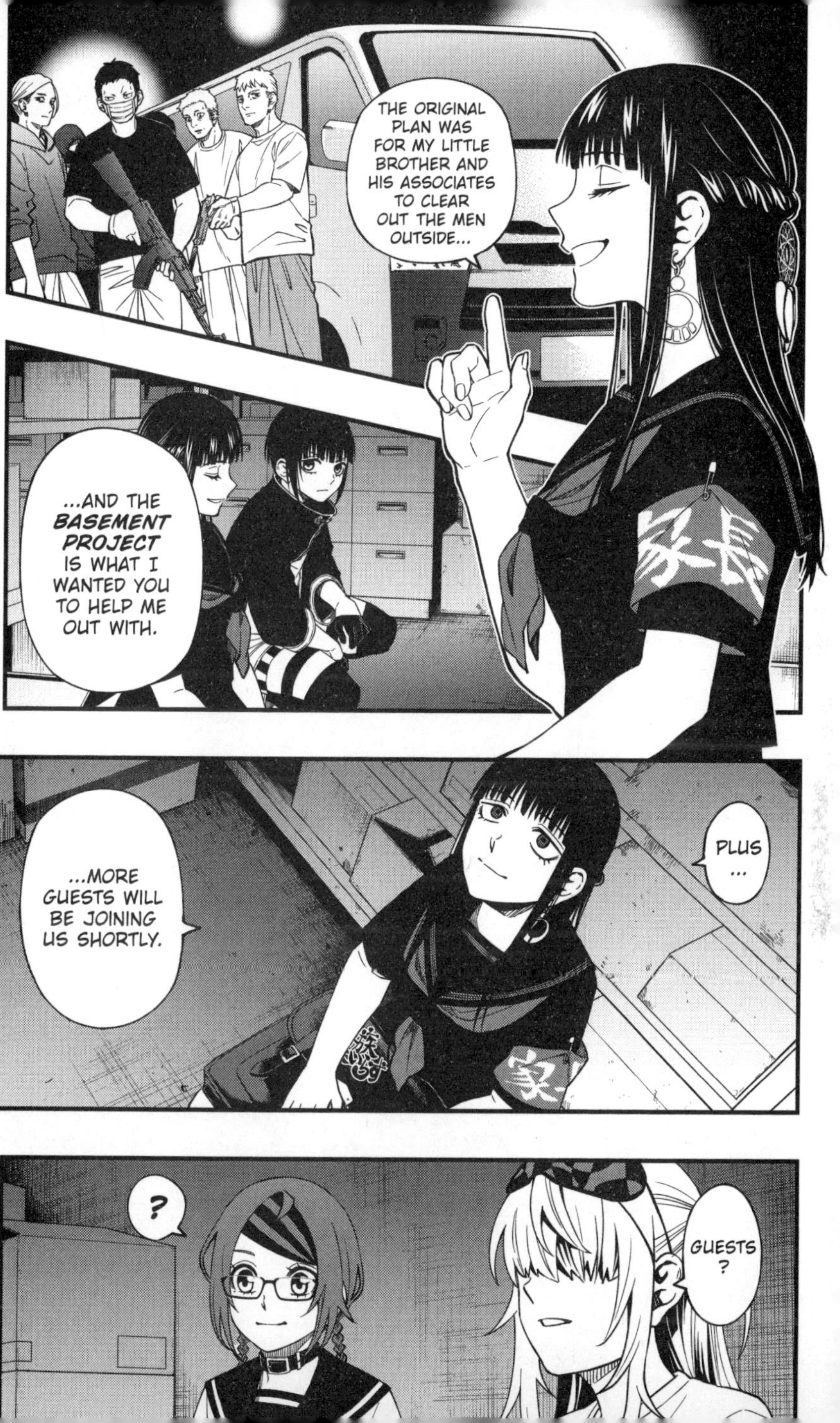
THE ORIGINAL PLAN WAS FOR MY LITTLE BROTHER AND HIS ASSOCIATES TO CLEAR OUT THE MEN OUTSIDE...
...AND THE *BASEMENT PROJECT* IS WHAT I WANTED YOU TO HELP ME OUT WITH.
PLUS ...
...MORE GUESTS WILL BE JOINING US SHORTLY.
GUESTS ?
?

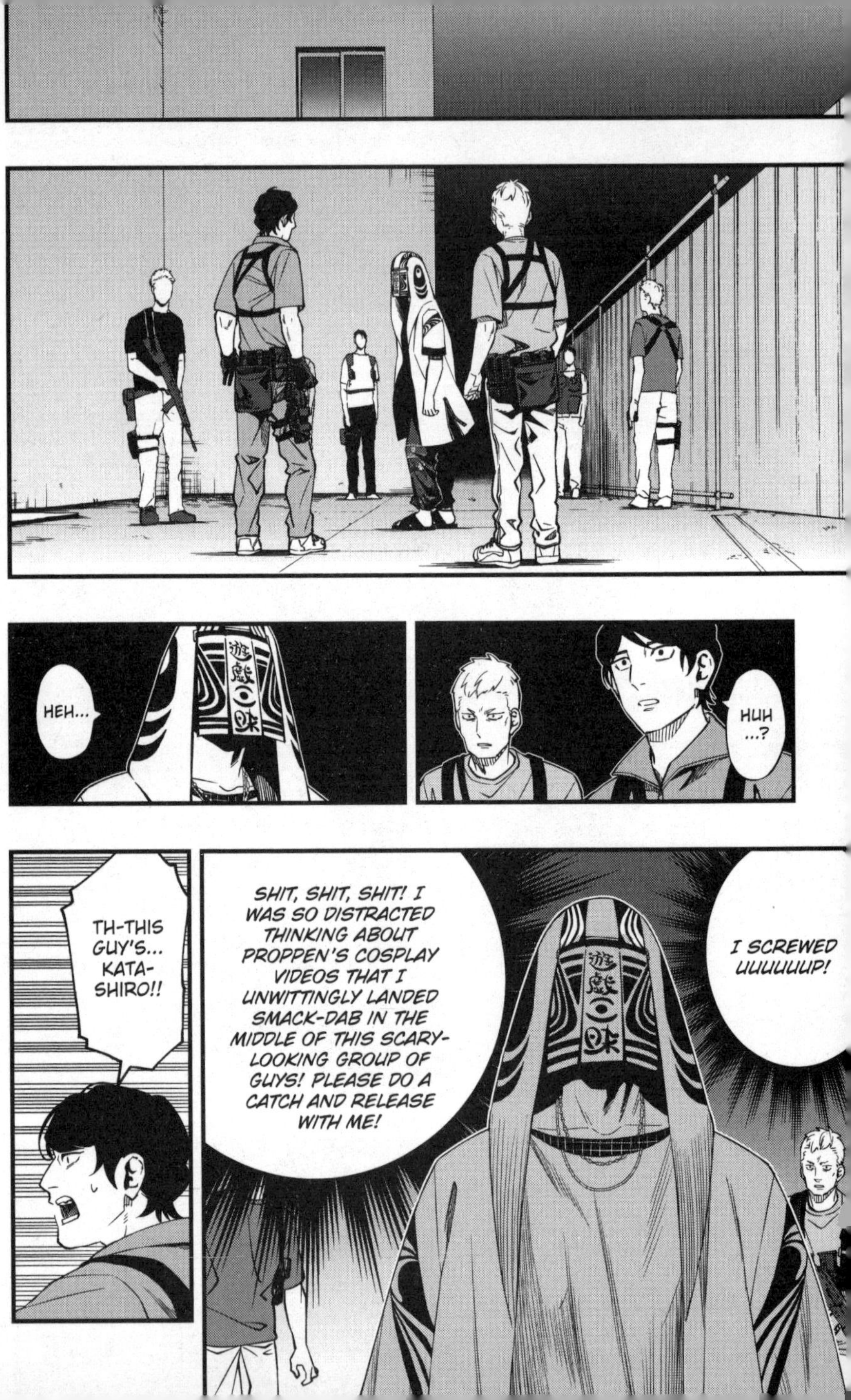
HUH ...?
HEH...
I SCREWED UUUUUUP!
SHIT, SHIT, SHIT! I WAS SO DISTRACTED THINKING ABOUT PROPPEN'S COSPLAY VIDEOS THAT I UNWITTINGLY LANDED SMACK-DAB IN THE MIDDLE OF THIS SCARY-LOOKING GROUP OF GUYS! PLEASE DO A CATCH AND RELEASE WITH ME!
TH-THIS GUY'S... KATA-SHIRO!!

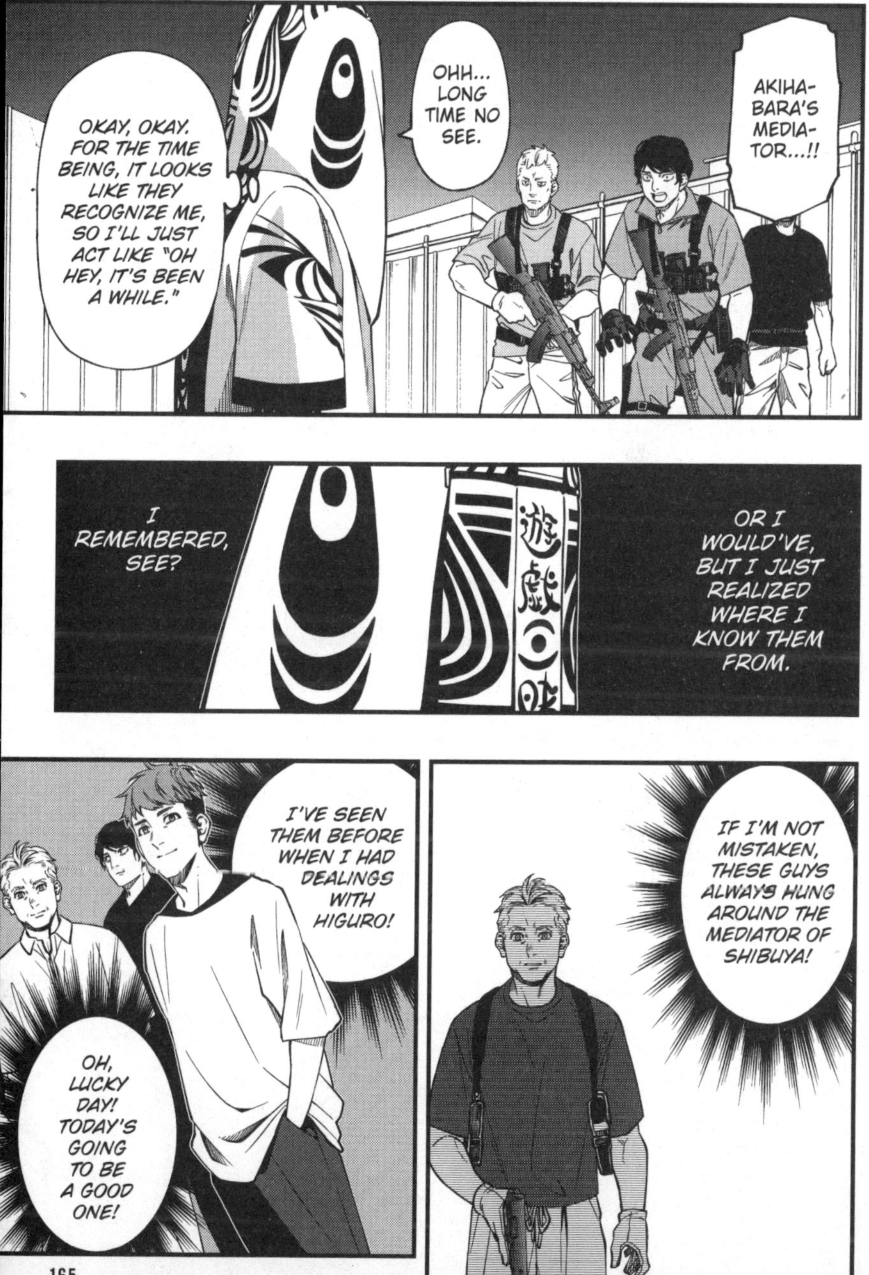
AKIHABARA'S MEDIATOR...!!
OHH... LONG TIME NO SEE.
OKAY, OKAY. FOR THE TIME BEING, IT LOOKS LIKE THEY RECOGNIZE ME, SO I'LL JUST ACT LIKE "OH HEY, IT'S BEEN A WHILE."
I REMEMBERED, SEE?
OR I WOULD'VE, BUT I JUST REALIZED WHERE I KNOW THEM FROM.
IF I'M NOT MISTAKEN, THESE GUYS ALWAYS HUNG AROUND THE MEDIATOR OF SHIBUYA!
I'VE SEEN THEM BEFORE WHEN I HAD DEALINGS WITH HIGURO!
OH, LUCKY DAY! TODAY'S GOING TO BE A GOOD ONE!

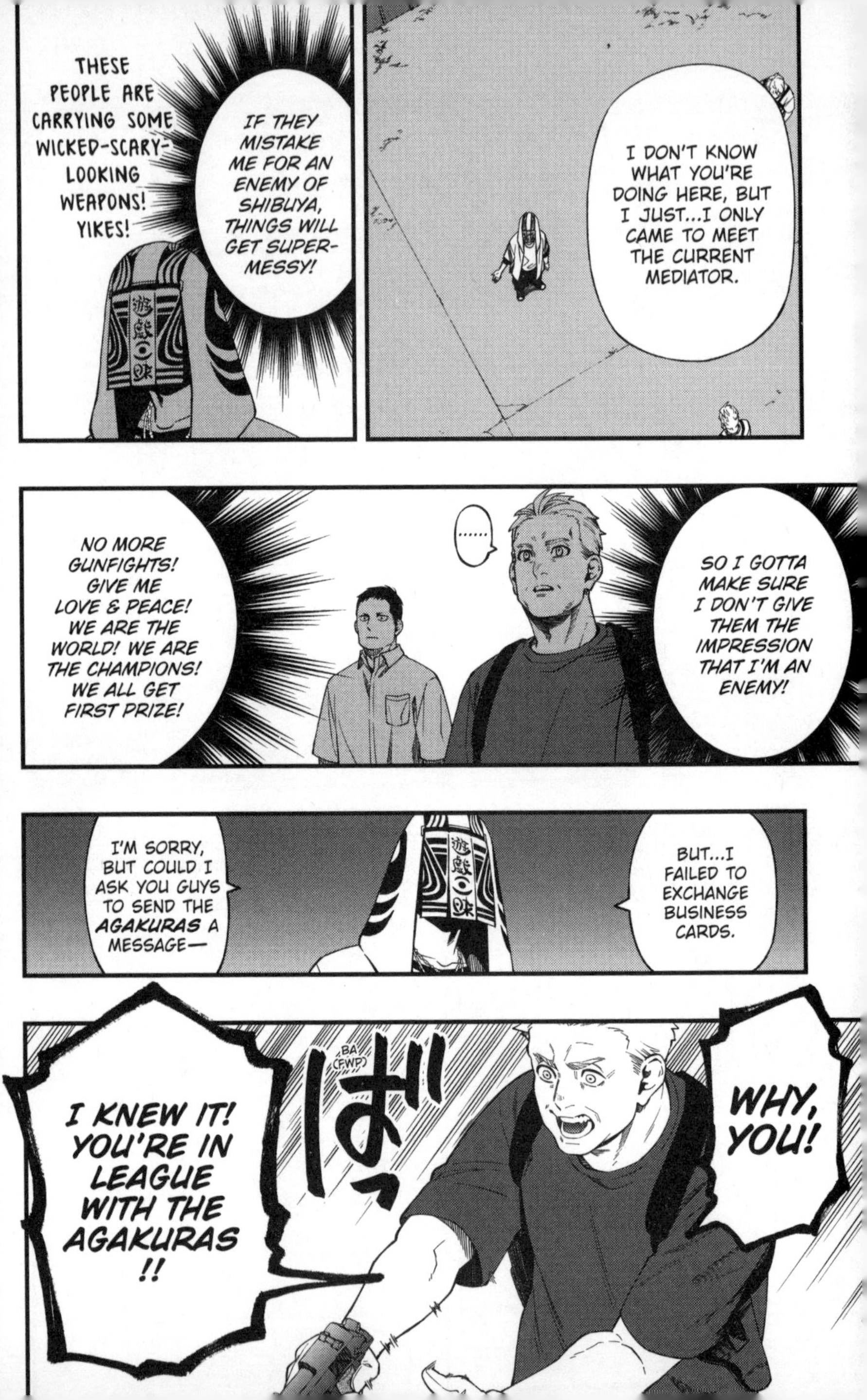
I DON'T KNOW WHAT YOU'RE DOING HERE, BUT I JUST...I ONLY CAME TO MEET THE CURRENT MEDIATOR.
IF THEY MISTAKE ME FOR AN ENEMY OF SHIBUYA, THINGS WILL GET SUPER-MESSY!
THESE PEOPLE ARE CARRYING SOME WICKED-SCARY-LOOKING WEAPONS! YIKES!
SO I GOTTA MAKE SURE I DON'T GIVE THEM THE IMPRESSION THAT I'M AN ENEMY!
......
NO MORE GUNFIGHTS! GIVE ME LOVE & PEACE! WE ARE THE WORLD! WE ARE THE CHAMPIONS! WE ALL GET FIRST PRIZE!
BUT...I FAILED TO EXCHANGE BUSINESS CARDS.
I'M SORRY, BUT COULD I ASK YOU GUYS TO SEND THE AGAKURAS A MESSAGE—
WHY, YOU!
ばっ
BA (FWP)
I KNEW IT! YOU'RE IN LEAGUE WITH THE AGAKURAS!!

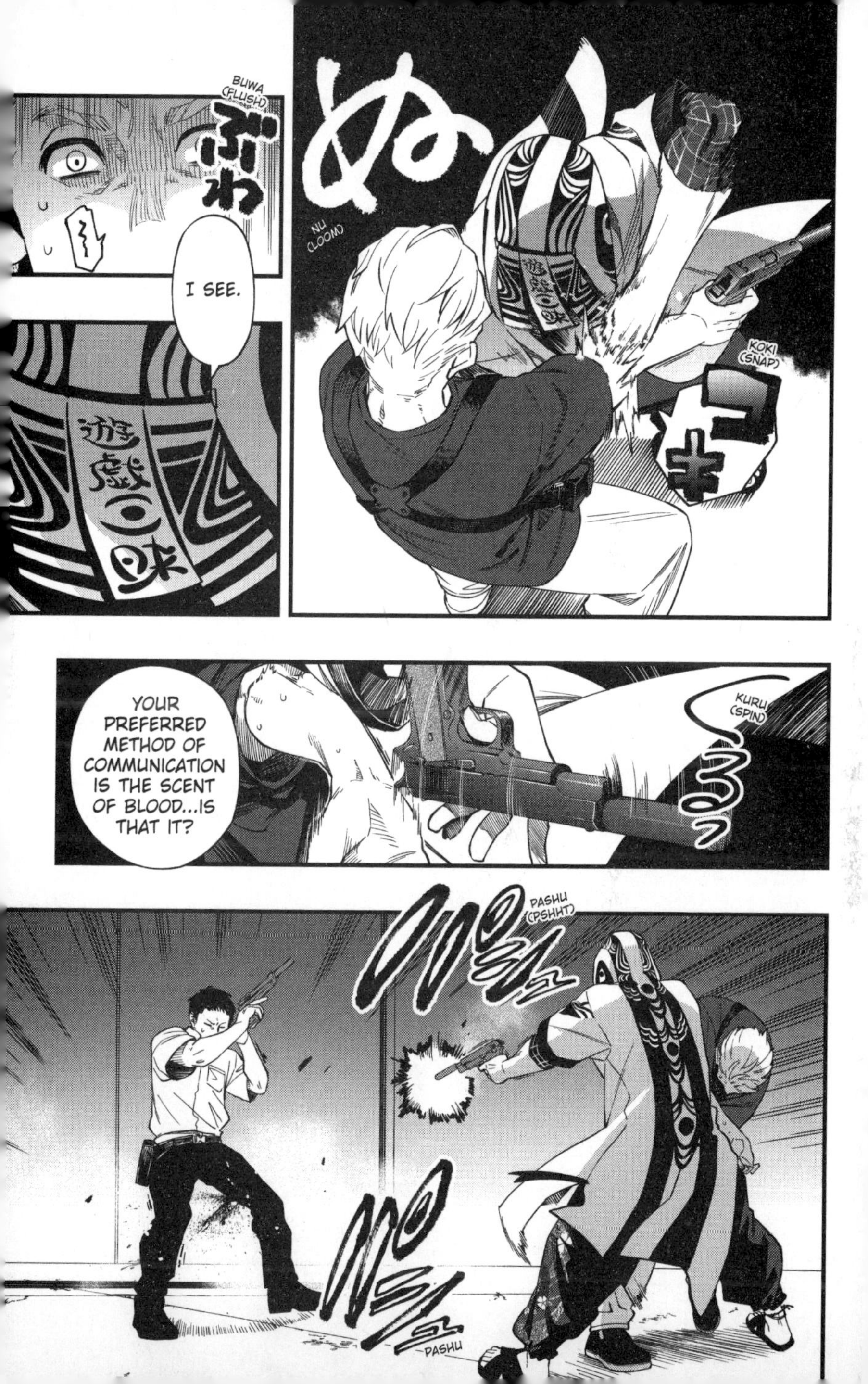

NU (LOOM)
BUWA (FLUSH)
I SEE.
KOKI (SNAP)
YOUR PREFERRED METHOD OF COMMUNICATION IS THE SCENT OF BLOOD...IS THAT IT?
KURU (SPIN)
PASHU (PSHHT)
PASHU

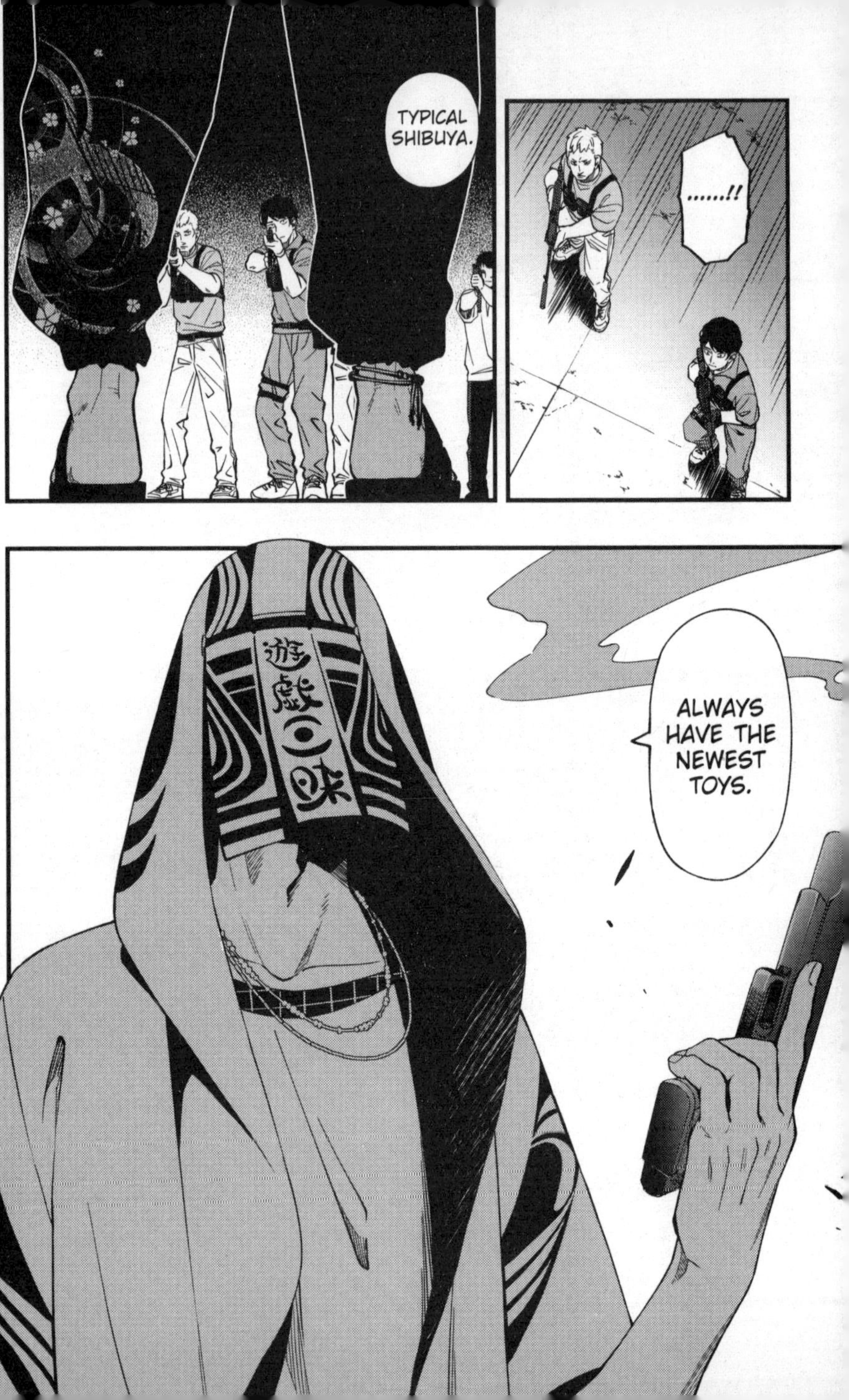
......!!
TYPICAL SHIBUYA.
遊戯三昧
ALWAYS HAVE THE NEWEST TOYS.

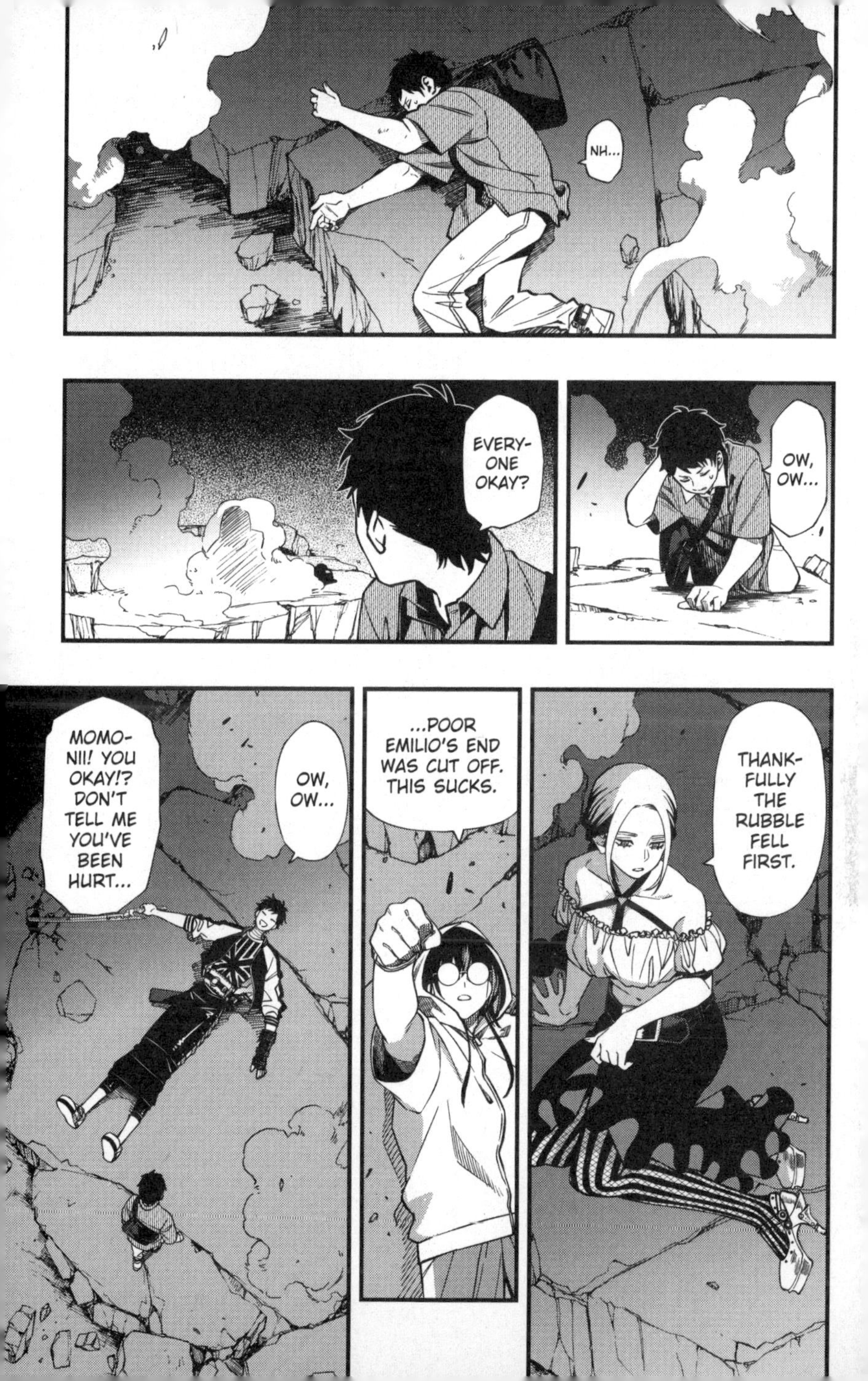
NH...
OW, OW...
OW, OW...
EVERY-ONE OKAY?
THANK-FULLY THE RUBBLE FELL FIRST.
...POOR EMILIO'S END WAS CUT OFF. THIS SUCKS.
OW, OW...
MOMO-NII! YOU OKAY!? DON'T TELL ME YOU'VE BEEN HURT...

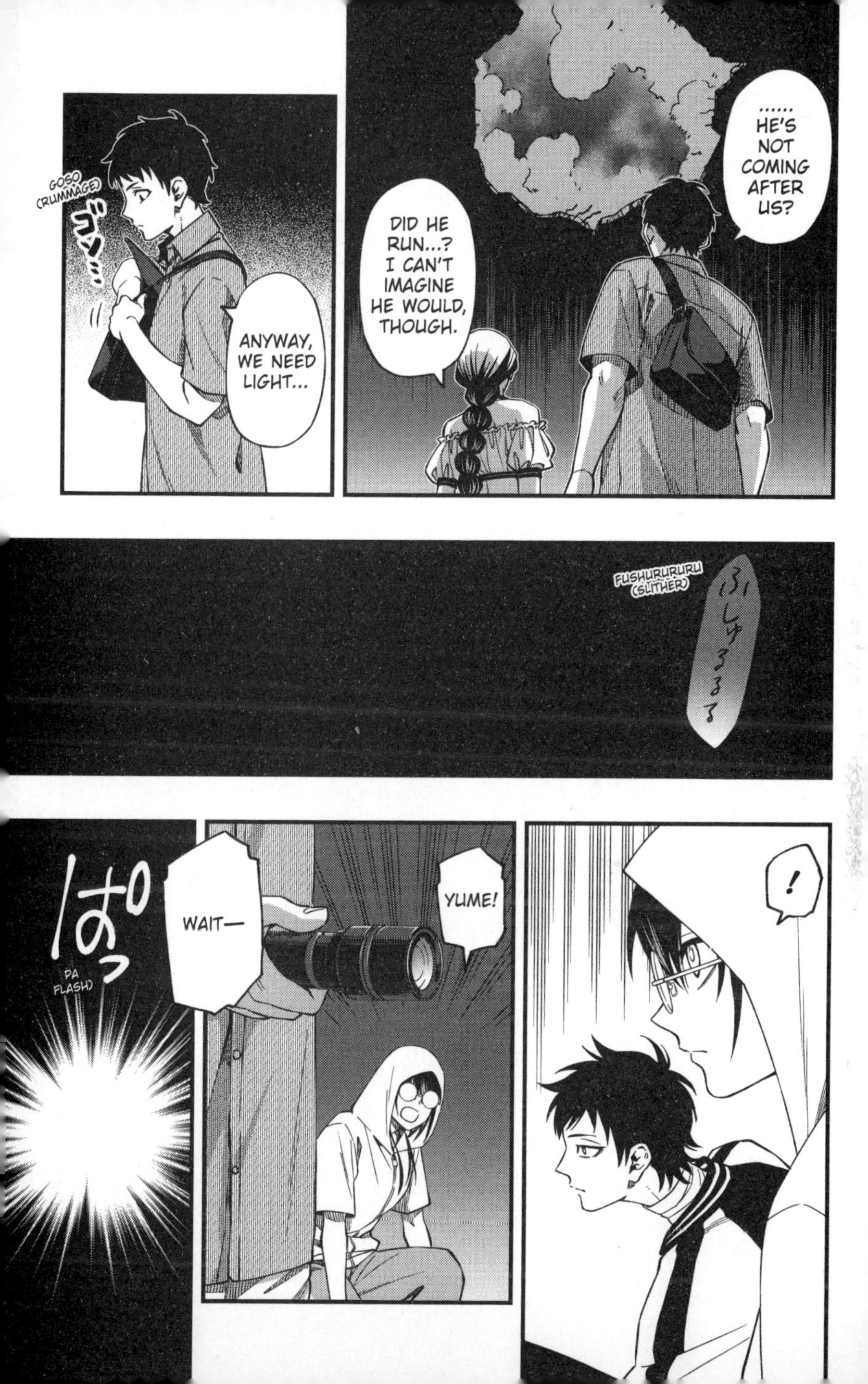
......
HE'S NOT COMING AFTER US?
DID HE RUN...? I CAN'T IMAGINE HE WOULD, THOUGH.
ANYWAY, WE NEED LIGHT...
GOSO (RUMMAGE)
ゴソ…
FUSHURURURU (SLITHER)
ふしゅるるる
!
YUME!
WAIT—
ぱっ
PA FLASH)

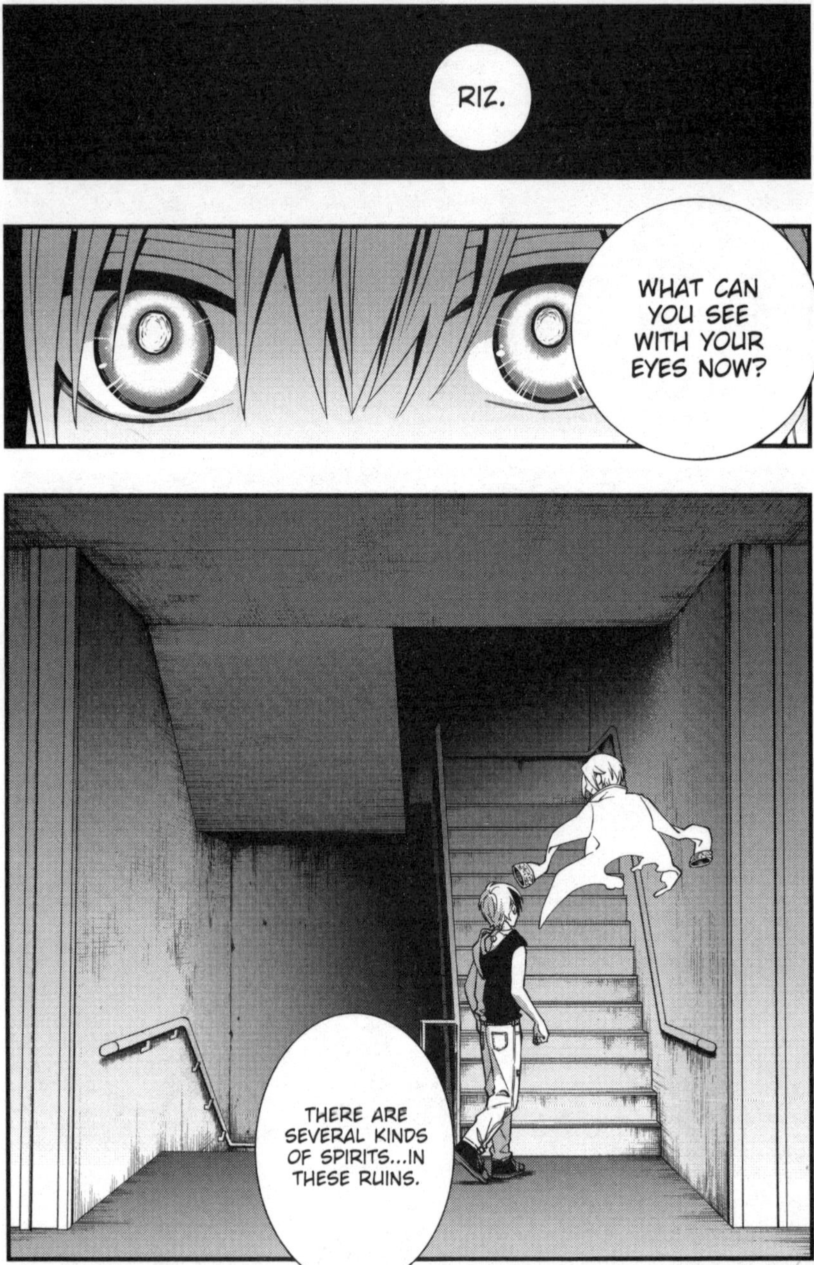
RIZ.
WHAT CAN YOU SEE WITH YOUR EYES NOW?
THERE ARE SEVERAL KINDS OF SPIRITS...IN THESE RUINS.

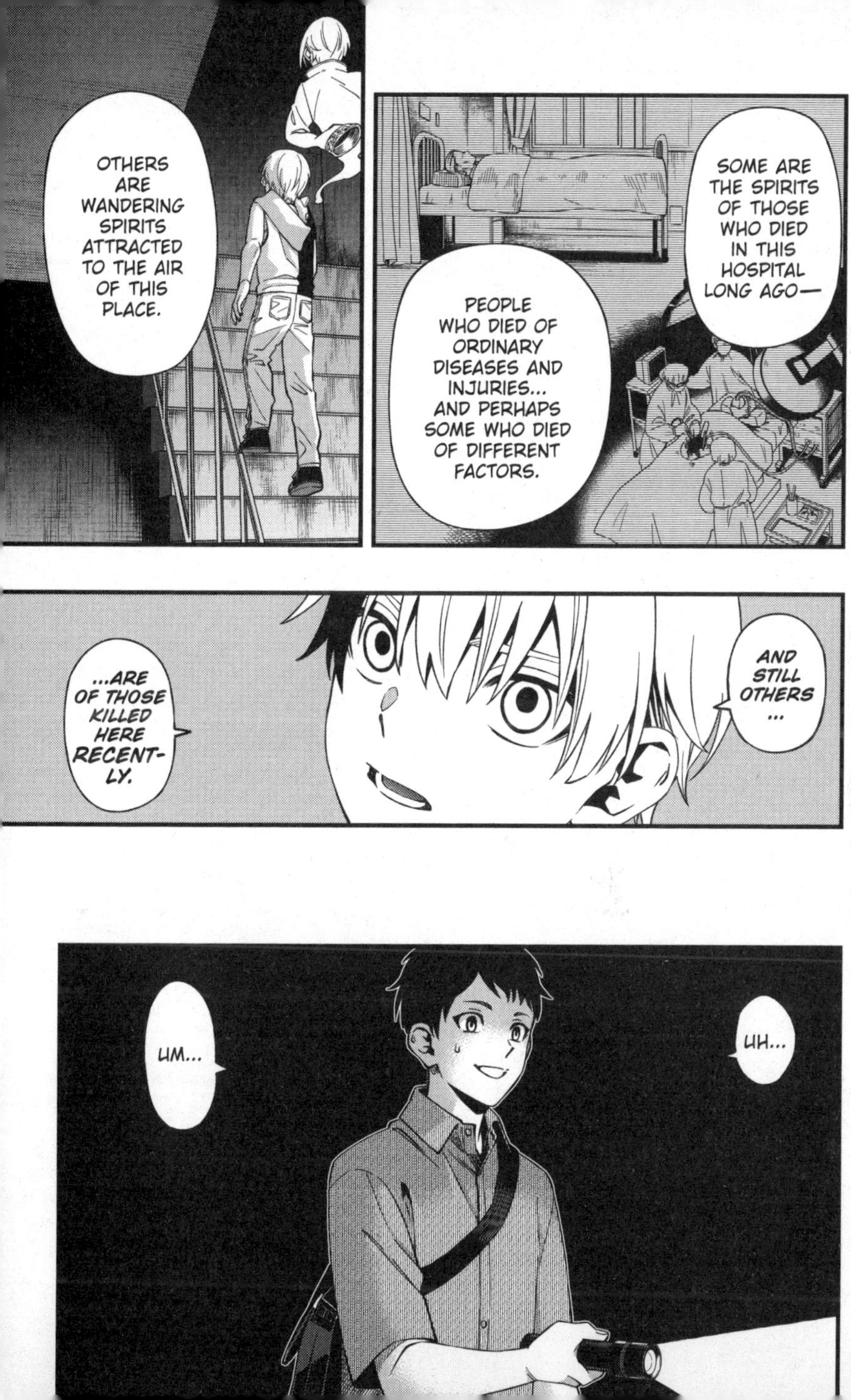
SOME ARE THE SPIRITS OF THOSE WHO DIED IN THIS HOSPITAL LONG AGO—
PEOPLE WHO DIED OF ORDINARY DISEASES AND INJURIES... AND PERHAPS SOME WHO DIED OF DIFFERENT FACTORS.
OTHERS ARE WANDERING SPIRITS ATTRACTED TO THE AIR OF THIS PLACE.
AND STILL OTHERS...
...ARE OF THOSE KILLED HERE RECENT-LY.
UH...
UM...

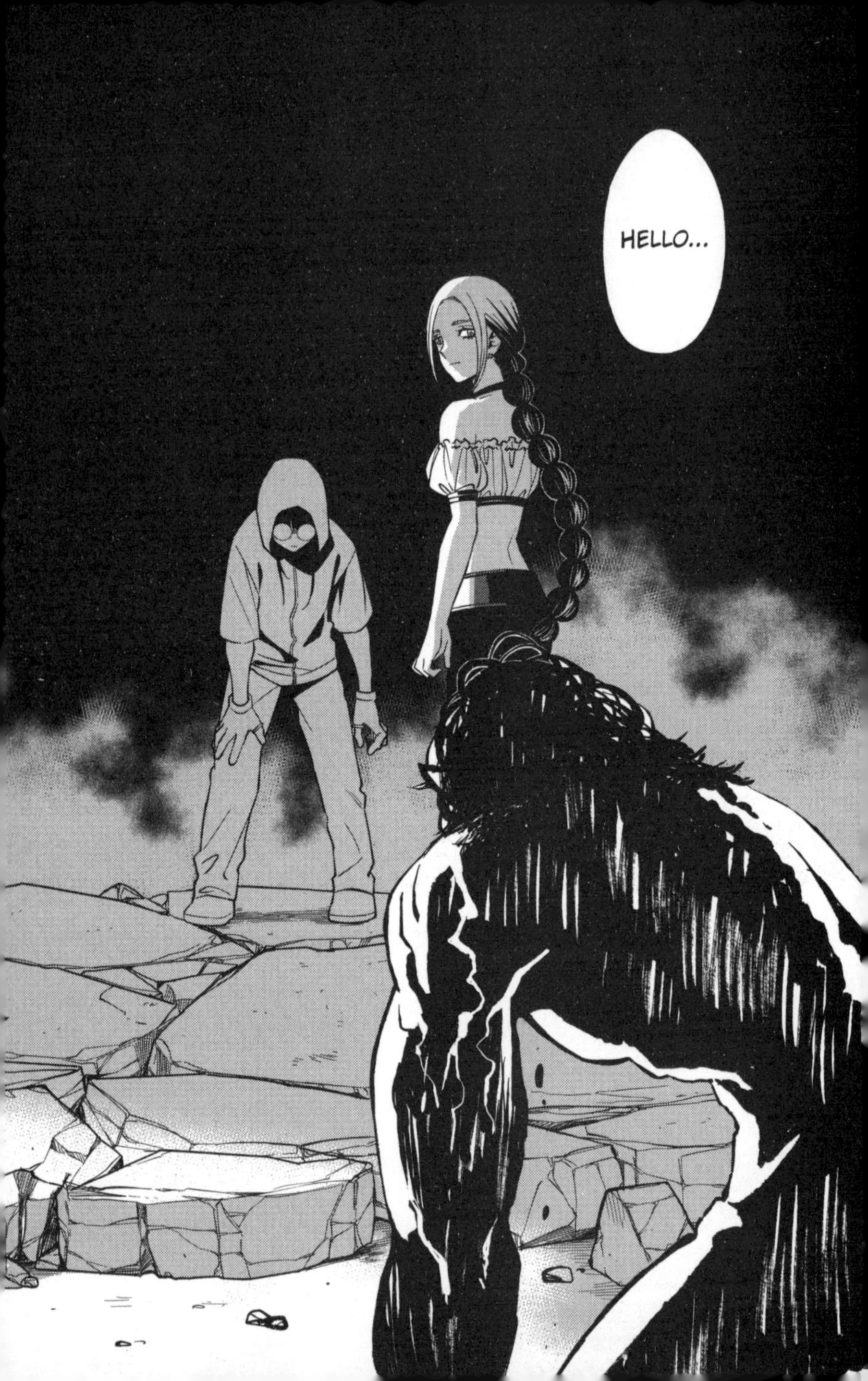
HELLO...

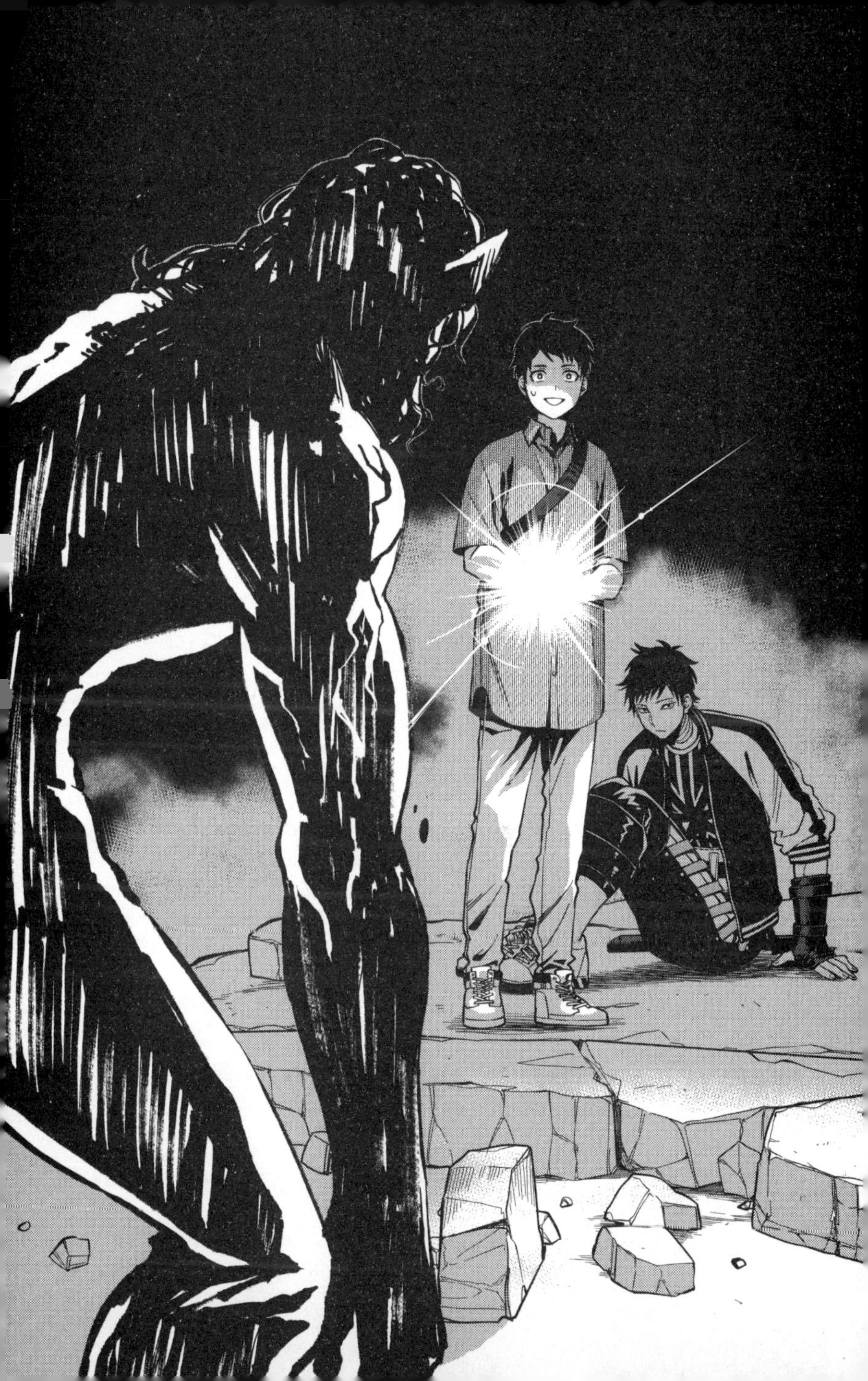

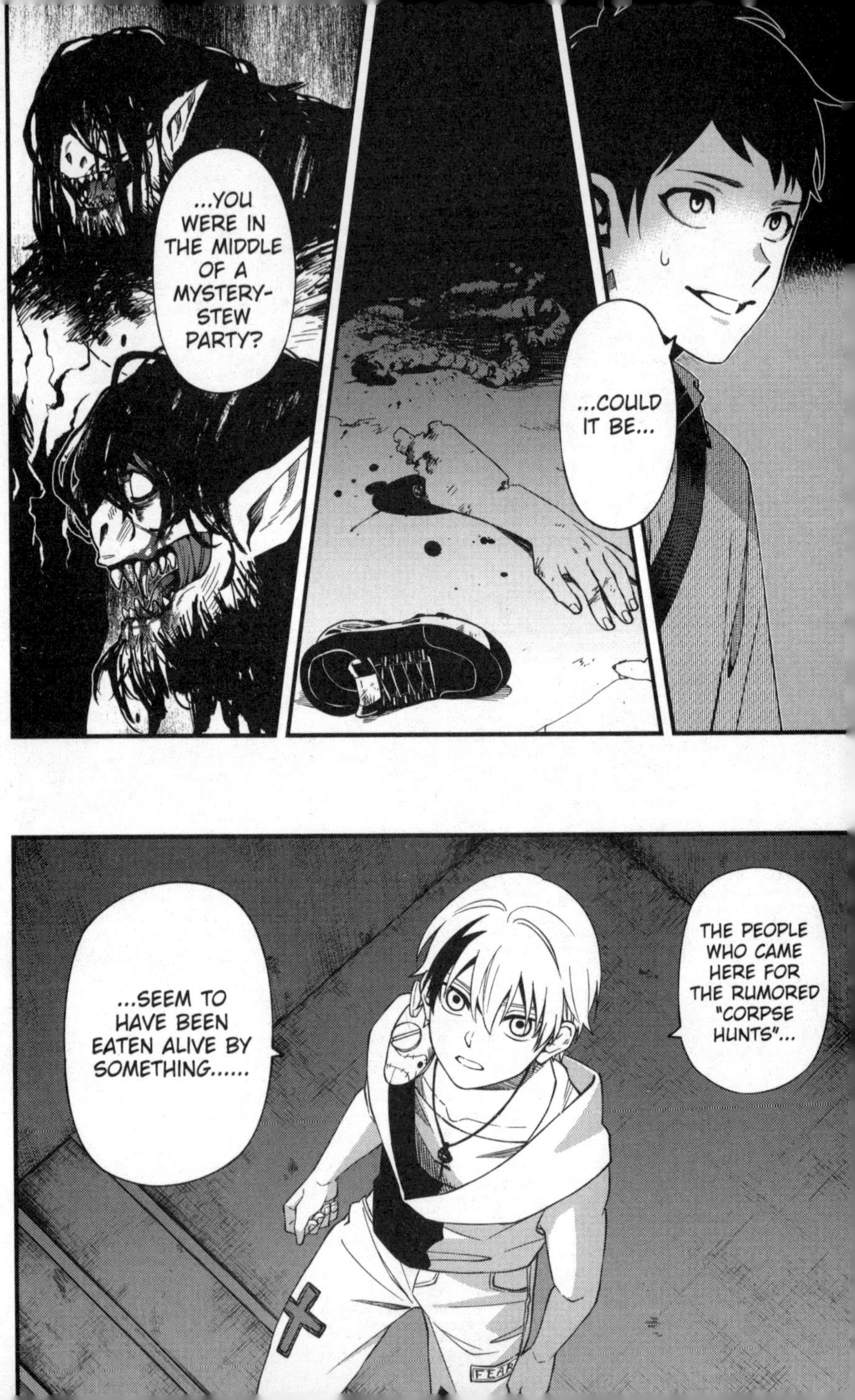
...COULD IT BE...
...YOU WERE IN THE MIDDLE OF A MYSTERY-STEW PARTY?
THE PEOPLE WHO CAME HERE FOR THE RUMORED "CORPSE HUNTS"...
...SEEM TO HAVE BEEN EATEN ALIVE BY SOMETHING......
FEAR

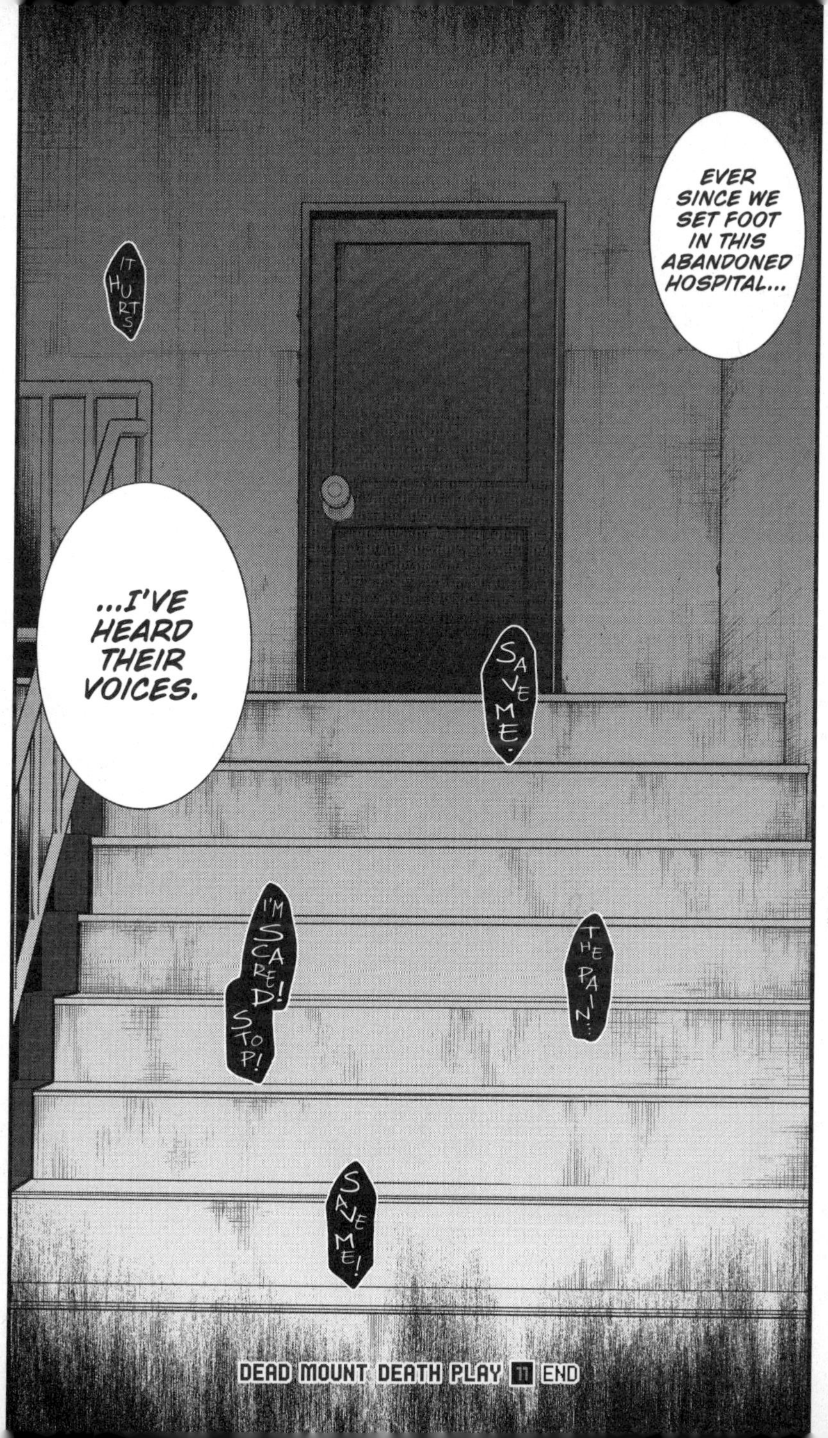
EVER SINCE WE SET FOOT IN THIS ABANDONED HOSPITAL...
IT HURTS.
...I'VE HEARD THEIR VOICES.
SAVE ME.
THE PAIN...
I'M SCARED!
STOP!
SAVE ME!
DEAD MOUNT DEATH PLAY 11 END

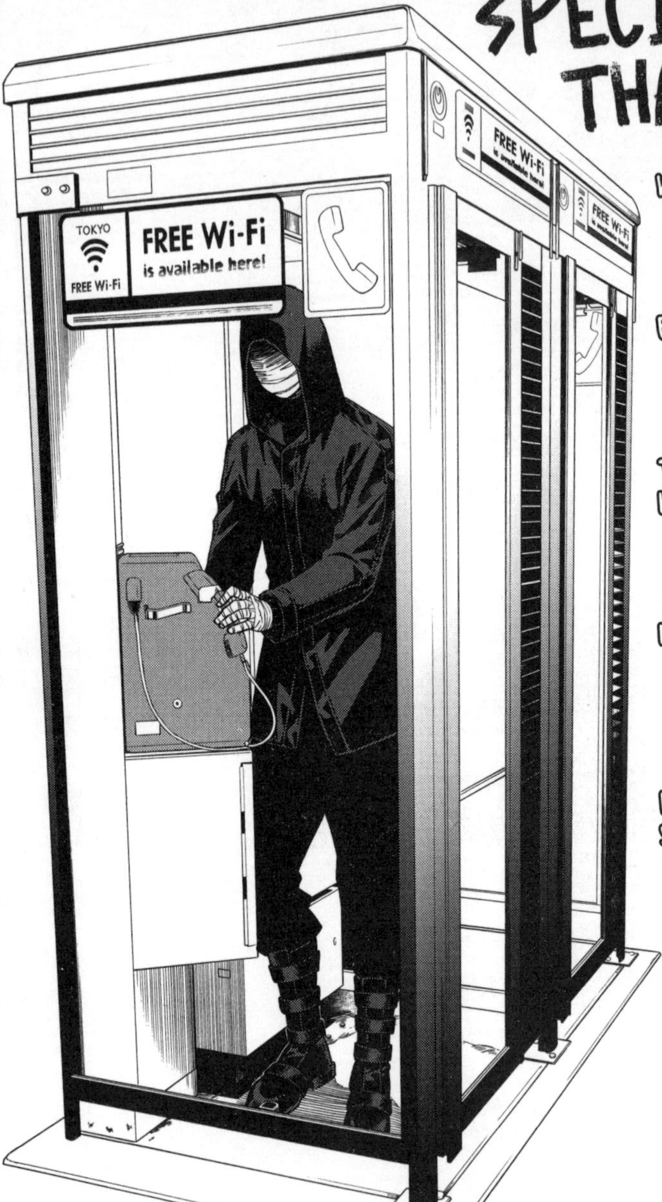
TOKYO
FREE Wi-Fi
FREE Wi-Fi
is available here!
FREE Wi-Fi
is available here!
FREE Wi-Fi
is available here!

# SPECIAL THANKS!

**WRITER:**
RYOHGO NARITA

**EDITOR:**
KAZUHIDE SHIMIZU

**TRANSLATION HELP:**
JUYOUN LEE
(YEN PRESS)

**MAGIC RESEARCH:**
KIYOMUNE MIWA
(TEAM BARREL ROLL)

**ILLUSTRATION STAFF:**
- YOSHICHIKA EGUCHI
- YOSHIE YUNO
- OTO
- NANAMI HASAMA
- NORA

# BEHIND-THE-SCENES OF #94

BONUS MANGA

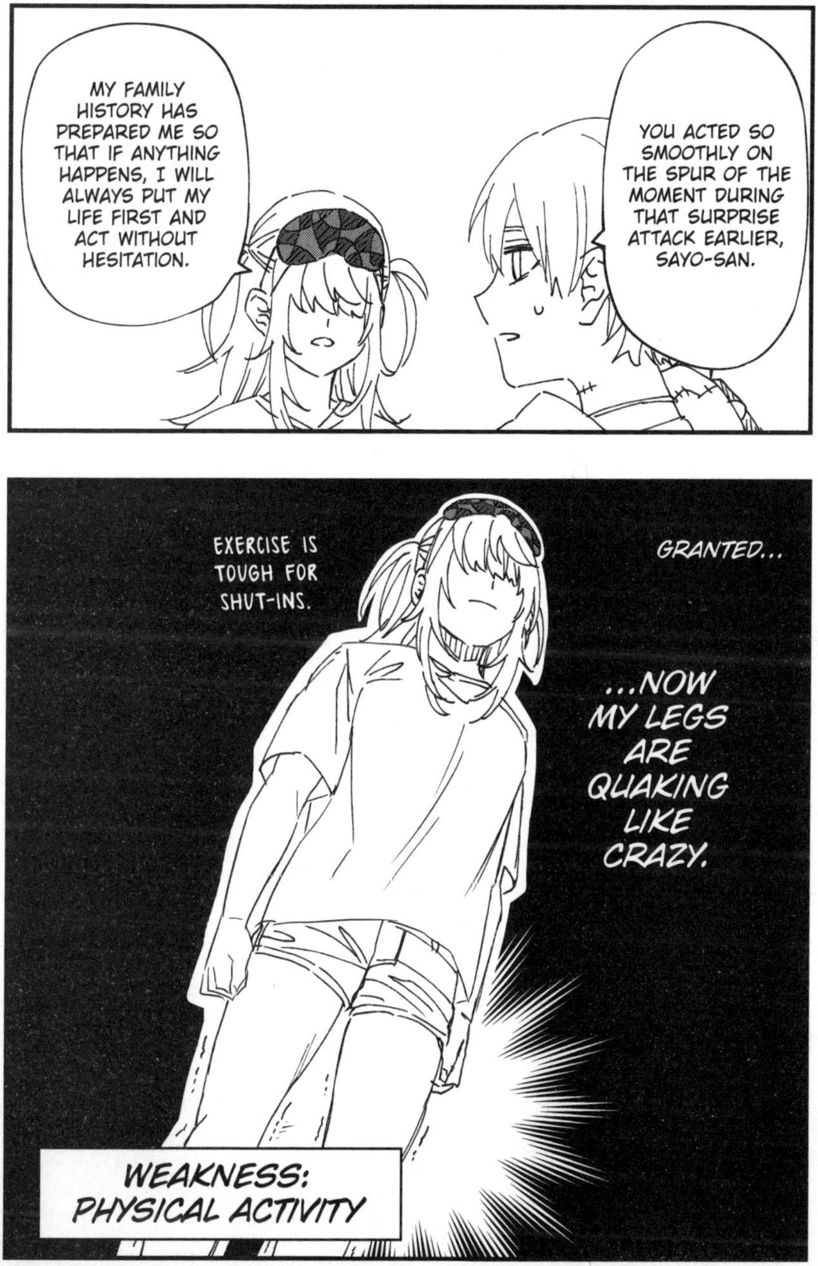
YOU ACTED SO SMOOTHLY ON THE SPUR OF THE MOMENT DURING THAT SURPRISE ATTACK EARLIER, SAYO-SAN.
MY FAMILY HISTORY HAS PREPARED ME SO THAT IF ANYTHING HAPPENS, I WILL ALWAYS PUT MY LIFE FIRST AND ACT WITHOUT HESITATION.
GRANTED...
...NOW MY LEGS ARE QUAKING LIKE CRAZY.
EXERCISE IS TOUGH FOR SHUT-INS.
WEAKNESS: PHYSICAL ACTIVITY

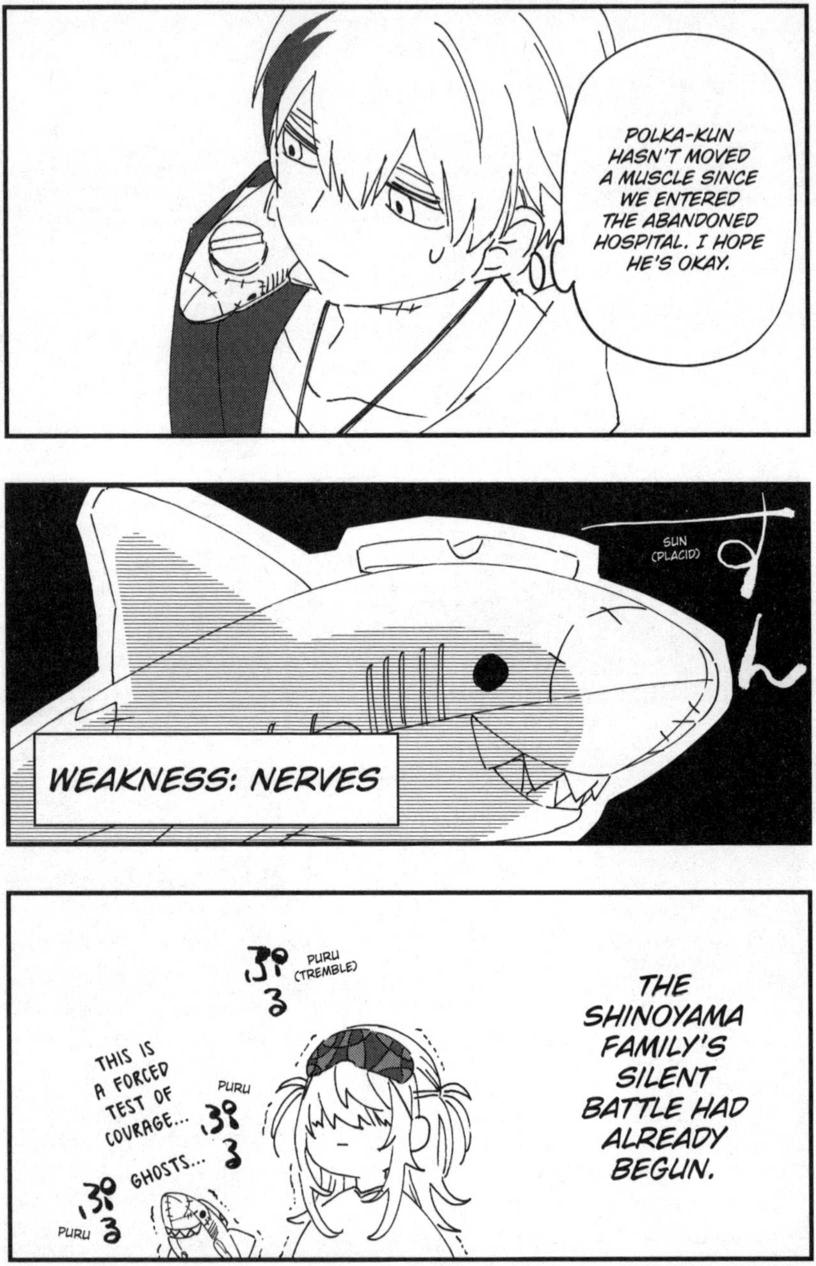
POLKA-KUN HASN'T MOVED A MUSCLE SINCE WE ENTERED THE ABANDONED HOSPITAL. I HOPE HE'S OKAY.
すん
SUN (PLACID)
WEAKNESS: NERVES
THE SHINOYAMA FAMILY'S SILENT BATTLE HAD ALREADY BEGUN.
ぷる
PURU (TREMBLE)
ぷる
PURU
THIS IS A FORCED TEST OF COURAGE...
GHOSTS...
ぷる
PURU

# Super-Fun Illustrated Guide to *DEAD MOUNT DEATH PLAY*

SPECIMEN

⑪

## ZUKUZUKU BONBON

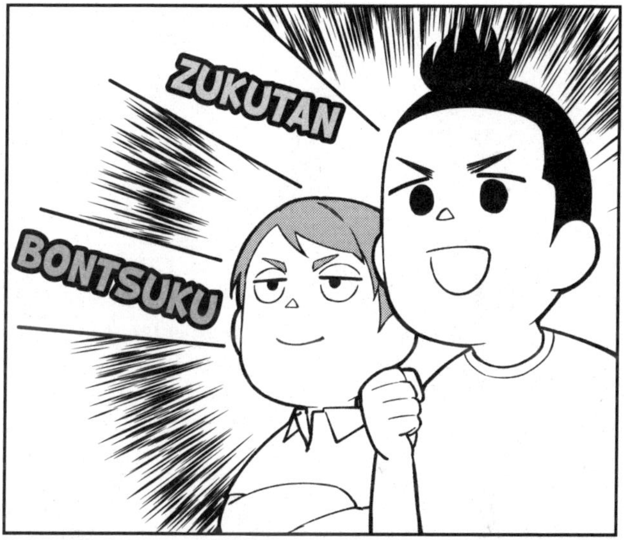
ZUKUTAN
BONTSUKU

Zukutan and Bontsuku were YouTubers who were struggling to build their channel's follower count, which prompted their decision to take on the hot new "Corpse Hunt" challenge. They're the "real dangerous guys" that Higuro mentions taking care of in Chapter 38 of Volume 5. Initially, I was going to put them right up there with Higuro in terms of evilness, but various things had to get cut due to length limits, and as a result, the worst they did was trespass in an abandoned building. It's too bad that they didn't even do anything all that bad and still had to meet that horrible end. Will their lost souls be able to gain viewers?

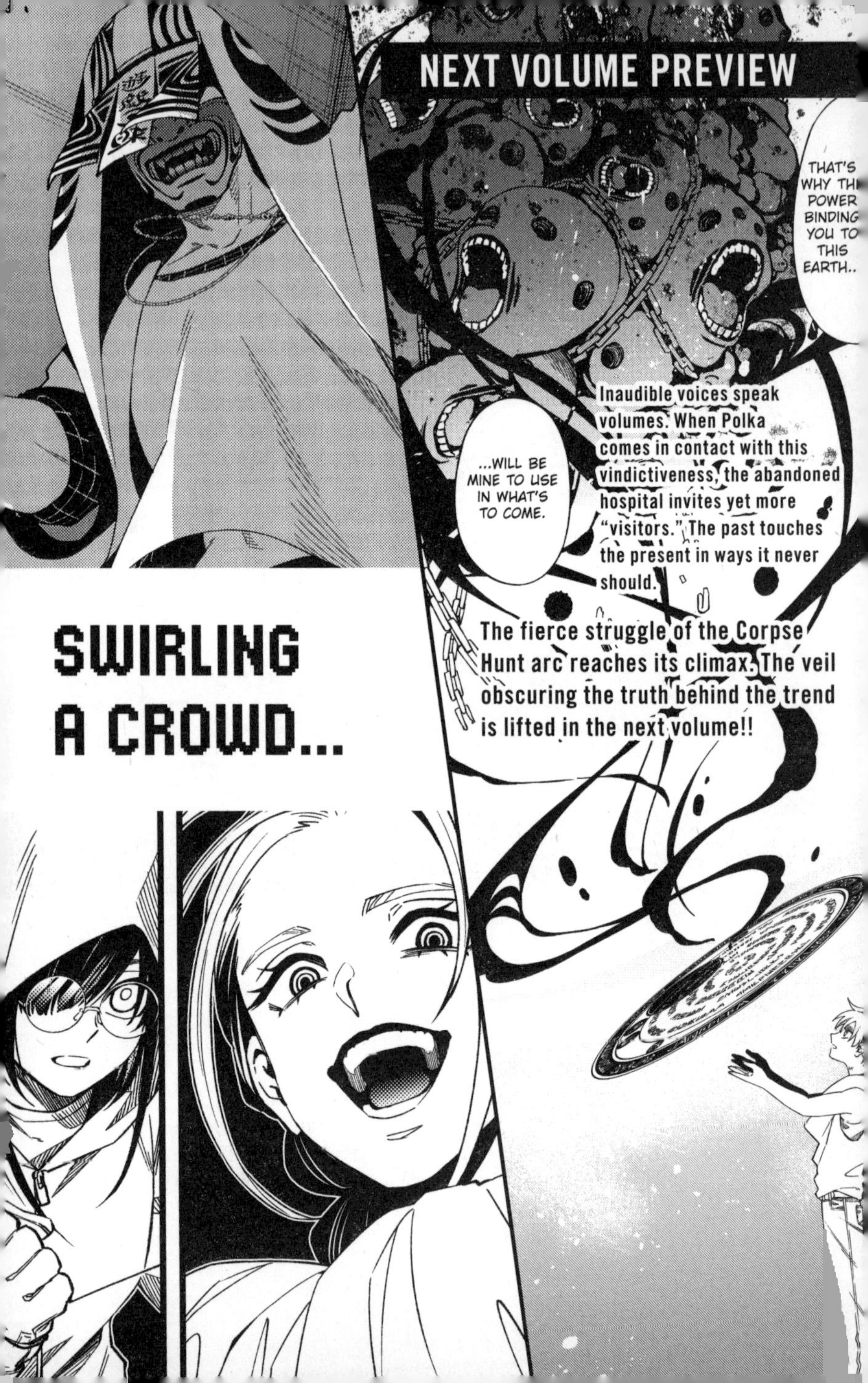
NEXT VOLUME PREVIEW
THAT'S WHY TH POWER BINDING YOU TO THIS EARTH..
...WILL BE MINE TO USE IN WHAT'S TO COME.
Inaudible voices speak volumes. When Polka comes in contact with this vindictiveness, the abandoned hospital invites yet more "visitors." The past touches the present in ways it never should.
The fierce struggle of the Corpse Hunt arc reaches its climax. The veil obscuring the truth behind the trend is lifted in the next volume!!
SWIRLING A CROWD...

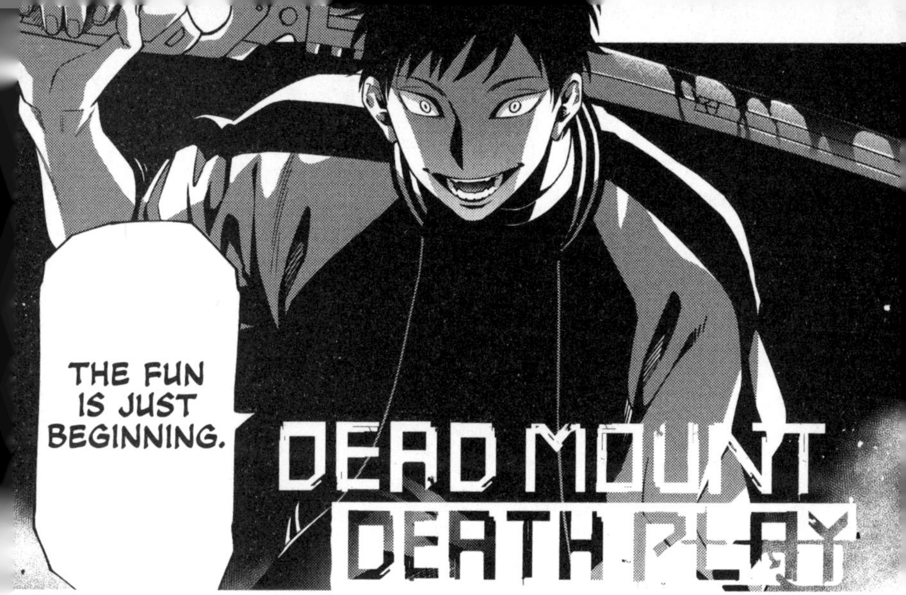
THE FUN IS JUST BEGINNING.
DEAD MOUNT DEATH PLAY

THE FEAST OF DARKNESS, WITH FOUL FEELINGS, DRAWS

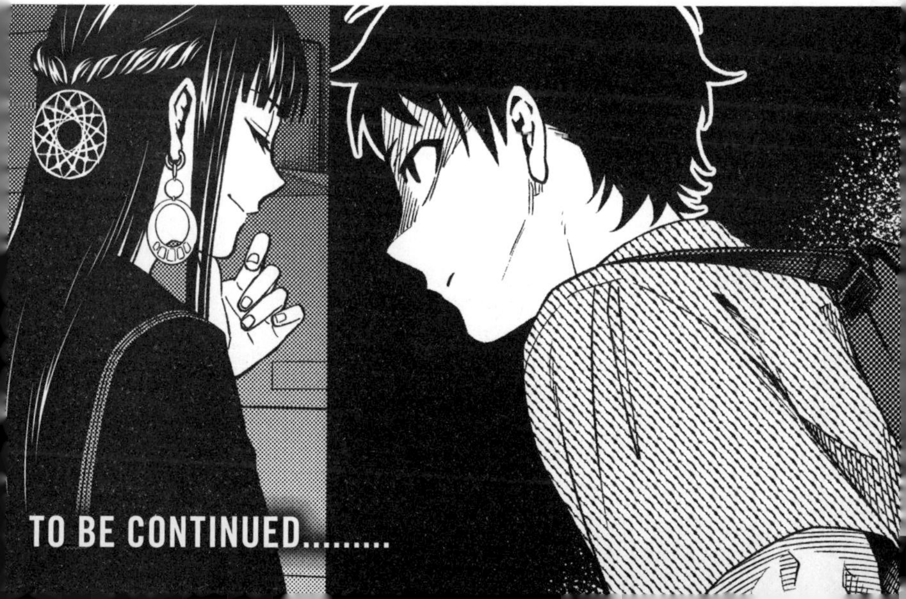
TO BE CONTINUED.........

# DEAD MOUNT DEATH PLAY

**STORY: Ryohgo Narita  ART: Shinta Fujimoto**

Translation: Christine Dashiell ✳ Lettering: Abigail Blackman

This book is a work of fiction. Names, characters, places, and incidents are the product of the author's imagination or are used fictitiously. Any resemblance to actual events, locales, or persons, living or dead, is coincidental.

DEAD MOUNT DEATH PLAY Volume 11 ©2023 Ryohgo Narita, Shinta Fujimoto/SQUARE ENIX CO., LTD. First published in Japan in 2023 by SQUARE ENIX CO., LTD. English translation rights arranged with SQUARE ENIX CO., LTD. and Yen Press, LLC through Tuttle-Mori Agency, Inc., Tokyo.

English translation ©2024 by SQUARE ENIX CO., LTD.

Yen Press, LLC supports the right to free expression and the value of copyright. The purpose of copyright is to encourage writers and artists to produce the creative works that enrich our culture.

The scanning, uploading, and distribution of this book without permission is a theft of the author's intellectual property. If you would like permission to use material from the book (other than for review purposes), please contact the publisher. Thank you for your support of the author's rights.

Yen Press ✳ 150 West 30th Street, 19th Floor ✳ New York, NY 10001

Visit us at yenpress.com
facebook.com/yenpress
twitter.com/yenpress
yenpress.tumblr.com
instagram.com/yenpress

First Yen Press Edition: January 2024
The chapters in this volume were originally published as ebooks by Yen Press.
Edited by Abigail Blackman and Yen Press Editorial: Won Young Seo
Designed by Yen Press Design: Wendy Chan

Yen Press is an imprint of Yen Press, LLC.
The Yen Press name and logo are trademarks of Yen Press, LLC.

The publisher is not responsible for websites (or their content) that are not owned by the publisher.

Library of Congress Control Number: 2018953479

ISBNs: 978-1-9753-8977-2 (paperback)
978-1-9753-8978-9 (ebook)

10 9 8 7 6 5 4 3 2 1

WOR

Printed in the United States of America

Turn to the back of the book to read an exclusive bonus short story by Ryohgo Narita!

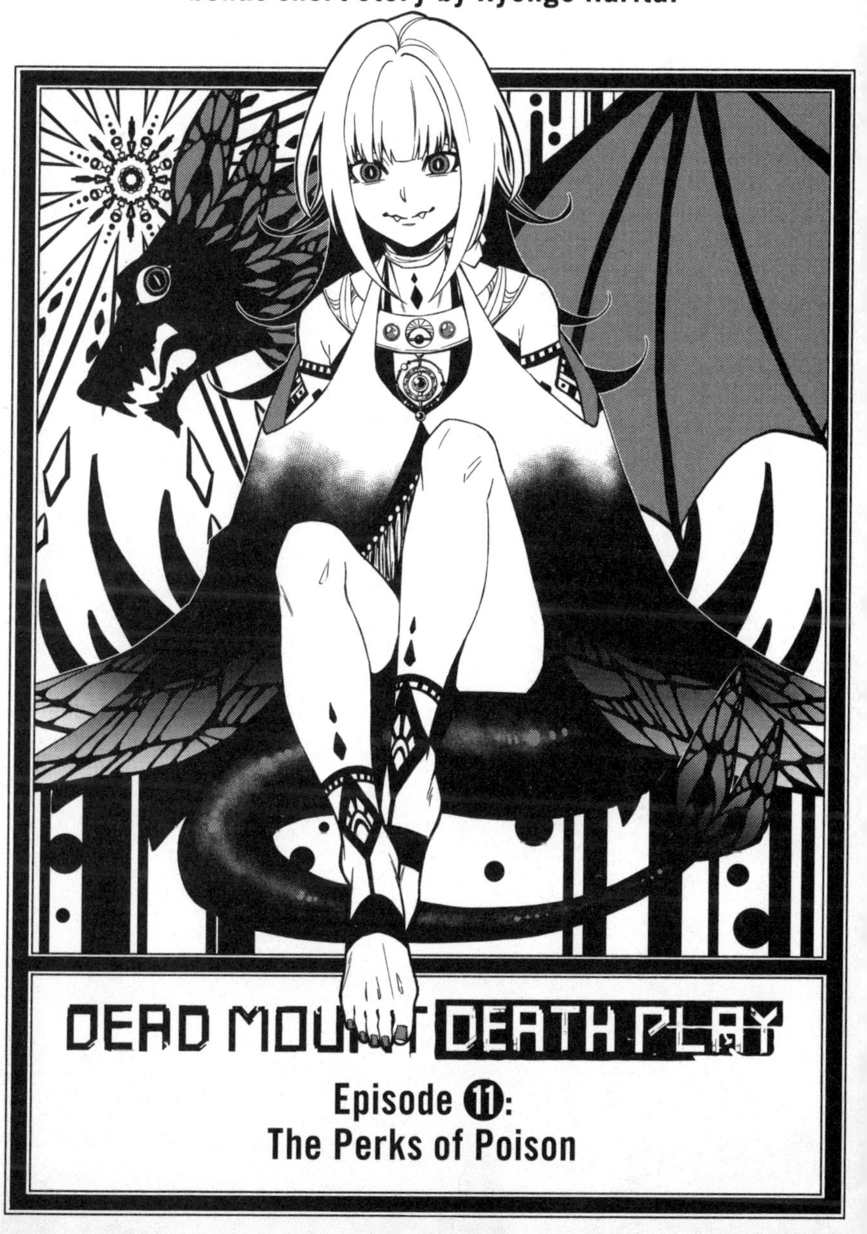

# DEAD MOUNT DEATH PLAY

## Episode 11: The Perks of Poison

spoken aloud, Silk asked directly: "Would you perhaps know…the whereabouts of my little sister?"

"…I can't say for certain." Lighting the tip of her pipe, Izliz spoke plainly of what information she knew.

"More than one hundred years ago…traitors of the empire fled to another land through a 'hole' that opened up here. At the time, it was said that some others used the 'hole' to cross over to another land."

"…! And my little sister was among them…?"

"As for Riddhe, I can't be sure. But it's possible. Rumor has it that many people saw a flock of bats that day."

While Izliz exhaled the smoke from her pipe, she disclosed all the truth she knew, including information of interest to many apart from Silk, especially to those from the "other land."

"Besides those who betrayed the empire…there are some I know for certain passed through the hole: *three dragons*—as well as an Imperial platoon and their commanding general who were carried off by one of those dragons, 'Homewrecker Dragon' Malfy—*and two Imperial Court Sorcerers.*"

Suddenly, one part of the corpse began to crumble like ashes. That started a chain effect, and at length, the corpse of the giant dragon began to disintegrate along with the many shadows. The whole of it dissolved into a rainbow-colored mist the same color as Pirawizzo's blood as it scattered across the land.

Pirawizzo had already been releasing his poison over the shadow dragons as he'd flown overhead. He'd closed the distance in an instant, disregarding even air resistance and gravity as he poured his "eroding poison" into his blood. By that time, it was all over, and whatever method he had used, the poison had spread to every inch of the giant dragon's corpse. It was as if even the time spent in its dispersal was disposed of by the poison.

■■■

Shagrua, who was watching the scene from the ground, grunted softly.
"…I knew he was going easy on me back then."
In his battle against Pirawizzo before, the dragon had never displayed such high speeds. Even with full preparation and readiness, and with the highest level of support from Recuria and her team in the form of body enhancement magic, it was a 50-50 chance that he would have been able to respond to such moves.
Shagrua, reaffirming his inexperience, clenched his fists as he looked at Izliz and the others who had come down.
Perhaps sensing his intentions, Silk sighed quietly.
*It seems Shagrua-san hasn't realized. You fought the 'Poisonous Dragon of Destruction' and survived, which means that you were not recognized by Pirawizzo as "a poison that consumes yourself." The fact that you were judged thus, even though you are not an ally, is… You can remain a strong force in your own life. Maybe that's what he decided.*
Every single person who had gathered on this abandoned peninsula was a monster.
Not counting herself part of that group, Silk walked toward Izliz and the others with one intention: To think more clearly about where she stood and where she was going.

"May I…ask one thing?"
At Silk's words, Izliz turned toward her.
"What's the matter? I thought you and Shagrua would be killing each other down here, but you're taking longer than I thought."
"…Yes. You see, I begin to distrust the reliability of my client." This confession

Shagrua's Evil Eye caught the intense trajectory of his soul.

Following the vestiges of the trail, he could see Pirawizzo was already soaring high into the sky, making his way to above the jet-black dragon.

■■■

"Hmm..."

Seeing Pirawizzo, who had suddenly joined them on the battlefield, Izliz, clad in numerous spirits of the dead that she had been using as shields or spears as the need arose, stopped moving.

"What have you come here for? Do you mean to interrupt?"

"Kuh-kah-kah. I'm going to help you out. Don't be so cruel. Save your anger for 'down the road.'"

Then, the spirit of a beautiful woman, the "Colossal Lightning Dragon" Urdwigia, drifted up behind Izliz, and said, "Now, what kind of flight of fancy is this?"

"Urdwigia, you feel the same way, do you not? It pains me to see our old friend enslaved and made to come back here only to rot away."

"Heh-heh. You too have changed quite a bit from the past. No matter, it's good for dragons to welcome change. Humans wouldn't understand, but as creatures who live eternally, we are prone to resist change."

"Why don't you also take on a new physical body?"

Urdwigia's spirit smiled at Pirawizzo, who spoke so daringly.

"I cannot do that. I still have over fifty years on my contract with Izliz."

"Such an eccentric."

Izliz, following their conversation from the sidelines, sighed as she dispelled the spirits that clad her, dispersing them to the skies over the peninsula.

"Sheesh. Spoilsport."

No sooner had she spoken than Izliz quietly wielded her magic to return the tall tower of skulls she was standing on back to the earth. Urdwigia's spirit and Pirawizzo flew down to the ground in time with Izliz, who descended gently at the speed of an elevator.

All that remained in the sky was the corpse of the 'Cycling Shadow Dragon' Blokadow, whose movements had completely stopped at the time the three began chatting. Not only the main body of the giant dragon, but also the numerous newly-created shadow dragons were frozen in mid-air. They did not plummet, nor float, falling prey to neither gravity nor the flow of time. There were utterly and completely still.

While Silk covered her face with her hands, Pirawizzo teased, "There, there, I know it's unpleasant for your life to feel it's being made a spectacle of, but it could be worse, you know? If that fool Norda had heard about it, it would be turned into a trilogy of plays, and the scripts would be sent to performers all over the continent. Compared to that, you got off easy. Anyway, it seems you've loosened up your tightly wound heart. Maybe now's a good time to talk with Shagrua and the others about the future in a somewhat honest way. Granted, I don't think it's necessarily good to fully relax."

"…You're one to talk, Poisonous Dragon of Destruction. You don't seem the least bit nervous about the fact that your old friend, Izliz, is on the front line in a fight against dragons."

It was hard to tell whether she was peeved at having her history be called a love story earlier or if she was genuinely worried about the current situation.

Either way, Silk turned her gaze diagonally upward to look at the battle between Izliz and the Cycling Shadow Dragon, who were still fighting to the death in the sky above.

But Pirawizzo, with a grin and a wry smile on his face, merely commented lightly, "Blokadow, whom you call 'Cycling Shadow Dragon,' is a being originally born from the shadows. If his soul were alive and well, he would not only control the shadow dragons. He would transform himself into a shadow and lurk on the underside of the world. He is too formidable an opponent even for me… But what's floating up there is only a corpse starting to rot. There is no way that Izliz, whom I have recognized as a worthy opponent, will lose, and therefore, there is no need to be concerned."

But there, his smile disappeared, and he pondered briefly, "…Hm. Thinking about it that way, even though it's a soulless corpse, it is too pitiful to see my brethren be forced to fight a losing battle against another… He has no obligation to play a part in the dispute between the Church and Izliz, nor is there any need to do so in the present situation…"

In the next instant, seven colored cyclones had swirled up around him, and Pirawizzo instantly reverted from human form to his dragon form the size of a carriage.

"Blokadow, my friend. Let me present some poison in a show of respect to the wreckage left behind from your journey of reincarnation."

In that moment, to Shagrua, Pirawizzo seemed to disappear. In the most fleeting blink of an eye, Pirawizzo's body vanished from beside him. But

As she spoke these words, Shagrua, who had been watching the battle above, turned his attention to Silk.

"...What do you mean?"

"That girl destroyed the country because she loved me. I know that she loved me as a member of the family. And I love her, too. That's why I must place myself in her hands. If even after that, she still cares for me... As her regret, her curse, her shackles..."

A dark redness welled up from Silk's feet.

"...this 'blood' that is a part of me will continue to be with her always," Silk said with a gentle smile on her face and a temporary lifting of the dark pall about her.

"..." Shagrua couldn't say anything to that, sensing a kind of madness in her depths.

But Pirawizzo, though he sensed the same energy, paid it no mind and spoke.

"What's this, now? Are we perhaps being told a love story masquerading as a redemption arc? Anyway, you could stand to be a little more nervous. Depending on how you behave after this, you too could become an enemy of the Geldwood Church, or Izliz and Shagrua here, you know? If you're destroyed before you can see your sister again, it will all be for naught."

Then, as if in response, a tree burst from the ground, and Romelka, her upper body peeking out from the tip of the tree, interrupted the conversation.

"That's right, that's right! Beautiful sisterly love! It's so romantic and wonderful to both be looking out for each other, and then there's you trying to shoulder the burden of your crimes all by yourself—you're like two ships passing in the night! I think Riddhe does understand your feelings, which is why she has kept her distance from her beloved sister, that is, you, Silk. Maybe as we speak, she's left the past behind and is living a new life under a new name or something? But, but! Don't forget! Even if she's started a new family and has new siblings in some new land, her big sister is the one thing she can't replace... Because even if she's forsaken her past, her sister is the one and only precious, precious Silk...! That would be the loveliest and best if that's what's happened! I would bet three fruits from the World Tree on it! Oh, but then again, that's probably what you want too, so I'd lose that bet, thanks for the food—*blargh-mmph*!"

Romelka was nearly suffocated by a floating sphere of blood that covered her face, and she withdrew into her tree.

Shaking her bloodless face, Silk squeezed out a near scream. "Wh—who says things like that aloud...?! The nerve! And right in front of me, no less! Oh goodness, why did I have to run my mouth off...!"

But Silk being Silk, that hostility rolled off her back. She thought for a moment before opening her mouth.

"...If you do not wish for me to take it from you, then what do you say to peacefully sharing?"

Pirawizzo's eyes narrowed in dismay at the extremely straightforward request.

"My blood is not something to be sampled as a product, you understand...? I think that's something you should request only after we've gotten to know each other a little better, don't you? Even Izliz, who I have known for a long time, would only get a small vial of the stuff."

"In that case, I would be happy to suggest a business transaction—no emotion, only money."

"For one with such a gloomy air, you're unexpectedly aggressive... I was told that you had been betrayed by your country and fiancé, and that you did not resist and remained faithful to your engagement even when you were about to be executed for a crime you did not commit... But I guess people change. Impressive. I shouldn't have expected anything less from the older sister of the 'Godhead Restorer'!"

Silk leaned in close to Pirwazzo, who was muttering to himself as he recalled the powerful vampire she'd encountered in the past. "U-um... I feel sorry for Riddhe that you should cite her when praising me. If you're going to praise anyone, please offer that praise to Riddhe herself. She did the unforgivable and destroyed our ancestral home, and I have to capture her for that. But that is another matter. She is an honest and sweet girl at heart, so please flatter her."

"Great, now you're complicating things. You really are sisters after all... You say you want to capture her, but your homeland has already been destroyed, hasn't it? The political center was destroyed, and the remaining vampire lords have supposedly scattered to the surrounding countries. No one would ask you to destroy 'Godhead Restorer' at this point. For the vampires, that's like saying, 'Blame and punish the day for famine caused by sunshine.'"

Silk shook her head vigorously, taking in Pirwazzo's eloquent words, but without any effect on her glum air. "That is why, as her family member, I must take the blame with her!"

"That's what I don't understand. The people who were destroyed in the first place got what they deserved, didn't they?"

"Still, she went *too* far. Or rather, I let her overstep her boundaries because I was not worthy... I might as well have killed the royal family and destroyed the country myself. Therefore, I must capture her... *And let her be the one to destroy me...*"

As Silk's thoughts drifted to her absent family member, she once again glanced toward Shagrua.

Her client had promised that if she killed Shagrua, he would tell her the whereabouts of her little sister. However, given she was being used as a diversion, she didn't know whether the deal would be honored or not.

Even if she tried to force the information out of them, the power of the Geldwood Church was too great. Shagrua, who was said to be the most powerful man in their forces, had defected from the Church and had come here, but there was no telling how strong the Church truly was behind the scenes. After all, there was the corpse of "Cycling Shadow Dragon" Blokadow, currently battling Izliz in the sky above, and the invisible device that had stopped functioning on the road a short distance away—even "Translucent Doll" Medeon had been sent to such a place as this as if disposable.

The Medeon lying on the ground was most likely a type specialized in stealth that had reduced combat power compared to its many replicas. That would explain why it was able to catch Izliz off guard. But what made Medeon truly terrifying was its ability to infinitely propagate itself and evolve into an "enhanced version" by joining its own duplicates.

If Medeon could be manipulated as a pawn, then of course there must be an "enhanced version" of it out there, and based on this encounter, it seemed safe to assume that the Geldwood Church still had a number of hidden threats in its arsenal.

*That's only my assumption, of course.*

Pushing the thought from her mind, Silk returned her gaze to Pirawizzo.

*The blood of the Poisonous Dragon of Destruction... If I could make it part of me...*

Instead of drinking the blood of her victims, Silk used it as an extension of herself. Whereas normal vampires took blood internally to strengthen their own flesh and spirit, Silk exerted her power to envelop herself externally in blood. Therefore, if such a poison that could penetrate any protection or barrier were added to her external armament...

"You shouldn't be thinking unnecessary thoughts, Silk Malacougar."

"...!"

"I am no stranger to you. I will not kill you without warrant, but if you seek to take my blood, I will resist."

"..."

It seemed to Silk as though poison was seeping from his very words. In fact, a weaker being would probably die of shock from the dragon's hostility alone, to say nothing of the words just spoken.

It made a nice sound, but even though he's the one who wanted a round of applause, he got pissed off. Sheesh, Norda is so selfish."

"That wasn't applause, it was abuse..." Silk glanced at the figure beside her with a gloomy expression on her face.

Her eyes fell upon an androgynous seemingly-human child.

But Silk knew.

What stood there was a being who stored all manner of poison—that is to say, "existences that corrode you"—captive within his own blood: the "Poisonous Dragon of Destruction" Pirawizzo.

Pirawizzo's blood was infamous as the world's cruelest poison. Even a giant could be felled by a single vial. It was a curse that destroyed the soul, and even aging and death. And it could send the strongest to their grave. When the destructive poison of his blood was boiled down and administered to its target...a vampire's body and an insect's were no different.

Silk possessed unparalleled physical fortitude compared to any on this planet, but she knew well enough that the being standing at her side was far superior to her. If anybody could hold a candle to him, it was a fellow dragon—or the handful of powerful people who had thrown common sense to the wind.

While Silk pondered this, she cast her eyes upon such "powerful people" standing around her.

One of them was "Calamity Crusher" Shagrua, her target for assassination.

Another was "Roaming Woodlands" Romelka, an Imperial Court Sorcerer of the fallen empire.

And then there was "Wandering Balcony" Izliz, who was currently cutting down a swarm of shadow dragons overhead.

Stood before this fierce group of people who had made a name for themselves throughout the continent, Silk sighed at having gotten herself into a mess that she really didn't need right now. In fact, Silk was as strong as any of them, but her naturally shy nature caused her to underestimate herself, and she fell into a gloomy mood upon reexamining the situation around her.

*If it were my little sister... If it were Riddhe, she might be able to put up a decent fight against Pirawizzo.*

In the midst of the scene, her one relative, her departed younger sister, suddenly came suddenly to mind.

Riddhe Malacougar.

Called the "Godhead Restorer," her little sister was said to possess powers equal to the ancestral gods of vampires. She might have been able to withstand even Pirawizzo's poison.

# DEAD MOUNT DEATH PLAY

## Episode ⓫: The Perks of Poison

### by Ryohgo Narita
Manga exclusive bonus short story

"And that's when Norda said things like this:"

"'Have you no pride as a dragon, Pirawizzo, to take human form so readily? So say I...that is, the great Jester Dragon Norda.'"

"'I could say the same to Malfy and Urdwigia, too; I abhor the increasing use of the art of humanification. So says Norda, the master Jester Dragon.'"

"'I would like to sound the alarm against the recent trend of dragons trying to curry favor with humans by taking on a cute humanoid appearance. So says the gorgeous Jester Dragon Norda.'"

"'In that respect, I'm different! So says the remarkable Jester Dragon Norda.'"

"'I have thus transformed myself into an antique printing press with dragon scales stretched across it! So says the elegant Jester Dragon Norda.'"

"'This is wisdom, this is sense, this is humor, this is genius! You ought to applaud me for this combination of originality and preservation of dragon pride, you know? So says the brilliant Jester Dragon Norda.'"

"...And so forth."
"So what did you do?" Silk, the vampire noble, asked the figure standing beside her as she looked up at the stormy sky.
"Hm. I said, 'Shut up and let me do what I want!' and slapped him all over.